7s

The
Secret Books of
Venus I & II

BOOKS BY TANITH LEE

The Books of Tanaquil
Black Unicorn
Gold Unicorn
Red Unicorn

The Blood Opera Sequence
Dark Dance
Personal Darkness
Darkness, I

The Secret Books of Paradys
The Book of the Damned
The Book of the Beast
The Book of the Dead
The Book of the Mad

Tales from the Flat Earth
Night's Master
Death's Master
Delusion's Master
Delirium's Mistress
Night's Sorceries

The Gorgon and Other Beastly Tales
Heart-Beast
A Heroine of the World
Kill the Dead
Red As Blood, *or, Tales from the Sisters Grimmer*
Sabella
The Silver Metal Lover
Sung in Shadow

The
Secret Books of
Venus I & II

Faces Under Water
Saint Fire

TANITH LEE

FANTASY

Published by arrangement with
The Overlook Press
Peter Mayer Publishers, Inc.
Lewis Hollow Road
Woodstock, New York 12498

Visit us online at http://www.sfbc.com

ISBN 0-7394-0699-x

PRINTED IN THE UNITED STATES OF AMERICA

Contents

Faces Under Water

I love all waste
And solitary places; where we taste
The pleasure of believing what we see
Is boundless, as we wish our souls to be:

BYRON

Contents

AUTHOR'S NOTE

In this parallel Italy, some names are spelled phoneti-
cally. But an <u>e</u> at the end of a name is always sounded,
(as <u>ay</u> to rhyme with <u>day</u>).

PART ONE

The Mask

1

"I spit on the Virgin. She's a whore."

The shadow of the bridge, ghostly in the pre-dawn, closed them over. And Furian thought quickly. *How wonderful life is.*

Then the shadow lifted. They were out on the canal, and the wanderlier was crossing himself. "Forgive me, Beautiful Maria."

Furian thought, *Am I so superstitious then. I must do it too? Tell myself a lie, like this man's extreme piety.* (For sometimes they only said, My wife's faithless, or I long to be impotent.)

But the Bridge of Liars, crossing or riding under which you must always lie for good luck, was gone.

Only the canal now, leaden pearl under a half-born sky.

"I don't think you will find anyone, Signore," said the wanderlier.

"No. You're right. It's unusual."

"My cousin, Chomo, he found two yesterday by the water steps at Santa Lala. A girl and a man. Lovers, perhaps."

"I should have hired you then."

"This was in broad morning, Signore. They were caught together by her hair. She had very long hair. Pale yellow. It was a shame."

Furian thought, *Shaachen would have liked that.* But he only said, "Never mind. We'll go towards the Primo. You can get another fare there easily."

"Thank you, Signore. You're always considerate."

Oh yes, thought Furian. *Always, always.*

The canal turned, and they came out into wider water. On either side, the dim, dark houses rose, peeling like dying flowers. Iron balconies hung over their heads like the empty cages of enormous birds. A lamp burned, one solitary pink ember.

The wanderlier sang mournfully some kind of sad song:

"And so farewell; laugh when you think of me,
"Who loved you better, better, better:
"He will make you weep—"

The voice of the wanderlier was muffled by the mask he wore, a cheap concoction of paste and board, the shape of a fish's face.

Furian was tired. He longed to sleep, and knew he would not do so, to attempt it would be foolish. Behind his own mask, that of a plain, grotesque white face with a long, pointing nose, he closed his eyes.

The lamp shone on his lids as they passed beneath. And like the Bridge of Lies, was gone.

It had been a fruitless night, from three o'clock searching the canals and pools of the island City for dead bodies to give to Doctor Shaachen. During the autumn carnival, there were often dead, usually murder victims, sometimes not even out in the water, let alone weighted down. Last year Furian had taken five in a night, one a young gallant who had been hanged from a lamp-standard, only his beautiful silver buckled shoes tip-toeing in the canal. The wanderlier yawned.

"My wife will be frying little blue fish," he said, "baking bread. But not," he added, "for me."

Furian grunted.

"Oh, Signore," said the boatman, guiding his wanderer, dark and slick as a dagger between two bulging leaning house fronts, "my wife hates me. She's in love with our son. He's at the University, you understand."

Furian said, softly, "I'm sorry."

"No, I don't mean," said the boatman, as if Furian had asked or insisted, "that she's incestuous. Only that her love is fresh for him. For me, burned out. And when I go home, she says to me, Look at you, Juseppi, you have the face of a fish."

Furian felt he must stir himself. "What does she wear for Carnival?"

"A mask like a dove, with black-ringed eyes. And she wears a white gown. The tops of her breasts are still soft and white, with marbled blue veins. When I touch, she says, Go away, you fish."

"Change your mask," said Furian.

"Last year I was a bull. She told me then she was afraid of me. She made me sleep in my boat."

Furian laughed. He said, "Forgive me. Why don't you take a mistress?"

"Yes. I'll do it. I'll make an offering at the Primo. The first girl I see. Thank you, Signore."

There was a faintly lighted window above, either a late window or an early one. The lattice cast a reflection on the water like black lace.

Just beyond, the waterway closed in again, a channel hardly wide enough even for the narrow wandering boat. But the sky was higher, a ceiling of whitish nacre, and something floated on the water like a blown blossom.

"What's that—look, Signore—a face in the canal."

Furian had got up, careful of the rhythm of the boat. Juseppi the wanderlier poked them forward with his oar, and firmed them in, piercing with the oar the sludge of mud and filth and history under the boat.

The wanderer stood trembling-still.

The water was black as ink here, rimmed with ripples like silver milk. The face floated, upturned, as Furian had seen many faces in this half light, at this season. Was it weed or black hair that wavered out behind? The dead eyes staring at the dawn, so far above, so useless to them.

"In God's name—" said Furian, surprising himself. He felt dizzy a moment, and the movement of his long hair, tied back at the nape of his neck, slipping forward over his shoulder—was like a serpent's touch on his skin.

"It's a *mask*, Signore."

"So it is."

"But it's been in a fight."

"Yes."

"Shall I search about—something may be down there."

Furian sat. "If it's down that deep, he won't want it."

For Shaachen did not care for the weighted ones, he liked them salad crisp, their lungs with only a little salty water in them.

But the mask was strange. It seemed to have been ripped and bruised. Yes, bruised, as if made of flesh. Skeins of black hair eddied back from it, but they were torn and ragged. About the eye-holes were scales of brassy sequins, but some had come off. One lay neatly on the water like a dull yellow tear.

The mask had been only half-face, resembling a sculpture, some god or handsome classical figure, a perfect nose, and chiseled brows, painted black—for a moment it looked familiar.

All across the right side was a slash, an old rusty color, as if the mask—had bled.

There was something very odd, very sinister in its appearance. But it was the sleepless nights, wine and brandy, the rocking of the boat, which made it nauseous and terrible.

Furian decided. "Use your hook. Bring it in."

"Signore—you want it?"

"Yes. We found nothing else. Let him have that."

The wanderlier gripped his hook, and reached for the mask. As he secured it, the oar let go of the mud and they drifted on.

Furian felt a spasm of distaste as the bruised white mask fluttered heavily off into the boat. Its dead hair spread over his foot.

The boatman crossed himself again.

"He's down below us."

"Perhaps. Or he went home with a bloody nose."

"Without the mask?"

To be unmasked at Carnival was, by the law of misrule, illegal. At least, you would be hounded, fined, even if you were rich, or holy.

"Well. Let's row for the Primo."

The wanderlier turned his wanderer through the narrow way, between arches, where three blind lamps hung down and the dawn shone in them, like mother-of-pearl.

Quickly they came out into a lagoon, the Laguna Fulvia.

The water was a sheet of lilac ice, and from it ascended wan palaces that seemed already drowned. So still was everything a moment, the reflections of the walls of Venus, City of the Sea, appeared more solid and more real than her vaporous buildings floating in twilight above.

Furian noted, as if he must, the huge white dome of the Primo Suvio, and beyond, the transparent veiled amber minarets of the Palace of Justice and the Temple of Art. But the sun was rising, yet one more gilded dome.

Furian shut his eyes. Damn beauty. He would give it all to the ocean for three hours of sleep. Or no. He would die for it, the longest sleep of all.

*　*　*

There was no need to disguise the find inadequately as a carpet, or something in a chest. Furian went alone, by the route of the alleys, to Shaachen's house.

To the south, steps led into the water, and there was an imposing pole to moor a boat, topped by a green iron Neptune. On the alley front, the palace looked mean, its windows narrow, sides stained, and scrawled by occasional graffiti. The narrow door, almost always open by day, led into the lower rooms, where Doctor Shaachen's free clinic was, as usual, full of destitutes and criminals. Drinking, smoking of pipes, and a card game were in progress. Elsewhere sat the desperate, jittery or slumped patrons. They would lurk here all day for the Doctor, ready to present their various ailments and diseases. Some he would cure, some, it was said, he killed. He was reckoned very clever, but would always say, (they said), Now, this medicine hasn't yet been tested. It may make you well, or worse. May do nothing. May even harm you. Go home, take it, come back in seven days and tell me what's happened to you. (And, they said, sometimes even the dead had done so.)

Ignoring the patients, who mostly ignored him in turn, Furian climbed the stair, walked the corridor, and rapped on a black door.

"Devil take you. Devil blast you, I say," Shaachen cried. "What do you want?"

"Nothing," said Furian. "Good morning and farewell."

He waited, and the door was flung open.

"Furian. Shit of stars. You have something? In that bag? A *head*? Come in."

Furian shrugged, and entered Doctor Shaachen's study.

The window faced to the south, across the canal, but it was filled by small squares of opaque, greenish glass. Against it stood a painterly array of bottles, liquid apricot, jade, and powdery mauve—an effect of pleasing color that was quite random. The fine orrery and astrolabe had been pushed aside, the old books jostled on shelves. Distillers' glasses stood on the table, crowded by the ancient stuffed turtle with a shell of agate. Papers littered the floor. Spider webs massed from the ceiling. The room smelled of stagnant brews, brandy, the canal outside, and of Shaachen's pet magpie, which was standing on the turtle's back, eating some raw shreds of meat out of its dish.

"So, Furian Furiano. Show me."

"It isn't what you think."

"Not a head? A leg, then? A *child*—?"

Shaachen experimented on fresh corpses. He found them handy. The City police did not hamper him, being well-bribed.

Shaachen leaned forward. He had on, as was normal, his black wig of long curls, under which he was shaved bald. Indoors, he went unmasked, and his face, like the black magpie's face, was that of a wicked old woman. Here and there in the alleys they said that he was truly two hundred years old, having sold his soul to Lucefero for knowledge. Probably he was sixty.

"You'll be disappointed," said Furian.

"That's," said Shaachen nastily, "what you say to all the girls."

Furian said, "It's not flesh. I couldn't find you any flesh to eat or feed to your bird. But I thought it might interest you."

"Give me," said Shaachen. "On the table there."

Furian emptied the bag over the small space on the table. The mask fell out and lay there. Shaachen's magpie flew up with a croak and blue flash from its black and white feathers.

"A mask. At Carnival he brings me a mask!"

Furian said, "If it's of no concern to you, I'll take it back—"

"Wait, wait. Where did you find this?"

"In the water. A street near Fulvia."

"Nothing else."

"Nothing I could see."

Shaachen peered at the mask through a magnifying glass. He touched it, but with a rod, a pair of tongs.

"Something strange. Something peculiar. I look, and expect his eyes to look back at me out of the holes. And perhaps, the reflection of his assassin in them. And perhaps they will. No, I forgive you, Furian Furiano. Something, some thing. I'll give you the price of a full-grown hand. How's that?"

"Very generous."

As Shaachen was unlocking his chest, he said, slyly, "In two nights, there'll be a Revel of Diana. At the full moon." Furian waited once more. "Do you want the work? Bring a companion with you. Only one should be needed. But a hefty fellow."

"I can arrange that."

"We won't meet here, but by the Centurion's Bridge. The Neptune side. Eleven, by the Primo clock."

There came a scratch at the door. Shaachen called in a more friendly voice. A well-dressed woman came in with a tray. She had the mask of a pigeon, and Furian thought of Juseppi the boatman, and his marble-breasted wife. Dull-brazen hair threaded with grey ran down this one's back. Shaachen had cured her of a growth, (he had said, by painting his member with a certain remedy and having intercourse with her). Now she brought him breakfast every day. There was a whole roast chicken, warm bread under a napkin, peaches. She set down the tray on the space from which Shaachen had, with the tongs, suddenly whipped away the mask.

The chicken was aromatic. Furian felt a hollow pang of hunger.

"Eat with me," said Doctor Shaachen.

"Thank you, no."

Furian picked up the coins. As he was leaving, the woman was slicing a peach into a cup of wine, and the smell of nectar filled the air. The magpie had come down again and Shaachen, calling it "Darling," was feeding portions of chicken to its black beak.

The City of the Sea, commonly called Venus, although her name had been Venera, stood—or drifted, in the popular view—on her seven islands. She was aproned by the three great lagoons which held her, Fulvia, Aquila, Silvia, and all through her ran her canals, cutting her in delicate pieces. Seen high from the air, as the sable gulls of the ocean saw her, she was like a broken mirror, reflecting sky. The broken, attributable mirror of course, of Venus.

In the market beyond Shaachen's palazzo, the early vegetables and fruit and fronded herbs were lying in sheets of color, that swam momentarily before Furian's eyes. He could have bitten into everything, the melons, the curled basil, (green, succulent), the purple legumes, the bosoms of young women bending, creamy, to their baskets, where just a slip, a shiver, and the whole breast, a globe of heaven, might be, for half a second, revealed. The inside of his mouth was wet, and he was suddenly hard under his clothes.

For this reason, he would wait. No breakfast. No woman.

He looked instead at the masks of the poor, antiques passed down through generations, kept sacred with the little Virgin statue, the medallion of Neptune, mended, patched. Sometimes only a band of black cloth with two eyeholes cut out. The beggars who clustered at the market's edge sported masks of straw or dead leaves. One had omitted the custom last year, and been hung up barefaced by the heels among the wrung-neck chickens.

Six weeks the autumn Carnival lasted. They were one week into it. He had missed the first five days, lying down with fever in his rat's nest. He must go to the rat's nest now, tidy the mess. Then to the Signora's, to copy her book for her.

A box-litter passed along the market's rim. Four men in ivory livery, holding up a doll in a wonderful mask. It was the shape they especially liked this year, that of an opened fan, narrow end at the chin, all silver lace tines, with the eyes marked in flares of blue sequins, the color that had been on the magpie's back, an alien blue. The woman herself was made out of white sugar. She had a little dog on her lap, fashionably also masked. He looked after her, remembering he could have had a wife like that, a mistress.

The clock was sounding seven from the Primo, several streets behind him. Round the spire the brass horses would be trotting, mechanically tossing their heads, one horse for each of the City's islands.

Furian wondered if Juseppi had made his offering at any of the Primo's pagan shrines, and gone out and found a girl, pretty and willing, in answer to his prayer.

Furian's present rooms lay in the Carpenters Quarter, behind Silvia, the smallest and most ominous of the three lagoons. Out of it, or her, at her sea-most end, the island of San Fumo rose like a black hump, curtained by funeral smokes. And under Silvia, as beneath Aquila, lay drowned places.

He had walked until no longer tired, then taken a wanderer to the water steps by the Carpenters' Bridge, crooked as a screw, where a small Neptune stood in a niche, with a votary lamp lit for him. Someone had left a dead crab, too. No one, or few, would rob the gods, and nature took its course with the crab, which had been there ten days, and now stank.

The houses pressed together, most, like his own building, now sheltering several tenants. Washing hung in banners across the alley, and birds twittered above in cages. Some children, quite dirty and seemingly happy, all masked—as cherubs, demons, sprites—were playing by the door.

They called him names when he wanted to get by.

Inside, the passage ran down deep, damp and phosphorescent from the canal under which it went. It came up in a courtyard with more washing, more children, more birds, pots of herbs, a pig in a pen, women at their wash-tubs. Two or three of these bowed to him. He was thought to be a gentleman, but God knew why. He had deliberately lost his accent years before, taking it out only to soothe old ladies like the books Signora. And he lived like a pig. Worse, for pigs, such as the one the Amari family kept, were clean and tidy if well treated.

The climb up from the court was a long one. The attics were reached by four flights of stairs, (Shaachen had christened his rooms the Apartment of the Sixty-Seven steps).

Once in he shut the door, and poured some water from the stale jug. His appetite had lessened. There was only a slight gnawing now.

Furian wrenched the sheets from his bed, slung them aside for the attention of the washerwoman, dragged the mattress to the window and hung it forth, like thirty others, to air.

He swept the floor. He pushed the two chairs into two new positions. He did not dust off the forty or fifty books. A dead rose crumbled in a crock. Last month, a girl had given it to him on the street, hoping presumably to be followed. But he had only come home and put the rose in water. Where he left it.

When he had finished with the two rooms, he went to get fresh water from the caretaker in the cellar. He lugged the buckets up, mopped the floor, stripped and washed himself. Finally, he took off his mask, to shave.

The mirror was small, but a fine one. If they had known, worth someone's while to steal. *He* had stolen it from his mother. He did not know why. A silvered glass, with a freckling in the upper circle, like little creatures trapped behind. The frame was knotted bronze, with gilding, and a silver lily. He had taken it up, this hand mirror, while she lay on her sofa weeping, screaming, and his father ranted, and the dogs barked below, stirred by the general din to add to it.

When he walked out, he had the mirror in his grasp.

Now he saw his lean body, his lean-boned face in it. What a fall it had had. The carefully-kept, powdered, smooth countenance of his mother, and a room rich with brocades. Now the rat's nest, and Furian. The eyes, long-lidded, dark but not black, the features long and finely cut. The mouth with its edge of bitterness. So easy to sneer with such a mouth.

When he had finished shaving, he wiped his face, put on the mask again with the pointed nose—his old mask, worn at Carnival for years, generally known like his face, by now, as Furian.

He combed his hair and re-tied it, and put on a clean shirt for the Signora, who would notice.

"Have another little cake, Signore Furian. Geletta made them just for you."

Since his hunger had abated he had eaten a cake, but he did not like them, they were very sweet. So he ate another, (His mask had been taken off; she was old-fashioned).

Today the Signora wanted only to talk about her past, when she had been young. About five o'clock she would grow exhausted by her former triumphs, perhaps jealous of her younger self. Then she would go, and he would start to copy the latest volume into her vellum book. Her tastes were many. He had copied for her frivolous novels and archaic treatises, in Latin, by former princes of religion, when the City's name was written *Ve Nera*.

But she liked him gone by six, for then, quite often, she would dress for a dinner at seven with her elderly acquaintances. She was of the most minor nobility. She took it all seriously, in a way he partly recognized.

Suddenly she said, "A terrible thing. A most wonderful young man has disappeared. Did you hear, Signore Furian?"

"No, Signorissima." He added politely, "Who would that be?"

"A marvelous musician. He is the son of a ducca. But his musical talent led him to give concerts. And sometimes to compose."

"I see." It sounded embarrassing. Perhaps someone had taken the opportunity of Carnival to kill this bore, as often happened, when all the world was in disguise. One threw off one's self with one's face. It was easier then to do what you really wanted.

"Cloudio del Nero. Ah, from his name one tells his Veneran ancestry. To a scholar like yourself—"

"You flatter me, Signorissima."

"He was so handsome and accomplished. They say," she lowered her voice—no one had spoken of such a thing other wise in her youth—"he had gone to visit a woman. A very mysterious woman . . . And he was to meet with other musicians at the Equus Gardens—but he never came."

"How unfortunate."

"Hope hasn't been given up. He was famous, you see, for his good taste. His beautiful clothing couldn't be thieved—it would be identified at once. And the mask—oh, his mask, of the most exquisite. Apollo, half-face, done in white and black, with brazen sequins about the eyes. It was one of the finest masks to be had, modeled on the Apollo at Aquila—"

Furian said, courteously, "And was the young man known to you?"

"Only by word of mouth, Signore Furian. A lovely example of youth, which all too often now, disappoints."

After this exchange, the Signora became exhausted early—it was only four. She went away and left him to his copying. And on the stroke of six the maid came in and told him he must go.

It was as he was walking down the steps to the waiting boat, getting into it, feeling the familiar rhythm of the water, which seemed to rock all Ve-Nera-Venus, that he saw, in his inner vision, the slashed mask floating upon the twilight canal.

Yes, it had been modeled upon a classic Apollo. Yes, it was a half-mask, ending at the upper lip. It was white with black, and sequined. It was, of its kind, impressive.

That then the victim who lay under the water—if he did— Cloudio del Nero.

Would it be worth while telling Shaachen? Having the canal dragged. Someone might pay to have up the corpse.

But Furian found this disgusting. To hunt for corpses for scientific Shaachen's pittance, yes perhaps. But to crawl to some great house, to make a pimp of oneself for death. To wrest away money (I know *where*), and feed off grief. To become for those Great Ones what they expected: rubbish. And Shaachen anyway had no care for cash. He had plenty, it would seem. And the corpse would by now be far too drowned to take his tinctures and sewings.

Let it lie.

2

The blissful melody woke him, but before he woke, he thought of heaven, so perfect, so unknown it was.

Then, coming up from the comfortless doze, he identified a coarse voice singing in the street, the tune distorted, lost—for a second it had sounded like an angel, not a drunk.

New songs came and went like days in Venus. They were sung to death, in rooms, in alleys, on the canals. Until this evening, it had been that dirge the boatman—Juseppi?—had maundered out—Oh I loved you better, better.

Now it would be this one.

Furian shook himself. He had fallen asleep for ten or twenty minutes in his straight chair. From the wine, probably.

There had been a time he enjoyed drinking, and had kept to abstemious drinking customs. Now he hated the taste of it—vinegar, wormwood—He poured another glass.

But the glass itself was fair. The smoky greenness of it, like some cleaner water in winter.

That song, it rang on in his head. No words, but the luminous melody, so slow; a largo. Even warbled by a drunk.

The clock struck from the church of Santa Lala across the lagoon. It was ten, here, and not much more by the Primo, for all clocks told different times. The sun was gone three hours. Oh God, the pointless melancholy of night.

Furian put on his coat—the mask stayed fixed to his face, its parted lips still moist from the wine.

He went out, and down the sixty-seven stairs. He had had his sleep, all twenty-three minutes of it, and would get no more. He would go instead about the City, and later maybe again search for corpses for Shaachen. He would need to find a ruffian, too, for the Revel of Diana.

* * *

It was true. They were playing the song about the City. He heard
snatches of it—unintelligibly at the drinking shop two streets from
his apartment, on the Silvia Lagoon, as he was rowed towards Santa
Lala—a passing boat with lamplit cabin, where thin high voices
fluted and chimed.

"That's a nice song," said the wanderlier who rowed him. "I'll
learn it tomorrow. It's about love, don't you think."

"I would guess so," said Furian.

The boatman was masked as a water-rat. Did his wife fear him?
Make him sleep in the boat?

As he walked through the byways towards Aquila, revelers
passed Furian. They were masked as gods and goddesses, nymphs
and satyrs. Not only faces, but wigs and bizarre clothes, horns. Their
rustic garments were of silk, and men with torches and clubs es-
corted them.

Furian stopped to drink at a bar that spread along the arches by
the Equus Gardens, and here he heard again the song, and some of
the words. They seemed strange. But the melody was piercing-
sweet, like pain. A man came by, selling song-sheets.

"I'll take one."

Furian gave him a bronze ducca, and the man said, "The last
he'll write."

"Who?"

"Some dead man."

"A dead man wrote this?"

"Dead now."

The seller shambled on and Furian scanned the sheet. It was
badly written and eccentrically spelled. Very likely it was inaccurate.
But the song seemed to have a story. A princess who would not
smile. Her lovers must win her by bringing an expression of happiness to her face. None could do it.

It was some old tale, transposed for music. Furian seemed to
recall it—surely the lovers, or suitors, had been beheaded or hanged
when their efforts failed. And indeed, the last line read, or seemed
to: *And he can only die.* As had the composer, presumably.

Something moved in the canal-depths of Furian's brain, like the
giant serpent supposed to haunt the water ways of Venus. But he
was into his third bottle, and did not attend to it.

He ate, without appetite, a bowl of soup at a restaurant he
knew, then walked on, up the streets. It was a boisterous night. The

houses were all lighted up, huge flakes of brilliance falling from the latticed windows, out of the opened doors. Lanterns burned. Rose-sellers came to him, insinuating he went to a tryst, and trying to trade with him their flowers, which in the dark and light looked black, and smelled stagnantly perfumed as the canals. He bought one or two. He always did. From the most wretched.

Finally, there was the square before the Primo. An amazing religious procession was going over to the great church by firefly candlelight, little boys in white, and the galleons of the orthodox priests of the Virgin, in their magenta, the jeweled crosses raised up on a sea of flames, an icon of Beautiful Maria held before, veiled in the same blue sheen that flashed from the wings of a magpie

Furian watched. He felt lonely as a child. What had the song said: *Before her darkness ruled me.*

But all men were children alone, and in the dark.

The priests glided into the Primo, the crowd halted to make way like a vast glittering flood, dammed up by God, crossing their hearts, bowing.

A wanderer had come stealthily to the fence of gilded poles below the steps.

"Signore—do you want the boat again tonight?"

Furian turned. It was not the other—Juseppi?—but the man masked as a lion—with one visible squashed ear. Furian recognized the ear. The boatman was also excellent to have on hand in trouble, and would be worth sounding for Shaachen's Revel.

"Yes. The long ride we took before," said Furian.

"Up and down the canals? That's fine for me, Signore. The same rate?"

"Yes."

Furian got into the boat. He was no sooner in than across the enormous night looking-glass of the lagoon, into which all the topaz window-stars had trickled, the Song came drifting like a breeze. There was someone on another wanderer, a mandolin, a strong, clear tenor.

It cut to Furian through the layers of clothes and flesh and wine. It clutched his heart. Christ, the Song was so beautiful. It was a wonder, a gem. And the composer had died.

"That's a good tune," he said idly, to his ruffian boatman.

"Yes, Signore. It's surely caught on. They say it's played in the Archbishop's palace. Del Nero wrote it, but they think he's dead."

Furian thought, *The man who wrote this music—I reckoned him a boor, an effete poseur, a fool, likely to be killed and better for it. But he was touched by God.*

The black roses lay on the floor of the boat.

Twelve had long since struck. They had found nothing. However, he had put to Squashed Ear the notion of attending Shaachen as a bodyguard, and the boatman had gladly agreed.

There was no moon. Stars slit the canals like knives.

Was it one, now? Morning? The lights were growing dim here, away from the great lagoons. So many black windows, or windows with just a faint bloom. So many lives, burning up or down, put out.

"Go that way."

"That canal? It's a bad place, there."

"You know it?"

"My cousin, he told me."

"Of course. But, just this once."

"You may be thankful I'm with you, Signore."

They went under the leaning houses, balconies. Here and there, an almost solitary lamp. The smell of the water was intense and horrible, a putrid tang under the accustomed foulness. He recalled the smell, which at the time he had not noticed. And there, the pinkish lantern on its hook.

He must have directed Squashed Ear indirectly, all this way, round and round, and in to this center. Unless he had mistaken. Certain parts of the City looked alike, even to one born here. Furian said, "Are we near to Fulvia?"

"No, no, Signore."

He was wrong then. Yet surely not. For there, exactly as it had been, over the wider pool of the canal, just before the narrowing of the way, that lighted window—The lattice of intricate small designs, like lace in the water.

A large house, one of the minor palaces, with high iron gates, and above the wall, the heads of old acacia trees, lending now an acid, resinous, autumnal odor.

They drifted by, and as they did, another boat, larger, came from some unnoted slip between the buildings, precisely into their wake.

Furian looked back. The second boat was mooring at the steps below the house, directly where the window reflected, The light fell clear on it, illuminating a fringed dark awning, brass fitments. There were six rowers. Furian heard the vague silky jangle of keys or bangles or chains.

"Get on, into the narrower canal," Furian said quickly. "Once we're out of the light, put down your oar."

Squashed Ear took this order without demur. Clearly he thought they were now after all on business. Perhaps they were. Just there, beyond the window, here now where the oar was going down to stay them in the mud, Juseppi had hooked the drowning mask out of the shadows.

Darkness enclosed the wanderer.

The water slop-slopped against the hull.

The gates of the house with the window were also catching light, opening. A servant came out with a lamp on a pole, like a melon-green moon hung halfway to the sky. And in its glow, his livery gleamed.

Then a woman's figure stepped between the gates and poised an instant above the water steps.

From his shadow, Furian watched. She was only thirty-five or forty feet away, lit as if on a stage by the prow-lamp of the waiting boat, the moon-lamp by the garden gate.

Like the magpie Madonna, her gown was of that same, alien blue. Her skin, the tops of her breasts, were like white alabaster with yet one more lamp inside. Her hair looked the color of polished pewter, perhaps a wig, or metal powder. Her mask was a butterfly that covered all the face, its pin of body stretched from chin to hairline, the wide outspread wings scattered with blue-eye markings, one pair of which would form the eyeholes for her own. There was something. What was it?

The wine buzzed angrily as bees in Furian's head. Impossible, stupid . . .

She was like the Song . . .

Piercing, the needle, sweet to pain. The colors, the textures, the way the lamp caressed her. Her graceful descent now into her boat.

And the oars started forward.

"They're coming up here, Signore."

"All right. Turn your mask away. We're waiting for someone else."

As the larger boat was rowed nearer, Furian partly turned his own head. He put his hand over the long, pointing nose of his mask, to conceal it.

The six-oared boat slipped by with the remotest tremor of the thick, mercurine water.

The most unnerving thing occurred. As the seated woman

passed, some fluke of their light lit up a brilliant blue spark, as it seemed to be, from her eye inside the eye hole of the butterfly. It must have been a spangle.

But for three seconds, she was near enough to touch. He had the impulse to pick up the roses from the wanderer's floor and cast them over into her lap.

There were albino sapphires, two or three, fashioned like stars, netted in the metallic hair.

Her left hand, resting on the rail, was white and young. It had no rings.

The boat was past them and had gone around a bend of the canal. Its spine-ridged wake faded. Only the gentle slop-slop now again, on the hull.

"A bad woman," said Squashed Ear. He crossed himself.

"Your cousin knows her."

"He's heard tell."

She was a whore then. Did that explain everything? Del Nero had gone to a whore, fallen out with her or her manager, been robbed and stabbed and flung down in the canal?

Furian stared at the water, where the wake of the other boat had gone, and where the mask of the dark and white Apollo had floated, face up. Things were simple. They were always simple. He felt a sense of desolation, agonizing loss, so that a cry plunged in his chest, wanting to thrash up into the air. He coughed dryly instead.

"Yes, it stinks here, Signore."

After all, Furian slept a couple of hours. Sometimes, on the fourth, fifth or sixth night without sleep, this happened.

At first, asleep, he was aware of the too-warm, gritty sheets, the uneven hardness of the mattress. Then that went.

He was in his father's house. He was fifteen, it was the day he composed the little harpsichord sonatella. His mother had played it, and they had applauded.

"This must be shown at the Temple. It should have a wider hearing." His father, proud and certain.

Now his mother and sister, in their white dresses. Was it spring in the dream? There was the scent of the statue-ed pool, and violets from the inner garden, and black dolche on a plate.

He said to his sister, older than he, "Why are your eyes so blue, Caro?"

"But my eyes aren't blue at all."

"Yes, bluer than violets."

He was very happy. He had never been curbed or treated unfairly. They had praised his achievements and bolstered his proper self-esteem. They had given him the True Religion, God, the Christ, the Virgin, and all the angels to care for him. He had beautiful clothes, lace on his shirts. He did not need to follow his father into the mercantile business which had made them rich. He could do what he chose, write music, write essays, walk among the charming wealthy people, attend to the fascinating adventurers who came into the house. One day he might select a lovely wife, or an adventure. He would want for nothing.

"My handsome boy," said his mother, all across the room. As a child, he had thought she, and his sister, the most gorgeous of all women. But now he knew there were other women more gorgeous, (as he knew there were other lands, and strange, discovered continents). This did not make him love his kindred women less. He felt a tender pity for these first two sweethearts, now set a little aside for others more rare.

His mother sang—a bird trilled in its cage. The bird was blue as his sister's eyes, but the bird had been grey, and his sister's eyes dark.

There was no reason why such happiness and comfort, such security, such pleasure, should ever end. Their house was strong enough to withstand storms. His elder brother, for example, who had taken up with a girl of the streets. She had been removed to a good apartment, taught manners and fashion. She was now a flawless mistress, who blessed them all, prayed for them daily at a respectable mass. His own youthful indiscretions, (older than fifteen now), had been laughed over, smoothed over. His father: "My children are God's gift to me. I value them. They can do nothing I will turn my back on." They had eaten guinea fowl at breakfast, and white honey from the hives of their estate. Tonight they would dine on charcoaled boar, apples baked with cinnamon. There was to be a concert, a famous singer had arrived to entertain them. A ship had come in from far, far away, another world. There were bales of silk, better than even the East could produce, silk so fine it could be run, yards of it, through a woman's ring. And outside were the games of the City. And beyond the City the playground of the earth. There was nothing to fear. Even death would be kind, and a hundred masses said to make safe the soul. None of it need ever, ever end.

3

He spent the afternoon and evening in Cupid's room. She was a prostitute, young and pretty, though not really to his secret taste, very slender, almost boyish, with short curly hair. She was skillful, but did not pretend, lying under him or over, if he preferred, with a calm friendly face. Once only, in an excess of desperation and lust, dead drunk and slow, he had made love to her for an hour before burying himself inside her. He had thought she was giggling, the curious bubbling sounds, until he understood she too had reached a crisis. She told him afterwards, abashed, she did not like this to happen. What she did was a sin, but the Virgin would forgive her, if she did not enjoy it. However, she offered at the shrines of Venus and Neptune, too.

Tonight, at the Revel of Diana, Furian knew what he was likely to see. He had needed to take off the aching edge.

Afterwards they sat eating apricots. He fed the fruit into her cunning little mouth.

"I wish you were rich, Furian. Then you could own me. Would you like to?"

"Nothing more," he said gallantly.

He knew—it was less affection than her desire to 'sin' only with one man.

Her bed in the dying light was the color of a dying pale yellow rose. She looked so young, but she was nineteen; she had told him her age two years ago.

She still wore her mask, which showed only the eyes, two swan wings threaded with cheap tinsel. He had hinged open his own mask, up to the nose, so he could kiss her, and eat an apricot.

"That makes you look like a duck, Furian!"

He thought of Juseppi, who had been a bull and a fish.

Between nine and ten, he dressed, and left her with a silver ducca. Downstairs, he went to the coffee shop near the Lamb Bridge, and waited for Squashed Ear to arrive.

A mandolin player was playing, badly, the melody of the Song Cloudio del Nero had composed. They would be sick of it in a week.

Squashed Ear was late. When he came, he looked not uncouth, black coat and black hat with a long blue feather. Furian had also dressed well, white stockings, the dark grey coat, and the hat with the grey plume. (He had, too, come armed.) Shaachen, he was aware, would dress in his worst best, the shirt with silver lace, earrings, God knew what else.

"Signore—I only discovered you by your long-nose mask."

"Yes. You're late."

"Your pardon, Signore. There was a to-do by the Primo water steps. A priest had to come out."

"Oh, yes."

"It was a woman, a boatman's wife. She had fine tits but she was howling and tearing her hair."

"There's a drink."

"Thank you, Signore. I need it, I tell you. We thought it was the usual—some man of us got her in the family way." Bored, Furian tossed back his brandy. "But it wasn't that. Shall I tell you, Signore?"

"If you like."

"Lost her husband, Signore. Gone missing. And she treated him like pig shit, was it any wonder. And Chomo, he says just this to her—the man's cousin, you understand, and she screams and screeches, pushed up his mask and rips his face with her claws. So Bollo runs to the Little Church by the Primo, and gets a priest, and the priest, he comes up, and he says, 'Quietly, daughter, you are a woman.' But she only says, 'What do you know?' *This* to a holy priest."

Furian had forgotten Squashed Ear was a gossip. In the long watches on the canals he tended to quietness, but became excited before other work. In his belt, was the sharp knife. He carried too a stout stave, as Furian had recommended.

"We'd better be going. He wants us at the Centurian's by eleven."

"Yes Signore. But isn't that like a woman. Doesn't want you when she has you. Goes crazy when you leave her. Of course, she's the boy at the University. He worked for the scholarship, but it took every penny Juseppi could put by—"

Furian paused. He glanced at Squashed Ear's lion mask.

"Juseppi, Signore, he's a steady one. I'd never have thought he'd go off and leave that sow, for all her bitchery."

"Maybe he found a nicer lady."

"Good luck to him then, Signore. Yes, good luck." And taking up Furian's bottle, Squashed Ear swigged from it heartily.

Shaachen was already at the Centurion's Bridge. He was not, as he had said, on the Neptune side, where the small bearded idol stood in his niche, but on the Maria side, by the lighted image of the Virgin.

He wore a plain mask, and carried his heavy bag of tricks, which he immediately handed to Furian.

"Stick close."

"You're expecting trouble tonight."

"Always I expect it."

Squashed Ear slouched behind them.

There were black gulls flying, some twenty or thirty of them, across the panes of black sky between the houses, so also reflecting in the black panes of the canals. The moon had risen beyond Fulvia, over the sea.

"You see," said Shaachen to Furian, "I have an enemy here tonight." Furian said nothing. Shaachen said, "Take note. It's the Prince Teobalto."

"A prince, no less."

"A tall thin one, with a wig like a sheep's fleece, and the sheep inside it. He may have set minions to upset my work."

Soon they reached the arches that ran along beside the Equus Gardens, and Shaachen led them into the bar, where they drank wine.

They heard the Primo strike eleven.

Shaachen got up and they went on into the Gardens.

The public walks were busy with sellers of brandy and lemonade and riotous masked patrons. Between the cypresses and yews, the lamps shone like burning flowers. Three old gypsy women crept through the throng, with faces like clever parrots, selling charms. Shaachen brushed them off, but Squashed Ear fell behind a moment to purchase something. "Does he want it to assist kick or prick?" Shaachen muttered.

Steps led up to the high terraces of the Gardens. Here the only horses in Venus were kept luxuriously stabled in a lofty palace with a

gilded chariot and four-horse team on its roof. They passed presently the ornate building, and next the wide enclosure where the
blue rhinoceros stood, arrogant and forlorn beneath a juniper tree,
staring back at those who stared at it. Over its tall railing ran a silver
plaque, that proclaimed it a type of unicorn. Shaachen knew better
and said so. The house of the white lions was noisy, although they
had gone to bed. Their roars echoed fitfully over the Gardens.

There was a rhinoceros-lion smell too, mingling with the roses
and night-blooming jasmine.

From here, you could look down and see the moon, round and
edibly white. She posed now on the dome of the Primo, so they were
momentarily twins.

Among the cedars, two police stood in their tricorn hats and
dark garb. They flanked the marble archway that led through into
the wild land beyond the Gardens, the Groves of Diana.

Shaachen, with his paper, got them by. But others would sneak
through, over the low fences, among the thick, black-green trees.
The Groves were a place of trysts.

Perhaps Juseppi was here with his mistress, the willing girl
Furian had advised him to seek.

A white arm glimpsed among the night shrubs, but it was a
statue. Few could make love to a stone.

Half a mile down, in the cultivated rough country beyond the
gate, they easily discovered the Revel, which had already begun. It
was an open pomegranate heart of lamps and so-far civilized noises,
with an orchestra playing. (On her plinth, marble Diana stood naked in her drapery, two marble hounds at her heels, the sickle disc
on her forehead. Her cold eyes looked indifferently away.)

It was the prince Teobalto, also plain-masked, and seemingly
with, as Shaachen had prophesied, a piled sheep upon his head, who
came mincing to greet them, with two satyr youths in silks and myrtle crowns gamboling after.

"You are here, dear Doctor. Do you have miracles with you?"

"Of course, Signorissimo. Everything's to hand."

"I expect great marvels. Better than your show for Floriano."

"Ten times better, Signorissimo. Or strike me." Shaachen
winked offensively.

Wine came, nosegays.

Furian looked long, and slowly, all about him. His eyes made for
him a shifting tapestry of lambent dresses, coats, hair piled in false
clouds, the flicker and stab of jewels. And to this, the orchestra

played accompaniment so mathematically, like a mechanical toy. It had four dolls, at tabor, at fiddle, at trumpet, even a harpsichord balanced on a floor of planks. While everywhere, half-disembodied and alive on their own, the masks of Carnival. A true unicorn to make any rhinoceros blush. A maned tiger. Gargoyles, Neptunes, dryads. And the fashionable new masks that were like fans, their spread tines rising into the plumes of peacocks and flamingos.

Furian had known all this, something close to it, only those few years since. He missed it still, the comforts and allurements, the sweet fragrances of pampered washed skin, and perfume from the Orient. He rubbed his sores against the splinters of his loss, viciously cherishing everything he might no longer have.

"Look there," said Shaachen. "Look, look."

"What? Which?"

"Her mask—the Principessa Messalina."

"You know their names, not I."

"The blond gown clasped with opal."

Furian looked. She was a tall woman, whose ziggurat of hair matched her dress. The mask was a wonder. A fan, but of fretted ivory, out of which partly emerged the outlines of a delicious ivory face, with dawn lips and evening lids.

"She has, herself, the countenance of an ox," said Shaachen. "No doubt the mask suits her better. Made, they say, such masks, by an inner circle of the Mask Guild. I've heard she keeps it on in bed, her husband, the prince, prefers it. Her lover, too."

Shaachen also was an old gossip. Furian turned away, to where a monkey was jumping over a cane, higher and higher, with apparent good will.

Beyond the monkey, at the edge of the clustering trees, blue glimmered on darkness.

He said, lightly, to Shaachen, "And who is that one?"

"Oh, caught your fancy, has she? I thought you only liked the bad girls, Furian Furiano."

"So I do. Isn't she bad at all?"

"Not with your sort. But I don't know her. Yes, a graceful line. But too slight. What does she live on, honeydew?"

Squashed Ear leaned forward. "There's supper over there. The sort of food I don't often see."

"Eat," said Shaachen, "don't gorge. There may be work to do."

Squashed Ear strode boldly behind the rows of dainty gilded chairs, to long tables holding pagodas of fruit, and a terrible greenish salt-swan from the lagoons, stuffed with spicy fish, no doubt, and dressed in its feathers. There came a rearrangement about the orchestra.

A goblet of Venusian crystal was in Furian's hand. Impossible turquoise glass blown with vapors like cirrus. He stared at it. He did not want this moment, because he knew now they would sing the Song. And she—she stood there against the trees in her alien blue. The woman whose eyes held blue fire.

He drank quickly. The wine was ancient and heady. It lifted up his skull so the moon, which now was sailing closer over the groves, could see in at his brain.

A little boy dressed as a Roman page was standing before the harpsichord stage. He had the fine, pinched face and pouter pigeon chest of a diver's child. They were trained to develop their lungs for swimming long segments of time under Aquila and Silvia, searching out drowned treasures of Venus. Sometimes one would be found instead to have a voice,

The orchestra rippled, and the mincing Prince Teobalto called out shrilly, like an elderly lady at the play, "Hush! Hush, if you please!"

Twittering, the party went silent, and the Song began.

He should watch her. Watch her butterfly mask, watch for the flame of blue tears escaping the eyeholes. Or would tell-tale blood, also as in a play, appear on her fingers or her gown?

With the orchestra supporting it, like a transparent bird, the child's voice—he had one, indeed—flew up the delicate notes.

Furian now heard all the words.

In his darkness, having found her, he could only try to win her. But she would not smile, he could not make her smile. Not at a jest, not in happiness, not even out of compassion. And so he must leave her to her solitary stony fate, and himself could only die.

At the last word, the boy held the note, long and long, the orchestra whispering, garlanding the silk-drawn hurt of its beauty. The audience held its breath. The vulgar ones counted. Not needing to count, Furian knew the child held the note for one whole minute, until he mildly signaled with hand, the orchestra coiled up the Song, and his voice sank effortlessly to an end.

They fell on him like loving hyenas, petting, stroking. The child, not out of breath, suffered it with dignity, until his gaudy guardian came up to lead him away.

The tears had pierced from Furian's own eyes. They had burnt him where they got out. The long-nosed mask hid everything.

But she stood immobile by the trees. Her own mask would hide nothing, for why should she care. And he himself was not moved, forgivably, by human tragedy, only by the power of music.

Shaachen said urgently, "Wake up. Fetch that lout." And primly, "How dare he use the nobles' tables as a trough? He should have gone to the servants' station. I must go down now and prepare."

In the beginning, Furian had been intrigued by Shaachen's alchemical and sorcerous talents, but he was too skilled. If they were tricks, you could not see through them, and if the magic were real, they inspired an idea of horror. What kind of world was it where evil and humiliation prevailed, yet a sun could be made to rise from a bowl of water?

The country was very wild here, had been let go, the trees enormous, primal flowers in long, tasseled grass, and here and there a statue artfully toppled, its hands snapped off, girdled by moss.

In a clearing, lit now by the moon, Shaachen went to a marble altar. It was perhaps fifty years old, looked a thousand, cracked and weathered, with ivy. Trees closed thick behind it.

Shaachen snatched his bag, and threw out handfuls of powder. He made over the altar three or four passes. Squashed Ear watched respectfully, suppressing belches.

"He's a gifted and wise man." Furian shrugged. Squashed Ear added, "I wouldn't like to get on his shadow side."

"Nor would he like you to. Just keep an eye open for anyone trying to spoil things."

The Revelers were eddying down after them now. The Princess Messalina came first, with a man on either arm. She was laughing raucously, tossing her head. The ivory mask had made her playful. Which was the husband and which the lover? Neither of either? Others followed, and some men with torches,

The orchestra did not come, only the tabor man with his narrow drum. He stood to one side, and began to tap a rapid little heartbeat.

The sparkling crowd surged and swirled. It was smaller. Not all had followed.

Prince Teobalto appeared, his silk covered by a long black robe, and his face, now, by a ram's mask with gilded curling horns to augment his fleece. He was to be High Priest of the Revel.

Furian felt a weary distaste. Once or twice, with Shaachen, he had watched such affairs before. At one, even, a lamb had been put to death, a 'sacrifice' which was unlawful, (Not for any ethical reason, the Butcher's Guild opposed it).

The torches were planted in the ground in ready slots.

Youths dressed as pagan altar boys lined up behind Teobalto. He raised his arms. The black sleeves swooped back and showed anachronistic lace.

"O Diana, look kindly on your worshippers."

No one mocked his old-lady voice.

Shaachen, tucked in by a tree, touched something in his bag.

A shower of silvery lights sprayed upwards from the altar, formed the shape of a crescent moon, and went out.

The crowd chirruped and lifted its cups of Venusian glass.

A part-naked girl came out of the wood at the altar's back. She was white and slender, with large, firm breasts. At her groin hung a fringe of scintillants, and she was wigged and masked in silver.

She leapt lightly on the altar, gestured to the sky. She sang a verse.

"Kneel and honor her, the goddess of the night."

Furian thought, *Where is the blue whore? I don't see her.*

More silver rain dazzled up. The naked girl now danced slowly, describing her body with her hands, and the Revelers swayed as if before a snake. Furian felt no desire. In the crowd he could not see the girl in alien blue. She must be above, her butterfly hinged up, eating and drinking with a greasy mouth. There were several who had no interest in *this,* preferred more private dalliance. Perhaps she was choosing for herself another victim. As they said, *The canals are deep.*

The first girl lay flat on the altar, and a shining crescent rose out of her body and burst in streaks of pale fire.

A hunting horn sounded deep in the wild park.

Now, then, for the show-piece.

Furian glanced about. Shaachen's way seemed clear. Why in any case would Prince Teobalto work out a grudge on Shaachen, who was less than a gnat to him, and here of all places?

Then the goddess Diana came racing from the wood.

She must be an illusion, but how conjured God knew. Yes,

Shaachen had genius as well as villainy. Maybe he was even in league with some supernatural power, as the alleys said.

Diana was tall, perhaps seven or eight feet in height. Her hair poured back from a diamond fillet, and the lunar crescent was iridescently blazoned on her forehead. She wore a tunic and buskins, as in certain paintings. She was white as snow, as the moon, all but her diamonds, and her eyes which burned a feverish nocturnal yellow-green, like a cat's. Behind her ran, or seemed to run, the white lions of the Equus.

The crowd scattered with exclamations.

Diana bounded over the altar and the cowering mortal girl, blew right through the clearing, and her train of lions and dogs after her, and other animals out of myth, even an icy unicorn, whose glacial horn gleamed like a drawn sword.

They were gone in a lightning through the Groves.

The guests of Prince Teobalto righted themselves in clamor, laughing and blaspheming. The prince himself, the High Priest, straightened from a terrorized crouch.

The tabor player, who had lost the beat, regained it.

Was this all? No. Another apparition was walking out of the wood.

A voice, better by far than Teobalto's, (trained), announced, "The folly of life. The unreason of flesh. These have brought you here. Behold."

The apparition halted. It was a woman in a dress of black velvet traced by jewels. Was she actual? Perhaps not. An unearthly music quivered, pipes, harps, to the rhythm of the tabor—which perhaps was no longer being played.

She wore, this creature, a fan mask, and all at once, drew it off. Beneath, another mask, this like a woman's face, rouged and powdered, with spangled lids. She drew off the second mask. Now her face was stretched, pure skin, taut as that of a young girl, yet sallow, like parchment. The eyes smoldered black. And then she pulled off the mask of skin. Below was the skull.

It was an ornate skull, set with a green jewel between the eyes. But the eyes were gone. Two hollows, like the black night hollow of the wood beyond the altar. White teeth grinned, lipless.

The androgynous voice announced, "Ah, what matter the world's sorrow. Smile, smile, Signorissimas, Signorissimos. I, a skull, tell you. Keep smiling. *I* do!"

The figure winked out. It had looked solid, but was a phantom.

Again, Furian pondered how it was done—a mirror in the wood, some image cast by lamps from another place . . .

One of the ladies was fainting. But the Princess Messalina had pranced forward in her ivory mask.

She vaulted on to the altar, and with two hands ripped apart the bodice of her costly gown. Two fallen breasts slid from the cage of corseting.

Messalina laughed. She stamped her foot on the altar. There was something quite mad about her. Something—unholy.

A thick-set man, masked and maned as a wolf, ran forward and seized her, dragged her down, screaming and laughing, and galloped her away into the wood from which the apparitions had emerged.

Furian stepped back.

Couples cantered past him. A naked, eagle-faced man hustled the naked girl from the side of the altar—and a wonder the princess had not trodden on her—his hands already busy on her flesh.

The sight of a skull had seemed to make them appreciate the flesh a great deal—

Teobalto, the ram, leaned on a tree, with one of his acolytes kneeling before him, the priestly black robe bundled up over his head.

Squashed Ear spat. Furian said sharply, "Control yourself. Don't be a fool."

Shaachen, like an over-dressed, demented gutter rat, sprang up to them. "They've ruined my show. I had more. We go now. Shake this dust off our heels."

The gilded horns of the ram scraped bark audibly. Already shrieks of orgasm spumed from among the trees.

A woman with a nymph mask and green tresses, half unclothed, rushed against Furian.

"Feel me! *Touch* me!"

But he put her off, and went by.

As they climbed up the slope, Shaachen scurrying ahead, cursing, muttering like a granny cheated of her treat, the form of the woman in the blue dress appeared. She stood solitary, unique, like a ghost. Tonight there were pearls in her hair. She clasped her hands lightly together at her so-narrow waist. He could have snapped her in half. The butterfly of her face showed only the most distant hint of eyes. Were they blue, or black? Or nothing, like the skull.

Shaachen fussed past her, not seeming to see. Squashed Ear strode after. In a covet beyond, a small rosy boy, unclad like a cherub, had unleashed his own desire on a pie. He rent it like a savage beast a deer, the gravies splashing like blood.

Furian said, "Who are you, Madama?"

Her masked face stirred a little, a blue-white flower on a stem. She said nothing.

Furian said, bleakly, "Keep smiling, Madama."

And went on up the slope.

"The god was to come, the deus of Carnival. Lust." Shaachen chattered as they climbed up the inner stair. The lower floor lay in lightless disarray after his latest clinic. "Then the planets of the City, Maxima Venus, Neptune for Pesci, and the moon for Cancro, and Vulcan for Scorpio. Ultimately, fireworks, without powder, naturally. But these drunken licentious sots, they can't wait. They must have off their garments and rut."

"Perhaps they were afraid of your powers."

"Afraid? He demanded it all, that booby."

"Teobalto. He didn't cause trouble."

"I expected to be set on. Certain things—showed I would be. And he, he's joined the Alchemist's Guild. He reckons to become a master, but even a rose petal in water, to make it moves beyond him. He's jealous."

Shaachen flung open his upper door.

The study loomed, dim as a tunnel, until Shaachen struck tinder to the candles. There was the clatter of wings.

"Ah, my darling. How are you? Did you miss me?" Shaachen, calmed at once by his familiar, stroked the magpie's demoniac head. "Tell me what time is it?"

The magpie, from its perch on his shoulder, split the black clippers of its beak and cawed twice.

"Ah," said Shaachen, "what minutes?"

The magpie shook its head, ruffled the black and white wings. Under its dagger beak and wicked head, its feathered breast was soft as a baby's first hair.

"None then," said Shaachen. He held up his hand. "Hark."

They paused, and after some thirteen seconds, heard the Primo strike the second hour of morning.

The magpie was infallible in its trick of telling time. It would even demonstrate the minutes, hopping or pecking up to thirty, raising the left wing to indicate the lapse before, the right to show the minutes after, the hour.

One more uncanny feat.

The colored bottles and vials massed black on the window. The bird had knocked one over.

Shaachen took the cover from a reeking dish of unpleasant scraps, and fed the magpie, which ripped and tore eagerly.

"He'll pay me. I'll make him pay."

"Meanwhile I must convey your thanks to the boatman below."

"Oh, give him what you want from this." Shaachen tossed a bag of silver into Furian's hand.

"You're generous again."

"I'm rich. You know it. Why have you never robbed me, Furian Furiano?"

"It would tire me, Doctor Shaachen. It's less wearing to be good."

Shaachen chortled, in a better humor feeding disgusting entrails to his bird. "Did you make a meeting with your blue skinny?"

He did not miss much.

"No. She didn't want me, as you warned."

"Courage. Perhaps she'll change her mind. I locked it up."

"What, Doctor, did you lock up?"

"That mask you brought. You see?" He pointed to a high cupboard, reachable only by steps, set like a jail among the squeeze of books.

Furian said, "You lost interest in it."

"No. My interest grows. It's a horrid, nasty thing, that mask. It carries a taint."

"A composer of a song wore it," said Furian.

"Songs!" said Shaachen. "It stinks of some awfulness."

"How?" asked Furian, despite himself. He had not wanted to think about the mask from the canal, the mask of Cloudio del Nero. But there was no chance in any case. His music sprouted everywhere, like a divine weed.

"Imagine," said Shaachen, "a gazelle with the head of an adder. Imagine an angel, with the wings of a moth, broken, falling. Imagine unseen scratching on a window."

"The mask."

"The mask knows an infamous secret. It holds the secret of the death. The filthy joke of some filthiest god."

Gulls were fighting in the sky. The tide was lushly in, smelling of sea and offal, and water sipped at the brink of the pavement.

Furian gave Squashed Ear his fee. Squashed Ear lingered "Those women. Those noble ladies. I heard they go with any one." Roused up, evidently.

Furian said, "Better get home and wake your wife."

"I'd rather wake Juseppi's wife."

Furian said, "The best fortune, then," and was turning to go, when he saw darkness-on-legs coming round from the wall of Shaachen's palace.

Below, the high canal, the pole with the Neptune and no boat tethered. One lamp, smashed, giving no light, and the moon down. It was Shaachen's lofty window which lit the scene.

"A difficulty," said Furian, to Squashed Ear. "We'll have to earn our money after all."

There were four of them, big fellows from the rubbish tips of the lagoons. He had a view of stained, welcoming teeth, an earring that glittered, and knives that glittered better. Then Shaachen's candles went out one by one above, the window died, and there was no light at all.

Thank you, Doctor.

As they lurched nearer, Furian saw that three came dedicatedly for him, as if to a prescribed meeting.

His belly was molten, but his hands were always steady at such a juncture. It was after he would shake. If he lived to do it.

He said, "Gentlemen, come on. Can't I buy you off?"

One stood grinning like the keep-smiling skull, in front of him. Two nudged closer either side, more serious.

Furian took a handful of the ink-stanching writer's sand he brought out with him on such nights from his coat pocket. He slung it in the solemn left-hand face, at the eyeholes of the half mask. Simultaneously pulled the knife free of his belt, and rammed it in the middle ones guts.

To the left, hawking, scrabbling at eyes. The other, still grinning under a paste-board nose, bowed over, his teeth darkening further in the darkness, from blood.

The third one was surprised. His own blade tore Furian's best coat as Furian stamped—the gesture of the sex-avid principessa—on his foot. Then Furian had got the hand with the knife. He dislocated three fingers, and as the man romped glugging sideways, cut the fatal vein in his neck.

He kicked sand-eyes in the chest, smashing the breast bone. It gave as easily as the rib of a cooked fowl.

The other one, the fourth, was standing over Squashed Ear, who lay full-length. His head had been stoved in, and the proud hat, the feather, were wet and bruised like a fruit from the mess inside.

"Fuck you," said Furian. He leaned forward and sliced the fourth man's mask and face wide open. But through his blood, dropping down, the fourth man flatly said, *"We'll see—"*

And out of the shadow again, like fresh pus from a bottomless wound, more of them were coming, five, six, seven, hissing and rumbling, and some light that did not exist snagging the quills of their knives.

Furian turned. He jumped off the pavement, straight down into the stinking hell-black cold of the canal.

Below, the water insistently closing, holding tight to mouth and nostrils and breath to shut it out.

He surfaced ten lengths along the waterway, and two knives plopped in beside him like friendly fish.

Then some stone they had plucked, unreasonably momentous, struck him a numb and deathly blow to the right side of his back.

Furian sank now, gasping in the poison of the canal, swallowing the piss of the sea god's night.

Christ and Maria—A bodily surge tried to eject the muck at once. His nose and throat were full of liquid ordure going two ways.

Choking, he came up, gagged, spat, went under a third time.

He swam in a panic-bright trance of oblivious, nauseous confusion. He kept down as long as he could.

Emerging finally he knocked against the stone of a house-side, and a little rat went neatly by him, happy in its element.

But the bullies someone had sent to crown the night were almost far enough away. Around a turn or two of the canal.

Furian forced himself down once more and swam until consciousness was almost out.

He came up by some ancient stair he did not recognize. No lamps, the rope-arteries of alleys. Fruit peel rotted on the water.

Under the wall, he thrust off his mask, sneezed violently twice, then brought up the fluid of half the canal, garnished by Cupid's apricots. Far above someone cursed him for a drunk. He crawled away down an alley, back full of black pain, retching and laughing, part strangled, wiping the slime from his eyes.

4

A fat pretty daughter of the Amari family, who he had fancied once, and once been allowed to fondle—but no more than fondle, she was virtuous—observed him without comment. She had a pretty mask too, a pink flower with eyes.

Then she said, as he turned for the door, "You shouldn't bath in your clothes, Signore."

"You'll have to show me how to do it properly one day, Fiamina."

She said, "Two men came, just after dawn."

"Two men—for me?"

"Yes, Signore. They wanted your rooms. They had something for you, they said."

"Did you show them?"

"Mumma did. All up the stairs."

"Are they up there now, Fiamina?"

"No. They came out. They were sorry to miss you."

Nothing was out of place in either of the two rooms. On the table was a duplicate of his mask, a white face with a long, pointing nose. It had been skewered to the wood by a cheap stiletto.

That was all.

It was enough. He was the mask. They had noted him, and would complete the task.

As he was rowed towards the Primo, Furian could smell the carpentry smell of Signore Amari's second coat. He had bought it from him soon after returning to the apartment. Amari had wanted Furian's best clothes too, even though Furian had been roaming in them, wet and stinking, for nearly three hours. He had taken a long and rambling way home. Not that it was home any longer.

The locked box that contained his books, the green glass and his mother's mirror—all he cared about—he left with the caretaker under some coins. "Not for sale." He left his rent too, sufficient for another month. By then something would have happened. He would be dead, or elsewhere, or all the trouble settled, whatever the bloody trouble was. For while Shaachen's (perhaps imagined) feud with Prince Teobalto might account for a roughing up, the band by the canal had been merchants of death.

He was cruelly sorry about Squashed Ear. He did not even know his true name, but presumably there was a widow.

It was another man's wife, however, that he meant to see.

When he stepped ashore below the heavenly white dome, no one took much notice. His clothes had the laborer's look, and his mask was different, a black dog's short pugnacious snout, complete with whiskers.

They had known the other mask. They had been at pains to show him so.

Of course, they could have waited. Bribed the Amaris to keep quiet. (Would the Amaris have done that? Probably.) Whoever wanted Furian so much was also in no hurry, perhaps even enjoyed this game with a quarry who changed his appearance and ran stealthily away.

"Is Juseppi about?"

"No. No one's seen Juseppi for a week."

"A day," said another.

A third wanderlier, a big man, came up whistling the Song. It was an omen. He bulked before Furian and said, "Hey, Doggy, I can tell you something. What's it worth?"

"What's the news?" said Furian, "and I'll let you know."

The big man, masked as Juseppi had been, but better, as a large bloated fish, hinged up his mask to reveal a fishy, thick-lipped mouth. "Clever, for a dog."

Furian said, "I heard he was in difficulties."

"So what? You're a carpenter from Silvia, I'll bet. What's a wanderlier to you?"

Someone, negating the omen, pushed the big fish aside and said straight out to Furian, "I heard he died, Juseppi. I was going by this morning. There was a row from his house. He had half the ground floor of the Palace Bertro. From his wife's family, you see. But she was screaming away. She's got a loud voice. It was Oh God, my Juseppi, what shall I do?"

"She's a slut," said another, "came down here, making a dance. She's got an eye for a man."

"Watch out, if you go there," said another.

"The Palace Bertro?"

"See, he wants to go there now, meet her. It's on the Blessed Maria Canal. Just behind the Little Church."

Dressed as he was, he should have very poor supplies of money, so he gave them nothing, and walked off, to barks and cries of encouragement.

The Blessed Maria Canal ran narrow and glass-green, and on the balconies above were flowers with the washing. The Palace Bertro had a courtyard before it, where an old woman sat in black like a suitable specter. She had a black cloth mask.

She paid him no heed. Everything was quiet. He went in at the door and was in a large room, its plaster peeling, shimmering with the water reflection through tall latticed windows. Three lean cats eyed him from a passage way out of which now rose a dull, ominous murmur. Then a woman wailed, long and rasping. It sounded more like fury than distress. He had come to the right place.

He knocked at an old door. There was silence now.

After a minute, a thin boy opened the door. He had lank fair hair and a terrified unmasked face. He wore the charcoal gown of the University. He was about fourteen.

"Juseppi," said Furian, clearly.

"My father."

"Will you let in."

"No, Signore. No, no."

"I want to help your mother."

"No—no—"

Then, behind the boy, a woman came sweeping and pushed the door wide. Her black hair was half up, half down. She wore a black lace veil over it, askew, and wrapped across her breasts that two men had praised. Her eyes were rusty from tears, her unmasked face coarse, beautiful, lined and raging.

"Who are you? What? Tell me! What do you know?"

"Nothing, Signora. I used his boat now and then."

"Then why are you here?"

"I was concerned."

She flung back her head on the rounded column of her fawn throat. She laughed roughly. The disheveled veil slipped and she yanked it back.

He saw her eyes were also half insane. There was a sort of blindness in their depths—she had been shown some thing that had made it hard for her to look at anything else, or give anything else her judgment.

"Oh come in. Come in. What do I care?"

The boy moved away from the door, and Furian walked into the room.

It was wide and gracious, like the chamber outside, with a terracotta floor, and one vast window where a glorious pot of basil towered. At a long table two men with eye-masks sat sullenly, grim-faced, and in the corner was another old woman, masked and wearing black, exactly like the one outside.

Things were scattered. A mending box, very full, (he could not picture her mending), a broom, a chest, open, and spilling sleeves, an overturned stool, soiled dishes set on the floor.

"Have some wine," said Juseppi's wife, loudly, scornfully. "Why not?"

"Calypso," chided one of the men. He got up but at once she let out again a huge almost inhuman scream.

"Leave me alone! In God's name, haven't I earned it."

And she tore her hair, violent, so a slender strand of it came loose in her grip. She waved this at Furian. "I'm not to be trifled with. Not now."

Furian said, "What happened to him?"

"Oh? You want to know that? You do?"

"Yes, Signora."

"Come here then. Yes, come and look."

And she reached out and grasped his hand in her burning claws, and began to pull him—he could imagine her doing it to any man, her son, Juseppi, the Ducem of the City—towards another door.

The first man said, "Calypso—it isn't fitting—"

The second man said more strongly, "The police will come back. No one else should see."

"I've seen—*I* have! Let this bastard look."

She hauled him into the other room. He would have had to use a lot of force to resist her. She was like a tigress.

The boy began to weep suddenly. And at that, her face collapsed like a shaken tawny rose.

"Hush—my love. Be still, Mumma is here."

Left alone, Furian turned, and saw he was in a bedroom. An embroidered rug hung on the wall, and an icon of Beautiful Maria in her magpie blue. There was a star on her forehead that appeared to be an opal.

Outside, the boy sobbed as if his heart were breaking. Perhaps he had held it in till now.

Furian saw what lay on the bed, and understood from where the smell had come. The butchering smell of the shops on the Street of Meats.

When he sensed the shadow at the door again, Furian said, "Is this how you found him, Signora?"

"Yes. No. My brothers helped me lay him out. And the women. They've seen worse. But he was below in the canal. In a chicken basket in the boat." Furian made an involuntary movement. She said, "If you're going to puke, lean out the window, if you please."

"I'm all right, Signora."

He wondered if she had done so. Doubtless not. She was a tigress, after all.

Juseppi had been cut in parts. Head, torso, both arms and both hands, both legs and both feet, (and his penis, under the towel?) had been severed, cleanly, maybe by a butcher's knife. Everything was now laid together, in the proper line of a body. The blood was old, black and dry.

His face, seen now, since he was maskless, was pathetically peaceful. His eyes had been closed, and had violet bruises beneath them. He was a good-looking, unnotable man.

"Who," said Furian, "did this, Signora?"

She came into the room and shut the door. The rose was reassembled.

"I don't know," she said. "Do you? Is this a threat? Are you here for them? He offended someone. Tell me what to do."

"I'm as much in ignorance," he said, "as you."

"That's a pity," she said. She stepped forward, graceful, took his hand. She put it over her round pale breast, paler than her face and neck, a breast like vanilla, sweet. And then she put her own hand into his crotch. "You like me," she said.

"But you're used to that," said Furian. He was hard, jumping in her hand.

She said, "I've got a nice mouth. Two nice mouths. I'd wrap you up, carpenter. Yes?"

"You didn't love him," said Furian.

Her lips were rouged red. He could taste them.

He took his hand off her breast.

She said, "He was a man."

As Furian went through the door, she slapped him hard across the back, exactly where the ones who wanted to kill him, and had conceivably killed Juseppi, struck him with the stone.

The boy caught his elbow.

"It's all right, Signore. Mumma's a bitch."

"No," said Furian, "she's a tiger. Remember that."

Outside he leaned over the canal and threw up again. The old woman in the black mask watched impassively. Somewhere a baby cried, as if it knew it should never have been born.

There was a child crying too in the doorway of the Boatman's Tavern. A little girl, about four, she stood in her rags while two burly men in eye-masks mocked her. There seemed to be no reason why.

"Look at the sow. Stinky little whore."

And the child wept in frozen, non-comprehending horror.

Furian went up to the men and pushed them aside. He slapped the bigger one hard across the face, so a thread of color issued from his nose.

"Hey—bastard—"

"You want more?" Furian showed the knife at his belt. But they were the cowards he suspected, and dead drunk. One herded the other away up the narrow street: "Don't tangle with him, he's mad."

Furian crouched by the child.

"It's all right," she wept. He picked her up and stood with her as she buried her wet face in his neck and hair. Even she had a little eye-mask, made of a rag, soaking now. She smelled of dirt and misery. But her skin was, under its filth, as smooth as his father's silks.

"Where's your mumma, Baby?"

She wept.

He carried her into the tavern. From its beams hung lamps on black brass cords, afloat in pipe smoke. A figurehead of Neptune, green-bearded, was propped against the bar.

"Whose child is this?"

The young woman with a lizard's mask said, "Mine, Signore. Useless, she is. You want to buy her?" It was only partly a jest.

He set the child on the bar, and wiped her face with his sleeve. She had let go of him at once, used to being abandoned.

"Brandy."

"Get to the dishes, you," said the woman to the child, who slipped down and hurried to obey.

Furian took the bottle and the unclean glass, and went to sit on a bench among the wanderliers. There were others there, tradesmen of various types, a poulterer reeking of fowls.

Furian sat thinking for a while. He listened to their talk. It was of nothing.

A man rose at length and loomed over Furian.

"What's your business, carpenter?"

"Take a drink with me. I'll tell you."

"That's fine for me."

They sat, and drank. The man pushed up his dolphin mask to the top of his head. He was barefaced, but no one challenged him. Here, apparently, it was a brotherhood. Furian would have to hope the two he had annoyed outside did not come back.

"Juseppi," said Furian eventually. "Is it true he's run off?"

"Why's that?"

"If he doesn't want her, I like the look of his wife."

"She's a cunt. But he's not run. He's dead."

Furian paused as if surprised. He said, "All the better, God rest his soul. What did he die of?"

"Someone's knife, I heard."

"No," said another man, leaning over to them with his pipe, "it was the Snake. It chomped him in bits with its teeth."

Hands rose, crossing hearts. They were superstitious, the wanderliers, about the giant supernatural serpent under the lagoons and canals of Venus.

Furian said, "Had he done something to anger it?"

"Anger *someone*," said the unmasked dolphin. "He'd found something, blabbed about it."

"Found what?"

"He'd rowed a man about, looking for Carnival corpses for some cranky alchemist."

"What man?"

"God knows. But Juseppi found a mask."

"No ordinary mask," said the other man, who had his eyes part covered by owl wings. He put down his fuming pipe, took the brandy bottle and filled his own glass.

"A mask's a mask," said Furian.

"This one was a-drip with evil," said the man.

"How?"

"He didn't say. He said he dreamed of it all night. It—howled at him. He said it was a portent of his death. He went to confess at Primo Suvio."

Furian's ears roared softly. The lights of the tavern swam through the air. The swallowed canal water had not done him good.

"Well, that's enough for me. If he's gone, she'll be lonely."

"Calypso? Not she. Heard tell she'd got another admirer already."

Furian got up unsteadily. They laughed and gave him a supportive shove. The dizziness passed and he walked jauntily out of the tavern.

There was no one in the street. He thought of the child scrubbing at plates. Probably, under her dress, she was black and blue with her mother's beatings.

You wanted to rescue them, all of them. But it was not possible. For everyone seen, there were a thousand more. All those blows, those tears. And God in his jewel-encrusted heaven, looking down, missing not even the fall of the sparrow. Smiling at its pain?

Juseppi had talked generously about the mask. He had made a confession of his sins. He had thought the mask foretold his death. It had.

Furian walked slowly. Long and warm and raw, the shadows of the houses slopped on him, and the noon sun sword-slanted between. It would be easy to drop down flat.

Like the slices of light and dark, the pieces of all this, whatever it was, swung round him. He glanced over them.

The mask lay on the water just beyond the reflection of a window. Cloudio del Nero's mask. The window of the blue harlot. And Juseppi on the bed, in ten or eleven parts. While the knives of would-be assassins glittered like the quills of porcupines, and again the stone struck him in the back, and he gulped the urine of Neptune and went down.

Furian leant on a wall. He needed some medicine. Shaachen would be excellent for that—Get to Shaachen.

But then, Shaachen was also caught inside the swirling of loose bright pieces. Del Nero's mask was in his cup board. Surely it was the mask which must give up the answer to all this?

5

Cupid said, "If I pay him, why won't he come? Look. I've got eighty-seven silver duccas saved, and all these brass venuses. Surely he would? You're not fit—"

"He wouldn't, Cupid. But you're a winged angel to say it. I shouldn't be here."

"Where else but with me, that likes you so?"

Furian lay on her bed, in the rose-death sheets, staring stupidly at the ceiling. His dog mask was on the floor but she still had the swan wings over her eyes, which were dark and anxious. A good actress.

He had gone to her by devious routes. Everybody went to prostitutes, for God's sake, it should be safe for her. Anyway, if questioned, she would betray him at once. It would be a code, not to be sentimental, and kind only where able.

She had been kind this afternoon. Putting off a client, albeit an elderly one she disliked, giving Furian clean water and the juice of plums. He no longer vomited, but the slight nausea dragged on. She said he had a fever, a white fever. She had sucked and licked at him until he jetted into her mouth, saying this would help to cleanse him. She was an adorable girl, with her gilded curly head, like a slender cherub. Of course, he paid her well. Some of the eighty seven duccas were his.

"Your Doctor Dianus is a beast," she finally concluded, "if he wouldn't visit you. And you're his friend."

"Maybe. Yes, perhaps. Or no."

He wanted to wait until the night came. He had a plain black eye-mask and a different coat, bought from a desperate Jewish tailor near Aquila. It was an elegant coat. Not his usual style at all.

There had been no one he had suspected, no attack all day.

Probably he had built events into a ridiculous importance. They were all coincidences elevated by the fever.

When the sun set, he sat up, and waited for the room to steady.

"You don't sweat enough. It should pour out of you to rinse off the poison. Those canals. They kill so many. Even a crab from there can kill you, if you eat it not hot enough. And you, to go *swimming* there."

"I was pissed as a king, my Cupid."

"Silly Furian."

She kissed him, and then helped him to dress.

"Don't—be careful who you speak to, Cupid."

"Oh? What's up?"

"I owe a man money."

Outside the sky was magpie (alien) blue, and stars made patterns that fever-moved now, fascinating him.

He would go across Fulvia. He would, better yet, take the other route first.

Something said within him, rankled, like the sober voice in drink, *Don't be a fool.*

He laughed it off, as one did the sober voice. To hell with it. He would.

The canal turned, and they came into wider water. On either side the phosphorescent dimness of houses like cliffs. Iron balconies. Night-faded white roses from an urn.

The lamp burned. No longer pink. It was grey, now.

As Juseppi had, the wanderlier started to sing, not the Song. *"If you were mine, my girl—"*

"Shut up," said Furian.

"Signore?"

"I don't want to offend you. But don't sing."

"Very well, Signore."

They were usually polite, in the boat. They wanted the fare. This one had the visage of a clown. It leered out of the shadow, its frown and down-turned mouth.

The window was above them. It was black.

"Put down the oar."

"Signore?"

A stupid one, this.

"Stop us here. Wait, until I tell you."

Furian stood up. The influx of new drink had contained the vertigo of the fever.

He looked at the window, and readied himself. It showed very little, only one faint-gleaming thing, just behind the lattice. Which might be anything.

Furian sang. His voice, untrained but sound, a light baritone.

"She is the moon of my evening.

"Before her darkness ruled me."

He knew the song. He sang it, both verses, with a slow intensity; largo. He wanted to make her smile, could not. She would not. He must die. He held the last note only for nine seconds, and when he stopped, there was a spike in his left side. But it went away.

"Oh Signore—bravo, bravissimo—"

"Quiet. Be quiet."

The gleaming faint thing was her mask, the butterfly with blue eyes and eyeholes for blue eyes.

In the moment he realized, he realized too she was not wearing it. It hung there in space, suspended by a ribbon from some hook, behind the lattice in the shadow.

He spat in the canal, and remembered he had only thought the truth—but what?—it was forgotten—under the unlucky Bridge of Lies.

Shaachen's palace was in darkness, and when he went around to the alley door, it was locked. Furian knocked a while. Shaachen had occasional servants, you could never be sure. On the wall someone had scrawled *Death to Lovers!*

When no one came to open up, Furian forced a narrow, weak-grilled window to the side.

He climbed in, went through a verminous pantry, and up a back stair. Twice he had had to use this way before.

The door to Shaachen's study was ajar, and inside there was no sound.

"Doctor Shaachen—are you there?"

Shaachen's voice muttered, elderly, hollow. "Who would know?"

"Furian."

"Come in and see." Furian went through the door. Doctor Dianus Shaachen, seated in the corner on the floor, looked up and said, "Am I? Am I Shaachen?"

The room was lit by one guttering lamp. It was a shambles.

The window that faced the canal, black now, had stayed intact, but all the bottles were broken. On the ground lay the orrery, buckled and ruined. Books were everywhere, torn, pages trampled, and smeared with excrement which stank, in a dry, thin way, hours out of date.

On the desk the heavy tortoise-turtle had not been harmed, but papers were scattered, some drawn, Furian could see, with crude moronic cartoons of sex and savagery.

A chair had been smashed.

Furian's eyes went up the wall, past a broken lamp, and found the cupboard like a jail, where the books had been pulled down. The cupboard door was off, hanging by one hinge. The place inside was empty.

"They took the mask."

Shaachen said, "Curse the mask. Do I want it. What does it matter to me, the death of human debris."

"He was—" said Furian. He stopped. In Shaachen's hands, as he sat on the floor like a tired child, was something black and white, stiff, and oddly folded like a poorly made cloth doll.

"You see," said Shaachen. He held it up. The lamp stroked a pearly gleam along white feathers, the shine of the canals over black ones. "They didn't touch him. He flew up too high, my darling. But when I came back, and come in, and find it, when I find all this, he flies down to me. Down to me, his father. And he puts his head into my breast. And then he dies. It was anger kills him, or fear. My darling. My only love. My magpie."

"Christ, Christ," said Furian.

"Fucks on your Christ. Where was your Christ when my darling died? Shits on him."

Furian went to the table. A decanter of deep blue Venusian glass held wine. He poured it in a goblet and took it to Shaachen.

"You drink. Would choke my throat."

Shaachen lifted the dead magpie to his lips and kissed the smoke-soft feathers. Its black eyes glistened, not yet dull.

Furian swallowed wine. He took more. He sat down by Shaachen on the floor. It was very dark, the lamp purple with exhaustion, nothing in the window but broken bottles and black sky.

"Gather your strength, Doctor. We should leave here. They wanted the mask, and might come back to punish you."

"What do I care. Let them come. I'll rip out their livers."

"That might not be possible."

"Let me alone."

They sat side by side, and the magpie rested stiff and weightless with death in Shaachen's old hands. The lamp filmed, flickered and went out.

Just audible, as if made louder by the lessening of sight, the glutinous constant murmur of the canal reached in to them. The sea would, in the end, wash the City away, would wash away everything.

Shaachen began slowly and carefully to speak. He told how he had seen the magpie in a too-little cage in the market, and how he had fed it a scrap of meat. And then they had let the magpie sit on his wrist and the magpie had pecked Shaachen spitefully, and the vendor swore at it and pulled on its leg chain hurtfully to correct it. But Shaachen had said, "Give him me." For the magpie had spirit and had been ill-treated, and anyway, was Shaachen's lost child. He told how he loved the magpie, its beauty, its strengthening flights about his rooms. How he took it to his bed, where it perched on the bedpost, nestled on his pillow, shat on the Eastern carpet and his wig on its stand. He loved its unmusical voice, its grace and insolence, its musty sometimes rancid smell. It came to know him. It trusted him. He alone could handle it, and when it pecked him he scolded it, then took it in his hand and kissed its bristly and wicked head. Its breast was warm and soft as a girl's. You could feel the heart beating like a tiny drum. It strutted and poked about. Once it had relieved itself on his dinner and then, with a delicate beak, eaten the compendium. You could feel its heart. And its eyes winked milkily when it blinked. And sometimes it had cawed in his ear and frightened him awake. And you could feel its heart. But no longer.

Furian got up, and went out. He checked the palace cautiously, knife in hand. No one was in the lower rooms. Bony pallet beds lurked in upper chambers. Also a chamber pot, months unemptied, was growing a curious fern. He did up the window he had forced.

Why had del Nero's mask had such value it must be traced, stolen back, killed for?

When he went up again, Shaachen was just the same.

"I'll bury him," Shaachen said, "I've a big casket. His little bones. I'll keep his bones. But they won't fly. They won't tell me the time. Darling," he said to his dead. "Darling."

Furian sat on a chair that had not been destroyed. He felt sick and weary. Later it might be feasible to lead the old man somewhere so he could rest.

He must have dozed, perhaps only a few minutes.

When he woke, there was a different noise in the room.

"Hark," Shaachen whispered. "Do you hear?"

Furian heard. It was the sound of wings, fluttering, over the room, up and down. The magpie had come alive.

"No," said Shaachen, as if Furian had spoken aloud.

Something flew over the window. It might have been a trick of fever-sight. Then came a light knock on the table, a slight dripping.

"He knocks over my inkwell," said Shaachen. His voice was light and breathless and young. "Always he does it."

Something scraped, scraped.

Furian half moved. Shaachen hissed, *"Stay still."*

The scraping ceased.

A flurry of wings beat up, up into the ceiling, and stopped in midair.

They sat motionless for some minutes.

Then Shaachen came to his feet. He went to a candle-stub, and lit it. Walking to the desk, he laid the candle and the dead magpie down there. "Look, Furian, you see?"

Furian got up. He crossed to the desk. On one of the papers a message had been untidily written, black on white, as if by the unwieldy scraping of a beak dipped in spilled ink.

"Thus," said Shaachen. He rubbed his face. Perhaps it was only magic, though he had seemed too feeble. Shaachen said, "The body is the mask of the soul. Eh, darling?"

On the paper were the words: *Don't cry. I live.*

PART TWO

The Face

6

Did the fallen angels remember their time in the house of their father, God, with shamed nostalgia? Had they been happy then?

The last day of his happiness in his father's house had been soon after Furian's eighteenth birthday. It was, in memory, a canary yellow autumn. His family had been at the estate for two months, and he had just left the University of Venus, and come there, along the dusty roads, to be with them. What a party they gave him. He could still taste, six years later, the meats and wines, the crystallized pale oranges in shells of rich, saccharine black dolche. He could see the fireworks let off beyond the terrace, showers of crystal on the dark. His mother, his sister Caro, with sparkling eyes. And his father taking such proud tender pains to treat him as a man. "My son." The coat embroidered by butterflies. Music.

At dinner, was his father's favorite agent, who had docked in Venus not seven days before. Lepidus was a gentleman, much traveled, a show-piece conversationalist. This time he had been as far as the Amarias, the mythical double continent dedicated to the Virgin.

Lepidus recounted his journey, after leaving ship at Candisi, and traveling overland. The trek had taken more than a year. He had seen broiling summers, and winters of such snows a man would sink and be lost in them as if in a lake. He had walked on rivers, and on the sea, iced ten feet deep. He saw the capital of Russa, with its core of metallic domes and green dragon-scale. Beyond, he crossed into the white land of Rus Parvus, Little Russa, (for it was Russa who had discovered the Amarias, two centuries before) traded for whale ivory figurines, the furs of bears, from the agate-eyed Argenti. Going south, by kayak and sled, he saw the great tent city of the tribal peoples named for brass, the Orichalci. One tribe now ruled the rest. They were called, in translation, plainly enough, The Enemy. They worshipped tribal gods, like the Argenti of the White

Lands. They believed, too, all things had a physical soul, internal during life, the supernatural essence linked to yet separate from both body and spirit. They were a cruel and noble people, living more in an unseen world of magic and powers than on the plains and deserts of the continent. Here he might trade for tobacco from the long blue leaves the Orichalci smoked in their ritual pipes.

One more year, and Lepidus reached the ultimate south, the second Amaria. Here were drugs and jewels and gold, and the cobweb silk which would pass through a woman's ring. Also the wonderful dark sweetmeat, black dolche. This came from a little hard bean, just as coffee did.

The table sat entranced by Lepidus' stories. Furian recalled, his mother had asked, "But surely someone has gone by now to convert these poor heathen to the religion of the Christ?"

"Oh yes, Madama. But they don't take to it, especially in the north. Their belief in a certain type of spirit is so strong. Do you know, they beg the pardon of every beast they hunt, and bless and thank it after a kill? They fashion spears that resemble the beast, to show respect to it. They have ceremonies in the dark, dances with masks and manes of feather. Every mask has the nature of some creature. They think all men are represented, on some higher corporeal plane, by a holy and non-physical part that yet is tied to the earth. The positions of the stars at birth, the nature of the man himself, these form his unseen psyche."

Furian's mother had turned uncomfortable, a touch ruffled. He could remember how he himself left an offering at the altar of Neptune in the City, minutes before he accepted divine communion at the altar of Christ.

"But can they comprehend the true soul?" asked Caro.

"Signorina, the soul to them is a stranger, something only to be regained with fleshly death. The *psyche* they constantly commune with while alive."

Furian's mind had drifted. There was a lovely girl among the guests, the daughter of one of his father's friends. She was too old for him, twenty perhaps, but he had wondered if he might have some chance of something.

The evening ended after the fireworks.

On the pillared terrace, with its antique fountain, (a Hebe pouring water), Furian's mother came and took his hands. "My dear, my dear."

After the mother, the sister. "Are you really home now? Or will you go off at once to travel? Stay a little."

And then, only the last of the night. It was almost four o'clock.

The servants were going round the garden, putting out the paper lamps, the candles under colored glass.

A bird sang somewhere, perhaps from its cage, or in the grounds, disturbed by all the lights.

His father's steward had approached, and said, "I'm glad to see you home, Signore."

"Thank you. So am I."

He had vowed to go out and visit the girl, and she had appeared to welcome this. She did not seem to mind the difference in their ages. She had allowed him, in the piecemeal shadows of a myrtle arbor, to stroke her upper breast, kiss the corner of her lips.

He looked up into the sky, where the stars were large and liquid, fixed and safe as diamonds on velvet.

Furian too might one day see the Amarias, and Russa. And he might begin to write the concerto. The first melody and the fugue had run in his mind all day. He knew himself happy. All his life after, he would recollect this fact. The sensation of happiness, full and warm. The past sound as a bell, the future gleaming beckoning before him, the present holding him in its steady safe hand.

He spoke a word of thanks to God, and crossed himself. And among the tress, a final lamp went out. Far off, the phantom of mountains had already an edge of bluish snow. It was the omen of a winter soon to come. He did not read it.

As he climbed the marble staircase, his hand on the gilded balustrade that showed fan-tailed birds—it was then. What had done it? The dying glimmers of the candelabra? The silence? The mystic last hour of departing night?

Between one step and the next. So swift.

Later, when he had tried to explain, they had said to him, all the ones he told, (the ones who shouted or pleaded, ranted, or mocked), that something must have occurred. Did he disremember? Had the lovely girl spurned him? His father insulted him? Had he seen something in the City which, only now, as night and inebriation perished, came back to him? But there was nothing, no explicit, appalling thing. No petty upset. No tragedy.

It was that he suddenly beheld, Here I am in this. But this— *this*—

Furian had paused, in puzzlement, trying to think, to think it out. It was elusive, ran before him, lashing its tail. A fearful monster. Yet it led him on.

A servant below, seeing to the indoor candles, had said, "Is there anything you want, Signore?"

"No—nothing, thank you."

And he climbed on, but the stair was a mountain now, with blue snow on it, and a black elemental clung to his back.

For the world was not this. The world was as he had seen it. The stench of the beautiful canals. The divers' children at Aquila and Silvia, their chests distended, and all their bones showing. The beggars and the thieves. The poor whores with draggled skirts and bare breasts and star-shaped patches over their sores. Old men who died. Young ones with knives. Children screaming in pain and some too weak to cry at all. A starving dog. A cat with a pigeon in its mouth. A drowned rat.

The world was trouble and hurt, age and decay and death. And since hell was already in the world, small chance it existed beyond it, or heaven either.

Furian felt and worried at these things as he climbed the stair, which seemed to go on for miles.

In his room, he stood at a loss, gazing about him at his rich man's possessions. They were no longer real. He inhabited a fantasy.

He had thought, *Oh, I'm low tonight. It must be the wine.* And he tried to go to bed cheerfully, clowning his drunkenness—stumbling, dropping things—which also was not real.

Almost as soon as he lay down, he slept. He dreamed a glamorous dream of walking through a garden, although not the garden of his father. The trees were made of Venusian glass. It was an hour after, and now he was wide awake. Presently he got up, and walked about.

Beyond the window and the balcony, a soft dawn wind was blowing up the Veneran plain. The sky was melting, and its lowest band was the color the fruits had been under the dolche.

If he tugged the rope, they too would get up and bring him a cup of hot black dolche, or a herbal tisane to help his slumbers.

He had only to ask, for all the doors to be opened to him.

But that was the fantasy again.

This was not life.

He sat on the balcony and watched the dawn flood up the sky like a blush. It was chilly. He shivered, but not from cold.

He was still reasoning with himself, and did not realize the days of lotuses were over.

All that morning he acted out his part, the performance of what he had, until the previous sunrise, been.

By noon his head ached and throbbed, and they indulged him, thinking he had got drunk at his party, and why not, why not.

He tried to write down the music that had been budding in his head. On the paper it looked as if it did not matter. Not because it was untuneful or inept, no, it was pleasing, gracious. But it was not real. The music of the real world was abrupt and sharpened, thorns without roses.

In two or three days he was sick. They called a physician who diagnosed a fever currently common in Venus, bred by her waters.

But when he had thrown the fever off, nothing had altered. The more he tried to push the being away, the being of reality, the worse it had hold of him. It was simpler to stop fighting.

He tried to tell Caro then. She did not grasp what he meant. At length, Furian approached his father.

"I need to go back there, I think. I need to live there. Not the way I did. In *their* way."

"Whose way, my son?"

Furian detailed the manner of real life. Poverty and lack, roughness and dis-grace.

His father laughed. His father told him Furian would do better to ride over to the estate of his father's friend. His father had heard a young lady there was pining for him.

Furian rode instead out into his own Father's estate. He watched the harvesters on the land. They were not, cared for by his God-fearing and generous family, so very wretched.

He found a wood, and stood bellowing at his father. Trying to vocalize the truth. But his father would never listen, or earnestly listening, would not hear.

Desperately, with a pang of horrible terror, Furian knew the abyss lay ready at his feet. And that he could only leap forward, into it.

7

Furian was dreaming. His father shouted at him. "Are you insane? What have I bred?"

And Furian's mother wept, her countenance a mirror of tears. Which he seemed to clutch also in his hand, the looking-glass that had reflected so often her face.

The new lodging lay among the slums near Silvia. He had gone away, and left implications elsewhere that he might have run further. Then come back close to home, as home had been. Was all this necessary? There had been nothing sinister since the murder attempt. They had the mask, whoever they were. Might that be the end of it, if he kept low, showed them proper frightened respect?

Shaachen had refused to move his ground. He let Furian supply five roughs, and chose a couple more from his clinic. These were to be Shaachen's guard. He had mixed, from unspilled stores, medicine for Furian's fever, then been busy burying the magpie in the iron casket, talking to it, calmly and lightly. It had shown it was spiritually alive, and so the burial was only for the sake of honor.

Furian was not sure what he had seen was to be credited. But he *had* seen it.

After swallowing Shaachen's bitter brew, Furian felt worse, perhaps a sign of its curative value. Once he had laid his false trail, he got into the dirty, lousy room, lay on the pallet, and slept like death for three or four hours. His dreams woke him, and flashing lights across his vision that only dispersed when he opened his eyes and sat up.

Mid-afternoon was in the slit of window. The heat was a hot syrup, and gladsome flies danced in the air.

He went and shouted down the house. The girl brought him a ewer of water to wash in and some food he did not want, so ate.

When he was ready, he called up the two fellows from the lower rooms. One had a silver earring and the mask of a pig. The other had only a whitish eye-mask. The pig was named appropriately Porco. The other one would not give even his nickname; invented one on the spot. "Call me Modest, Signore."

"I'm going out," said Furian. "You'll come."

"You've put on a nice coat, Signore," commented Porco. He ambled forward and fingered the sleeve the Jewish tailor had set with such pains. Furian slapped Porco off. Porco apologized.

"Three of these each," said Furian, showing the money. "More, if there's trouble."

"What if they kill you, these people?" asked the cautious, ugly Modest.

"Then you can take what you want. But I'll probably haunt you. It's your work to see I survive."

Porco crossed himself and made the trident sign to Neptune. "Don't joke about that, Signore. My brother's uncle was haunted just that way."

Modest swore. "When you're dead you're dead."

Furian thought of the magpie. He said, "Better hope so."

They went out.

Either Shaachen's drug, or the illness, made it seem to Furian as though he walked through thick clouds of liquid. How fitting here, in Venus. Between the dirty stooping shacks and sick tenements, came sudden vistas of the Laguna Silvia, inky green, with pieces of distant buildings seeming afloat on her like tiered ships. A city resting on water.

Whores squawked or cajoled them from balconies. This too had some relevance.

The satchel, with other things Shaachen had supplied, from secret drawers and places behind the wall, seemed heavy as a boulder.

They were rowed across, walked, walked.

Modest grumbled. He did not like this sort of exercise. Porco tried to cheer him up, telling him it was good for him, and perhaps the Signore would stop and let them all have some refreshment at a tavern.

Furian said he wanted them stony sober.

"One little glass, Signore."

"No."

When they reached west into the City, they saw, or Furian did, across the stretch of the Laguna Fulvia. There, before the Primo

Suvio, the masses had, more than six centuries ago, gathered to hear their priests exhort them to set out and rescue Christendom in Venus-built ships. The First Cry to the crusades. But now the white dome also floated, confectionery.

Furian felt dizzy. He wanted a glass of wine as desperately as Porco.

He was not sure of the way, coming in this fashion, along the alleys and narrow streets. He recognized a side canal all at once, as if a veil fell from his eyes.

"Has anyone been interested in us?"

"No one. I kept my eye out. One slut followed us a couple of streets, to see if we were worth pinching from. But decided she'd better not when Modest polished his knife."

A wanderer was idling by the steps of a ruinous old house. The house lamp hung almost in the water, reflecting like a silver pear.

What time was it? The little clouds above the Primo had been daubed with honey.

"We'll take that boat. We come to a house with gates and a garden. You'll stay by the gates, and I go in."

But do I? he thought. *Who's to say?*

The wanderlier eyed them distrustfully. Porco took up the place of two persons, but lean Modest less than the place of one.

Furian sat further up. He had the familiar sensation of how easy it would be to drop back in the canal and let it conclude matters.

Having described the house, Furian asked the wanderlier if he knew it.

"No, Signore. Some palace."

The sky had the quality of the dense, almost brown, gilding inside the Primo dome. Sunset then, or nearly. The tethered boat bumped gently by the steps, and Porco and Modest had got out, and were standing against the ornate iron gates, polishing, both of them now, their knives.

"Stop that. Stand over there."

Offended, they went along the pavement, and stood in the shade of a huge old acacia that towered above the wall.

Furian jangled the bell on the gate. He waited, looking into the garden. Beer-colored shadows wove the trees together. There were wild roses, blue wisteria turning now away from flowers to a russet autumn mantle. A slender path ran through, and there was a statue at its turn, a Pan playing the syrinx.

No one came. Furian rang the bell a second time.

To his right, above, in the pastry architecture of the house, the tall window with its lattice, seen sidelong. The window was opaque white, the others stood in a row, these shuttered tight. He had not noticed them before.

It was so dangerous to have come here he had not bothered. Of all the things he could have done, the chanciest, the least clever. They would not have expected it of him. Or had they?

If no one came, was no one here? Was he prepared to climb up the gate? With Porco's help he could get to the top. Could swing over and down in the garden.

But no, someone was coming. Out from the side of the house as if from a flat wing of scenery in the theater.

An old, grey-haired servant in a leather apron, with some keys. "What is it? What do you want?"

Furian wore the good coat. He was clean and combed. He had on yet another mask, a plain black oval, the eyes cut out, and a chiseled nose, and lips that must be hinged up for food or drink.

"Is your lady at home?" said Furian.

The man, who had a well-made mask in the form of a cat, said, "My lady? Who do you mean?"

"The mistress of the house. Madama of the butterfly mask. I don't want to name her. I wouldn't presume."

"If she were here," said the old man, "Why do you want her?"

"I have some things with me," said Furian clearly. "Things useful to her work. To enrich her beauty. To assist her in reading the fates of those she must deal with."

An ordinary harlot would be intrigued. Or uneasy. Furian added, because probably she was not an ordinary harlot, "I sang her a song last night. Perhaps she heard me. Go and tell her, and see what she says."

He slipped his hand through the bars of the gate, and held out the bright piece of money.

The old man took it without a word, and then instantly, shaking his keys, unlocked the gate.

"She said you'd come."

Furian thought distinctly, *Into the cage. Conceivably she has someone waiting.*

He felt a galvanic rush of fear, and of readiness. The fever made him reckless, or his life. He said, "You don't object if my men wait just there? I wouldn't suggest they come in. Unless I have need of them, of course. They're rather . . . boisterous."

The old man said nothing. Furian walked in at the gate which was locked behind him.

The shadows were heavy in the garden now. They rippled against his eyes and he wondered what they concealed. Then the servant led him inside and through a tall dark doorway, into the house of the blue whore.

After all he had sunk in the lagoon, and through time also, for this was the water of Ve Nera, as it had been once, clear and cool.

Her sala had walls and floor of blue marble, mottled and clouded with richer and more transparent blues. At the four corners, high up, was a carved woman's head and throat, a light cobalt blue powdered by gilt. Each was subtly different, crowned with a diadem, her blue tresses caught with fruits and leaves. One had a silver crescent moon on her forehead, one a quartz star, one a sun of pale amber, and one the magic emblem of Venus herself, shaped in glimmering electrum.

There was very little furniture. A sofa, a desk, a few chairs, but these were fine. Before the window hung a sheer curtain of white silk from a rail. And before this had had been placed a harpsichord. It was painted indigo, with a scattering of flowers in various ghostly, faded tones. The keys twinkled the distilled and sinking sunlight.

She was not in the chamber, no one was, which gave him leisure to look at it. There would be no way out save the two slim doors, for the lattice of the window would resist flesh and bone.

Looking at his reflection in the marble was like standing on water. Had Cloudio del Nero died in this luminous room?

The second door, as he had expected, opened. A cat-masked girl stood aside, and the woman entered.

Her dress had loose sleeves, a long loose train. It was a creamy flaxen color, a few shades whiter than her hair. The hairstyle, like the dress, looked artless. Some drawn up, most left lying shining on her breast, down her back along the train. It was marvelous hair, but streaked with sheeny darker strands that he took at first for some affectation. But they were not. She had begun to go grey, like her elderly servant.

Somehow this disturbed him. He recalled her hands, noted them now. They were young. She was not more than twenty, if so old.

Her mask today, like his, was plain. An alabaster face, lovely enough in a soulless, unliving way. It covered all her features, but, as she moved across the floor, he saw again her eyes.

They were the most extraordinary, impossible, *brilliant* blue, breakingly blue, like some flower or gem.

"So generous, Madama, to let me in—"

But she held up her hand. She sat down at the desk, took up the pen, and wrote. He watched the white feather. Its motion was dreamlike. And when the servant girl glidingly brought him the paper to read, this too was like a peculiar dream.

But even the magpie had been able to write, after death.

The words said, *I do not talk. Ask what you wish. I will answer as I may.*

Furian laughed. "You astonish me, Madama. How novel. I'd better make my questions as entertaining as you yourself. Is it a game?"

She wrote. The girl went back, replaced the first paper, took the next paper, brought it.

No game. You must be patient.

He said, "You don't need this assistant, surely. If I come closer, I can read over your shoulder."

Naturally she would refuse.

No. She nodded to the girl, who went directly out.

He went up to the desk, but then she again held up her hand. She placed the paper before him. It said, *Stand there.* He was to be before her, not at her back. Furian bowed.

He said, carelessly, "In my satchel here, I have some wonderful things, cosmetics, unguents, some of them from the East. If you'd like to try any sample, in privacy, Madama—"

She wrote.

Upside down now he read the words, *Is this why you sang beneath my window?*

Furian smiled behind his mask. "To gain your attention, of course. How lucky that I succeeded. And I thought you'd like the song."

She wrote. *Why?*

"Why? Well, Madama. It was composed by a talented man. And, I thought, composed for you."

She raised her head. Through the white mask-face her eyes— her *eyes*. They stared into his unblinking, without one flicker. They were the color of the aquamarine glass in the Madonna window of

the Primo. Or perhaps the forget-me-not pane above the shrine of
Venus. They were like holes into the sky of some other world.

He held her gaze. It was too easy. She was well trained, for
there was no innocence in her look. She might have been blind . . .
or some creature that could draw out your soul by its stare.

He had the urge to glance away. Wanted to very much. But
somehow could not now let go—

She lowered her head. The alien lamps were bent on her paper.
She wrote, *The song was not for me.*

"Oh, lady. That's not what I heard. All Venus says the song was
for you. And the poor fellow died. Did you know?" She wrote. He
reached across and caught her hand. She had been foolish enough
to let herself be alone with him. Her skin was cold, satiny. He
smelled a perfume, something warm and shadowy, like the sunset
hour. "Won't you talk to me instead, Madama. Tell me your name,
maybe. The song doesn't say what it is."

She took her hand out of his. She wrote, *I do not speak. I indicate the song was not for me, not that it was not about me. The song
was about me. My name is Eurydiche.*

"Do you care to know mine?" he said.

She wrote, as he had anticipated, *Furiano.*

"That isn't truly my name, Madama," he said. "Only what they
call me."

She wrote, *It is a perfect name. You are full of desperate fury.*

He flinched, as if she had struck him. And, as if she had, wanted
to strike at her in turn. He said, quietly, "If names are to be suitable,
then, Madama, is it death to look back at you?"

She rose to her feet. The brow of her mask was level with the
upper lip of his. She was slight as vapor, her waist looked small
enough to fit between his clasped hands. Only her breasts were
fuller, covered by a crossing of lace.

Simple to dash her to bits. Or push her down and stab her
through with the alternative weapon of sex. But he did not want her.
This damnable iciness that was a warmth, the chill fish that must
swim in her pale azure blood

"Never provoke one who's furious, lady."

She leaned down and wrote swiftly. *You have the legend wrongly.
The musician Orpheus went to fetch Eurydiche from the kingdom of
the dead, but he looked back at her, which broke the laws of hell, and
so he lost her, and she him.* (He noticed her head moved as she
wrote, attending the pen.)

"I know I had the legend wrongly, Blueness. I thought it suited you better that way."

She looked up again one second at him. Her eyes flashed as they had that time in the darkness. They were phosphorescent, like the evil canals which had poisoned him. The eyes of a sorceress. But she was only a trull.

Then she wrote again. *We are not speaking, Signore Furian. Now, as you said, it is a game. Perhaps you will leave.*

"And someone is outside the door to help me along with a blade?"

She wrote, *No one like that is there. And your friends are ready by the gate.*

"Yes, it was wise of me to bring them, wasn't it. And I might also have friends among the police."

He turned and walked across the floor and everything tilted, as if he did indeed walk on water. He felt her eyes attached to him still by a long aquamarine cord.

He thought, *Let go, you trollop. I've not done with you yet. This isn't over. You send men down into nothingness. A Medusa whose glare turns them to rock, not a Eurydiche. But perhaps I have the Mirror of Venus to show you your own face and so kill you.*

He did not look round. He opened the sala door where he had come in, and no one was there but the old servant, to conduct him through the house, and out the gate, to Porco and Modest, fretting in the sunfall.

8

San Fumo was smoking like a chimney in hell.

The crematory fires were underlit a rotten rose. Even as he looked down, a lamplit funeral rowed out across Silvia to the Island.

It was showy, each black carven boat prowed by a black carven horse with nodding jet ostrich plumes. The "Charons" dealt their poles. A drummer sounded for the oars-beat, as they did in the slave galleys. Women were weeping.

Furian turned and walked back to his new lodging.

On the stair, a boy handed him a letter.

"From whom?"

"An old chancer with a bald head."

The seal in the wax was a profile of the goddess Diana. It came from Doctor Dianus Shaachen.

Furian read the note by candlelight, sitting on his rickety pallet.

'Come just before midnight. I mean to try the Arts for an answer.'

The Arts meant alchemy, black magic perhaps. Furian would be strengthless against any supernatural aggressor. No, it was, he thought, that Shaachen liked to show off.

Why go? Shaachen might pay him for attendance, but he did not need the cash.

There was, though, nothing else to do, save sit here, or prowl about the City, cautious for assassins, his brain ticking with ideas about the blue-eyed woman.

He looked for Porco and Modest. Modest refused to be of use.

"He doesn't like walking," said Porco.

"And you?"

"My woman's cooking my supper."

Furian left them and went out alone. Nothing had occurred. Even in her house, nothing. An instinct, maybe only obvious common sense, told him they were holding off, to see what he would do. (But why?) In any case, Porco and Modest bored him.

Nevertheless, Furian had dressed in slum clothes, and wore a rag mask that covered eyes and nose.

He went on foot around Silvia—Modest would decidedly have been aggrieved—went on through the alleys and over the bridges. There was a large party at the Castello Barbaron. From the long windows flames pealed molten. Torches dazzled up and down the street. They were playing music.

Furian looked up at their lights, a wolf out on the dark plains of Venus.

It was nearly eleven before he reached Shaachen's quarter.

In a wine shop a swarthy eye-masked man watched Furian sullenly. When Furian got up, the man followed him out. By a canal, Furian turned and felled him without comment. The man lay sprawled. "Give me a penny. Just a penny. All I wanted." Furian threw a handful of bronze to him, and went on.

"Come in at once. Stay to the room's edges."

Shaachen had showed him up by the dim dregs of one candle, but in his study things had been tidied. There were two toughs at the downstairs door, and Shaachen had assured Furian the others were about, one even on the roof.

The casket with the magpie stood on a cabinet. It was locked. It gleamed in the candle stutter, wriggling as if with life.

"You're to be my witness," said Shaachen.

"To what?"

"I would have done it with the mask, but they took that."

"You want to call Powers and inquire why del Nero died."

"That too."

"You might have been wiser to have gone to ground, Doctor."

Shaachen was lighting more candles. They burned up everywhere, on shelves, tables, the corners of the floor. There would be plenty of light.

"Don't you smell it," said Shaachen, his not-recently shaved head tufted and bristly as the magpie's had been, "don't you sniff an element of pride?"

"Whose?"

"They might kill us, or not. They like someone to know what they did. How clever they've been. And the little people, tiny insects

who can't cause trouble. To us, who'd listen? It's safe. They frighten
us, then let us be. To *know* and admire, and tremble."

Furian nodded. "Perhaps. And who are they?"

"I know one thing. I surprise you—the old fool, what can he
find out. Who would want del Nero dead?"

Furian waited. Shaachen only peered and poked at the open
circle drawn on his tiled floor.

"He was a nobleman's son," said Furian. "But he became a fine
musician and composed a tune the whole City started singing."

"Jealous, someone," said Shaachen.

"Yes, it could be. Some member of the Musicians' Guild, angry
at a rich man having fame and success as well."

"Come in the circle."

"If I must."

"Better than to be outside. Things will go on outside."

Shaachen's paraphernalia lay within, jars, boxes, a stand with a
book. Magic needed many props. Furian stood well clear of it all to
let the Doctor work. The room already prickled with energies, and
Furian's fingers seemed full of pins.

"How is the fever?"

"It's well. I'm bad."

"You look like the painting of a sick saint."

"Thank you."

"The one with arrows through his belly."

"*Thank* you."

"Take the medicine."

"I think I prefer the illness. The last thing you gave me was full
of crushed flies."

"It worked," said Shaachen, which was true.

Furian kept to one side. The wine he had had helped to hold
him fairly steady. The nausea was gone, he was only cold, with a dull
hot coldness, and every candle had a fever halo.

Shaachen seemed cheerful, bustling. Now he took up a silver
shaker, and shook it. Little bells sounded. He cast something powdery down and fire broke at intervals along the circle. Shaachen
closed the circle with chalk.

He read out from the book on the stand a list of long, grotesque
names. The tongue was now Latin, now perhaps Egyptian, now
some scratching Eastern thing, now mere noises, clicks and gut-
turals, hisses.

You did not laugh. For all this idiocy would work.

One of the first things Shaachen had shown him, years back, was a frost-blue angel misting through the window. It had a fiery sword in one hand, a brazen apple in the other. It had gone out like a blown flame at Shaachen's command, but sent a sort of imp to bring what Shaachen requested, which that night was a vial of holy oil.

It had certainly been oil. If sacred, it was debatable.

During former rituals the magpie was shut into the bedroom. Safe in the casket, perhaps it watched, at last.

A bubbling sound had begun in the room's four corners. Up the south window and the wall went a shadow. Solidifying there was a gigantic tortoise. On its back, a translucent jade ball, in which was light.

North, Furian heard the rustle of the black feathers of a crow. West, he glimpsed the white crocodile, and East the curious beast with a rat's head and spraying down of tail. These were the room's four guardians.

Shaachen spoke a disjointed, partly-rhyming litany in Latin.

The guardians faded, and directly beyond the circle, on the widest space of the floor, the three Zodians of the City appeared in a glowing triangle.

Scorpio, the sea scorpion, gleaming bronze, under his black iron planet of Vulcan; Cancer, a genderless veiled human form, holding in its arms the moon pearl; Pisces, the smaller fish visible within the sea-green womb of the greater fish, balancing the emerald radiant of Neptune.

Shaachen cast out through the circle, in at the edge of the zodiacal triangle, a piece of parchment. On it had been written the name *Cloudio del Nero*. There was a rush as physical matter met the energy of the psychium. The paper flared up, took wing; It was a black butterfly. It fluttered fragile as two charred leaves, on the softly-flaming ground.

Slowly now, a girl's shape, wound in a blue mantle, with the star of Venus on her forehead, formed between the City Zodians. She walked on air, through shadowy pillars, and dissolved.

"There is a woman in it," said Shaachen.

"Didn't I tell you?"

But Shaachen held up his hand—as she had done, that very woman—for silence.

A wind blew through the columns that were noticeable only by their absence. It blew into the faces of the men in the circle. A hot, sulfurus and cindery wind, as if swept straight from San Fumo, the Isle of the Dead.

Furian covered his mouth and nose with one hand.

Shaachen stood braced, leering. He spoke another incomprehensible word.

A black animal shouldered up out of the wind. Its eyes were like wet lava. It had curved horns and a mane of spikes, six sparking hoofs, a dragging phallus capped with a barb.

"A beast of rage," said Shaachen.

Furian's body shuddered, separate from him.

And then, where the butterfly lay on the parchment, pinned flat now, motionless, the mask evolved, exactly as Furian had first seen it, in the wrung-out, lavender water darkness at the onset of dawn.

Its black false hair spread out from it, the curls pointed up with gilt. The spangle-rimmed eyes and classical god-like nose and mouth. From the lips ran a trickle of ichor, shining. From the eyes ran raindrop tears.

A horrible moaning lament involved and possessed the air. It was a distortion of the melody del Nero had fashioned, played upon white-hot nerves by needles of probing steel. Unbearable embers of notes scattered. The mask *bled*.

Gradually, as they watched, it split in two agonized segments, and out of it crawled worms with beaked and eating mouths.

The image was so tangibly foul, Furian felt himself choking on it. He turned his head, and as he did, a voice screamed through the chamber.

"Crossed! Clogged! Unstitched! Undone!"

A sound came also between Furian's teeth. He felt his body bending double. He wondered, with a last horrible cynicism, what would he do to the magic if he puked inside the sorcerous ring? And held himself together with a mental fist.

But the horror was over. The lights had danced up bright, and when he looked, all the swirling pictures had vanished.

Shaachen too seemed bleached. His nose was standing out like a horn-shell.

"Now you know everything," said Furian.

"Ah, no. Not yet," said Shaachen. "Thank God." He spoke a prayer, and some other murky filmy something lifted from the room and was gone. "Let us sit. Sit, sit. There's wine in the decanter under the cloth."

They broke the circle. It had crumbled a little, and portions had run like old white dye. But it had kept them safe.

Shaachen said, "Evil was worked. He wasn't murdered in the usual way. But murdered, murdered for sure. What was done leaves an echo that continues. The mask knows—"

"You told me this before," said Furian.

"The mask knows, for it was the one who made the mask that killed him."

"A mask maker," Furian said, slow and stupid. He coughed, and righted himself and poured the wine.

"The Guild," said Shaachen, staring away to the astral landscape of some incarnation not this one, a prophet on a mountain. "The Guild of Mask Makers. Or that elite group among them who makes such masks as the dark Apollo."

"Not jealousy then?"

"Jealousy and fury were its friends."

There was a stain on the tiles, deep, acid green; a strange burn that might, by morning, have faded.

On the grimy grim bed, Furian tossed and turned. He had twenty minutes sleep before the girl woke him, pulling his shoulder.

"Let go, you harpy. Damn you."

The sun he had seen rise was of course still low, the sky yellowish nacre. A charming day, for anyone who had slept.

"I'm to give you this," said the girl obstreperously.

He took the paper. Shaachen again? It seemed not. The writing was characterless and careful, the sort you could purchase from professional scribes at street corners.

Go to Aquila, and see the sight.

"Who gave you this?"

"The flayer's boy."

"Who gave it *him*?"

"I don't know." The girl flounced.

He turned her out.

He stripped and washed in old water, shaking with fever and the previous night. His head was hollow, and full of the resonance of some *thing* that had no sound. (The echo of evil Shaachen had detailed.) More medicine. It burned now like that mark on the floor.

He put on a clean shirt, the decent coat. The black eye-mask.

To go where the paper said was madness. So he would go. Go and admire and tremble. They could have had him any way. Killed

him. Perhaps he really did not matter to them, except as something
to toy with.

Porco was at breakfast, a fine one shared with none, not even
the slattern who had cooked it. Chicken livers in saffron. (He had
profited by Furian.)

"Come on."

"Ah—Signore—"

"Look. Yes, silver. You'll come."

"I will. May God, Heavenly Maria and Neptunus forgive you,
Signore."

Aquila was the great lagoon. Beyond, you could see the ocean, in a
curve like the smoky iris of a green-blue eye. But Aquila looked
leaden, and on the water drifted broken pots, weed that had been
netted in, and a dead octopus fishermen were hauling to their hungry boats.

On the shores, and slid on platforms into the water, the buildings were picturesque in their depravity. Barnacles re-enameled the
scaling walls. Everything but the lagoon had a green tinge. Even the
sun.

Under Aquila lay the church of Maria Maka Selena. A little
before noon, when the sun passed over, you might see at low tides
the tilted clock face, a hundred feet down, looking up into the sun's
eye. Old silver-leaf, the figures of maidens, all green now, malachite
girls under a peridot sun . . .

"Bear up, Signore."

"Shut up, Porco."

What was he here to see? Presumably he had to hang about,
and while he did, someone might come up and stick a knife in his
side. Years before, there had been a plague of glass daggers—which,
snapped off at the hilt after the blow, left few clues. There was a
song too, *A dagger of glass thrust through my heart—*

A song was coming from nearby. A rushed song. Too fast.
Furian realized, it was del Nero's largo, played on an uncontrolled
and squeaky violin, at a trot.

All the petals of its beauty screwed into those hurried meaningless phrases. As if to have it over.

"That's splendid, that is," said Porco. "They're all playing it that
way now. It was a dreary old dirge before. Some fiddle-player from
the Musician's Guild, he started it fast, they say. It's better. You
want to have a smile, don't you." (Keep smiling, *I* do.)

Furian groped after this. He said, "Which fiddle-player?"

"Don't know, Signore. They're all one to me. Scrape out a tune. He's got a lovely mask, they said. As nice as any you see."

The green bubble sun winked. It was blindingly white.

On the Laguna Aquila there had started a commotion.

A big boat was pushing off, and on the deck a woman shrieked, struggling to pull herself in two.

Furian focused on her sluggishly, unevenly. Her hair a tousled tortured fairish mass, and her clothing half ripped off her, so people on the quay were laughing and pointing at her now. Her sagging breasts were bare, and one long thin leg—she was a parody of allurement. Her hands had been tied, probably to prevent her wounding herself or another. He grasped where she was going in the guardianship of her black-tunic jailers. The Madhouse lay behind Aquila, against the sea wall.

Poor bitch. There were jewels hanging on her dress, and a sparkling chain. She had a beautiful mask too, still demurely fixed for Carnival over her shrilling, screeching features.

It was made of ivory, the mask. A fan, fretted, out of which partly emerged the outlines of a delicious face. It had dawn pink lips, sultry evening lids.

He knew her mask. The Principessa Messalina. At the Revels of Diana—she had leapt to the altar, tearing her dress in the same wild way—

She swayed, writhed. He thought of the worms.

Porco was jeering.

Furian said, "Her name's Messalina. For the Madhouse, presumably."

"Heard she ran half-naked in the church. Wanted to have the priest on the altar. And all the men after. Some thing about her namesake."

"Messalina had all Rome in a night. The old empress, that is."

Furian realized it was not Porco who had delivered this information.

"Is it the Princess Messalina?"

"Oh yes."

"What happened to her?"

"Gone mad," said the newcomer. He had an odd familiarity. A brown lower face, and scrawled lips. There was a bruise on his jaw.

"And why did she go mad?"

"Women," said the man. "They're all mad anyway. But I'll add, Signore, those pretty masks, the best ones—they're unlucky."

"In what way?"

"The composer who died—or who's missing and supposed dead—he had one of those masks. An Apollo or Bacchus. And she—that one down there—she had her special mask from the Guild. Last year, the last autumn Carnival, there was a prince, I forget his name, he had a mask of some dead king, and he stuck a knife in his throat one evening at dinner."

"Did he have cause?" said Furian gently. "Indigestion, perhaps." He knew the man. Furian had knocked him flat the night before, then thrown him coins.

"No cause. He was rich as Pluto, and he had a goodlooking wife. Fancy boys, too. Unlucky, the masks."

"Unlucky for some," said Furian. He reached across and took the man by the crotch, very hard.

The swarthy half-face grew mottled.

"Tell me," said Furian, "who sent you here."

"No—one—you were rough last night. Then you paid. Will you—pay—now—?"

Furian twisted his hand and the man fell on the paving. People skirted him. Venus was callous, particularly during Carnival.

"Where are you going?" gabbled Porco.

"To a jolly place."

"You want me? It's—this walking—"

"Go and worship your chicken livers."

There was a water-mill in the canal. The water was curded like fleece, splintered like glass, then running in calm, humped waves.

The wanderlier cursed the mill. They bumped against the steps, with an iron-studded door directly above.

Furian got up to it and rapped with the brass mask knocker, which was in the shape of a twelve-rayed solar disk, with hollow eyes and snarling mouth.

A lackey came. He wore a mauve coat. He looked sidelong at Furian.

"You understand," said Furian, going past him with a slight collision into the passage beyond, "I'm here on someone else's business."

"This is the Guild House. Only the Guild comes here."

"But I'm in."

"You can go out again."

"Is that so?"

Furian was not amazed when the mauve menial called, and three strong men in dark leathers appeared along the passage.

"My master," said Furian, "will be disappointed."

"He must send in writing. A meeting may then be arranged."

"With whom?"

"The Master, or his Captains."

"That's warlike. Why's that?"

"These are the proper titles," said the lackey.

The strong men stood in a well-made fence.

Furian nodded lovingly. "We will write."

Outside he stood and grinned, on the narrow pavement. He did not know why he grinned.

The water wheel churned the water.

Somewhere there was a violin player who distorted the Song of Cloudio del Nero, and perhaps it was he who had aimed at him, from jealousy. And somewhere were the husband and the lover of ugly Messalina, who both might wish her gone. And elsewhere, one year back, a dead man who might have had countless enemies, each powerful enough evidently to write to the Mask Guild, to meet with the Guild's Master, or his Captain.

A mask was made for friend or lover, either as a gift, or because they were persuaded to take one. And as the artisan worked, he worked out too how to accomplish a death. A very clever death, by madness or suicide . . .

For such a mask, so wonderful, there would be many fittings, choices. Talk, probably, things let slip.

And from these things the artisan, who was also the assassin, devised their ends.

But Virgo was in it, was she not? Virgo with glittering Venus on her brow and clad in alien magpie blue.

. . . Was that a little movement? There, by the side of that house, where a slip ran through, one canal mating with another . . .

Furian walked, not so very quickly, along the pavement.

The Silk Market lay behind this place. He knew it well, how not, from long ago early days. There would be a crowd and obstacles, and they were not to be despised, at this moment, in the hand of God.

9

A column stolen from Egypt dominated the Setapassa. It was crowned by a sphinx of black basalt, forty-three feet in the air. Below, the silks, velvets and brocades hung like sheets of water, sky and sun.

At the edge of the square, the lacemakers palazzo raised ornate stone arches that rivaled the lace. West lay the glove-makers' booths, and tiny caves of shops squirreled away along the side streets, everything tasseled and sequined as in some Eastern fairy tale.

Furian had no interest in the market. The crowd, made up mostly of the more valuable citizens, had some attraction.

He slipped among them, by the noble with two milk white dogs on leash, the woman in her litter, pointing, with a pale yellow glove, at cloth the color of decaying lightning.

There was indeed someone behind him. He could mark it, the slight tumble through the crowd that followed him.

He got close to a gambling table, under smoke-banners of gauze, paused as if to watch. When he looked up, the crowd moved at its own pace, unbroken, but there was a woman standing not two feet away.

Furian recognized the boy first, in his grey University garment, and the plain half-mask scholars were requested to wear. Then, she.

Her gown was black velvet today, perhaps rather hot. It had tourmaline buttons on the bodice in the image of scorpions. Her mask was a black lace fan. In the eyeholes, her dark, greedy, lovely eyes sprang from his.

"Why, *Signora*," he said.

The boy jumped. Calypso, Juseppi's widow, did not.

She said, very low, "Get away, Signore. It isn't safe for you."

"But wonderful for you. Juseppi must have put all his fares aside to buy you such a gown."

"I've got a new protector. What do you care? You didn't want me."

"Ah, Signora, I tore a hole in my breeches wanting you. But you're such a stinking leech. I didn't dare."

"Fire be on you," she spat, still low and throaty as a dove.

Then he saw them coming for him again, the tell-tale crowd pleating slightly to this side and that.

"Farewell, Gorgeous," he said. "May God bless you."

"Fry and die. And fry."

The little caves jolted by, much faster now, for Furian strode at speed. They seemed full of monkeys, who called to him, and cunning paws fluttered things which shone.

Where was he? Not far from Fulvia now.

He glanced back.

They were a blot in the general mass, about five of them, shouldering on. They looked, it seemed, like any parcel of rough men with a pocket of money, out for a day's sport.

Here was another open place. Veils hung down smelling of the incense of the East. Furian brushed through them. A cat on a perch spat at him as Calypso had done.

Then he was up against a line of booths. The busy crowd swilled and rocked against him, and beyond lay a canal, and over there it broadened, with boats going up and down, two or three close to the bank.

An idea was forming in his mind. It might be the fever again, (which made everything ripple and churn, made the sequins crash with nearly vocal violence, made him want to laugh), but then, there were these women, this scorpion bitch in her velvet, taken up with some wealthy man directly over the coffin; and the other one. The other—

A hand clenched possessively on his arm. He had waited too long.

Furian turned, smiling under his half-mask, and saw a friendly deadly half-masked smile returning.

"Signore. Won't you come with us? Eh?"

Furian put his knife, (ready, although he had forgotten it), between this one's ribs. The man dropped leisurely, keeping his friendly look.

As Furian tried to step away, another hand snaked across his eyes. A snatch. The sun—

The day was all over Furian's face. He had been unmasked.

The lout guffawed. And two others shouted: "Face! Face!"

It was too late to grab back the covering. Furian saw a sea of masks turning like cannon mouths.

"Where is it?" thundered a man, one of the crowd, playful, threatening.

Another screamed "No excuses. He's a bare-faced liar."

Hands leaped on him. They had his coat, his flesh. Round his throat—

He twisted, thrust them off, danced, dived, came up through a welter of material and curses, and fled.

The crowd was now a boiling pot. Fingers, claws, feet and punches, blows—They whistled and hooted.

All the world of the Setapassa was after him. It was a crime to go unmasked at Carnival.

He ran, striking out, towards the bluish break of the canal.

The cry was up behind him: *Face! Face!*

Bodies pelted aside—sweat, scent, breath—they saw what he was—lawbreaker—tried to trip and bring down. At least to impede. And they were laughing. He was fair game for anyone.

Something hurt in his side—had someone knifed him? No, he would not be running—his lungs tore. The sun hit his forehead with the mark of Cain—

Two women, excited, grappled him—"He's a pretty one, no wonder he won't mask—" their hands prying, feeling—he pushed them off—

He reached the edge of the water. About nine men thumped into his back, chortling and swearing. "String him up with the silks. Apostasy! Bloody bugger—"

Furian plunged out from the pavement into the nearest boat, which reared and galloped under him. He shouted at the wanderlier—surly, backing off, wishing him in the Inferno—"Row me. *That* way. Two silver duccas—"

"Bare-face. Get out."

"Five. Do it."

"It's not fortunate. Stupid fucker—"

"Six—"

The men on the street were leaning down, lighthearted murderous brawny arms. Furian pounded them off. They came back. To use his blade now would mean death anyway.

Behind the lethal merriment, he marked the masked grins of the gang who had followed.

"Seven duccas. Or I swim."

The wanderlier slashed the tether away. Still bucking, they spun out on to the canal.

Furian sat down and put his arm over his face.

The crowd cat-called and maligned him. There were no other boats filled yet. There would be.

"I'll take you to the Lace Palace back door, over there. No further. Show us your coins."

Furian flung them on the planks between the seats. Hoofs of the few horses kept in Venus pounded through his skull.

Another boat had drawn close to the pavement. A knot of men dashed over into it, yelping their vigor. At least three belonged to the following gang.

If the crowd took him now, he would be helpless, and then, so simple for someone to cut him, slip away. Even a romantic glass dagger—who would see until it was too late? *The bastard's dead. Serve him right for going unmasked. The punishment of the gods.*

These vulnerable, malnourished and pathetic people, for whose misery he had thrown away his life. These *scum*—

They passed under a bridge.

"No further. Get out. They'll hole my boat."

Above, the whey-pale palace with its lacy arches. Beyond, an alley.

He left the boat and raced for it.

He was sure where he was going now. The only place possible. He recollected that other walk, the necessary waterway. He had a start on them. The alley twisted. They always did.

A woman on a balcony saw him and squalled, *"Face! Face!"* It ran from side to side over his head. Inside his head.

He stumbled, and a thin dog rushed from his path, snarling.

His heart was a stone, which beat.

As he ran, he rent away part of his shirt sleeve. Under the lea of a dripping wall, he cut two eyeholes, tried to tie it over his upper face, succeeded. It might last.

He identified these byways from instinct only.

He might be wrong.

The chase had seemed to draw off, but he was not sure for the buzzing and hammering of the forge in his head.

Another wanderer. Dipping . . . dipping alloy of . . . water.

"Where you want? Who after you?"

"Mask slipped," he panted, "an enemy."

The man accepted him, rowed off up the backwater.

Furian saw, near, far off, the mirror faces of the houses repeated, and, in the depths, Venusian weed that clung and floated like hair. The mermaid hair of Venera.

"City of Met Darkness," Furian said.

"What you say?"

"That turn there."

"That's a bad canal. Got bad reputation."

"I know. It's why I'm going there."

"Get out here and walk."

Furian dislodged himself from the second wanderer.

"Pay me, you bastard drunk."

Furian smiled and cast down some coins.

"Not enough."

"Enough to buy something to poison yourself."

To the ring of threats and maledictions, Furian swung on.

The pavement became so narrow he could slip over, and in. Did not want to quite yet.

He coughed. No blood. That was encouraging, and a surprise. No pursuit either.

Meant to chase him here? Back to the source. Why oh why?

Pavement too narrow now to walk on. Into this alley. Round, and along. High stones, blind windows. Somewhere a woman sang in a thin, hateful voice. Not the Song. Some hymn to deaf God.

Back up from the alleys. There, across the widening strip of water. A garden behind iron gates. A window behind an iron lattice.

How to cross. A puzzle. No bridge, no boat, no wings to fly.

Furian looked at the canal. If he went into it he might not come up again. But there was no other way, and for this moment he did not care. He would care tomorrow, if he lived.

The canals had already done most of their worst to him.

He eased over and took the water with a curious liquid agility that he was much aware of, seeing himself from far above, swimming couthly, barely stirring the water, the ripples of juicy green spreading like carving in chalcedony. And already . . . the bank.

But he could not pull himself up now . . . yes, but he could.

His muscles were made of white fire, and would do anything, and there was music in his head, the Song at last, going too quickly.

Up the bank—it was done. Now only the gate to scale. The Black Gate of the Blue Trollop.

He put his foot into the gate's mesh and climbed. Pain lanced through him. It did not belong to him. He had two tops of the gate in his hands, pods or acorns. He dragged himself again upwards. Somehow the garden was there, and he dropped over into it. He landed on his feet. The impact met the impact of the hammers in his head. For an instant there was nothing. Then he was there again.

Furian slung himself against the sideward door of the house. Once, twice. He kicked it, and the door gave way.

The old servant was running at him, cat-mask lopsided.

Furian stopped. He said, hearing himself, voice clear and sound as a bell, "Out of my way, old man."

The servant stopped, too. He whined, ridiculously, "One day you'll be old."

"If I am, old man, you'll be dead." Furian felt the water of Venus sliding like glass over his skin and soul. "But celebrate. One day, I'll be dead too."

He went past the old man, who allowed it.

Furian walked up the stairs. He felt light as air and pain did not count. Minute diamonds lit and went out across his eyes, but at the top, after a little, when he reached the door of the sala, they cleared.

He could hear a harpsichord. Probably only in his brain. He opened the door.

The room was just as before, a haven of blue. Yet set now, motionless, inside a pane of ice. The drift of white ice was at the window. There before it, the frozen harpsichord, and the figure seated, playing slowly, somehow without movement.

The notes dripped and rippled. Water notes. Had she not heard him? No, he was made of liquid. He was a ghost.

But so was she.

The pale hair with its lines of grey, he saw it, drip-rippling like the water and the water-notes, as her shoulders tensed and rested and tensed. Strange melody, without form, a wandering descent. It was very sad. It was a mist, and these crystalline uncurlings in the mist, a search for what might never be found, a loss that might never end, a question, offered over and over, unheard, unspoken.

He realized his makeshift sleeve-mask had come off in the canal. His hair hung wet-heavy round him, made of lead. Water shimmered along the floor. It had no aroma, only something faint, like burning leaves—he could smell burning—

He spoke to her clearly, as he had below.

"Here I am."

She left off playing, and the ice-pane cracked.

For a moment her head glimpsed about, he saw the line of her cheek, the insane blueness of one eye.

She wore a gown like that, also, deep, drowning blue.

"Won't you greet me, Madama. I came all this way. You could say I was herded here like a sheep. Where do you run when the City's on fire? Into the fire's heart."

She turned. All at once. One second he saw the back of her, and then the front of her.

He had noted already she was unmasked.

She made no attempt to hide her face.

Furian felt his blood rush down within him like a flight of comets.

Her face—

She was as white as white marble, and she had been carved from it. She was like the women at the room's corners. She was not alive.

In the perfection of her pallor, the blue eyes scorched. Large, unblinking, the color of ecstasy or exquisite pain.

She was so beautiful, so unconscionable, that she was terrible as the face of the moon. She was not real. She was truth that was not real. Reality that was not real.

She was not alive, yet she lived. Nothing of her moved. She was a statue. Medusa, *changed to stone.*

He must—he looked away. He saw the floor, and great circles of it were rising and splashing upwards, and as they did so, soft as a cloud, the ceiling came down.

Furian fell to his knees, then forward. He lay stretched on the blue marble at the feet of unliving life, unreal reality. But did not know it any more.

10

Cancer the Crab, its genderless human guise and smoky Eastern veil put aside, walked sideways through the sea. Scorpio the bronze warrior stood on a column. The two fishes played, revolving in esoteric patterns. Furian swam strongly, against the silken current. It stroked his face with coolness. Eventually, he would need to come up for air. Not yet. It was so pleasant here, the City seen only far above, through half a mile of water. One day, the ocean would cover all Venus. It would be like the Flood. Then the City would lie looking up, as he looked up. Safe under the sea for ever. Streets and domes, towers and squares. The boats grounded. The beautiful faces under green drifting layers, like a flowery paving of lilies, or masks. All struggle done. It would be marvelous to sleep here. But he had better go up, and breathe.

Furian surfaced slowly, without tumult.

The bed was hard and smooth. Under his cheek, the warm silk pillow, firm and ungiving, yet oddly *not* hard. And the current, still stroking, cool and rhythmic, his forehead and his face. There was a low floral scent.

He opened his eyes. He moved his hand, across the living firm pillow of skirt, and woman.

Furian knew at once. He was not amazed. As if it had been prearranged.

"How kind of you," he said. "You're too generous. I haven't even promised to pay you yet."

The scent was her young, fragrant body. Irresistible delights. He was in her lap, like a child that had fallen. She had been stroking his face, quietly.

But she stopped. A shame, he had liked it. Now what?

His muscles gathered themselves—and nothing happened. He lay just as before.

"It seems I can't move," he said.

Her gentle hand came down and touched his lips with one finger.

At her touch, one part of him did move after all. The uselessness and ribaldry of this made him laugh softly. He had not seen her face again, thank God.

A bell was ringing. It penetrated his head and every thing broke in shards and went floating down.

When he came to once more, a pair of men in comely cat masks were carrying him up a staircase. This struck him as very funny, and his laughter now was louder, and put him away again.

He dreamed he lay on the sea, over downed Venus, with the drowned faces staring up from below. But a fearful moon stared down. He could not escape its appalling beauty or the two glistening, unblinking eyes that gazed through it at him, like razors.

When he woke he was comfortable. Nothing mattered. Someone had put a drink to his lips, which was bitter but appropriate in some essential way. The taste perhaps of healing herbs remembered. Or else a toxic draught to see him off. He went. He was in the sky now, and Venus-Virgo lay below, a woman in a blue dress with blue hair, eyes closed.

"How long have I been here?" he said to the girl, who might have been the servant he had seen before, or the slut from the slum, abruptly washed and in a proper gown.

"It was yesterday you came. You fainted in Madama's sala."

"I know," he said. (He had thought that was a dream, too.) "Anyone would, wouldn't they." She made a prancing motion. She would say nothing. Or would she? "She's very pretty, your mistress."

"Some think so," said the girl.

"What do you think?"

She blinked a glance at him. He was intensely aware of all the movement of her face, the constant flicks of the eyelids, wet slide of the eyeballs, quirks of her mouth, even the slight distension of her nostrils as she took air in and out.

Furian said, "I suppose you're used to her."

The girl snapped, "She's modest. She stays covered mostly."

"And only goes out at Carnival, a few weeks in autumn or spring. When she can be masked."

The girl said, "You must drink all the water in the jug there. No food until tonight."

He thought, *I'll be gone by then.*

But after she left, he turned on his side, and slept like the dead.

In the evening he woke, and knew where he was, and recalled what had been said. When he sat up, the room was quite steady. It was probably not the ministrations of this diabolic house, rather Shaachen's medicine bringing on a crisis, now successfully past.

He looked about. A cup of wine stood on the chest by the bed, and an apple with a knife, (they trusted him?). Across the dim room, which was an ample one, an enamel bath had been filled by water that steamed.

They had taken his garments, and he had slept adequately without his shirt, but there in the corner, absurd on a pedestal, was a suit of clothes the like of which he had not seen for six years.

Furian ate the apple without using the knife, but he might keep the knife. It was a poor thing, but could be useful. The wine was thin with fresh water. She must have a well here, and a good one.

He went and sat in the bath and laved himself with the warm water. Nearby was an attendant razor—trust indeed.

The girl came in on a knock as he stood shaving cautiously at the unlit mirror, naked. Of course, she would have seen him in the bed. She began lighting lamps.

"Are you mine with the rest?"

"*No,* Signore!" She flushed to her hairline above and between the cat's ears.

"Only she's the whore, then."

"She isn't!" cried the girl. "How dare you say so! She's been charitable to you."

"I wonder why."

The girl hung her head.

"When you're ready, you're to go to the room to the left of the corridor."

"Am I."

The girl bridled. She said, "There are strong men in this house. Be careful."

"You mean I can't leave here until I'm told I may. You mean I can't have any of you until I pay."

The girl picked up a shoe from beside the suit on the pedestal. She flung it at him, but a little short. For a slave, she made free. But then, she thought nothing of him.

He said, "All right. I'll be obedient. Don't be cruel to me. You were so charming when I was sick."

"I was not," she rasped. "*She* was."

"Tell me why," he said.

"Why do you think?"

Confounded, Furian stared at her. Though she was masked and he not, he could see the blush again on her forehead. It was deep.

He said, "You think she likes me."

The girl lowered her head. She made an angry gesture. "*Yes.*"

"I'm flattered. But bemused. Why should she?"

"Who knows why one likes another one?" said the girl. Then, "She's been fair to me, all my life. You don't know her, I won't talk to you any more."

And she *ran* from the room, slamming the door.

Furian put down the razor. He walked to the small window, which he had already examined. Through the half open shutters, he looked out at the canal, but did not see it.

A new game? He thought of the delicacy of her soothing hand, the way she had drawn him in on her blue beach.

He thought of her face.

Furian cursed her.

But she had been cursed already.

Presently he put on the fine-spun shirt and linen, the elegant breeches and satin coat, the stockings and the buckled shoes. His hair, rinsed of the canal, he left as it was, for there was nothing to tie it with. And no mask.

He drank the last of the watered wine. He wanted something stronger, for now, presumably, he must go and stand there in a room with her again.

If she would have the decency to mask herself he did not know.

His own hands in the embroidered cuffs, (the nails so clean), reminded him of his father's house. His youth.

But nothing, not even memory, could come between him and her. Nothing at all.

It was a small, gracious room, the walls brocaded in watered primrose, the ceiling high, and painted with cloud-blown gods.

They—or he—was to dine. At one end of the short table, the silver knives, a fork with a pearl set in the handle three goblets, two with stars, one of dull violet glass that held the candlelight in a single damson drop.

At the other end of the table, the ink, the quill, some sheets of paper.

There was a decanter too, and he filled his first glass, turning it almost black. Then drained it, and filled it again.

When she came in, he must thank her. For although it almost certainly *was* a game, it might not be the game he had thought. Perhaps she had loved del Nero, after all. Perhaps del Nero had been as petrified—strange, apt, horrible word—as Furian. The Song, an apology not a lament. Why then a murder?

The door, with its brocade panels, was opened.

Eurydiche came in through it.

She had on white this evening, the bodice sprinkled by little brilliants. Her breasts nestled above like doves. Her hair was powdered with silver, piled up, one long tress curling down and down.

She wore the plain white mask.

He bowed to her. He said, "You've been a saint to me, Madama. I didn't deserve it, naturally. But the saints, I understand, are always impartial."

She stood, looking at him. Through the eyeholes, her scalding eyes. He held them. Waited.

She went to the table, seated herself, and wrote. She pushed the paper to his place opposite. Her wrist was so slender, ringed by topazes, to match the room?

He too must go to the table. He picked up the paper.

It read:

Will you permit me to remove my mask? Can you bear it?

For a moment he felt the dizzy weakness threaten him. He said, "I'm at your mercy, lady."

She wrote.

The paper came over the slight width of the table. (Seated, they would not be much more than four feet apart.)

He read the paper.

That is not what I wish.

He said, "Then I must leave."

She wrote. *You are not a captive. You were not stayed before. You returned here.*

"I was *driven* here, I think. Why?"

She raised her head.

He had a sudden ghastly desire to see it again, the carven slender moon of her face. He filled the glass. He said, "Take the thing off. You're discourteous to me, you didn't give me a mask."

She sat quite still. Then her hands went up, weightless. She undid hidden clasps, and let down the mask's inert poreless camouflage from the inert poreless mask beneath.

For her *face* was a mask.

She bowed her head again, and wrote. It took a little space. Then she pushed the paper with her fingertips and he took it up.

You saw at once. Not everyone has done so. I will never grow old, at least, I will not seem to. Do not be afraid of my eyes. The phosphorescent look of them is from the distillation I must use to bathe them in. I never blink, they are never refreshed except from a little bottle I have. I cannot eat, only absorb liquid, that from a special vial. Of course, I would not let you see this. Please sit down, and be at ease. This thing you behold does not make me wicked. Imagine if you will, I am here behind this face, smiling, wishing to speak, and to listen.

An uneven pulse throbbed through him. He looked at her. It was like looking at the sculpture of the most beautiful, or the face of the most beautiful who had died. She was made of stone. She was perfect. Her eyes did not blink, her lips did not part. The breath that was sucked in and out came by the effort of the lungs and throat. No doubt she would pour the liquid food into her throat, and the muscles there, able to work as those of the face did not, would carry the prescribed sustenance into her.

She could never be spoiled, it was true. No ugly frown or grimace or stupid amusement would ever mar her. The scars and wrinkles that perpetual expression made upon a face with age, could never come.

He raised his glass.

"I never saw anyone so beautiful." He drank. "A million women would envy you, Madama."

She wrote—it was her last page.

Envy me that a man faints at the sight of me? Envy me that I can never laugh or cry, or close my eyes, even when sleeping? Call me Eurydiche. I like to hear my name. Few others ever say it.

Furian said, "Surely Cloudio del Nero said your name? He's under the canal. The princess he couldn't make smile—why did you kill him? Was he unwilling?"

She stood up.

Her face and eyes burned with lunar nothingness. But her whole body was on fire with mute, trammeled emotion.

It startled him.

She made a beckoning gesture.

He saw it was the papers she wanted back, to go on writing.

Furian picked them up. He held them and said, "But, my dear, I don't know how much of this I can stand."

She came about the table, with the pen in her hand like a dagger.

Emotionless—in ferment. He felt the passion in her like the held-back vortex of some colossal tidal storm. She seized his hand and wrote across the palm in the uneven ink: *I cry. I live.*

They were almost the words of the magpie.

She let him go, and stood, flaming, empty, brimmed. Yet even her breasts did not move quickly with her breath. She could not breathe as she needed to. She turned away from him and caught the table and let go.

Then, after a moment, she walked silently across the room. She went into a corner where a marble goddess stood upright in the shadow.

She stood beside the goddess, and let him see, how alike they were. (How different?)

Furian said, "I don't want to distress you. Show me I misjudged you. There's darkness all round you. Will you talk about that? This isn't the time for courtly conversations."

She came back over the room. Her step was brisk. She seized a page out of his hands, took it to the ink well, dipped her pen and wrote.

She left the page lying.

"Wait—"

But she was gone out of the doors.

Furian bent to the paper.

Eat what you wish. Leave my house when you wish. I will die of shame for trusting you.

He turned when the door opened again. But it was the dinner coming in, silver trays and salvers, and the jewels of wines.

He watched them place the dishes, fill his plate, pour out the first mellifluous alcohol.

When it was all done, he sent them away.

He sat in the chair as the food went cold, reading over her words. He read the words on his hand, too, which, from closing it, had copied themselves in reflection. *I cry. I live.*

There was a water clock in the room, over in another corner. The soft dripping he mistook for the canal, while a gilded galleon rode up a stem, and at what must be midnight, its top mast struck a tiny bell.

Furian had been drinking the purple wine from the purple glass. He had not taken very much, because the wine was good. All the lamps were guttering.

The door opened. The girl came in. Even her cat mask seemed swollen and moody. She put a parchment before him on the table, turned and went out with slapping skirts.

Furian picked up the new paper.

'Signore Furian, you are aware I know the name by which you are called. Also I was informed you are no common adventurer, but the son of a respectable and powerful man. How am I cognizant of these things? There is one person to tell me. Let us leave that for the moment.

'I have few dealings with the City or the world. You will guess why. But Cloudio del Nero was my lover. I met him in a strange, unwanted way, but he took a great interest in me, and even offered me a secret marriage. I was fond of him, but no more, and did not agree. If he has died, I do not know the means, or even if it is so. Perhaps you will believe me. And that I am sorry.

'This I do comprehend, though not the reason: You are in mortal danger. You must trust me this much, while you remain in my house I may protect you. I was too proud before. I ask you now to remain a day or so, until perhaps your friends, or your estranged father, may be brought to assist you. I vow that you need not once see me while you are in the house, only my servants, who will go about your errands as is necessary, in order to invite aid.

'Forgive my former unwise words. Accept my help, and forget me.

—Eurydiche'.

At the bottom of the paper she had written an afterthought, very small. *It is hard for me to act well in the human world. I was born as you see me, a freak. I have no measure, but expect nothing.*

Furian did see her, but as a child in a white dress, her face an ivory doll's face. She could not cry, save in her heart and mind.

He screwed up the paper and tossed it down. He went to the door, opened it. The corridor was in darkness, but for one other door at its opposite end, which stood an inch or two ajar. A mild light hung there, straight and still as a wand of magic.

Furian moved towards the door. He stopped and rapped on it quietly.

He heard the stir of a dress, pushed wide the door, and stepped in.

Eurydiche stood all across the room, which was her bedchamber. The bed had ebony posts, a painted lid, long drifted curtains. Candles burned on a table, where she had been writing. He shut the door.

Her back was to him, and as he took another step, she held up her hand, and the topazes on her wrist blinked as her gemstone eyes could not. *No closer.*

Her hair was undone, but the powder in it yet, so it glittered eerily as a moonlit wave.

"We'll say I did misjudge you, then," he said. "Why do you want to help me?" He stood looking at her back. She did nothing, and then she shook her head. Even she might say Yes, and No. "Your maid," he said, "thinks you fancy me." As he spoke the words a shower of brilliant lust went through him, but he felt again the draining weakness the illness had brought. Two disparate pangs.

He did not want her. So might have her. Yet also he wanted her as he had seldom desired a woman. For she was all the beauty and the misery of the world in one. Horror and pleasure, punishment and redemption.

And she? She could not say a word.

He walked over the room softly, but she detected him, and whirled about. *Her face—*

Furian came up against her, so her body met with his. He put his hands—the fine hands of his youth—on either side of the slender ivory disk. Her skin was firm and silken, cool as the autumn morning.

He leaned to her slowly, looking at her, into her death-blue eyes. His shadow put them out. His mouth was on hers.

Eurydiche did not push him away. She did not struggle.

He kissed her very lightly. She tasted of distant wine and cold fruits.

Furian drew back. "You can show me yes or no. Is it Yes?"

She put back her head on the slim pillar of her throat.

Her eyes blazed on his. Her head went up and down. *Yes.*

Furian took hold of her. He ran his arm behind her neck and put his mouth on hers again. It was possible to enter her mouth by a gentle pressure. She was lucid and sweet to the taste, her teeth unflawed and her tongue smooth and pliant, but moving only at the insistence of his own.

In the seconds when this utter laxness excited him to an unbearable pitch that might be the preface to aversion, her arms roped round his back. She gripped him, the coat, his hair, and her body gave way. Her weight was slight but he took all of it. She was heavy as a sleeping cat might be, a swathe of velvet. He picked her up off the floor and laid her on the bed. She would not let go of him. She pulled him back like a mermaid, intent on drowning, smothering him, drawing him down to the depths of the sea.

Beyond the room was the earth.

They spun in this microcosm, like a planet.

He brought her from her wrappings, thrust off his clothes. The garments lay tangled on the floor, like scraps of paper.

Finding her body, his desire now caused him pain. As she clung to him, her hands straying, clasping, he saw above the landscape of her flesh the visiting moon of her face. The face absorbed him. He returned to it, from her cupped breasts with their petal tips, from her flat soft belly, the pearls of her hip-bones, the tender feet with nails like shells, from the core of her with its rough fine pale amber hair, that did not match the greying flaxen of her head. He returned to her face, her beautiful resistless mouth, kissing her, kissing her, eating her tongue, devouring her narrow cheekbones and the silver lashes of her windowed eyes.

Of course, no change in her, nothing. Yet he heard the breath rasp now in her throat. Her limbs quivered. A stream of arousal lit her groin and the buds of her breasts pushed into his palms, on one of which the words had blurred, (*I live*). But the face was remote. The face *listened* high above their world of shivering and searching and straining on, above her hands which teased his sex, practiced and cunning, her fingers that fluttered on his spine like wings, and sought inside him, so he must lay her out, open her wide, crucify her on the bursting burning pin of his body.

As he worked within her, the room and next the City fell apart. He heard the rumble of buildings fallen in canals and the insurge of the ocean.

Her hands leapt and seized him. Then fell away, strengthless. He felt long spasms rushing in her loins, but her up-tilted face watched blindly, far away. From her throat came a sound. One sound. And beneath his chest her heart gurned, striving for air she could not take.

As the crisis left her, he saw the opacity beneath the corundum of her gaze. He knew, she was unconscious in his arms as he had been in hers, but could not stay for her, went down in her, down to the ocean floor, where upturned faces lay with starry eyes, deep, deep below the water.

They lay half entwined. The house creaked stilly. Far off a bell sounded for three, but he did not know which church had given it voice.

"Is this dangerous for you?" he said. "If you faint at the peak—have I hurt you?"

She caressed him, his check, neck, shoulder. Along all the line of him until he came erect again inside the silk snare of her hand. She shook her head and spread herself, abandoned, arching her back.

Their race was swifter. They dropped together. He could not have stopped, he thought, to save the life of either of them.

"Who told you about me?" he asked.

She pointed at the table, where all but one candle had gone out. The pen was there. They forgot the pen.

"Eurydiche," he said.

In the dark which came, he said it over and over.

When morning bloomed, a silver haze at the narrow window, he saw her again. He lay face to face with her, staring at her, in and in at her. It seemed to him he himself did not blink any more, but when he said this to her, she hit him lightly with the back of her hand. She would nip him with her fingers, tickle him, tease him. She had almost every ordinary playful sexual skill.

He kissed the wide lids of her eyes, described with his tongue her brows, nostrils, lips.

His kisses were like stains of crushed lilac flowers along her groin, her breasts.

Outside it rained.

Daytime noises disturbed Venus. The canal filled and slopped on the pavement. Bells rang miles away.

Someone brought food, and after she indicated this, pointing at his mouth and stomach, the door, gestures bizarre yet amusing, he went and brought it in. He ate, and she, taking up a little glass with a spout that reminded him of Shaachen's alembics, poured the contents through her lips and back into her upturned throat. There was nothing ungraceful in the procedure. It pleased him. He too did it

with the cooling dolche, and laughed at her, saying she was not
mysterious. But then he told her she was a mermaid, and Venus, and
Virgo, the goddess of the zodiac.

She must have tasted the dolche from his mouth. He asked if
she liked it. She nodded. He licked out the cup and gave her more.
(He wondered if she had done these things with Cloudio del Nero.
But she had been fond of del Nero. Furian she had wanted.)

They slept through the afternoon when the window was peach.

In the dusk, when the window was steel, she mounted him. He
watched her, her breasts, the face of the moon, the eyes of the stars.
She drew him to a pinnacle that made him cry aloud.

Afterwards she lay on top of him, the face against his hair.

Some deep melancholy of divine pleasure made him weep. She
watched, and putting her finger to his tears, placed them just within
her mouth.

Later he lay over her and killed her again, and himself. For he
felt himself near death with her. A wild febrile strength, born from
the fever, now took all of him away, and it did not matter. He did
not think beyond the room. Time, although it passed in colors at the
window, had ceased. Life had drawn aside, as, for the dead, it does.

When he woke in the morning she was gone, and he turned into the
bed, breathing up her fragrance from the sheet.

He found the next paper folded on a tray of food the girl bought
and set outside the door.

'My love, make yourself ready. Tonight we are to go away. Trust
me with your safety.'

She had spoken of trust before. Did he trust her? No. Not at all.
Trust had no part in it. He would have to do what she said.

He rolled out of the bed. When he was dressed, and had eaten,
he went about her room. He took the sleeves and skirts of her
dresses out of a closet and nuzzled them. He observed her mirror,
which had reflected her. Beyond a few garments, some gems, combs,
a book that lay on a table, the pen and paper, she had left little of
herself. What could there be of her. He had found that. What she
was. A kernel of pure, cool, rushing fire.

Soon he went out to look for her, and met the old servant in the
corridor. The man stood foursquare. Disapproval? Fear?

"She's gone out. You must wait, Signore."

"Will you send someone with a letter for me?"

"If you wish, Signore."

He wrote to Shaachen rapidly at her table.

'Blue-eyed Virgo I found. The one you know of. All is well. Who cares? Be wary yourself. I will write more when I can.'

Then he added, 'The Madonna, whose face is made of alabaster. Better speak some spell for me, or say some prayer. Amen.'

It was dusk. They had not lit the lamps.

As she came into the sala, he crossed the room, and took hold of her.

She was mantled in black, and masked—the butterfly.

"Take the mask off. Let me look at you."

She did as he said.

He covered her mouth with kisses. He tried to ease her back. He would have possessed her against the marble wall.

But Eurydiche gently pushed him away; she said "No," and he let go of her.

She put into his hand another paper. But he shook for a moment with desire, and would not read it. Then he carried it to the veiled, darkening window.

'Flavio will come in with a cloak and mask. Put these on. Will you trust me as I asked?'

"No," he said.

He looked at her and she was masked again. She made a little redundant graceful gesture.

"You don't believe I don't trust you? But you might be taking me to my death."

She advanced slowly to him, and slipped her arms about his ribs. Turning her head, she laid it on his breast. Then, looking up with her whole face, as she must, she put her hand over his racketing heart.

"It's not fear," he said. "Lust."

And she leaned against him once more, probably feeling the lust quite well in its lower station.

Finally the door opened again and a young male servant entered. He too wore a black mantle and a plain black mask. The black cloak and eye-mask he carried he handed to Furian with a quick half bow. The sort of bow Furian had not received for years and did not want now.

"Where are we going?"

Flavio said nothing, only went out again. Eurydiche led Furian to the desk. She wrote quickly. *Where you will be safe. I think no one else can assist you—and I was given word.*

"By whom?"

She wrote *Wait*.

"If I won't."

Her hand flashed up, impotent and angry, and caught his arm. She squeezed his flesh harshly.

"All right," he said. "It's all right. I'm at your mercy. Have I said that before? You can kill me any time. You've made a love-fool of me."

She shook her head rapidly. Another woman would have laughed, cursed him, perhaps shed tears. He took her hand and kissed the palm and closed her fingers on the kiss. He put on the half-mask and the cloak.

The sala, when they left it, was lost in indigo darkness.

11

There was little light.

As they descended the palace, he saw the servants had not bothered with any of the lamps.

There were no sounds.

Her man, Flavio, went first, then she. Furian came last. It seemed to him they moved stealthily. And yet, too, the gloom and shut doors of the house led him strangely to infer that no one, any more, was there.

In a passageway below the rooms, he sensed the water of the canal. They were certainly under the paving now.

Presently there was a door which Flavio unlocked.

A flight of steps ran down, wide, shallow and damp. A smoke rose from them, and there was the stink of bad water. A trickling susurrous came on all sides and beneath was blackness.

By the stair a lamp hung on a hook. Flavio took it down and lit it. This seemed an accustomed procedure. The steps lit three by three as they descended, and Furian heard the canny rats of Venus skittering away below.

They were in a long tunnel. Arches ribbed it over, and a bluish fungus grew on some of them, giving off a useless lightless glow. Not only under the canal, down into the lagoon, perhaps.

They walked without a word.

Sometimes Furian glimpsed rats as they fled away. They were albinos. There began to be other tunnels, narrower than the main channel, branching off. All were ignored. It was a secret thoroughfare, old sumps and sewers that had dried out, or places made purposely for just such clandestine travel. Though he had heard of such things, Furian had formerly avoided them.

Then they turned at last into a broader stretch, and there were new lamps hanging up at intervals, infused with a thin, green, fluttering glare.

This was a general walkway, for in a minute or so, two shadowy masked men came strolling up to them, and passed without a greeting on either side.

Later another went by, this one with a rat-white (masked) dog at his heels.

Other stairways now began to appear, and narrow tunnels that sloped straight up. Some were marked by signs. One of these tunnels Flavio chose. Its entry was marked by a distinctive emblem, a snarling sun of bronze with open eye-slots; a mask: the symbol of the Mask Makers Guild. Furian checked.

She had brought him *here*?

But she turned and beckoned him in her mute, eloquent way. And he—he was a love-fool. He would do what she wished.

He followed her, and the servant, up the tunnel.

A bold gleaming lantern hung from a lion-shaped hook. There was a stair, the stone kept clean and quite dry. Having climbed it, they reached a slit of door, only wide enough a woman slender as Eurydiche could go through without turning sideways on.

Flavio knocked at the panels. A man's voice came at once. "Whom does the night give up?"

"Seekers of the risen sun."

"Name yourselves."

"Madonna Eurydiche, her slave, and one companion."

The phrases had an antique quality. The first had been apparently a password. Now there was the sound of bolts drawn, and the curtailed little door swung in.

Flavio turned himself and went through, Eurydiche went after, and Furian, grimacing, after them.

It was a tiny chamber, fitting the door. Two lamps lit it, and a man stood in a black apron, on his head the fearsome visage and wig of some ancient monstrosity. The mask was excellent in its way, fanged and tusked. The eyepieces had black glass in them.

Furian anticipated more preamble, but the door's guardian merely indicated a second door.

"You're expected, Madama."

The second door was of a normal size, and beyond was a stone passage, lighted at intervals by naked torches. The City knew, the palace of the Mask Guild was very old. Another flight of steps, these broad and white, took them to a double door.

Without hindrance they went through.

Beyond lay the Guild hall.

Furian thought, *Why be modest? Display is power.*

The ceiling looked high as a sky. It was painted as one, a green sky of tempest shown in panels, with boiling clouds. A sun set in fulvous glory to one corner. At the opposite corner a moon rose in a flock of stars. Every one a faceted glass that dazzled and winked.

Pillars held up the sky-ceiling on capitals of silver acanthus leaves. The tops of the walls had a frieze of Roman marble, centaurs carrying off maidens. There was also a chandelier, fragile as some ornate gigantic jewelry, budding with thirty or fifty candles, everyone ablaze. Everything reflected in a floor like water.

On the walls were a hundred or more masks. They resembled terrible unmarred faces, staring, with tongues out or pursed lips, with rays for hair and horns like the moon, the snouts of beasts, or the loud, dumb beauty of the damned.

They journeyed through the hall, over the reflecting floor, (minuscule figures), and went through another door, along another corridor, to a tapestried wall that had no door at all.

Flavio stepped aside. He settled into a small alcove, and sat down. He set his lamp on a table there, familiarly.

Eurydiche turned to Furian. She touched his lips softly with her fingers: *Be silent.*

Then she knocked three times and three times again on the wall.

There was a sigh of sound, and the tapestry quivered. The wall had moved aside behind it.

Imperiously now, it seemed to him, inimical and unknown the woman glided through without a glance. Furian walked after her.

Death, Furian thought. *A whole room of it.*

In the bright shine of candles on gilded stands, a background of dark green serpentine, and resting there in rows, the countless yellowed smiling skulls. Beneath a dark window, forty-seven skulls that were black, no longer smiling, their teeth all dropped out.

My welcome?

She did not seem at a loss. She stood before a big man's shape, which was seated, almost idly, in a chair. But her hands had come out from her cloak. They darted over the air, describing various forms. And the man had also raised two hands, one with a black ring upon it, and did the same.

They—were *speaking* together. It was almost instantly plain. A language that did not need tongues or lips.

She must know him well, he her, for this to be between them.

His hands were not young, nor old. Strong, spread, callused workman's hands, with cuffs of silver lace, and a ring worthy of the Ducem.

His face was masked oddly, a circular plate of deep blue glass, cut with two eyeholes and a gash for the mouth, having a hooked and bulbous nose. Beyond, his hair was strictly tied and streaked by heavy grey. The eyes were dark and veined, long-lidded, the containing skin creased and sallow. The eyes and hair and hands of a man in late middle age.

Furian did nothing, standing attending on their unfathomable conversation.

The conversation stopped. She turned her butterfly face towards him, seemed hesitating. Then she moved away. A curtain hung down and she went by it into some other room.

The man spoke at once.

"You are Eurydiche's lover."

Furian was unnerved. The voice—there was something to it . . . did he know it?

"If I am, what are you to her?"

The man said, flatly, "Her father."

Furian replied, "That warns me to be wary."

"It should not. She's told me everything. Besides, I expected nothing else."

Indeed, the voice was familiar. It stirred up the past, long avenues and vistas of gardens and fine chambers.

"Then you'll expect to abuse me," said Furian, levelly.

"Why should I expect that? You were always one who took what he wanted. Even when you wanted *nothing,* you took that."

"You know me? How interesting."

"And you know me," said the man. He undid the fastenings of the mask. It came off in his large hand.

It was a lined, audacious face. A gentleman's face, an explorer's face, for the tracks about the eyes had been formed by seas and sun and vigil.

An instant scene formed fast about him. It was in Furian's father's house. The long table draped and laid for some dinner. The oranges in dolche, and the musicians playing a little divertion. *Who?*

"You don't remember me? I was of so little account."

It came.

"Lepidus," Furian said.

His father's agent and captain, the man who had traveled so many lands on his father's business, even as far as Rus Parvus and the Southern Amaria. The silk that passed through a ring—

Lepidus. Now here, a maker of masks, the father of the woman whose face *was* a mask—

"You seem to know it all," said Furian, "but I'm in the dark."

"Surely not so much. You went hunting murderers."

"I only found a mask on a canal."

"You found my daughter. Do you still think she killed him, the composer of the song?"

"No. It isn't in her to kill."

"You think not? Ah, but you're right. She can only kill with a look, my child, can't she?"

Furian said nothing.

Lepidus got up. He went to a table and poured wine into two goblets of clear Venusian glass.

"Choose which you want."

"You think I'll suspect poison."

"Won't you?"

"I'm defenseless here anyway."

"You trusted her to bring you here." Furian shrugged. He took one of the glasses and drank it down. Lepidus refilled it. "You drink that way now."

"You know everything about me."

"I know something about you. That you left your father's house on a whim. I was on my own little estate at the time, but I heard of it. Your father wrote to me. Now and then, I've come across you in the City. You didn't look up from the gutter you were so determinedly in, to see me."

"My father asked you to watch me, then."

"Something like that. But later, you went your own way. It was Juseppi, your wanderlier of that night, who spoke of you in connection with del Nero's mask."

"He was, I think, made to speak of me."

"Perhaps."

"And then I was to be killed. And then, I was *not* to be killed. I'll assume that, since I'm not dead."

"That's because Eurydiche likes you. And it seems that you in turn like her quite well."

"Del Nero seemed to like her."

"He loved her. But she had no true feeling for him."

"A strange motive for murder."

Lepidus said, "As you guessed he was murdered for another reason. Someone was jealous and wished him away. A musician, you'll understand."

"But you had him killed on this jealous musician's behalf."

"I, and others."

"You had him set upon and thrown in the canal."

"Nothing so crude. It was wonderfully subtly done."

"*How* was it done?"

Lepidus smiled, in the broad raconteur's fashion that long ago had enchanted the supper tables. "That's another story. We may come to it. But not yet."

"Have there been others your Guild—and you, Lepidus— killed?"

"You know as much."

"Name them. Number them."

"Oh, five or so. Seven or so. The names might mean nothing."

"Messalina is one?"

"Yes."

"But she's gone mad. She's beyond you."

"Never think that, Furian. Shall I call you Furian? Since you call yourself that now."

"Why do it—why murder? If not for yourself?"

Lepidus drank his wine. He said, "But it has also *been* for me. And for the others who do as I do—also for them. We have our personal reasons, rages, thorns, for wanting this power over others, the God-Power of life and death. To toy—as we've been toyed with. It's become—our art." He paused. He said, "Let me tell you something about myself. That night of your dainty party, when you came home to your father's house, when you were going to your bed, I was riding to my estate. I hadn't been back to it for thirteen years. This is often the plight of the dedicated traveler. On your father's ventures, and on my own, thirteen years away. I had a wife. Of course, you didn't know. Why would you bother to know, I was only an occasional guest. But I hadn't seen her, you perceive, for thirteen years, or the daughter she had borne me in my absence. Yes, my wife sent letters to me. She praised the little girl, said she was pretty and quick. And I, like any guilty parent, returned them gifts and money. The night when I came home, I found no daughter at all. All those years my wife had kept her with the nuns of Santa Dolora. I could not at first get from her why."

Furian waited, but Lepidus was silent.

Furian said, "So you went to see."

"She was brought to my house. She came veiled over like a frosty flower."

"But you took off the veil."

Lepidus said, his voice no longer urbane, but rasping and very thick, "I didn't lose my senses, as you did. But I crossed myself. I babbled to the Virgin. I broke out in a white sweat and had to void my bowels. They call it Fachia Pietra—Stone Face. It happens now and then, in every several million, million human things. The muscles are dead in the face. They may be moved manually, or how else could they feed, but in no spontaneous way. It never changes."

"She told me this."

"Stone Face," said Lepidus. "My daughter. An only child, did I say? My wife hadn't given her even a name. The nuns christened her Maria, as they did every foundling girl. Then a number. Maria Una and Maria Dua, and my daughter was Maria Setta. But the other Marias were afraid of her."

"However, you took her in."

"Did I? No. I gave her to paid servants to bring up. But as a lady. She wasn't meant for a nun-house. In her first letter to me she wrote *Dearest Father, I am quite happy now.*"

Furian's belly turned like a snake. His heart twisted. He said only, "And the language you make with your hands?"

"I learnt it in the Amarias. I learnt it for entertainment. The Orichalci invented it, for the speechless among them. She mastered it quickly. She'll teach it to you."

"To me. Why to me?"

Lepidus leant forward. He was heavy now, a tree at the fullness of its growth, stiffening. An angry raging tree. "You have a choice, Furian. She needs a protector, a man of her own age. A lover, a husband. I'll give you this, if you want it."

"Del Nero wanted. He was a prince."

"I told you. She didn't want him."

"But me she wants."

"You spoke to her in some garden. You were masked. But from that moment. You sang under her window. You were playing the love-game even then, though you may not think so. And you came with her here."

"That was perhaps unwise."

"Or sensible. If you won't have her, you can still live. Either way, there's only one course for you."

"Which is?"

"To become an initiate of the guild. Once its oaths and terrors bind you, you're safe to me, and to my comrades."

"I see that. Then I must. I don't want to die."

"That's new. You seemed half to want death a long while."

"But now I'm enslaved of your daughter."

"You were always perverse," said Lepidus.

Furian thought, *Perverse to love her then, so he thinks, For he does not. He hates her. This is a duty or some earthly trial.* (I am quite happy.) *In God's sweet name—*

"Well then," said Lepidus, "take more wine. You'll dine among us tonight. The rite that will place you in the Guild is a difficult and savage one. You must be prepared."

Trapped like a wasp in sugar. No way out. Not yet.

"Whatever you say," said Furian.

And he's pleased to see me so. Those days and nights at my father's table, my family like lords, and Lepidus our actor, performing his life risked so often only an enthralling tale. And I with my eye on some girl, not properly attending. He does like it so, this. The poor wasp in the sugar of his daughter's skirts.

And what has he seen, spying on me? Flat drunk, sick, playing with knives—the men I've killed myself, the women I've had, depths to which I've sunk—my bloody dreams—I am a worthy punishment, he judges, for this daughter who shamed him with her beautiful deformity.

12

The dining chamber was dark. The somber silks were from the East, and sables hung from ceiling to floor. His father would have appreciated it.

On the table the vessels gleamed. There were clams in a honey and garlic sauce, greens from the farms, peacock roasted and dressed with their feathers, calves livers, a dish of the peculiar floury *Batata* from the Amarias.

Furian ate sparingly, just enough to confirm his (demanded?) respect.

Eurydiche sat to his left, her mask obscuring her, eating, of course, nothing.

There were five others.

Lepidus, the blue glass mask hinged up to his nose. Three further men sat about the table, dressed richly enough, satins, lace, wigs, pins and rings and earrings. Each of these wore only an eye-mask, two quite plain, as was Furian's, and one in the form of a gilt half moon. The fifth person was another woman, who sat beside Moon-Mask. She wore a black velvet dress with decorations of tourmaline sea scorpions. Her mask was a fantasy of a black fan. Calypso?

She gave no sign she had met with Furian. Unlike Eurydiche, she filled her plate and goblet, yet did not shift her mask to eat. She was restless, moving and rustling in her chair. Now and then she reached for her silver fork, or the glass, left them lying.

Once she spoke, very low, to Moon Mask. "I must take it off."

"Do what you want, dear heart," he responded. "Why not. Let me feast on your loveliness with the food."

But she did not even then remove her mask. Her fingers tapped the fan and fell away.

Was it Furian she was afraid to reveal herself before? Did she recognize him? Had she been told the truth of anything? Whatever else, she had come a distance from Juseppi's Osiris death in pieces and the open sunny rooms of the Bertro Palace.

Lepidus smiled on and on, a short, graven smile. The candles made rivulets on the rust brocade of his coat, as if he had come out of water. But that was not he.

He had had, Furian thought, none of this aura—of weight, of biding malice—at the tables of long ago. Or had Furian only missed it?

The men talked in a sort of code. The dialogue had the same antique ring as the phrases employed at the entry below. It was another new language, from which the uninitiated was excluded. He could not follow, could not enter, though he might hear every word.

This too they did for him, he believed. To demonstrate the well-walled kingdom he was to try to enter. But he had been promised a rough passage. Acolytes of any guild underwent traditional rituals and ordeals, and were sworn not to speak of them. Enough leaked out to make one chary. But now there was no choice.

Unless he and she might escape. Was that possible? Eurydiche relied upon Lepidus, her father. She had had to. If Furian proposed they should mislead and evade him, would she attend, or be able to disobey?

"When we are midway up the mountain, the fire may be seen," said one of the plain eye-masks. (No names had been given, not even Furian's—but then, they would know of *him*.)

"A ram caught in a thicket," said another man. "We must praise God for the fairness of its eyes."

That was how the talk was. Furian did not really heed. Nothing was to be got from it.

Calypso put her hand on her glass again, and again withdrew it.

Did she know these men were the ones who had ordered Juseppi's death, had had him tortured, then cut into bits and sent her in a basket? She must know. How else had she met her swain?

"I can't," she said.

No one gave her attention.

The mask she wore, had worn in the Setapassa, was exceptional. Every tine of the fan was fluted by the lacquer of black lace. The eyeholes were in the shape of roses. Her eyes behind were opaque and wandering.

"Four ships came to harbor," said Lepidus. "Now a fifth ship comes. We honor it." And he bowed to Furian, ironically. But the other men at the table also bowed. Furian at a loss, bowed back.

They like a clever dog. They want it to beg for the bones.

Calypso rose suddenly. She pointed past Furian into the shadows of sables. "Something's there!"

Her eyes were wide in the mask now. Furian could see their whites were inflamed, as if she had been in smoke.

"Nothing's there. Sit down," said Moon Mask, off-handedly now.

"It's a monkey. I can see a monkey."

"Sit down. There's no monkey."

Lepidus said, "Perhaps the ghost of some animal that haunts the room." He touched Calypso's arm. "The hour's late. Our friend may wish for his bed. There are things to do tomorrow."

The men got up. Each nodded to Furian as he passed him, going out. Calypso walked behind the moon-masked man. She drew her skirts in close, away from invisible things which ran along the floor.

The door did not quite shut. Lepidus said, "The man will show you to your apartment. A little cramped, I fear. Perhaps you're used to that nowadays."

"Perhaps."

"My daughter will go to her own room, which I keep for her here. You see, the proprieties must be observed under this roof."

Furian said, "The lady in the black dress—"

"Juseppi's woman. Yes?"

"She seemed uneasy."

"Of course she is. She's a coarse woman and not fitted to be here. But one of our number lays claim to her, for the time being."

The servant had come to the doorway with a light. Furian must evidently now go. He turned to Eurydiche, and took up her hand. It was cold. He must go, and leave her with her hating father, but again, no choice.

He leaned and kissed her hair. Her fragrance disturbed him utterly. So much license had been abounding. He had thought they would still share a bed. Lepidus took him to the door. He whispered, "At last, of them all, one you can rescue."

Outside in the corridor, the black-aproned man led him away, up a stair into a maze of twines and doors.

The room was certainly small, and bare. The bed was hard and narrow. On a table lay a Bible bound in black leather and a Neptunium, the book of prayers to the god of the ocean. A silver cross hung on the wall. In each corner, high up, was the symbol of Venus, beside the trident.

A barred window looked squinting on to darkness, but he heard the race of the mill along the canal.

There was water in a decanter, but belatedly cautious, he did not drink it.

He sat on the hard bed. With her, he had slept as mortal things are said to sleep. Alone, he did not think that sleep would come, nor wish to court it.

Furian listened to the water-race. Below that sound, the noises of the Guild House were stifled.

Despite what had been said, they might come up here to murder him—it had been admitted, power over life, to *toy* with it, appeased them. Or they begin their initiation ritual in the midst of the night, merely to unhinge him.

Did she know how much Lepidus hated her, loathed her? Probably she thought it inevitable and natural that he should. Yet she was brim-full, a poured fountain, of love.

His eyes clouded with fruitless fatigue. He would have given anything to have her here. He must speak to her tomorrow, if there were a moment's space. They should be gone. Her father had seemed to say he killed to work out his rage at her, upon mankind, like an angry, maddened god. And had she never known?

He dreamed of a green salt-swan swimming alone along a night lagoon. The walls of ruins stood up, not a light showing. The swan parted its mouth, and screamed like a woman inside his head.

Furian lurched off the bed. This fresh habit of sleeping—he had slept despite himself.

He flung the door open and stared out. Feet were running, up and up. They became a boy in a black apron and plain black mask.

"Signore—come—come—"

"What?" he said. He caught the boy's shoulder.

"The lady—she'll need you—" cried the boy.

"Which lady?"

"Madonna Eurydiche."

As they rushed downstairs, along the corridors, he thought that she could not scream, could make scarcely any noise. If he had truly heard it, perhaps it was not her?

The boy was pulling him into a room. All the while, the boy

choked and muttered in fear. No sooner was Furian inside than the boy ran away.

All Furian could see at first was Eurydiche. She wore a long pale night-robe, and her hair was loose. Behind her, the things of a bedroom—it must be hers. A tapestry on the wall of Diana hunting with white hounds, shone oddly in the light of the lamp. He saw the tapestry was askew, and why. A man lay under it and had wrenched at it in falling, it seemed.

The man was Lepidus. Still in his glamorous rusty coat, the ring on his hand which somehow yet clutched the edge of the hunt . . . A big, able body, and the hair, undone now, streaming out, but its grey discolored.

Eurydiche stood with her hands loose at her sides. When he spoke her name, she moved at once. She came at him. He saw the unhidden disk of her fearsome loveliness, the glitter of her inhuman sapphire eyes. Then she was ripping at him, beating him, struggling.

He caught her, held her still.

"I know—I know. I heard you screaming. I can hear you weeping. I *know,* my love. I can hear."

At this she dropped against him. He held her as her body shook itself to quiet in his arms.

She would tell him presently, writing erratically at the small table, how she had woken at a little noise, and seen the lamp alight, and then seen—this. Her father's body under the tapestry, still dressed and jeweled, but the hair undone and stained with blood, and all the face, from the fore head to the chin, cut neatly away, skin and flesh, muscle and sinew, features, mouth, eyes, (brain), leaving only one more grinning, dull-white skull.

PART THREE

The Skull

13

"**D**on't leave me," she cried, so desperately. "How can you leave me? Do you want to break my heart—kill me—how can you go—my son—my darling—"

Furian lifted himself out of sleep. He was not used to sleep, for years it had been so evasive. Eurydiche had taught him how to slumber again, and how to eat if he were hungry, and how to drink more for pleasure than excess—But the dreams. Could she have kept the dreams away?

He said aloud to the blank room, "I left you, Mother. I'm sorry. I expect you recovered."

Had she? He had never inquired. He had heard nothing of them. Presumably Lepidus had known, before he removed from their service to make masks, and murder. But Lepidus would have to be tongue-tied now.

The room was long and low, and nets hung from hooks. One brown candle burned. The mattress was on the floor, and verminous.

Was her chamber as gross? Possibly the one who had got them away had made sure it was not.

He would never have placed Moon-Mask in the role of savior, but that was the one who had come in, as he held Eurydiche in the long silence.

"It's treachery. Enemies everywhere. Who knows who struck him? But you two must get away at once."

"Very well."

"Not by your own means. You must do what I say. Or you'll die, and so may she."

They went down, cloaked, masked, two more of those secret wanderers by night for whom the slinking boats of Venus were named.

Moon-Mask did not go with them, only his three men, their leader masked like a bull, as dead Juseppi had once tried to be.

The boat stole between the dark stone curtains of the houses, over the stony mirror water. It was a journey of hours. At last they passed into the Laguna Silvia.

Furian became aware, by the turns they took, they were going among the haunts of the fishers, the Divers Quarter.

Nets hung from windows, in the dark like spider webs. The smell of fish was dense. On the tethering poles, Neptunes stood up, moving a little, some with Filmy pearls put into them. On the sides of houses, on broken shutters, the City Zodians were painted, Scorpio, Cancro, Pesci. From one greenishly lit window thin as a pin, a child's voice fluted out, singing long cadences, being taught to breathe even by night.

But sunrise was coming by the time the wanderer's oar went down. They tied up at a reeking, crumbling pile of tenements. The upper story craned over, and up into this they went.

In the large communal room, men and women clothed in rags and remnants, sat amid an early breakfast of wheat porridge and bubbling rice kettles, turned to stare at the refinery of a woman smelling of perfume and masked like a butterfly. A huge eel lay on the table, its head off, still quaking. Children played shrieking with the writhing tail, pitiless in a pitiless world.

For some reason it reminded him, true incongruity, of the Orichalci, in their city of tents. The ducal tribe known as The Enemy, who honored the beasts they killed and spoke a blessing and a prayer for them. In their wild ceremonies under enormous moons, naked but for their sacred masks and manes of feathers, they invoked a quarry and called it to dance soul to soul with them.

They were taken up a stair, and put into separate chambers.

For they were not to lodge together. It would not fit with the 'proprieties'. A man guarded Furian's door, and another probably hers. He realized, slow and stupid, cursing himself, they had become prisoners.

When a skinny diver boy, in a rag mask, with huge chest and vivid eyes, (a necklet of blue pearls over his torn shirt), brought in a dish of polenta, Furian offered money. The child—he was not more than ten—laughed. He had a wonderful laugh, rich and full from large, sound lungs.

"Barter here, Signore. A fish-head, or a treasure from the drowned palaces. That's all we like."

"There's money under Silvia," said Furian indolently. (He had none, anyway, it had been left with his old clothes at her house.)

"*Antique* coins, Signore. Duccas from three centuries ago. Capitas from the Ancient Romans. *Those* I'd take. But still not let you out. The Maskers are mighty. How would we dare go against them?"

"You know then it's the Mask Guild."

The boy flirted with his eyes, saying, unspeaking, *You are the dupe, not I.*

When the boy had gone, and Furian had eaten some of the porridge, he went to the slit of window and peered down. Outside was the building's back, an encrusted alley strung with shreds of washing.

The window was like a keyhole, too narrow to provide an exit. The drop anyway was some twenty-five feet.

He thought of Eurydiche. Was she mourning? Had her grief been for loss, or made more of terror, dislocation. Was she truly an innocent? How could she be. It was a fact, with her face she could never have misled him, by a false yet winning smile, an unreal expression of pain. But, conversely, she might hide it all.

Carnival. The word itself—farewell to the flesh that was, a practice for the grave.

He needed to speak to her, as best they could. He needed—to know . . .

There was an old beggar man coming down the alley, stooped over, his head bound in a dirty turban. He used a stick and had a scruffy satchel on his shoulder. There was something untidy, black and white, attached to the strap.

Furian could do nothing but wait. Maybe, if he asked to see her, it would be allowed. But no doubt, they would be observed.

He was half turning for the door, to speak to Moon-Mask's hireling outside, when he heard the beggar singing below. It was del Nero's song, rendered very horribly. Furian was at least able to tip the leavings of porridge on the old devil's head—

The man leered up. He wore for a mask a strip of cloth. His face was nearly black, and covered over with blemishes and warts. One bright eye like faceted glass glittered up into Furian's. The thing on his shoulder resolved itself. It had been preening, and was a magpie, smart as the most fashionable hat.

Furian stayed dead still.

The beggar reached into his satchel and brought out a little folded square of paper. He gave it to the bird, and pointed up. Furian heard the words, "There it is, darling."

The magpie shot straight up and landed in the narrow window. It was young and cream-smooth, and had the sheen on its feathers, unearthly blue. Its eye was sharper than the beggar's, like a sliver of black steel. It dropped the paper in the room, and Furian saw the words there, written on the back, *Ask him the time*.

Furian stared at the magpie. He said, "Tell me what time it is."

The bird cocked its shining head.

It cawed throatily eight times, without hesitating. Furian had heard the bell faintly from Santa Lala, not long before, sound the same number.

"What minutes?"

The magpie thought, raised its right wing to show a lapse after the hour, and pecked ten times.

Furian had the urge to touch the magpie, which had been dead, but was now alive in the flesh, doing its former trick. But as he stretched out his hand, the bird veered from the window and dived down again to the alley.

Furian pressed his face through the window.

"Shaachen?"

The old beggar—Shaachen in extravagant disguise—gave a cackle. He limped away along the alley, the magpie on his head.

Damn him to hell. Was this the hour for theater? Where in God's name was he off to?

Furian, with nothing else to do, picked up the folded paper. Opened it.

'Furian Furiano, you were not so difficult to find. I had one watch the Guild, and so by night he followed you. You are in deep now. I have not forsaken you. It is a plot thick as the best fish stew. Take note. The Principessa Messalina died today.'

Furian softly cursed. A glance showed him the rest of the paper was all about the magpie. He read, fretfully, how the bird had flown in at Shaachen's street door and upstairs. How it resembled the dead magpie in all ways, and could do, outright, all the same tricks, particularly the trick of time-telling.

The letter ended, piously, 'Consider this creature, and this sign. Fear nothing. The world is an illusion, and we may pull off the veil. Find you I will. Keep this letter.'

Furian sat down heavily on the uncertain stool. He put the letter into his coat, and started soundlessly laughing. Of all the things

Shaachen might have done, he had chosen *this*. A demonstration of the afterlife and the miraculous recurrence of things. Rescue had obviously been too paltry, too normal an act to attempt.

Soon after, the door opened again. The Guild man in the bull mask walked in.

"These quarters are uncomfortable, but you need only suffer them until tonight."

"Where is *she*?" said Furian.

"The lady Eurydiche is safe."

"I should like to see the lady."

"She's occupied. At prayer for her father. Better not to disturb her. The priest is with her now."

"Oh yes?"

"Tonight we go over to the Isle. Lepidus will be buried in the Guild mausoleum."

"I see. And I?"

"Go with us. You're under the protection of the Signore Lunario."

Moon-Mask—probably the name was not his given one.

"We have a chapel on the Isle," said the bull-faced man. "There, the death of Lepidus will be examined."

Furian said, slowly, "You mean you'll hold your own trial? Nothing so banal as the Ducem's justice for the Guild."

"We exert certain rights upon our own."

"But I'm not your own."

"You were to be so."

"Am I suspected?" Furian said.

"You may say everyone of us is suspected, Signore. You, with the rest, were in the Guild House."

"Why would I kill Lepidus, my protector?"

"Who knows. Perhaps *you* know, Signore."

Furian held back his anger and the creeping coldness. "And she?"

"She was his child, Signore. She accompanies us, appropriately, to honor the funeral."

When Bull-Mask had gone out again, Furian sat down once more, and cursed Shaachen more thoroughly. But Shaachen might have had, after all, difficulties. The Mask Guild, like all the guilds, was powerful indeed, and in any case, Furian could not leave the girl alone among them. Despite what had just been said, she too had her motives for harming the manipulative and unkind father. To be de-

spised did not make one generous, no matter what gifts of cash or
security, even of common speech, were rendered in place of love.
Besides, Lepidus was himself a murderer—and with a long reach.
Even the Princess Messalina had not been safe in the Madhouse.

Had Eurydiche known all that? How not? She was not simple,
she was not blind or deaf.

Tonight they would be taking her, whatever her guilt or blame-
lessness, will or aversion, ferrying her father's corpse across Silvia,
to the Isle of the Dead.

As the lights of the City drew away, the bell was tolling from Santa
Lala. Above, black gulls flew in silence, escorting the vessel.

It was a charon, a funeral ship. From stem to stern, a craft of
forty feet, heavy in the water, painted for darkness and trimmed
with brass stars. At the stern and at the prow, their pallid arms
outstretched with gilded wreathes, stood two wooden angels of
death in black robes, heads bowed under curving, brooding wings.
Aft, the cabin, with its silvered tassels and marble-tinged drapes,
where the coffin lay under black velvet.

There were three oarsmen, clad in the single black garment that
dehumanized the body, and cloaked the head, leaving only the mask
of a skull, its eyeholes blotted by somber glass.

This, for Lepidus, an omen extra. It had come to Furian, as he
paced out the day, that he had heard of it before, this cutting away
of the face of a man, the scorching out of his brain with hot iron, to
leave only bone. It was a practice of the Orichalci, their means of
slaying a dear foe. He had learned of it, at his father's house, and
from the lips of Lepidus himself. That was not a dinner. Lepidus
had been telling his traveler's tales in the inner garden. Furian,
fourteen then, had halted to listen. He had thought the mode of
murder had been described so fully for his sole benefit—the man
kept glancing at him, gauging whether or not Furian was distressed
or thrilled. And Furian had walked away.

But from the eventuality there had been no escape.

Eurydiche sat distantly from him in the charon, by the cabin
with the box. Moon-Mask Lunario stood beside her.

They had brought her a black gown, a plain white mask. Her
hair was garnished by silver powder and a string of opals.

She had not made any move toward Furian. Nor had he spoken
to her. Masked, dumb, they had seen each other. Nothing else was
possible.

The water of the lagoon seemed half solid, yet the oars moved in it without effort.

Trickles of the dim lamps of Venus ran alongside, next slipped behind. In another country, a fishing boat stole from the lost shore.

But ahead, the Island glared like a volcano on the water. Her crematoria were busy tonight. Although some miles in length, there was no room for all the City to lie there. Most must go into the fires, and accept a little bed, one foot square, for their ashes to rest in. Long, long ago, a special dispensation had come from Rome, promising that, on the Last Day, God would reassemble these fragments into wholeness, for what was God, but a great magician.

The Mask Guild had other means, the powerful usually did. A mausoleum, a chapel. Rich men, they said, sleep *long* on San Fumo.

The old-blood light began to make a path along the lagoon for the funeral barge to take.

We are rowing towards hell.

Furian tried to put the thought aside. *For all I know my father may be there. In a cramped merchant's tomb, buried upright. Buried, for all that. Or—Oh God—my mother—Caro—*

Thoughts wrung his mind. He pushed them off. He must think of her.

It seemed, he thought, they were at the middle of the lagoon. Venus was a curve about the water, two loving arms, dull-braceleted by lights. The Island—hell—lay ahead. And beyond, the sea wall, and so the sea.

It might—it *might* be feasible to get away. Some boat, the ocean. A galley, putting out for Candisi or the East, might take them aboard. His lush coat, her opals, payment. The galleys were wanton ships, rowed often by slaves, half lawless. He would need to bluff them in some way, but then, his life had been a bluff, until he came to her. To Eurydiche.

And the song: *Before you, darkness ruled me.*

He turned to her involuntarily. She sat like a doll. But Lunario Moon-Mask was picking over the deck towards him.

"Are you at ease, Signore?"

"No. But who would expect me to be?"

"I regret, in a few seconds you will be less easy than now."

Furian felt two pairs of hands seize him. Unsensible, he had been gaping only at her. But after all, there were ten men on the boat, and none his friend. While bloody insane Shaachen—

"Don't resist. If you upset the boat, *she* will go into the water. She doesn't swim. Did you know?"

He let them manhandle him. He looked again towards her.

The plain white mask was tilted to him. But that was all. No movement. No expostulation. Not even the glimpse of her uncanny blue eyes. She must have known.

As they stood him up, his feet tied at the ankles, and supported him carefully, and the boat, a very little, rocked, he thought, *A day and night of sexual pleasure. That was all she wanted. She had it. Now I'm meat for them.* And he said aloud, "Farewell to the flesh."

The last stooping man stood up. (Into the water once again.)

Lunario said, solicitously, "The weight he's tied to your feet will take you to the bottom. You'll see many interesting sights as you drown."

Furian said, "Choke on your own blood, fuck you, you thing."

As they hefted him high, he wanted to shout at her, but nothing could get up his throat but a taste of the mud to come.

Then the night wheeled over. The sky unshawled, and the City was in the sky. He hit the fire-pathed wet before he was ready. There were no prayers to say. He took one huge breath of air as he went down. For beneath the lagoon he must attempt to cut the lead weight from his feet—but he had not even brought with him the little apple knife. Not trusting her, he had trusted her. Love-fool—love—

Night and water and death closed over his head.

14

It was so cold, the water, so viscous and clinging. It was like despair. It probed him, his nose and ears, into his open eyes. He leaned to the weight to which his feet had been tied. As he fell, he took hold of it and wrestled with it. But the rope was strong and new, and the attachment was, as he had thought, a chunk of lead. Heavy as a hundred years it dragged him down, impervious to his struggles. His mask, dislodged, was gone. As his life soon would be.

There was no reason to fight. More philosophical to give up, take in draughts of the water, and die as thoroughly and swiftly as he was able.

But no. Lungs bursting now, he still tried to pick away the rope, to pull out his feet, shoes off in the water, kicking.

His sight was darkening. He could see nothing, only the silvery bubbles that were the last of his air.

And then the sea was alight, and out of the light, grey figures slid towards him.

Were these great fish from the outer ocean—the mythical serpent of the canals—come to devour him fresh?

In the panic of drowning, Furian now fought with everything, the rope, the weight, the salt water of the lagoon, the hands that came and took him, and grasped his ankles, and forced over his head one enormous bubble of the wasted air. At his neck was a pulling, a tension.

He could not hold off any longer. His lungs rucked, spasmed, gasped, and the fluid rushed in.

But he could breathe the fluid. It smelled bad and had a color, which was a sort of fusty brown. But he could breathe it—his head cleared a little. How—

The hands let him go, he spun a brief way. His sight came back in green pulses. The light was green. He beheld a fantastic vision.

Three rag-masked divers, one a boy, the boy with the pearls, hung in the water close to him. The boy was grinning a shark's white teeth. They could hold their air, trained almost since birth to do so. The two men held up, in curious glass globes, oil torches that burned with a sea-green splutter. One of these globes—Furian touched it, disbelievingly—they had crushed down over his head. It had air in it, and kept it, the opening secured at his neck with a leather brace closed fast. The rope and lead had been cut from his feet.

One of the men made a spear-like pointing gesture.

They had saved his life. He was to follow them.

He did exactly as they commanded.

He had dreamed of this, but not expected to see it awake: subaqueous Venus.

They had dropped further into the cup of the lagoon. The torchmen swam ahead, the boy after. Furian behind them.

Their lights lit first only the outer darkness of the water, formless, fathomless, secret. Fish came from it, and flared away, like crystals, like butterflies. Long curtains of weed trailed down, and through the weed they went, and things hung in the weed, God knew what, huge fish or octopus—they were amorphous specters, shining with their own soiled luminescence.

There began to be a sort of general glow. It was the phosphorous of the sea.

First he saw a tower appear, manifesting dim and beautiful as nothing seen on land. It had been a campanile, and in the filigree of its head he noted the tumbled bell, green as a bottle, chained with weed.

After the tower, they moved between high walls. Furian looked down into a square, the buildings partly fallen, but there was a line of arches, luminous and gilded, and there a column with a white sphinx, a pale sister to the sphinx of the Setapassa.

From ice-glassed windows, buckled lattices and balconies of black lace unrolled. The weed made banners, now turquoise blue, now glaucous green. A staircase shelved away, on every step some eccentric prize, a broken urn carved with goddesses, a pitcher of battered silver, a drowned boat, (a wanderer), with barnacles smothering her like lusterless gems.

They sailed through the upper story of a gutted palazzo. Below, were marble floors, Furian saw skulls down there, not lilies, not faces or masks, skulls looking up with wide open eyes.

The boy squirmed back and tugged at his arm, indicating upward.

They rose, the men, the boy and he, up by the spire of a coraline church, past its leaning cross, the gargoyles with weed-bearded fangs—even the Devil had drowned here.

One by one the men came up through the skin of the lagoon. They were behind a small islet with fishing boats. The open water lay spread beyond. Across the surface, the stain of San Fumo's fires. There was no sign of the funeral barge.

One of the men undid the lacing of the leather brace, and lifted off Furian's globe. Its air was oven-hot and sour, and meeting the cleanness of the night, he coughed.

"We must go down again, Signore. For us it's nothing, but you needed to renew the breath in the globe."

"Thanks for my life," he said. "Why did you?"

The speaking man smiled. "You're all one to us, Signore, you're landsmen. Say perhaps we judged you weren't ready to die. Not in a state of grace."

The other laughed. The boy looked serious. He said, overriding the uncaring adults, a serious teacher, "Breathe much now, Signore. As though you drank when thirsty. It's another long swim."

He did as the boy told him, and when they put the globe over his head once more, the air smelled cool and clean and raised his spirits like good brandy. He was happy to descend again. He wanted to see more of the water City. He was alive. He had lost everything else.

They dived.

The lagoon was changing color again, bluer here.

Beyond the sunken church, and the hill that supported the tiny fisher island, was an avenue of pillars. On each was mounted a marble statue. They were of gods and heroes, classical, with faces melted by a century or more of the lagoon.

He passed them marveling, looking in their hyacinthine sightless eyes that seemed to follow him. He sensed their heads turning on white limestone necks. Could not catch them at it.

Fish small as fingernails, bright as mirrors, flushed between. He swam seventy feet above the place where the street had been, when men walked there.

He wanted to sink further, root through the palaces, among the waterlogged gardens where flamy anemones grew and caught their light, sift through his fingers the capitas of vanished emperors, the bronze pennies slung overboard for luck.

But the air was stale again, and he kept on after his guides.

Another shape came in his way. On a pedestal sat Neptune, turned to verdigris. Furian punched the trident and it broke off, spiraling down to the paving of the swallowed street below.

Nothing else was important. The world did not exist. You need not think.

He saw a transparent mermaid behind a wall. An hallucination probably, the dying air, or not.

And then the plan of streets and masonry gave way, and there unrolled beneath him an incredible vista of the ancient earth—an amphitheater of the Romans, many hundreds of feet across and more in length, an oval, whose tiers of seats cascaded to a dubious hollow floor. What cheering and screaming, what scenes of battle and death had been there, where now the milky water curled, and fishes eddied in their own cool and indifferent crowds. To go down to this was almost an imperative, to press on the stone and penetrate the walks beneath.

But just past this place was a wavering forest of the weed, and into it the divers were just now flickering.

Years on, would he recall this sight, and how he had been cheated of it? Maybe not. For there were other memories above.

He followed into the weed. As he did so, he saw the tendrils were strung by diamonds, emeralds, purple jacinth. Next moment the jewelry fled. Fish. After all, how like the bloody world.

A black tunnel roared. The divers proceeded into it.

Why go on? Why go on and come to land. Why trouble.

But instinct was too vigorous. He propelled himself also into the tunnel.

After a moment they were rising up again. Something sucked at them, some current from above.

They emerged into a chamber of blackest water, and the boy swam straight up and pushed at a huge lid in the roof. The lid unfolded, unhinging like a clam shell.

There was somber and unwelcoming light. Furian shot into it and his head was above the water.

The boy helped him out on to a shelf of wet stone, and undid the brace again from about his neck. Furian pulled off the globe and breathed a stinking clammy atmosphere far worse than staleness.

"Where is this?"

"The tomb vault of the ancient Ducemae of Venus," chanted the boy, crossing himself. "They're buried in lead boxes under the water."

Furian thought of the lead weight. He glanced about below, and saw through the water now, or thought he did, black coffin shadows, each surmounted by a prone granite figure.

"The Island of San Fumo."

"Yes, Signore."

The two others bobbed easily under the opened lid. They watched him, impartial yet unfriendly.

"I'd pay you," he said, "but alas. I think I may have been robbed in your house."

"You would have been, if you'd had anything."

"And you'd have earned every ducca."

The boy took Furian's globe, securing it to his belt. None of them was out of breath.

"The door to the vault is simple to force," said the man who talked. "It's already ajar."

The other did speak. He said, "All the men you know from the Mask Guild came to the Island. But their guild chapel is a mile or two away to the east from here. And they think you're dead, wouldn't you say."

"Yes, it's nicely convenient."

"But then," said the boy, "there is your lady."

"Which lady's that?"

"The butterfly lady."

"Oh, yes."

Furian shivered. It was dungeon-chill in the vault, and the water seemed finally warm. It was better here than the canals, and he had swallowed none of it. (And that was as well, because no one here would fold him in her arms, tend him, bring him back to health.)

The best course would be to go around the island, find some wanderer or fisher, get out to sea, to the larger shipping.

As for—as for the butterfly lady—she had shown her concern for him this time. Sitting at peace in the funeral boat as they flung him over.

"It's a shame," said Furian, "love doesn't last."

The boy said, "My sister told me, the lady wouldn't cry, though her father was dead."

Furian stood up. He said, "If I prayed any more, I'd speak for all of you."

"There are too many gods," said the talkative man.

He drew breath in one long, rushing, inward sigh, and sank straight down. The other did the same. The boy lingered.

"What is it? Do you want my coat?"

"Keep it, Signore. Try to light a fire and dry it. The night will be cold."

"You're too conscientious."

The boy spoke softly. "My sister said, your lady walked up and down, up and down. When a priest came, she sent him away. She wrote something, but then a masker went in and she hid it."

"She isn't my lady."

"Then she has no one now."

The boy drew in breath, leapt, turned in the air like a dolphin, and clove the water. He disappeared at once.

They had left Furian to replace the lid of the hidden entry. He did so, then climbed the passage from the stone shelf. Above was a ruinous chapel, full of loose stones and ivy. The iron door, as promised, cranked ajar, and needed only a shove or two to let him forth. He wrenched it back where it had been once he was out, and turned to see what the world now offered.

He was in a walled grove of elderly unflowering myrtle trees. On the gate was an old escutcheon of Venus, the star and goddess symbol, and the coronet of a Ducem. But the gates too were half open.

Beyond he saw the sweep of a hill, drenched in night, the cypresses standing like black pens, and the fields of little humps and markers and tiny statues, and here and there the great ghostly summerhouse of a mausoleum, fluttered by the merciless wings of basalt angels.

Over the slope, about two miles off, the sky was terra-cotta red, and the malevolent smoke funneled into heaven all the way to God.

The night smelled of ashes, and of dew. Of roses also. Of the most bitter and unacceptable flavors. But it was cold. And the boy had been right. A line of woods ran away to the left. He must make for those, (shoeless, maskless), and set to work the tinder he had somehow had and they had let him keep. Light a fire. Dry himself. Think of where next to take himself. Since it would not be back to her, then where?

15

The Isle of Death was all in this fashion, the endless grave yards with their miniature graves, the occasional tall and imposing tomb. Through everything, the woods and orchards of the Island threaded, old trees girdled by late flowers, a statuesque oak, a beech, a pool of water with some funereal nymph, a willow leaning in sallowing autumn hair.

By night, everything was grisaille, or black or coal blue, or lit by the hell fires russet and priestly magenta.

He made his own fire soon, under the trees. He stripped when it was alight, and rubbed himself with clumps of the sandy grass. He dried his clothes, put them on again. He longed for brandy, more than any lost love. Or less? If she had been with him, would he have cared only for her? He would have held her, lain over her to keep warm. Sex for food and drink, and her sweetness to hold in faith.

Let her go. She was a bitch. She was insane and all the filthy things he had ever thought. She had let him be sent into the water. One shudder, one outstretched arm, however powerless. But not. Not she.

Her hands, so white. Her stroking, her caressing, her teasing of his body. Her full warm breasts, her slenderness, the wonder of the core of her. Her face. Which he had thought he had begun to read like his Bible.

Let her burn in hell. Let her *go*.

Something was moving in the wood. There had been bear and lynxes once on the Island, but no longer. (Although now and then, they or their revenants were sighted.) Probably rats, a large bird—But they did not wear boots.

Furian got up. He stood aside into the shadow of the trees,

leaving the fire to burn. He had made a makeshift weapon, a stick sharpened in the flames. He toted it, ready.

Into the clearing came a man. His head was shaven, shining like tarnished copper in the firelight. On his shoulder was a magpie, also color-changed, black and pink from the glow.

Shaachen walked straight to the fire. He posed beside it, capering a little. "A friend and he hides." His little old female face stretched in an evil grin. "Come out, handsome." And the bird cawed.

Furian walked into the light.

"If you're here, I hope you'll be useful."

"What am I? Your saint? Of course I shall be useful. See what the old bugger has brought you."

Shaachen unslung his satchel. Out came a loaf and some cheese, a brandy bottle and a bloated skin of wine.

"Thank God," said Furian. He let himself down on the ground, and took the brandy, drinking off five or six raw gulps. "Last time you were no use, under the window acting beggars."

"My darling brought you up a letter."

"That was so much what I needed."

"The paper was invisibly traced with symbols of magic to keep you safe. It seems it has. Where is it now?"

"In my coat. It got wet." Furian felt for the letter and found a dryish mush.

"Keep it still," said the Doctor.

"And how did you find me this time?" said Furian. "And why did you bother?"

"I enjoy you," said Shaachen. "You are so flamboyantly much what I anticipate. It's like the play."

"My thanks."

"Don't mention it. As to finding you, I knew they would come here. I waited, watched. I saw the charon off and came after in a little fisher boat. At the Island all of them come forth—but for my dear Furian. So, you have escaped them."

"Didn't you see something drop in the water?"

"The charon was some way off. But yes, perhaps. Was that you?"

"It was me."

"You jumped and swam."

"They threw me in with lead on my feet."

Shaachen had sat down. He fed cheese slowly to the magpie. He said nothing; then, "But why would they do that?"

"Unlike yourself, they don't care for me."

"They hate you, doubtless. But I'd thought—perhaps not already having slain you—they must want to keep you. Didn't they offer to make you one of their own?"

"Yes. And how did you know *that*?"

"I too have been searching out, asking here and there. The guilds are known, in some form, to each other. I am an alchemist. Within my own circle, I may hear things not broadcast on the street. I might have warned you, but you went too fast. Straight in at her door, the Virgo with blue eyes. There was a rumor too, of her. Is it true, her face doesn't move? Fachia Pietra. A fascination."

"Her face. Her heart."

"Another rejection?"

"She was willing enough. But when they drowned me, she sat by serene as Sunday morning in the Primo."

"I begin to see," said Shaachen. "I begin to. Not quite."

"They kill for hire," said Furian. "Those who wear the most celebrated masks seem to be their victims."

"Yes, I have that already. They are of few numbers. Three or four men, forming a secret guild within the Guild. Not all the rest are so tainted. This limits their scope a little. You may trust me on this. But they kill for hire, you say?"

"And to gratify some foul urge for chaos, power, viciousness. God knows."

"And he—the raging one who showed his animal in our rite?"

"What rite?" said Furian. He took some bread and ate it. But he was hungry, and put it by . . . there was no longer any reason to behave logically with drink or sleep or food.

"You forget it so soon. When the Zodians towered in my chamber, and I told you the murderers were in the Mask Guild."

"Oh, that time. Yes. I remember the animal with a barb on its penis. That was him, was it? Lepidus? Well, he was angry with her. With me. With everyone who had something he hadn't, or cheated him in some way, as he saw it. He must be a bellowing ghost. He's dead."

"Ah!" Shaachen exclaimed. "I see more. How do you know he died?"

"I saw his corpse and so did she. Its whole face was off. He was our ally, or presently he was. Someone didn't find pleasure in that, and had him seen to, and I was next. But she knew. Either that, or she didn't mind it." Furian stood up. He said loudly, too loudly for the wood, "She sat and watched them throw me over. She couldn't speak, but in extremity she could make a sound—I know, I heard it over and over in her bed. She didn't even rise, or *fidget.*"

"But they had hold of you," said Shaachen. "Two or three of them, surely, to be certain. And there were the other men on the charon. What could she do?"

"Nothing, nothing. But in God's name—not one flick of her hand."

"Sit," said Shaachen. "Tell me how you came here with lead feet. I've been searching you out for a great while."

Furian sat. He took the wine skin and drank. He told Shaachen of the divers and the underwater entry at the tomb of ancient Ducemae. All the glamour of the journey was gone now. He knew Shaachen would have been avid for descriptions of the drowned City, the statues, the amphitheater, and withheld them meanly. Furian was tired with the old tiredness which precluded sleep.

Shaachen did not inquire anything about the swim, the tomb, apparently aware of this. The magpie drowsed on Shaachen's shoulder. It was young and splendid as a new-minted coin, and knew the tricks of the dead. The loyalty too. Some were loyal. Could you only expect it from a beast or a bird?

"Did you keep the fishing boat by the Isle?" Furian asked. "We can use it to go back. Then I have a choice, it seems to me. To make inland from the City, or take ship elsewhere. I might evade them now they think they've done for me."

"This is your sole choice?" said Shaachen.

"I think so. They revel in what they do, but I'm a small enough fish to them."

"But no," said Shaachen, "I think not."

Furian blasphemed softly and obscenely. "I've had sufficient of this, Dianus Shaachen. I'm off to save my worthless life."

"And hers? Is that also worthless?"

"To me, yes, if she thinks nothing of mine."

Shaachen took the magpie from his shoulder. He held it in both hands and cooed to it and kissed its demonic head. The beak, which could have taken out his eyes, stayed still as carving. It made back to him a silly little love-cackle.

"Consider," said Shaachen, "unlike other women, she can't speak to plead for you, or beg you to await her in heaven. And surrounded by the men who are enemies, she is without physical recourse. Consider, perhaps, she's as shocked as yourself to see you suddenly bound and thrown to your death. All of her turns in terror to stone. You pierced her body, but did you possess her brain? How do you know she betrays you, or has no concern. Perhaps, as you sank, she fell dead on the deck from the agony of what had happened."

"You saw them leave their boat. Was she dead, then?"

Shaachen said, with grizzly lugubriousness, "She walked heavily, like a woman sick or half asleep."

"She was a little tired. Bored by such an uneventful day."

"No, Furian Furiano. She walked as if she were laden down. With lead."

Furian slung the wine away.

"She has no friends with them, that's all. Dreads them. She had a friend in me and didn't want me, any more then she wanted del Nero that she let them kill two feet from her sublime blue sala. Or in front of her, even, as she thought I'd been."

"Only suppose," said Shaachen, "there is one chance you may be wrong. That she loves you and her heart, which isn't stone like her face, but glass, like the hearts of all lovers, is in little bits, cutting her breast. Only suppose she's in the Mask Guild's grip and thinks you dead, and can't cry her tears of alabaster. And you sit here to speak of foreign ships."

"In Christ's bleeding name—"

Shaachen let the magpie loose. It flew round the clearing, with claps of its ink and paper feathers, gleaming with fire, sheened red now, not blue.

As they walked the night Island, Furian swore at the ground, bombarding his shoeless feet. Shaachen muttered. Finally, "Give me back the paper I sent you."

"That letter is porridge."

"Scrape it out. I want it."

Furian did as Shaachen said, scooping up the glutinous, crumbling mess from a pocket. Shaachen took it and stowed it in his coat.

"You think I won't need your magic symbols of protection any more? Why didn't you bring boots?"

"You'll need only Doctor Shaachen."

"Oh well. I can't argue with that."

The hills coursed up, whorled with the tiny, circling graves. They passed a monument to some great family of Venus. The goddess herself mourned them in marble. Pines and cypress pointed at the black sky, where stars were hung out like sparkling masks. (Too far off to see their eyes.) A nightingale sang.

Furian thought, *I said I'd go to her, because of what he said to me. Why is he here? He experiments on the dead and on the living. One more experiment?*

The wine-bloom of the burning chimneys had lessened. They went east towards the Mask Guild chapel.

It was, in any event, a lost cause. And probably she was as base as he had thought. But if not, if not—

Dawn turned the smokes of San Fumo violet. Birds spurted their music, and it was possible to sense the lagoon's lapping, as if only darkness had muffled it.

There were groves of trees, and then an open slope, the autumn grass turned to the sun, tobacco brown. Above, a walled garden with acacia and cypresses. From these, a golden dome rose like a sun's egg.

"The Mask Chapel," said Shaachen, complacently. "How do you mean to proceed?"

"Limping. Look about. Do you know anything?"

"The chapel will be difficult of access. Your best means are to go knock on the door."

"You think so?"

"It will save you time."

Furian said, "My one advantage was, I thought, they believed me dead."

"Don't be too sure," said Shaachen. "Maybe not."

They went up the slope, carelessly. There was little cover, some small groups of parched trees turned towards the lagoon, which now they saw far off. The water was blue and the City lay over it, a transparent vertical map of towers, floating, as ever, like a flock of ships.

Beyond the dome of the chapel, one smoke rose.

Shaachen spoke unintelligibly to the magpie. It lifted straight up, and flew back among the trees.

There was no gate in the wall. An arch showed a flat path, set with mosaic chariots racing—they were chariots of Death with sable horses. The building at the path's end was simple but ornate, a windowless box. But there were windows sliced narrowly in the dome. Behind, buildings clustered in the garden.

A woman was coming down the path, unexpected and incongruous. She wore a festive blood-red dress, and her face was hidden by a black fan mask.

She hurried, and as she came closer, Shaachen stood away behind Furian. Furian glanced at him and saw the Doctor had put on a comic mask, a rabbit with tall ears.

"What are you playing at?"

"I'm now your servant, a poor old fool. Call me Diano."

Calypso reached them. She put out her hand and lightly prodded at Furian's breast.

"Is it you?"

"Who?" he said.

"You must come in quickly. I don't like it outside."

She took his arm, and snuggled against him. As she pulled on him, they began to walk, and rabbity Shaachen crept behind.

The black and gilded door of the chapel had opened and Lunario Moon-Mask was there, with a couple of men behind him. These men carried staves, but Lunario's hands were empty.

"What a long while you were," he said.

Calypso made a scratching movement at her mask, as if it itched. She kept hold of Furian.

"I made haste," she said. "There—are creatures in the garden. Was that why you sent me?"

"Hush. I refer to our guest, who dallied."

Furian said, as they came to the door, "I had to return from the dead."

Lunario laughed. "But I know that's a lie, Signore Furian."

Furian eased Calypso off his arm. She turned abruptly and slapped his face a hard, stinging blow, then stalked into the chapel, past the grinning half-masked men.

Lunario said, "She's got a strong arm. Did you feel the slap? Does it prove to you you're alive?"

"I supposed I was meant to be drowned."

"Not at all. The divers rescued you as they were paid to do. You came ashore at the old tomb. Then you might have run away, or run here, but you delayed. Now you've arrived at last. Who's this one?" Lunario gestured at Shaachen, who was hopping and twittering at Furian's back.

"A servant. Somehow he followed me. Senile, as you see."

"Senile but clever. Well, he can come in." Lunario stood aside. The men with staves stood aside. How welcoming.

Beyond them, a black stone vestibule gave on a second massive door, shut fast.

Lunario turned and moved into a narrow passage. Calypso went after him, ignoring Furian now, and the men with staves gave him one friendly urging. He followed, and Shaachen, gibbering, perhaps dribbling in an excess of theatricality, scuttled at his back.

They ascended steps. A lamp burned dully on the wall.

"Wait here. Your servant may wait, too."

Lunario crossed the space they had entered, and was gone into another corridor. Only one of the men with staves remained. But Calypso slunk against Furian. "I see things. They're there. Only I can see them. There's something black clinging to you. It has claws, but no face."

"Go after your master," Furian said.

Calypso bridled. "This mask," she said, "sees better than I do." In the eyeplaces, her own eyes darted, inflamed and congested, seeming half blind.

Furian sat on a stone bench by the wall. He smiled down at the floor. In a few more moments she scudded away, her bloody skirts sweeping up the old rank dusts off the paving.

Diano, the insane servant, crouched on the floor. He had taken out some dice and was throwing them, grunting and giggling at the results.

"I'd have them put down," said the man with the stave. "Once they get like that."

"You're right," said Furian.

"You wouldn't keep a dog like it."

"No."

"How did he manage to follow you?"

"He comes over to the graves sometimes. He has relatives buried here. It was just bad luck we met."

The man with the stave approached and bent over Shaachen. "Eh, rabbit. I'd wring your scrawny neck." Shaachen Diano looked up at him. The rabbit mask leered. "And he's a Jew. Shit-scum. I'd burn the lot."

Furian got up. He had nothing to lose, it was mostly all gone. He hit the man with considerable force, and in a shower of gore and broken teeth he went over and lay there. Furian picked up the stave, and at that moment another man came in from the corridor. This one laughed luxuriantly. "I can't leave you alone for one moment, can I? Didn't the wetting cool you down?"

"Evidently not."

Furian observed this newcomer. A stocky man, with the mask of a wolf. Its maned fur passed over his head and down his broad back, concealing hair and throat. The voice nagged, for it was known—and the mask known too. It came in a flash of seconds. The reveler in the Groves of Diana, who had seized Messalina off the altar, nearly nude, and galloped her away into the wild park.

"You're here, I think, for her," he said now, the wolf, in his rich, *known* voice.

"Who's that?"

"Your girl with blue eyes."

"But I was meant to be here," said Furian.

"If you cared a lot for her, you'd come after her. Simple enough. And you haven't disappointed."

"Or drowned."

"You were previously warned, Furian, an ordeal lay before you, your initiation into the Guild. So far, you've come through the testing well."

Furian took a breath. "The drowning was—an initiation?"

"A part of it. There's more. For now, you should take rest. There are things you must be told."

"Which I shan't credit."

"I think you may."

He made a short, dismissive motion. On his hand a black ring blazed like a living eye. It was the ring of Lepidus. He had, too, the wolf, the voice of Lepidus.

Furian said nothing.

The wolf said to him, "Come with me now. No tricks or snares. My daughter's waiting for you in a little room."

As they walked, crazy Diano rattling in their wake, Furian said bleakly, "Who was the man you killed, the man whose face you cut away?"

"A custom of the Orichalci," said the wolf.

"I know. You told me once."

"I didn't think you listened."

Furian was trembling at a numb and somber distance from himself. Had *she* known it too, all along? That her father lived, that Furian would be saved. The lagoon was only a *test,* the sorcerous alchemical element of water.

"But the man," he said.

"Someone who resembled me bodily, somewhat," said Lepidus the wolf. "A ruffian, of no great use. We gave him a good dinner and drugged his wine. He was peacefully dead before I took off his face."

"Oh, then, it was inoffensive. As with Juseppi, too, I trust. A good dinner and some wine, before the torture and the Death of Osiris, the cutting in ten or eleven segments."

"Eleven, of course. It served only one most urgent purpose, to terrify, to close up doors and seal them. But it was done ritualistically because, for us, ritual has importance."

"And the faceless man I took for you, why that? Why not you aboard the boat, and throw me in yourself?"

"To come at you, Furian. To play upon you."

"Consider me come at and played on."

"I see you underestimate yourself. The hub of alchemy is the changing of lead into gold. But first the lead, which is so dark and set and strong, must be softened."

There was a door.

Behind it, apparently, she was. But was he ready for her?

The wolf put a key into the lock. And that might be one more illusion, a pretense that she was her father's prisoner here.

"There's so much to tell you, Furian. You'll marvel at it."

"I'm already overwhelmed."

"And now, the love of your heart."

The door folded wide.

It was a little side room of prayer, with an icon of Beautiful Maria.

She—Eurydiche—sat in a wooden chair. She wore still the black gown from the charon, and the opals dressed her hair. Her face was unmasked, but turned away. Perhaps she had turned it even as the door opened, as a normal woman might, to hide what, in her, was always anyway quite hidden.

She appeared untouched. Like the icon on the wall.

"Now, Doctor Shaachen," said Lepidus mildly, "let's leave these lovers to their reunion. There's much to do, and I can allow the eager young man only one hour in her company. But it should be private."

Mad Diano babbled.

Lepidus said, "Or, if you prefer to be senile, Doctor, I can put you into a sewage pit we have here, for just such emergencies."

Shaachen straightened. He said, "Why join the Mask Guild and not my own, the Guild of Alchemists?"

"I was too modest, Doctor, to essay your guild."

"But you're easily wise enough," said Shaachen. "Some join us who can do nothing. And you can do so much."

"I shall have to see to your death," said Lepidus.

"All men come to death," said Shaachen, "I've been shown, it's nothing. Only let me see the ritual through. The *spell*. I'd like to witness your skill to its full."

"Since you ask so nicely, perhaps. Meanwhile, someone must take away your satchel."

The door shut and the key turned in the lock. Shaachen and his death, Lepidus and his life, were gone.

There was only the small room, and Eurydiche sitting there, her face turned away.

Furian looked levelly around and into every corner. It was an instinct. There was no method for her to write. Someone had been very sure of that. Or else she had not asked. For what could she say to him?

Shaachen, the idiot, had sold himself to a murderer for nothing. And it was Shaachen who had persuaded Furian to this spot. The word of an idiot was worth what his death had cost—nothing.

Yes, there had been *one chance* she was innocent and in despair. But she had known it all, and been accomplice to it all. This now, was simply to be more softening of the lead.

He walked to her chair and stood looking down at her. "I'll ask you my questions, and you must nod or shake your head. If you won't, then so be it. Of course, what you indicate will doubtless be a lie. But even so, I want it from you. I want to see you tell me the truth or the falsehood. Because you are the reason for all my woes, and for all the woes of all this story, aren't you, my little stone doll?"

16

Eurydiche raised her head. She rose, and he drew back. Only the edge of her dress brushed over his hand, and at the touch of it, he shivered.

She made no other gesture. Her arms hung at her sides. Eyes. Face. Doll indeed.

"Very well," he said, "Yes or No, then. When he lay on the floor of your room, I mean the man they killed and defaced, did you know this wasn't Lepidus, your father?"

Her head moved instantly, side to side. No.

So, it was a game she wanted.

Furian said, "Thank you, Madama, for your first delightful lie." But she did not move. He had already explained he would not believe denials. Perhaps this enhanced her clandestine amusement. (Had she always laughed at him? Even flat on her back? But no—her physical heart and her loins could not lie. There at least she had told the truth. A slut who would take pleasure from any able man.) "Tell me then, when they threw me over, did you know I was to live?" Her head, side to side. Obviously, deliriously, No. He said, smiling, "Why then, if you didn't know, did you show no sign of alarm? Let me suggest—you'd lost consciousness from shock and pain." But her head went side to side. He said, "You were quite helpless and didn't dare to move? Overcome by your enormous grief, you sat mourning the two deaths—his and mine."

At this, her hands did come up. It was a strange almost involuntary movement, as if she wished to grasp at something. But nothing was there. Her hands fell. She nodded very slowly. Yes.

"Poor girl," he said. "And not even able to weep at your hurt. Losing me, your great love."

A tumult rose in him and he gripped his brain and blood and held them down. He wanted to strike her face as he had struck the sneering globule of the Jew-hater. He wished to smash the porcelain of her. And he clenched his hands upon his arms as if he froze, to keep from killing her.

"What a bitch you are," he said. "You've known it all. That he slaughters for hire, and for his fun. Now a rich patron cretinous enough to order a mask from his artisans, and now a fellow off the street, solely in order to upset little Furian the dupe. And you, you were at the Revels of Diana, to watch as he prepared some filthy plan for that woman there, poor bloody Messalina. In some way he works through you—How? What does he do? But you can't tell me without your pen and paper, and anyway, I doubt you would."

She shied from him all at once. She sank back in the chair, and put one arm over its wooden side, and put her head down on her arm.

"I've distressed you. I'm so sorry. We were such friends, weren't we. And I came back here for you. Or could I even have escaped? Perhaps not. The plot's as thick as a stew, as the idiot said. Could I even trust the trees of the Island?"

In turn he put his back to her. He stood before the door, to wait out the hour.

As his breathing calmed, he heard her breathing, then. It was throaty, stifled.

Furian knew a moment's terror at what they had come down to. He could not harm her. Her beauty was more dear to him than his life. God knew why. The beauty of her inner self, the being that had looked out at him through blind-blue windows. The being he had held and loved.

He said, harshly, "Don't be frightened, Eurydiche. I won't assault you. You've been more cunning than I thought. I'm still in thrall to you. I'm yours. A worthless gift, I know."

Some while after, she came to him so softly he did not realize, lost in his thoughts of nothing, until he heard her gown on the floor.

She moved about him and took his hand. As once before, she let her head droop on his chest. He said, "Let's not, Eurydiche. It's enough I'm enslaved. I won't play your game any more. Go back and sit in the chair."

At this she left him. Her warmth, her perfume, and her self. He did not look.

In the furnace, the lead melted down. But Furian was not a substance to be changed to gold. He knew as much. He knew they would fail with him, and then he must die. He did not quite see how it was to be, but that it must be.

All his life among the dark had led him here. At eighteen, when he left his father's house, he had been on the road to this.

He could have ended a hundred ways. Of some knife. Of some sickness in the warrens of the City. Even, once or twice, of starvation. But no, fate brought him to the Isle of the Dead to die. Fate was a poetess.

When, seemingly, the hour was up, the door was unlocked. The man masked as the bull loomed there, with two unknown others.

Furian went out, and the bull conducted him downstairs and out of the chapel building, across the guild burial garden whose markers showed large and pale between the acacias and the stiff sculpted yews.

Stoically, almost sleepily, Furian made no attempts at action or evasion. He was taken into another building with a lesser dome, this of lapid blue, and so to a chamber with hospitable appurtenances, a couch, a bath, even some books laid by.

The bull offered him a steady hand to shave his face. Furian laughed. Said No. The bull insisted. For business to come, he must be at his best.

"Oh, *yes,* then. Watch the razor doesn't slip. They want their meat unsliced."

Afterwards there was a meal, with wine, and fruit.

Would it be achievable, the state of sleep? How could it be. That phase was over. And soon, a longer sleep. (The same for Shaachen, who thought it would be otherwise.)

Yet Furian dreamed for five minutes in a chair, and saw Lepidus' substitute skull, symbol of all death.

Fresh linen had been left out, and a new set of noble clothes. He did not bother with them. If they wanted his refinement, they would have to insist.

The body anyway was the suit of clothes, and under the body were the indecent bones. And under those, a soul, perhaps, or not a soul.

The day gathered and spun towards an evening, long skeins of light that put gold-leaf on to the high unseeing slot in the wall. Once a bird passed by. Was it Shaachen's magpie? A symbol opposed to the Skull, one of everlasting existence and renewal. The Virgin's bird also, Virgo . . .

He thought of insubstantial, anguished things. His mother's outcry when he had gone away. Cupid in her rose-yellow bed com-
plaining that he had given her up and heaping invective on him.
Men he had cut open. The child crying outside the tavern because
two bastards abused her with words, too young to answer or know
how to run away.

Sunfall, dusk, these went on and on. A man before his execu-
tion, Furian felt obliged to look at them, take note. How saffron
gave way to madder, and so to mallow.

But he was impatient with life now, parading herself. Another
beauty trying to deceive, when reasonless night was so obviously
close.

17

Midnight had just struck, when they came.

They told him this.

But he was waiting.

No comment was made on his unchanged garments, stained from the lagoon and the smoke of a fire. He had put on the shoes only. There had been no mask.

They went back the way they had come, and so out into the garden.

The sky was blackest blue and the moon had risen, waning and fragile, a slender, graceful girl. Moonlight spotted the tombs, leopardine shadows. They reached a wall of the chapel. There was a door, and this they undid for him. He was to go through.

Lepidus was in the room, standing, a genial host. One recalled his faultless manners as an agent and traveler. His wit and finesse, and how he had never seemed put out, with all the resentment and contempt smoldering, invisible.

He too was unmasked. Perhaps he had extra entertainment in acting this out, his face schooled to such spurious and insulting, avuncular charm.

"Furian. Take a seat, and try this wine." Furian took the seat, and the wine. He drank a mouthful and put it by. "So abstemious all at once? Well, that's to your credit. You may want to be able to think."

"Yes I may."

"I have to tell you of certain events. Before we come to guild matters."

Furian said, "What's next? Fire, earth or air?"

"Nothing so straightforward. Consider the lagoon, if you will, as fluidity rather than the element of water. The mutable and transient—Neptune. There's only one more trial of you. You may not even mind it. May like it. We'll see."

Furian said nothing.

Lepidus sat down in the chair opposite, and poured himself a glass of the wine. The chamber was not large, but hung with sober velvet. Another door led somewhere. The lion's den?

Lepidus spoke low, in an encompassing and companionable way, (Furian was put in mind of some priest benighted with him at an inn).

"Almost, Furian, I stand as a father to you now."

"A father. But I left my father."

"So you did. And why was that?"

"A complex and irksome tale, Lepidus. I don't have your flare for story-telling. I won't weary you."

"Then I shall tell you, Furian, shall I, your own story?"

Furian said nothing. But now he waited.

Lepidus said, "Once or twice, I saw you as a boy. You were impressive for your years. I remember, you had a special talent for music—"

"You embarrass me."

"But also you were very impertinent to me."

"Was I. I don't recall."

"Of course not. They were little things."

"I didn't always stay to listen," said Furian.

"That night," said Lepidus, "that night you were eighteen and newly home, you spent your time gawking at a young woman's breasts across the table."

Furian laughed shortly. "I do remember that."

"Well, you were immature, and had been studious. I was wrong in what I did."

Furian said, too swiftly, "And what did you do?"

"I've got your interest now. I'm glad. I did a foolish thing, almost what a woman might have done, if able. I put a little spell on you."

Furian's throat closed hard. He tried to swallow, and could not. He sucked air into his lungs and said, off-handedly "To make me love you instead?"

"I might not have minded it, Furian Furiano. A taste of you in your youth. There are more pleasures that way than one. But no, it wasn't for love."

Furian waited again. He did not dare to speak, and in his breast his heart was clammering, in tight iron strokes. Had he always partly guessed? *Something—*

"When I was among the Orichalci and the Argenti of the Amarias," said Lepidus, leaning back, the raconteur again, "I learnt some of their formulae, their arts. To get anywhere with them, a man had to take on some of their nature, and go through particular endurances. It was worth while, although I carry scars, both physical and of the psyche, to this day. A treacherous and wondrous people, that tribe, The Enemy. It was only a little, little spell. The sort they'd use to turn a man away from their hunting grounds, or from a woman. Or from his kindred."

Lepidus paused, and Furian heard the silence of the close, draped room, loud as a whistling gushing wave from the sea.

"And to turn me from what, exactly."

"Your then life. Its happiness and content. To make you dissatisfied. Disturbed. Want other things. Oh, maybe I had some notion you might seek me out for adventure. I would have liked it, Furian, to show you the world as I'd discovered the world to be. But it was a fact, your passion was too strong for me. It took my tiny hex and turned it to a massive stroke. You left everything and ran into the dark."

Furian looked away. He looked into the insubstantial, wavering past. To his father's estate, the stairway in the folding up of the candles. A score of pale wings fluttering down, and there, *between one step and the next.* So swift.

(He had been puzzled. Trying to work it out. It was elusive and ran before him, lashing its tail. Yet it had led him on.) Disillusionment. Guilt. Emptiness. That dawn at the window and the soft wind blowing up the Veneran plain. The days of lotuses over.

But it was not possible that Lepidus had been so accomplished. To drive him out of his mind, to exile him from his family, to diminish him among the slums and sinks of Venus—*to make him into what he was—*

He said, very dry, "I'm to believe all that was your doing, then. How you amaze me, Lepidus. And I thought you only a showy vagabond."

Lepidus bowed. "You're at liberty, of course, to disbelieve. But I've had you in my fist since that night. When I watched you, when I forgot you, you were mine. I created you, Furian. Even your actorish name."

Furian took up the wine. He had a pair of mouthfuls. Lepidus observed, amused, it seemed, or so he pretended.

The simplest means to get a man into your power was to inform him he was there already.

And Lepidus began to talk again, as if he enjoyed this so much, he could not hold back.

"Even with her, with my daughter, I like to think it was some element of my labor on you that drew you precisely to her. Even to finding del Nero's mask on the canal that *fateful* morning. A dog follows its master, even when he doesn't call."

"I'm not your dog."

"Are you your own then? Eh? Would you say so?"

Furian took another mouthful of the wine. He had finished it after all, and his tormentor saw, and came at once, so solicitous, to refill the cup.

Furian said, "That was a quaint story. Now tell me one about Shaachen."

"The Doctor? Oh, he must die. I think he knows not only what our inner guild does, but perhaps just how we do it."

Lightly Furian said, "Can't I buy you off with something? He's an old dunce. Nearly what he was acting for you with his rabbit mask."

"I don't think you mean what you say. A fool, yes; or why else come here after you. But a learned fool. Among his books and potions I wouldn't trust him. But he carries little in his head, save curious illusions for drunk princes."

"Let him live. You promised me my life. Or is that changed?"

"No. I'm like any kind father. You're to be my heir. You'll have my daughter, and a function within the guild."

"But I don't want your daughter."

Lepidus beamed upon him. "You must understand, I have servants in her house who are useful to me. Do you remember the girl who threw a shoe at your head?"

Furian got up. He stood by the chair. He said, "So it was all spied on."

"What else? Your idyll sounds most enchanting. You were made for each other, it seems . . . both by me. The musician loved her but she was only generous to him. You've no notion how apt this will be. The hatred you feel for her, the love, the distaste, the distrust— the fury."

"Like your own? Or don't I measure up to you?"

Lepidus now laughed very loudly. He looked hugely tickled, gratified.

"Can it be you deduced so much?"

Furian hesitated. "What do you mean now?"

"Let me tell you then. I've had her. She was fifteen."

Furian felt a panic-stricken cacophony rising in him, black as the pits of hell, and with their heat. He pushed it away and said, but his voice sounded cracked and old, "You fucked your daughter."

"Divinely, three or four times. I was so disgusted by her, but she was so dewy, soft, so arousing. What else?"

In the depths of his mind, Furian saw the animal of rage with the barb upon its phallus, rearing amid trampled sparks.

"You want to ask me, did she like it. How can I know? She didn't resist. Or encourage. And naturally she neither wept nor frowned nor screamed out in pain or ecstasy. In her writings to me after, she never once referred to it."

Furian picked up the wine. Then he let the glass fall, shattering on the floor.

He said, "You made her your whore, and then the whore of others, to come at them. Del Nero and who else? You meanwhile lay over the others who were women, such as Messalina."

"And a man or two . . . but otherwise you have it. Yes, Furian. Sex is a component of what I did to them. You see, these weren't like the little spell I set on you. These are the arts of murder."

Eurydiche, whore and accomplice. Maybe the willing mistress of her father. Eurydiche—disgust, arousal.

Furian stood behind the chair.

Lepidus sat drinking at his ease. He looked well-fed. As if he had just been dining.

A huge wind of fire seemed to have rushed through the room. But it was gone.

A knock sounded gently on the inner door.

Lepidus put aside his glass.

"Let's go down now and complete the ritual."

"Yes, let's, since I haven't a choice."

"The technique of it I'll explain to you, at the proper moment. But you're primed."

Furian turned to him. He said, with no control, hoarsely, wildly, like a boy of eighteen, "Don't trust me, Lepidus. Don't ever do that. I'll be obedient. I'll keep my place. One day or night I'll settle with you."

"I'll look forward to it. You and I and a little tussling. How appetizing."

Outside the door, a wall, and one more corridor that ran in two directions. Lepidus went away to the left, and Furian was led decorously to the right by the bull-masked man.

Furian was compliant. Without argument or struggle. For what was it to be now—some rank magic, some vicious, scar-making infliction learnt from the tribe called The Enemy—what significance did it have? He had revealed his namesake fury, fury and shame, his weakness, all of it. He had retained nothing that could be handy. Even if Lepidus had lied about his 'little spell', (he had lied, he *must* have lied), he had made Furian his creature.

The inner hall of the chapel was of some size and perfectly round. Above, it rose into the arena of the dome, which here was faced with black marble, like all the chamber. Eyelets had been cut in the fabric of the dome, but they were small, and revealed only further darkness, the black marble ceiling of the night.

Below, the floor was glassy, like polished obsidian. Shallow black steps rose from it, and around the walls at the top of this terrace, were placed a ring of braziers that leapt with bloody flame. And the flames reflected upward into the roof, downward into the floor.

Within the black circle of the floor was marked, by narrow inlaid tiles, a white square. At the point of each angle, on the terrace above the steps, bulked a black marble chair with a high arched back.

Alchemically, conceivably, these points and chairs marked the Cardinals of the compass, North, South, West and East.

There was nothing else in the round hall but for the three human shapes left, as if stranded, on the lower floor.

Each poised alone, isolated, like a chess-piece on an emptied board.

Furian saw the woman Calypso, in her black fan mask, and scarlet dress. And perhaps twenty feet away from her, the woman Eurydiche. They had changed her clothes. Now she was clad almost like the Virgin, a white gown, and caught from a coronet in her hair, a blue smoke of veil. A diamond spangled on her forehead, the star of Venus. She was not masked. Yet, masked.

Shaachen, sitting near the center of the floor, had kept his rabbit's face. Also kept up or put back his invented character. He was idly tossing his dice on to the floor with an annoying, unbearable clinking, retrieving them, throwing them again. The satchel was gone, and anything it might have contained with it. He looked very small and black, a pathetic, pitiable form. Of all of them, he should not be here. But then, he had asked to witness the ritual. A show-off himself, he had unerringly sensed the same in Lepidus. But as Lepidus had guessed, removed from his props, powders, tinctures, chalk, book—Shaachen was powerless.

Furian did not go down the steps. He looked at the upper tier on to which he had come out. The door was no longer to be seen. Now his eyes grew accustomed to the braziers' jumping arson, he saw golden outlines traced on the inner dome. All the beasts and figments of the zodiac were there, and the constellations, gods in chariots, unicorns and dragons, which seemed to move—his head reeled. He turned his glance back to the floor.

He looked at her. But Eurydiche made no movement, if she noted him. Her body was still as a stem no wind could blow.

His eyes left her. And he beheld, with sudden surprise, almost affront, Calypso's bodice had been altered. Above the scarlet stuff, her oval, heavy breasts were sumptuously bare. She did not seem to notice. Keeping to where she had stood or been put to stand, she turned her fan-face here and there, up and down. She called to Furian in a fish-wife's screech: "Be careful of them! They sting."

He thought, *Her breasts perhaps. Yes, they'd sting.* He thought of filling his hands with them, playing the tips of his fingers over them until she clutched him. She liked men. It would not take long.

But these thoughts did not belong in this place. (What had been in Lepidus' hospitable wine?)

A fearful sound stamped in the hollow chamber. It was a drum. It beat once, then over and over. Its tempo was like a heart. The heart irresistibly picked up its rhythm.

Four figures were at the Cardinal points of the square, on the terrace at the top of the steps. They had come in through the walls at other now invisible entrances. In the dancing flame-light, such appearances were manageable.

Each figure was naked, and each was masked, the entire head covered over. Four heavy muscular men, (the fourth with curious, well-knit scars on the tawny material of his body). They had each been shaved of every hair. One had the head of a shark, of silky slate grey. One the head of a white bear, whose fur ran down his neck. One had a face composed of a black vapor of bats with tiny winking eyes. The fourth one was a red wolf, its pelt pouring to his shoulders.

They walked about the chairs and sat in them. Four living statues with the heads of demon animals. And one, only one, the wolf, with his member swollen, ruddy and upright, which as he sat, he fingered, approvingly. A golden ring surrounded his erection, ornamenting and maintaining it. Lepidus. Lepidus in the station of the East, for the East was the wolf, the east wind howled with its voice. And the bats were the evening West, the shark the oceanic South, the white bear the cold and legendary North, the White Lands, Argenti masks, Orichalci.

From inside the head of the wolf, Lepidus spoke. His voice was almost a whisper, but the chamber carried it.

The words were Latin. Furian did not comprehend them. From Shaachen's mysteries he recognized the first swirling prickling of the air, and what might come, but did not care. Probably he could even understand the chant, for they had taught him Latin once. But he had made himself forget—

Whatever was wanted, he would have to do it. This was what he had confused with death—the death of the will. Until that day or night he had prophesied. Then he would rebel and Lepidus would kill him. Tonight anyway, he had lost all of himself.

And was she laughing? Would she like to have him after. The slave brought in chains to her bed. And again, the stab of desire, so he was erect as Lepidus, under his clothes.

The Guardians of the Guild chapel were rising. They were only partly visible, red and roiling, with fires for manes. The drum beat and the heart ran with the drum. A new chanting came, far, far off, across the continents perhaps. There were feathers in the flames and faces almost of men, painted black and cobalt and crimson. Winged men, and men with the lower bodies of stags. Things from the otherwhere. Sacred images of The Enemy.

Calypso was turning about on the floor. Maybe she thought she saw only what she had already been seeing. Some thing had taken hold of her mind; possibly she had truly seen these things before they were conjured.

But Eurydiche stood like stone. Familiar, all this, to her?

And Shaachen the alchemist sat in his rabbit mask, the unmagical dice put away now. Very likely he was only intrigued. For the magpie had shown him he would live beyond death.

The Guardians merged into a laval fog. Behind each of the four chairs towered, for a moment the effigy of the mask, red wolf, great bear, a writhing shark, a flight of huge bats. Then they were gone.

Furian looked straight up again. In the dome, the zodiac and the stars and planets were wheeling slowly. The chariots jolted, the archer took aim, from the pitcher poured a torrent of fireworks. And Virgo was courted by the unicorn.

"Furian," said Lepidus intimately, in his ear.

But Lepidus sat on his seat of blackness some feet away, fondling himself with a deathly constraint.

"Furian, come here. I'll tell you the final secret, and what you must do."

On the floor, Shaachen turned his rabbit face to goggle at the wolf.

Furian, subject, went along the terrace to Lepidus.

"What's the secret? Do you want me to toss you off? My apologies."

Lepidus laughed. His laugh was honey.

"You can't break the sorcery, little boy, with little jibes. The energy is too strong. We four keep all the Guild at bay. We four will presently rule the Guild. All Venus, why not—worlds and powers."

"I'm here. Tell me the secret."

"Don't be impatient. Look at Calypso. Isn't she a splendid dish?"

"But you've sent her crazy, like Messalina."

"Not I, Furian. Not I. *It's the mask.*"

"I thought so. Like the others."

"Like the others. The prince who slew himself and the lady who hanged herself. Del Nero who drowned himself and lies under the canal, looking up through the water. And Messalina, whose heart just stopped in the Madhouse. And so on. Always, the mask. Shall I say how?"

"By all means."

Furian's mouth was dry. The brazier heat was like hell for sure. And in the upper air, the golden elementals coiled about each other, and the furnaces of the Orichalci shifted with eyes and paint. Who wanted wine? Wine was red and hot. Water. Water from a stagnant pool. The poison of the canal, where he had swum to her, and del Nero's face had been turned up to him unseen, below.

"Listen," said Lepidus. "A mathematic. We learn intimately the facts of each victim. Their day and hour of birth, their totems and signs, their preferences and antipathies. Their deepest fears and joys. Their concealed perversities. Which planet rules them. How their inmost life is shaped. This is a minor exercise. Men love to talk of themselves, and where not, their underlings adore to betray them. There is magic too, a helpful knack. It's possible to discover, now and then, that which even the victim does not know of himself with his waking mind. When all *is* known, we make the mask. It's exquisite. It is the best of them, superficially. They must have it. They are complimented on all sides. But oh, the mask, where it touches them, on their skin, *there*. It has been made against everything they are. Against name and nature, condition and desire, heart and spirit. At the wrong phase of the moon, under the most unsuitable star. At an hour abhorrent to them, in the worst planetary conjunction our arts reveal. If they are up, we make *down*. If their tone is sweet we make *bitter*, and sweet for sour. A color they hate, present though never seen, a scent they loathe but will never smell—yet something of them smells and sees. Visualize a window set crooked in its frame. A wound that is unseen but never heals. It grinds, it grinds on them, and they never know how it is that it does. Evening for morning, day for night. And while it *grinds*, it stays a partner to what they are, inevitable, attached, like the shadow thrown on the wall. It binds them. Them must wear it, that mask, like no other. Even in love, even asleep. It looks so fair. Sometimes one of them will tear at it, but they can't take it off, can't, can't. Sometimes they reach inside and rend their own skin—most of them, at the last, did this. The face or the mask or both, with scratches, cuts, bruises. It rubs, *rubs*, like grit in the shoe that makes a sore. But this makes sores on the *soul*. I gained the knowledge from the Orichalci. I went through steel and thorns, biting ants, and fire and blood to gain it. I gained it whole and entire. Their shamans use such things only in great extremity. A clever people, who can call out the psyche in their ceremonies. A cruel people. Cruel as God. Do you see?"

"Yes."

"Before Carnival is over, those we select are eaten away as if a rat had been gnawing them. They kill themselves, or only die. For del Nero, that rival you love so well, it was his need of my daughter, or so he thought, that clawed and chewed him out. Only when he went under, when his lungs were full of green mud, did the mask fly up. And you found the mask, my dear. You found the mask that had killed him. And so came back to me like my little lost dog."

Furian stood by the black marble chair. He felt nothing. He had known, it seemed. The masks, what else. The masks were themselves the murderers.

"But one other small magic was in it," said Lepidus the wolf. "In a moment, I'll say. First, I insist you look at Calypso. Lunario had her. But so did I. What a pot of dolche she is. But that wasn't why we took her, not from affection, I regret. No one paid us to kill her. But she is to be killed, you see. This very night."

"Your explanations explain nothing. It only gets blacker."

"Yes, it does do that. You could have Calypso now. She'd be so willing. And luscious. And poor Eurydiche—so *mortally* jealous, watching *you* at work on another woman."

Furian felt Lepidus' burning hand fasten on him through his clothes. Lepidus fondled Furian just as he fondled his own self.

And Furian was hot as fire, cold as a grave, yet he twitched and filled to bursting, in the grip of his enemy.

Lepidus said, "Eurydiche is the focus for it all. I made her mine. She became the Venus mirror. I shine the light of sorcery on her and she reflects it back, on *them*. For this reason she has always met each one. With some she has been more than courteous. In Messalina's bed—she was there too. Did she like it, you ask again. Who knows. I told her she must."

"I don't follow you," said Furian. He did not bother to move away and Lepidus let him go.

"But you do follow. You're familiar with magic. What is Eurydiche but a symbol. And through the glass of her speechless void, through the abyss of all her screaming silence, *this* passes, and is magnified. Go down and take your pleasure with Calypso. Eurydiche will see. That will be enough, with *you*. The masks kill slowly, but this once, very fast. Take Calypso in the mask—it will finish her. Send her down to Juseppi in Avernus. He'll like that. She'll have to put him together as Isis did Osiris."

"You do it," said Furian, "if it takes your fancy."

"But you were to be obedient. Obedient or dead yourself. And you've killed quite often and easily. I tested you twice, and saw you do it."

"Why? Why do you want me to—"

"To assume my mantle. I've done enough. Even the masks have done enough. Calypso is to be the first, your test. You'll kill those I choose, through Eurydiche and through your own appetite. Better than a father, a *lover*."

"The masks kill—but you say, not without her. You say that Eurydiche—that *she* kills them—"

"*She.*" Lepidus stroked his penis. "I made her. I had her. She never knew how I used her after. My lust, all lust, caused such turmoil in her poor breast. And the turmoil must get out again—but how? She has no speech, can't even blink. Such surging emotion will find an outlet. If not through the lips or eyes, then through the *heart*. Each sun of pain or fear, even the fear of an unwanted, demanding love, reflects into her glass. And is sent off from her so fiercely it can start a fire. Did she know it? No. How could she? She met these persons and never even knew they died, living put away as she did. But then—ah, Furian. You appeared. With you, she's different. With you, came love and healing, and her mirror turned to coolest, purest ice. So you see, there must be made more strife. Terror again, and agony. Out of such bliss, twisted, can emerge a scythe worthy of the Angel of Death itself. She'll only need to see you put your hands on Calypso. And you'll have your revenge, on my daughter, for all this quagmire into which, unwittingly, she dragged you; She knows now what she is and has been. I told her she was a murderess, that same night, yesterday, when I walked into the room and showed her that I still lived, and told her so did you. She knows how I've employed her, the lure and the weapon, both. Not only her use in their beds, their *gravemaker*. When you met her in that little room, did you find her more strange? Did you wonder why she had no paper and pen to write to you? You abhor her and you love her. Go down and straddle the red sow. And Eurydiche will weep and shriek behind her living mask. And Calypso's peppery brain will explode. This, my Furian, your final initiation into my service. This, or your death. Choose."

Furian turned. He looked at Lepidus. The thick body was bloated with its feeding. On the stroked rod, a pearl of excitement had broken out. Furian breathed, and even at this intake of air, fragments of rotten, sizzling power sprang to protect the monster, round its chair. Furian put one finger to them, and was burnt.

Furian lowered his eyes. "I've chosen. Kill me."

Lepidus rocked with some sudden turbulence. The mask only snarled.

"Are you sure? Sure? It was my best wish, to hear you ask for death. Even better than ruling your life, wearing you away."

"Then get on with it."

And now Furian shut his eyes, and put out the fires, the figures, the black room, all the magic, the chaos.

Something seized him. It was like the pressure of twenty nailed hands. He was swung up and up. Vertigo forced him to open his eyes once more. He hung in the boiling ceiling among worms of scalding gold. There was ice and flame together there, but he was stretched head downwards. He could not move. He heard the drum, and felt the horror of utter darkness, and of white light, of cessation and eternity. And waited for one ultimate blow.

All the gods were taking exercise by lashing him with golden flails. His ankles were held in manacles of gold that were not real, yet were stronger than iron.

He swung a little at each lash, but none of these were the final blow.

His head was full of blood and in his ears the drums pounded.

Below, perhaps only thirty feet from him, he saw the little figures. He did not worry about them. He wished to be dead.

But Furian's brain, his mind—not his soul—seemed loosened from his body. He moved away from the self hung there like a dead hare in the Butchers Quarter. He saw, without eyes, more clearly.

Lepidus had got up from his black throne, though the other three beast-men sat as they were, to North and South and West. He was coming down the steps, his member standing out ahead of him. He went past Eurydiche, and, as if she could not help herself, she turned her head to watch.

(He might have lied once more. There was no proof she had not known. She might revel in all of it, the foreplay and the death.)

Lepidus walked slowly towards Calypso, weighed down by his indicating lust. He fancied, and would see to it himself. And Calypso, her head darting up and down and about like a bird's, awaited him, her hands already alighted on her breasts and holding them up like ripe fruit for his attention.

But Shaachen was busy at something too. He had gone scampering forward. He caught hold of Eurydiche. He turned her about, with one hand, to look at him. Furian heard Shaachen's voice, "Come here, come here." He was drawing her to the middle of the chamber. Shaachen pointed up. Up to Furian's body hung from the dome. "Look. Who's that? You see. Look at him. He'll die like that. Handfast, unable to breathe. The blood to the brain bursts it." (Furian thought, vaguely, *Oh, only that then.*)

Eurydiche's head was raised, tilted back on her white throat. The veil came undone and drifted to her feet. Her face, its eyes. Even now, hung here or separated from himself, he wanted to kiss that upturned, pliant, lifeless, singing mouth. Her eyes were so brilliant, as if with tears. But her tears were locked inside.

Shaachen had got something out of his coat. He looked so exactly a rabbit, hopping about Eurydiche, scattering bits untidily on the obsidian floor. Where they landed, spread little puffs of luminescence.

The funny scratchy rabbit voice was mumbling.

These were the pieces of the ruined letter, the dried mush from his pocket. No one had bothered with them. But they must be magical still. Shaachen had formed a circle about them both, the girl and himself. He took her arms and said, "By almighty God, don't move. You must stay still." Her face went down and she looked at him. And in that instant the shark-masked man stood up and shouted in Lunario's voice.

The words were something arcane. A gust of power not light, not motion—streamed across the room and hit the paper circle. At once a snow-white, transparent globe swam up and covered Shaachen over and covered over Eurydiche.

"Lepidus!" Lunario thundered.

The other Guild men had also risen. (One, the bat-faced man, had an erection too now, perhaps not from desire but startlement.)

Lepidus' wolf-face looked over its shoulder. He paused, his penis still nosing at Calypso's scarlet skirt.

"Why, Doctor. You're inventive after all."

Shaachen did not answer. He called in a high childish voice, "Come *now*, darling!"

Furian, out of his strangling body, and still in it, felt a sharp light smack to his cheek—a wing. He saw a black and white fluttering, sprung through one of the eyelets in the dome, now dive towards the floor.

It was the magpie. It swooped to Shaachen's shoulder, strutted there half a second, and jumped free. As its black feet touched the circle of damp paper, the magpie altered.

Rising up, it *rose*. The occult bird of Virgo. It grew like a black tree dashed with white, up on the black legs like inky coral, up past Shaachen and the girl, up above them, until its black-hooked head stood the height of a tall man higher than they. It spread its wings of coal, and from its back shimmered the rich, the alien blue. The scissors of its beak opened. It cawed once, and the chamber groaned.

The shark, the bat, the bear, stood by their seats. Lepidus stood with his hand upon the breast of Calypso.

Shaachen took hold of Eurydiche, viciously now. He shook her a little.

"Furian will die. Your father will make that happen. Do you want it?"

She was only stone, and then the wind blew her back into a stem. The flower head tipped side to side.

"No? *No?* Be sure."

Quickly now she shook her head. The diamond shrilled on her forehead. The coronet fell from her hair and spun away to the paper circle's edge, with a lick of fire.

"I can do as *he* does," said Shaachen. "I can use you as my mirror. But I'll kill your father instead." She was motionless inside Shaachen's hands. Shaachen said, skittish, "He spoke to me about my props. Don't need them if I have you. But it will take all of me, and more of Eurydiche. It will kill you outright. But Furian will live. Do you hear me? *He* does. Furian hears every word. Lepidus or Furian. And if it's Furian, then be positive, your death. What do you say?"

Her head fell back. Furian saw again into her face. She was expressionless for a cruel God had made her so. And yet he read it all, the tempest within her, the racing tide.

Furian's body roared for her—"*No!*"

But the head of Eurydiche was lowered, went up, then down. She had nodded.

Lepidus let go of his victim, wolf's head fully turning and out of its eyes his own, looking like two snakes.

But Shaachen was gobbling, gabbling, and showers of light and flame shot up and up. The magpie fanned its giant wings.

Furian struggled. He struggled to fall and break himself and all this.

There was a noise like shrieking. A thousand voices of the damned were in it. It split the drums of the ears. At the outer circle of the room, the brazen redness of the Orichalcian magic bubbled.

Furian could not help but see. Tossing in the sorcerous chains, he must behold her, the woman he had loved, standing beyond Shaachen's squeaky ranting, changing, changing into crystal. He could see through her now, as through the thinnest pane of glass.

A sapphire ignition where her eyes had been flared downwards and up. And suddenly, out of her glassy nothingness there shot four bolts of the coldest and most unearthly blue. To three of the four Cardinal points they ran, to shark, to bat, to bear, straight as arrows. And to a fourth point where a red wolf balanced on the hind legs of a man, one dazzling ray hurled like a spear.

The air sizzled and shattered. Its red periphery went almost to black.

Furian felt himself turning in the height of the ceiling, then dropping, slow as a feather, through a welter of nauseous lightnings. He hit the floor softly, and curled on his belly.

From here he saw that the mask of the shark had come alive, come alive and turned inward. Lunario was screaming, fighting with it. Blood fountained out from under the blue grey head, which with its ivory teeth, was tearing off his face.

Three others screamed as he did. The bats were free, feeding voraciously upon the man who had fallen, ripping at his face and eyes. The white bear was twisting off the entire head, and next, through the pandemonium, the crack of a man's neck bone was piercingly audible.

Lepidus, on his knees, wrestled howling and retching with the mask of the red wolf which tore out his throat.

"Stay where you are," said Shaachen, miles away. "Don't touch the circle. Be quiet."

"Eurydiche," he said.

"Silence," said the magician, in the voice of God.

Furian put his head on his arms and said no more.

When all the screaming ended, the beasts of the four masks flowed off from the wreckage they had made; they fluttered and rolled down the steps and met together on the obsidian floor. And here they tore in turn each other apart, fur and wings and skin and pelt, eyes and teeth, and as they rent and twined and sundered, they melted down like lead in a fire, but not to gold, only to a filthy clinker, which finally, mercifully, was without life.

Furian assisted Calypso to sit up. She had gone down not far from the bloody mess of Lepidus. Her gown was wetly splashed, but it did not show.

"Let me alone," she said. "Get away."

"Yes, but first this comes off."

He eased at her mask. The fastenings were complicated. She had knotted ribbons in under her hair, to be sure.

"No—no, don't. I'll die."

"You'll die if you wear it."

"Take it off and my face will go with it."

Furian leaned and kissed the tops of her soft breasts. She moaned. He said, "Trust me, it won't."

When he pulled the mask away, she was pale and wasted.

In her autumn countenance, the lines had deepened. Her eyes were sick, yet lit now by two waking stars.

"Am I alive?"

"Alive."

He kissed her lips, and standing up, got her to her feet. Abruptly she put her refound face into her hands and wept. He heard in it the name of Juseppi. He left her, and walked slowly to Shaachen across the floor. The paper circle had burned up. It was charcoal. Shaachen was kicking it aside, while the magpie, only of usual size, sat clucking on his shoulder and letting go clotted streamers of clean green excrement.

"Birdshit, the gobs of God," commented Shaachen.

"Why did you use her?" said Furian. "But then, you don't mind the occasional death. It's science, isn't it."

"If I might save a life, I take the risk. To live is worth a risk. But this Mask Guild within a guild, to kill was the pastime. So I came to see to them, if I could."

Furian looked down. Across the circle, Eurydiche lay. Her hair had come loose, and spread like white silks in the sinking light, from which all redness had been bled. She was made of milk-white flesh, not glass. In her eyes the flames winked blue, as if her lashes fluttered as they never could. Ashes of white roses. Ashes of the moon.

He knelt beside her and brought her against him and held her. He stared into her face.

"She was willing to die for you," said Shaachen, "you can never forget it. Is this love?"

Yes, love. Insane and unspeakable and undeserved, and unbelieved, until too late.

"And so she's dead."

"Touch the neck. Do you know nothing?"

Furian put his finger against her throat. The pulse of Eurydiche was as faint as the beating of a moth. Even as he felt it, it stumbled, ceased, turning his bones to water. Then resumed, reluctantly. If she breathed, he could not see it.

"Dying then. She'll die."

Shaachen flapped his hands. He was as ever ruthless, experimental. "I may save her. You saw. I'm crafty."

"You can't. You blasted her apart. She'll die. She's dead. Even you can't bring her back from that."

"Don't look back into your past," said Shaachen. "You've lost what you cared for, so must lose everything? Don't you know the story of the first Eurydiche? Her lover glanced back at her, though warned not to. They were coming up from the Underworld, no less, and she was yet half dead. She couldn't, that way, bear his eyes, and was driven down again. If he'd waited, the sunlight would have made her whole. Impatience. Men are fools."

Furian put his face into her silver hair. He thought, *And after you darkness.*

EPILOGUE

The Heart

As the weeks passed, the season faded into winter. Along the canal a wanderer now and then went up and down, sometimes a boat with vegetables and fruit, once a procession with priests and incense, bearing an image of the Virgin Maria, to bring the rain. The Carnival was gone, like a gaudy cloud, behind the pale lemon sun.

While she lay in the narrow bed, the girl, recapturing the ability to breathe and be, thought of her small life. It was a dream, and glided before her in a dream's fashion, sad and surreal. She remembered the first house, among the fields, the mountains far away with their salty snows. But her mother was a memory less actual than the pious nuns, who were callous to her, telling her always to thank God and Christ, although she did not know for what. This era ended in the blaze of glory, her father. Another house followed, comforts, pleasures, learning. Until the summer day the fire was turned upon her. The rape. How she had blamed herself. Her fault, his savagery, (although again, she did not know why). And afterwards she was bereft, for now she could never love him any more.

Her life then, without love. It was filled presently by the panoplies of sex. How awful, this vast procession, colors and glitters, ways and means. Hollow, and worse, for now, here, there, for one second, some mirage of sweetness—never to be found. Mostly, let it be said, abjection, misery, and shame.

All the mystery of the City and the earth lay beyond her secretive house. She thought her father took her to these feasts and festivals of Carnival, to punish her, since she had brought him down.

She knew he used her as a whore for others. Some were partial to her sort, her freakish looks. Returning, she was drained as a leaf hidden from the light. And from light, she hid herself.

She had no scope for other things. She read of other worlds she might not enter. What was crying like? This constant weightless passage of unliquid tears, the *phantoms* of water, through the caves of her heart?

For she was empty. She was not alive. She lived, moved, and was asleep. Always, always asleep. She knew no other state.

One night. One night at her father's bidding, present at a place of masks where she might wander, among the groves and lamps, a man approached her.

He too was masked—and yet

At once she knew him. As if she had known him since her childhood. As if he were her brother. He spoke to her beneath the sheltering trees.

"Who are you, Madama?"

She could not speak, of course. Yet her heart broke, at the wonder of his known and beautiful voice, into a stretching ache, a flowering hurt of smile. And he said, cool as her tears that never fell, "Keep smiling." As if he knew it all.

From that moment, even as he left her, she became a part of him. And when at last she saw his face—mad from fever and anger, white and stripped of everything but nothingness, it was yet the face of the lover she had always had within her. Her own face, only made other, made male, made *human*. Made divine. The guardian angel vowed to her by God.

Nevertheless, within her sphere, Lepidus remained a power. It was he who had told her so much of Furian, explained that Furian, if with her, would be kept safe—although Lepidus had not said from whom or from what—*himself*. So she gave Furian over to Lepidus. And at the first, (lying) death of Lepidus, when all the temple—harsh and barren, the palace of some heartless god—crashed round her, adrift, she clung to Furian. Then lost him also, as she had dreaded she must, for in an earthquake nothing stands. As the lagoon closed over his head, too stunned to feel, she had known merely the sentence of desolation that is in the gift of every limitless desert.

Later, when Lepidus reappeared, reborn, and told her that Furian also lived, a terrified lightness dashed her up. And as she hung from these killing talons, Lepidus told her all the rest. What she had been constructed to be, his focus of murder, Nemesis. (This, the second rape.) In her newest hell, she did not blame herself, did not question. She wanted only the incredible miracle that had released her before, love—Furian—to cleanse her and repair her. As he had cleansed and repaired her of all injury and sexual taint. Furian alone could give her back what the heartless always take away—her heart. And when it seemed Furian, although he said he loved her, did not wish to love her, would not believe or accept her, she began to die. To which death, the death of her life before was a shining thing.

It was Shaachen who offered her real death in exchange for Furian's continuance. Paramount had been her wish to save her lover. But also it was her honor. She had been the cause of death; this then justice. But more than that. To die for Furian would prove to him forever what she could not otherwise display, that she loved him more than life. Even he could not argue with her death. He could not distrust her. Though he must remain alone, he must always know he had been *loved*.

The Jewish alchemist, in the winter days when he began to talk to her, told her firmly that he had promised her death because her sacrifice must be total in order that his magic work. She did not mind. She thanked him, writing in her fine controlled hand, for the opportunity he had given her of vindication. Not once did she inquire how she had been saved, what bizarre sorceries and medicines had brought it about. Nor how they had escaped from the Island of Smokes. She did not therefore know at first that Lepidus was no more on his pinnacle. How the hirelings of the Guild, flying in fright from the sounds in the chapel, had given no trouble. Of the reeking fish boat. Of arms locked round her, of silent words pressed into her skin and hair. She did not even know she was in Shaachen's disreputable palace. She asked only one thing, she asked it every day. *Will I see Furian?*

"Not yet," said Shaachen. "Not until you are entirely alive. He doubts me. I won't let him near, till he can have no doubts."

Nor would he speak much of Furian. Only that Furian had written to his father, and been answered. Only that Furian had gone to this church or that, or to the Primo. That he had prayed.

For what? she asked.

"For you. For himself. For all the world."

At last Shaachen related to her that Lepidus was dead. He did not describe the manner. She knew that it had been through her, and by her consent. When Shaachen seemed reticent, Eurydiche wrote, *My only father is Furian. He is my brother and my son. My other self. I need no one else.*

"One day he'll die," said Shaachen, moving from the reticent to the crass.

Then so will I.

"Not for a long time," said Shaachen, perhaps compassionate. "Not now for a long time."

Occasionally she saw the woman who had been on the Isle of the Dead. Unmasked she had a handsome face, which day by day took on a bloom. She wore fine gowns and grew sleek. Once this woman, called like Eurydiche by a Greek name, Calypso, put her hands on her hips and spoke at some length. She had the story to give she was a rich man's daughter who had wed for love and so lost everything but for a crumbling floor in some palace. Her husband had been too good for her and died. "Now I'm here," she added, bridging her tale obliquely. "You'll think I'm a harlot, living off an old man. Well, he's fair to my boy. And he may be elderly, Signore Shaachen, but he knows more of the bed than any young one."

This educated old man one morning showed Eurydiche a letter he had written, dedicated to no one. Perhaps Furian was to read it, or the Alchemist's Guild. Shaachen's hand-writing was crabbed, and the magpie had trodden on the paper, further muddling some passages.

Shaachen's gist was that the Orichalci tribe, The Enemy, had put Lepidus under their curse for his presumption in appropriating their magic, and his villainy in misusing it. This curse drove him on to make all his mistakes. To hazard his powers against the rogue force of Furian, and the colossal force of true love. While blinding him to the talents of one such as the canny and venturous Shaachen. So such curses worked, little in themselves, building from the flaws of character, the inner qualms, of those on whom they had been set. He might have taken a lesson from what he had done to Furian at eighteen. Lepidus had been played like an instrument and sent at last out of pitch

After she had read this—it took a while, there were long portions of self-congratulation—Shaachen stood her up.

She wore a dress of jasper velvet, and he fussed a moment with her sleeves, like an old servant woman. Then told her she was now alive, and might go into the other room and try the harpsichord he had put there for her.

The room was long and reverberant, and veiled with webs and dust, through which the inconstant winter sunlight ebbed or flamed. The harpsichord was old, unpainted with stained yellow keys, where lay a black feather sheened with blue.

She touched the feather, then sat down.

It was a song she tapped quietly from the instrument, but not the lover's song Cloudio del Nero had made for her, which now the faithless City had quite forgotten. This was a tune of her childhood, and in her head she heard the words she could not sing.

If he is mine then he will come to me.
If he is mine, I will be his.
If I am his he will be mine.

She heard his step, as once before, and as before, made out she had not.

He put his arms about her so tenderly, so unbelieving. He drew her up, and turning to him, she saw the face of her father, her brother, her lover, her son. Furian. Her other self.

"You are alive," he said. "You are. In God's name, you are."

He was empty as a shore from which the sea had gone, the emptiness that had been in her, so long, so long ago. But now, her eyes on his face, and as he looked at her, she saw the sea return, the waters of great oceans, and cover him with truth and light, with strength and happiness and life. And with eternal life.

Saint Fire

The law of the Dreamtime is yet the law.

FROM THE KOORI (Aboriginal)

Contents

Contents

AUTHOR'S NOTE

In this parallel Italy, some names are spelled phoneti-
cally. But an *e* at the end of a name is always sounded,
(as *ay* to rhyme with *day*.)

The Latin phrases should be pronounced as Medi-
aeval Latin generally was-*V,* for example as in *very,*
(not as a W), *ch* as *K, ae* to rhyme with *eye*. (It should
be noted too, the Latin used in this book is also that of
a *parallel* Italy.)

For the revelation of the connections between the
Hymn to Aten of the Pharaoh Akhenaten, and Psalm
104, the author expresses many thanks to Robert Scott
B.Ed.

PROLOGUE

And priests in black gowns, were walking their rounds,
And binding with briars, my joys and desires.

WILLIAM BLAKE
Songs of Experience

A bell was ringing Luna Vigile from the marshes. The inn was not noisy at that moment, they heard it clearly enough. Some crossed themselves. Many grew quiet in a restive respectfulness, until the bell fell silent. Then they picked up their cups, drained them and called for more.

"Another, Ghaio?"

"It's late. I'll be getting home."

"A last draught to light your path, Ghaio."

Ghaio Wood-Seller glanced at the merchant Juvanni. Juvanni, who had established a name but not much luck in trade, had just negotiated a hefty loan from the wood-seller, a trader in much lowlier goods. But a city always needed kindling, especially now on the threshold of winter. Ghaio, who dressed scruffily and lived in a slum, was haughty, and said to be rich.

"If you like, Juvanni."

"Yes, yes, my friend," fawned Juvanni, and snapped his fingers for another pitcher of wine.

When the girl brought it, she leaned low to the table.

"Be wary," she whispered. *"Sweet smell."*

Juvanni's red agitation paled. Even Ghaio looked put out.

"In *here*?"

"Coming here, the boy says."

"He'll go by."

"Maybe not. And not *he, two* of them."

She slipped away, to carry on her task of warning valued customers.

Juvanni looked into his brimming cup. Then took their previous, empty pitcher, and thrust it under the table.

"Someone else's," he said. "This is our first, eh, Ghaio, and we're abstemious."

"Damn them, I say," said Ghaio.

Juvanni shook his head. "Hush."

"Eyes and Ears of God," said Ghaio. "I have nothing to fear from them." He smiled long teeth at the merchant. "I've just gifted the Church a hundred silver duccas."

"So much? I would to God I could still—"

"Yes, yes, Juvanni. Well maybe you should give up your trade in sweetmeats and try something more serviceable. But then, I never had your schooling. I can't read much, and I add up on my fingers. I expect that would make the difference."

The door opened. Into the ruddy warmth of the inn came a breath of cold night. The torches faltered on the walls. A new silence began.

Really they had not required the girl's warning. The fragrance of incense that came from the two black-robed creatures in the doorway was potent. Sometimes, it was true, such men moved through the City in disguise, and without even the whiff of sanctity to betray them. But this was blatant.

Their faces were bare, the candle-wax masks of priests. One raised his hand over the rigid figures of the inn, blessing them.

The innkeeper had come running. He bowed low.

"May I assist you, holy brothers?"

"There is nothing your house contains of attraction to us," said one of the priests.

The other said, "Except for the souls of men."

With the cold air of the Silvian Marshes, the words of the priest ran like a shudder from wall to wall.

Although not far from the marsh church of Santa Lallo Lacrima, the inn had been seldom visited. But the Council of the Lamb stayed always vigilant. Recently the Eyes and Ears of the Council were seen more frequently in most spots. There was talk of war. At such times, the Church grew particularly sensitive to the sins of Ve Nera, City of Venus.

A third figure had appeared behind the priests. Against the vagueness of the outer dark, it was only tall and lean, wrapped in black. As it stepped forward, there came three gleams of pallor, from white-blond hair, from a pair of brilliant gray eyes, from a sword swinging in a sheathe of steel and ivory.

The priests turned, and shifted aside.

Juvanni sucked his breath.

The inn-keeper straightened, seeming relieved and alarmed together. "Good evening, Soldier of God."

The Soldier of God nodded.

One of the priests said to him, "You are familiar with this sty, brother?"

"Yes, brother."

"You come here to *drink*?"

Ghaio Wood-Seller noted the blond man's long mouth twitch with what might have been distaste. Certainly not fear. "Yes, brother. The inn well has the purest water in the marshes."

The priests had settled all their attention on this man. He was, in station, their equal, yet subtly above them, a priest-warrior of Christ, one of the elite who prayed but also fought for the honor of the Church. On his shoulder shone, white and gold, the badge of the Lion, the Holy Child astride it. He was young, not more than twenty-five or six. Strong, and sheerly masculine as no swordless priest could be. All this Ghaio assimilated, for he liked sometimes to study men, if only to bring them down.

And this one was regal, was he not, due for a fall.

But the priests drew away, and one softly said, "Does your Magister know that you're here?"

And the Soldier of God turned to the priest a face of stone.

"You may ask him, brother. It is Fra Danielus."

If it had been a play in the street, the inn would have laughed. But even street plays never mocked the priesthood now.

They were retreating though, these two, going out. Fra Danielus was one of the three Magisters Major, who lived high in the Golden Rooms of the Primo. This soldier of God came from the Upper Echelon.

Now he walked through the inn, straight through, the innkeeper hurrying beside him. As a leather curtain closed them away, the inn perked up.

"He has his own business here, then," said Ghaio, curious.

"I have been told—" Juvanni hesitated, "he visits a woman here."

"A *woman*?"

"Oh, hush, Ghaio—"

"And they vaunt their celibacy. Well, it comes as no surprise." He downed his cupful of wine. "And now I'm off."

"You won't forget . . ."

"Your duccas? No. Send your servant tomorrow. They'll be ready. I'll trust you'll be diligent with my interest."

Outside, Ghaio's torch-boy, hired for the trip, emerged from a doorway, shivering.

They went up the alley, the torch lighting them luridly and fitfully.

The Silvian Quarter was bleak at this hour and this time of year. The slop of water in the canals had the turgid sound that promised ice in winter, as in the summer it promised stink. In a gap among the house sides, Ghaio saw, black and thin on water, a Styx Boat, and the two Eyes and Ears of God seated in it, being poled away.

From the marsh blew the smell of a frigid salt sea. Last winter, and every winter before that for five years, the ocean had partly flooded the marshes here. An old Roman temple on a hillock had provided a fine crab pool, for those with the mind to row out to it.

The sea was eating, or drinking, the City. They said in a hundred years or less, these marshes might become Ve Nera's third lagoon. But Ghaio would not be alive in a hundred years and had no time for the future.

"Cristiano," said the woman. She rose and went to him at once, the Soldier of God, and put her arms about his neck, in a cloud of hair not quite blonder than his own.

"Yes, Luchita. What is it this time?"

"So cold. Winter-cold. Do they freeze your hearts in the Basilica?" He waited for the familiar tirade to pass. Tired of it herself, the woman let it go. She only said, "You're my brother. Who else should I turn to?"

"Your husband."

"That sotten pig. He drinks more than he sells here."

Cristiano waited again. Luchita remembered how he had always waited like this, even when a little boy only two years her senior. Infuriating, his cool, calm uninterest, the sense of his impatience always held in check because it was—like everything, or so it seemed to her—a sin.

She said, sullenly, "This new tax, Cristiano, on food, on drinking—the Tax of Pleasures—"

"The Council sets it."

"You serve the Council."

"I serve God."

"God—do you think God wants us to live in misery all our days—Christ knows, they'll tax screwing next."

He shrugged. Although she knew, with his high-flown and impossible ideals, she had probably offended him.

Outside, a song was starting up, the one that was popular this month, about the pagan goddess Venus, and the god of war, Mars.

Every year, new taxes—on drinking, and fine food, on property and on luxurious garments—no trouble to Luchita there, God knew. Soon a tax on songs? Well, it would not amaze her.

"I'm sorry, Luchita. I can't help you. Every inn will have to pay it, and pass the cost on to the patrons in the price of beer and wine."

"And then the patrons will go elsewhere, where they can find inns that cheat."

"I have no say in the Council. My work is other."

"Couldn't you—some exemption—he's often sick—"

"From drunkenness, according to your own words."

"And I may be with child."

Startling her, he looked sudden and hard into her face with his sword-pale eyes. "His? Or another's?"

Luchita glanced aside. "God excuse me, I don't know."

Cristiano stared at some invisible distance.

Outside the words rang clear.

When your heart is mine,
You may do as you will to.
When my heart is yours,
Then wish the world good-bye.

It was a corruption, he thought, of all things, of a holy plaint to God and the Virgin. The giving of a whole heart set against the turning of the full eye of Heaven upon inadequate man, among whom even a saint was unworthy.

The next verse, from its sounds, owed *nothing* to a priestly plaint—

"Well. If you won't help us—"

"I never can, Luchita." He came back, and pushed aside his cloak. As always, as all his order were, he was garbed in a soldier's maculum of close-fitted mail. He set a bag which clinked on the table. "Take this."

"God bless you, Cristiano."

"He won't, for that."

"No, God wants only suffering from us. So you priests tell us. And guilt and shame for any joy we snatch. Isn't that so?"

"And anger is also a sin, Luchita. Especially when directed at Heaven."

She wanted to hurl the money in his face. Afterall, the pig would have drunk it in a dozen days. But she held her hand down. Her brother had done his best, in his pure and remote manner. (Heartless.) And whatever he said, he was the most, the only powerful man she knew.

After he had gone, some tears ran from her eyes. She rubbed them away and went out into the inn to serve, singing.

His house stood on the Canal of Seven Keys, a mixed blessing. In deep winter, if it froze, you could cross it or walk along it, on foot. In summer, it matured, and dead dogs, even men, sailed up and down with the tides. The house itself, fixed firm between two others, was peculiar in that the walls were of a dark red. Ghaio's Red House, locals called it.

Over the door hung his sign, painted with a bundle of wood tied by a cord of gold: wood-seller. The gold had faded on the sign. But only there. Ghaio, as several suspected, was wealthy. He owned three houses, the two on either side his own, and one further along, and took rents from the occupants, although sometimes only in wrung-neck chickens, or other flesh, female and alive. He also owned the broad yard at the back of the Red House, which crowded out the back premises of the other buildings.

Once inside the house, Ghaio glared about him. The room was quite dark and the walls peeling a little from damp. It had no look of affluence.

But then, primed by his tread, his slave woman arrived to light the yellow fat candles.

"Late, you slut." He slapped her. "It doesn't please me to come into a house black as pitch."

"You said—"

"Never mind that." (He had told her never to light the candles when he was out. He was a miser, but a contrary one. She was supposed to guess the time of his return—and sometimes did from mere desperation.) "Where's my supper?"

She pointed mutely.

Ghaio's views on food, and one or two other matters, were not miserly, when applied to himself. The table, now lit, showed a trencher of black bread, a white loaf, a dish of olives and cheese, a haunch of cold roast pork. And wine of course.

"All right." He sat and took up a grabful of the food. He chewed.

Candles cast shadows. In the corners there seemed very many tonight.

Confound those priests. Like shadows, they were everywhere. Soon they might come knocking on the private doors of such as himself. But he had his gambits ready, including the flail he used on his three slaves, this woman, the old man, and less often, the woman's ugly, snotty child. "See, saintly brother. I perform penitence on my own body."

And he had gifted the Church. Gone to the Basilica, the Primo Suvio, great temple of God's crusading knights, and *paid*. One hundred silver duccas. Even God should be delighted.

But Ghaio did not like to think of God. Though not sure that He existed, yet He stayed for Ghaio a tiny, nagging doubt, like the little pain in a tooth one felt years before it changed to agony and must be pulled.

"Tonight," he said to the slave woman, "you come upstairs." She said nothing. He said, "You hear me?"

"Yes, signore."

It wouldn't take long. Against the wall even. She was hardly good enough for his bed.

When she opened the door to go out to the kitchen in the yard, Ghaio caught the briefest strangest glimpse of something, outside.

What in the name of the Lamb—

But no, no, it was nothing. It was the woman's child. The child he had called *Volpa*—Fox—for its filthy reddish hair.

It must have washed that hair. The brat had been waiting for its mother, and as it moved back from the door, the hair—uncovered by the usual rag—caught the candle light, like a flick of fire.

The door had shut now.

Ghaio thought, after all, a flick of fire was to be expected here. The Wood-Seller's house.

He sank his teeth in the pork. How old was the child now? He seldom saw her. He had bought them as a lot, ten years ago, got the price of the woman down, since the child, he said, was no use to him, only an infant.

The woman kept the child hidden from him mostly, he thought, not to annoy, and it—she—performed the most menial tasks, emptying night-soil, washing floors, walking after the wood-cart the old man slave pulled to market.

Hidden, he had not thought of the child much. But it—she—was older now. Twelve—or thirteen, even.

Perhaps he should look at the child.

A wind seemed to be rising outside, bringing the tide along the Canal of Seven Keys, the salt sea licking at the islands of Ve Nera, City of Venus the goddess of lust.

Soon it would be midnight, and the bell would sound again from Santa Lallo Lacrima. Two hours later it would toll the Prima Vigile for the priests to go on their knees once more. Those at least not prowling the byways, searching for drunks and whores to chastise. It was of no account to Ghaio in any case. Fed, and eased of sex, he would be long asleep by then.

BOOK ONE

Alter Mundi

PART ONE

Instead whereof thou gavest them a burning pillar of fire . . .

WISDOM OF SOLOMON
The Apocryhpha

1

First, she saw the mountains—not knowing what they were.

The sky, perhaps. Yes, probably she thought they were the sky; stones built of thin fine ether. The foothills of Heaven.

Two thirds of the year, there was white on them, snow . . . clouds. In high summer they darkened and there was no white.

The farm was in the earthly foothills, and here the slaves worked, among the brown grass and the yellow stalks of grain. Her memory was of sitting, of running, of carrying things.

She did not know what occurred, and after, her mother never explained. There was anger and fright. Mother weeping. So she wept too.

Then a market-place, down on the Veneran Plain, in a town of stumbling little hovels and mud. It rained.

She was four.

Presently, the journey to the great City, whose name meant *Meeting Darkness,* or *To Travel By Night:* Ve Nera. The carter had a nickname for the City. Venus. He made jokes about Venus—now a city, next a goddess. Not the Virgin, the only goddess the child had heard of until then.

Finally, the carter lay over her mother in the cart.

Outside the awning rain lashed miserably.

The carter grumbled, "Took you on—hope you're worth it. And that pest of a baby, that little curse. You women. Breed like conies. Don't dare bud from me. You hear, I'll beat it out of you."

The carter was Ghaio Wood-Seller. Master.

In memory, entering it, the City was indeed a darkness. They were put into a boat—never before felt, the motion of a canal. Arches of shadow, and blocks of night. Water rippling black.

Christian slaves did not matter, the Church had said so. Bodies might be in chains, souls stayed free.

A month later, Ghaio beat her mother. He made the child, already new-named "Fox," watch the proceeding, as a lesson.

Volpa's mother was never pregnant again. Perhaps the beatings saw to that, or simply the generally harsh life in the Red House. Yet, although life was bad, they clung to it, as if to some granite rockface. The alternative was to fall into the abyss.

Or was it? Volpa's mother, in the early years, spoke sometimes of God, and sometimes of the Virgin. Later, she mentioned them less.

"We suffer on earth," said Volpa's mother, "so that we can be happy in another place."

But why must we suffer? Volpa might have asked. Possibly she had done so.

Certainly an outlandish answer seemed to have evolved to just such a question: The world is a school, a cruel and exacting one. Only here can we learn from terrors and mishaps, which, beyond life on either side, are never encountered.

Why then learn? Why is it needful?

"Because only then," said Volpa's mother's sweet tenor voice, "can we be one with God, who has already experienced, and surmounted them."

So God did not send sorrows against mankind to punish or chastise?

No, simply to cleanse, to refine. God, lonely in omnipotence, longed for the company of creatures purified as He had been. He wished that every single soul should achieve such greatness and such wisdom as were already His.

Ghaio, truly, was a diligent exponent in God's school.

Master. Apt title?

Volpa knew to fear and avoid him from the beginning. But it was normally easy, since she lived in another country, the kitchen and the yard.

The yard of the Red House was almost entirely filled with timber, logs, bundles of wood, and the shed where the cart was kept. There was also a cistern to catch rain, whose water was not of the best. (Nicer water was fetched by the woman from the nearest public well.) Over Ghaio's cistern, however, there grew a fig tree. In summer the leaves were like dusty metal. Green figs appeared irregularly in autumn. Bare in winter, the branches had a rheumatic look.

Whatever the season, on nights of the full moon, when Ghaio slept or was from home and the other houses dark, Volpa and her mother would dance about this tree in a strange, silent circling. The old male slave, coming across the yard to the privy one night, saw this, hid his eyes and went away, Volpa had no other indications that the dancing might be profane. Unlike the lesson of God, she never queried it. They had danced in this way, she thought, in the foothills long ago.

Ghaio slept with her mother—that is, had swift, rough intercourse with her mother—two or three times a month, in the early days. In the past four years, far less often.

Volpa saw and knew nothing of these couplings. Thus once, Volpa's mother said an odd thing. "He'll be too old before you're grown."

It was less a statement, of course, than a prayer. Ghaio had shown no inclination to violate the child, who, besides, was kept dirty and muffled and as much from his sight as was feasible.

But time, which leached off some of Ghaio's libido, and some of his strength, was working an opposite magic on the woman's daughter.

Volpa, who had never seen in a mirror—would not be able even to recognize her own face—was at first aware only of slight changes. The ill-treatment which had, perhaps, kept her mother barren, delayed the onset of womanhood. But finally it came. Soreness blossomed into breasts. A thunder of pain broke like a crystal and spotted the straw Volpa slept on with ruby drops.

Then she saw her mother with her hands to her lips. Afraid.

"What have I done? Mumma—I'm sorry—I didn't mean to." (Like the day she broke the pot—and was whipped.)

"No, it's not your fault. It can't be helped. It's what I told you of—do you remember?"

"That? This—is *that*—"

"Yes. Don't cry. It's good. As it must be."

"But *you're* crying, mumma—"

"Only from the sun in my eyes."

For Volpa's bleeding had begun in her birth month, late summer, the time of the sun lion, patron of the Primo, the great Basilica of Ve Nera.

Volpa—even her mother now called her that—was fourteen.

Soon, trudging up the alley after the old man, who hauled the cart, behind the creaking wood and picking up any which fell out, Volpa heard fresh abuse. Before she had been pushed about, slandered as a slave child. Now she was man-handled as a slave who was a woman.

In the market-place boys and men stole up on her and cupped the shallow rounds of her body, breast, thigh, buttock, in unloving hands. Squeezed her like the vegetables. "She's a hot piece." "No, not ripe yet." Sometimes she was glad when the black-robed priests moved nearby, although they spread fear like the aroma of their incense. Then men left her alone.

The adult Volpa did not confide much in her mother. Intuitively she knew her increasingly silent parent had enough to bear. Volpa bore her own dismay, unspoken. It was life. It was God's school.

But sometimes she thought of the story her mother had told her, at the farm in the hills, and maybe again, once or twice, in the first two or three years of the Red House.

The mother was the heroine of this story. It was a real story, true.

Already carrying her daughter in her womb, but not yet knowing it, Volpa's mother had been one night at dusk on a hill.

The day's work was over, and perhaps she was in those days then, allowed rest; she had never said. But pausing, she had looked up above the bare winter fields, into a pale sky that had seemed, she said, the color of the emeralds on the fingers of the mightiest priests. And stars were set out in this polished sky, fierce, and prickled as hedgehogs with their lights.

Suddenly the air, which was cold, grew warm. A warm wind blew up the plain, thick as the gusts of summer. And on the wind, high, high up in the orb of the emerald that was sky, Volpa's mother saw a flight of angels pass.

"At first I took them for birds, Blessed Maria pardon me. They were against the light, and yet they had a gleam on them. And the wings, moving slowly, as gulls' wings do when they catch the currents of the air above the City. But they didn't have any shape of birds, beyond their wings. They were long, like men with their legs stretched out, their arms crossed over the chest. And on the head of each, a flame—like a star come detached, and going with them."

This story of the angels never varied, or only here and there an iota. Now and then some slight extra detail was added—as of hearing a cock crow in the valley, as if at sunrise, and thinking the cock had seen them too—but never anything left out.

"Where did they go, mumma?"

"Away, upwards—into the dome of the sky. Until they grew so small they vanished."

"Did they look at you?"

"I don't know. Perhaps."

"Why did you see them?"

"Because they were there, and I was looking up," Volpa's mother had replied, with dignified simplicity.

She had told no other.

Now she never spoke of it, and Volpa never asked to hear. In imagination only, Volpa relayed the flight of angels. She had seen it so often with the inner eye of her mind, that now it too had become one with the earthly memories of her infancy in the hills. As if she had witnessed it at her mother's side.

That winter, after Volpa turned fourteen, was very bitter.

Ice—they said—formed on the great Laguna Aquila, and the smaller lagoon called Fulvia, and ice pleated the hem of the sea beyond the bars of sand and the sea walls.

The canals froze solid. Even the cart was able to be pulled along them to the market, not needing the alleys, slipping a little.

In Ghaio Wood-Seller's kitchen in the yard, Volpa's mother kept the hearth going as long as she was able from the meager allowance of wood the master gave them. They were supposed to use it only to cook his meals. However, the old man slave stole, a few twigs here, a log there, from the tempting mounds in the yard. Ghaio presumably never guessed. In any case, they were often cold.

During this winter, Volpa's mother began to cough. She tried never to do it when serving Ghaio, for then he struck her: "Shut your noise!"

One morning, the air seemed to break. Suddenly a softness came, like breath breathed on a rich man's glass goblet.

Volpa, waking on the straw at first light, went into the yard, and saw a single pale flower, some weed, that had pushed up against the house.

When she returned with the first unfrozen water from the cistern, she saw her mother still lay asleep.

"Mumma—wake up!" And she shook the woman's arm because no slave could lie abed.

But the man slave was there, gray as a cobweb gone hard.

"Don't shake her. Don't shake the sleeping or the dead," said this old man.

And reprimanded, a little aggrieved—what one took from master one could not bear from another slave—Volpa stopped. Then she saw the straw was dark under her mother's head. As had happened that time with herself, blood had poured out on the straw. Now, though, it seemed to be all the blood the mother had kept in her body. And the soft new light showed her white as the ice which had melted away.

Ghaio blasphemed and complained. She had not lasted eleven years, this useless, slave bitch. He had her body sewn in the customary sack, and thrown on a boat for the Isle of the Dead, where the bodies of slaves were only burned, there being no room for limitless burials.

Volpa stood stunned and weeping. The boat was rowed away in the gray morning. The old man slave said to Volpa, or to the air, "Cry for yourself but not her. Her pain's done. She is in God's world now."

Volpa wept. She said, "That's no better."

"Oh yes," said the slave. "Why else do you think He damns us for suicide? His world is the best of all, and we must earn it." Volpa only ever heard this man say two meaningful things, and this was the second. (The first had been about the shaking.) Then, as they returned through the alley to Ghaio's yard, the old man said also a prophetic thing, "How I long to get there. Would this could be done. I won't raise my own hand, Lord. But fetch me—by any means you like, by whatever awful way. The road's stones, but the gates are pearl. Fetch me, Lord. Amen."

The wood-seller had a collection of debtors, among whom was no longer Juvanni the sweet merchant. *His* house Ghaio had taken in lieu of the loan that winter. Where Juvanni and his family had gone was anyone's guess.

Ghaio did not want the better house, though. He preferred his hovel. He sold the other, and put the deeds and the money into a chest in the upper room of the Red House, which was reached by a ladder, and full only of a bed, some candles, and many, many similar chests.

In the evening after the mother's corpse had been rowed away for the crematory, Ghaio had Volpa serve his meal.

He took no notice of her, but neither did he strike her. This surprised Volpa, who had tried not to displease him, but knew she had been clumsy.

At last, Ghaio sat back.

"You'll have to take your mother's place. I won't waste cash on another." Volpa waited. "How old are you?"

"Fourteen years, signore. So she said."

"Now I see you, you look less. Skin and bone. Skinny red fox. Let me see that hair." Volpa drew off her scarf with reluctance. "Ah, you're nothing," said Ghaio. "Worthless. I might sell you. What'd you bring me, though? A copper venus and a sneering laugh." Then he said, "Go up the ladder and open the chest nearest the door. It's not locked. Inside is a paper with a list of men's names, men that owe me money."

Volpa did what he said. Her whole life had been molded in obedience to him.

She knew he looked at her as she climbed.

In the upper room, she glanced about. She had been there often to wipe the floor and collect the night-pot, but always when the Master was from the house.

There was a tiny window, shuttered against the weather and the dark. The bed was low and spread with a moldy fur—normally her mother would tidy the bed, but today the man slave had done so. In the room was a bad smell, not merely from its enclosure and the accumulation of bodily stinks. It was a corrupt smell.

When Volpa came down the ladder, Ghaio again looked at her. She had to lift her skirt away from her legs to manage the ladder. She gave him the paper.

Then Ghaio reached out and took hold, through slave's tunic and shift, of Volpa's center, the mound of her sex. Her instinct—entire and vital—was to leap away. But she was property. She kept still, as she had mostly had to do in the streets and market. Presently, apparently dissatisfied, he let go.

But, "We'll see," muttered Ghaio, as if promising her something. He was.

*   *   *

That night, Volpa dreamed.

Generally it seemed to her she never did. Rather it seemed that she went—elsewhere. And coming back at sunrise to the Auroria bell over the marshes, she was dazed from a long journey, exhausted by her slumber. And this lethargy mostly only left her gradually in the hour after she rose.

The place or places she had gone to in sleep she recollected only in fragments—some glimmering piece, like a bit of a broken dish, made of some costly substance, yet worthless since broken off. Besides, it soon faded. As she revived, she lost all memory, all *sense* of the countries of the night.

Her dreams she considered differently, and they were rare—or rarely did she recall them intact. The last one which she could at that time remember had been dreamed at the farm or estate from which her mother and she were sold off. Volpa had been then less than four years old. She was, in the dream, in an orchard, where all the trees were bold with fruit—perhaps only like the orchards of the foot hills and the Veneran Plain. Yet on one tree, at the orchard's center, was an unfamiliar crop. The globes that hung from its boughs were of gold and silver—the image not of metal, but of sunlight and moonlight. (Told of gold and silver once by some traveler at the farm, she had only been able to picture them as such.)

The tree of gold and silver, of suns and moons, attracted Volpa in the dream. She went to it, and began the slow circling dance her mother had taught her for trees.

Then, high in the branches, something moved that also shone. She thought it was a cat at first, but then she saw it had no legs, or ears, and instead of a pelt it was smooth and sheened as any of the fruits of the tree.

As she had told her mother this dream, the mother had grown anxious. "What did you do? Did you pick any of the fruits?"

"Oh no," said the child, "they would have burned me, I thought."

"And the snake?"

"Was it a snake?"

The mother nodded.

The child said, "It slid down and stared in my face. It had such beautiful eyes."

"But did it speak—or offer anything?"

"No, mumma."

Her mother's face had eased.

"And then?"

"Then you woke me."

"God forgive me that."

The night after her mother's death, and going up the ladder with Master looking up her legs, Volpa dreamed she was on the plain again, under the foothills.

Now, however, there were no villages or towns, and the land was covered by warm powder, or dust, very deep, so that as she walked, Volpa's feet sank far into it. Also there was before her only one mountain.

Realizing this, Volpa halted.

The mountain was astonishing. It was long, and had a curved, flattish top, and was colored a lucid flaming red—like a hearth or a sunset. A scarlet red, that had fluted shadows chiseled in it, and veins like living fire.

In wonderment Volpa stood, watching the mountain, which seemed to reflect the passage of clouds and suns. Then, she saw between herself and its incredible rock, figures dancing on the powdery plain. They were black, as if being by the fiery mountain had burned them. But something touched Volpa's foot, and looking down she saw a golden serpent rippling away through the sand.

When she woke, it was night, yet through the high window of the kitchen a full white moon was blazing. Somehow the contrast of its color scorched the dream of a red mountain into Volpa's brain.

She got up silently. The male slave lay sleeping in his corner. The houses were soundless, but for the lisp of the spring canal.

When she went out, the whole City of Ve Nera, Venus, seemed laid to sleep. Nothing stirred. No human voice nor cry of any creature, not one bell.

Volpa went to the fig tree and danced slowly around it, as she had done with her mother.

The boughs were silver with moonlight, but showed no hint of renewal.

On the Isle of the Dead her mother would be ashes now, and tipped in some hole. But the people in the dream were so black, surely they had been in fire and come back out of it, whole, and far stronger, better.

Once she had danced, Volpa leaned on the tree, holding it, and crying noiselessly. Her pain rose and fell like waves, and it occurred to her that perhaps God noted this, and the height of her suffering, and that by her grief she helped to buy the life beyond life in God's perfect world.

Then something rustled, up in the bare tree. And for half a second, Volpa thought it was her mother, become now an angel, perhaps black, and leaning through the branches to say something kind.

But when she looked, Volpa saw it was a scrap of some refuse, blown up there in the winter, now coming apart and so making movement and sound to deceive her.

2

As spring took hold, Ghaio felt new optimism. This was almost always to do with money. The untamed scents of sea and fish and sap that now filled Ve Nera, put a bounce in his step, but only so he went up the ladder more quickly to count the money.

Having counted it, he selected a bag of silver duccas and one gold venus, and dressed himself in his tatty best.

(There had been some talk of an edict against usury, when practiced by Christians. Ghaio did not think this could come to anything, but it was wise to stay friendly with the Church.)

The hired boat ferried him out on to the wide Fulvia lagoon. Ghaio Wood-Seller looked about. How much of the City could he now buy? How soon could he buy more?

The gift to the Church was a sensible insurance.

It was almost midday, and Ghaio was going to attend Midday Mass, the Solus, in the Primo.

The lagoon was a sheet of green silk. The very sort of silk for which Ve Nera had become a rival in the cities of Candisi and the East. After the winter, the buildings crowded round the lagoon looked dank and draggled, matted beasts that had slunk to drink. Then the shore-line opened into the great square, swept, and tinted like Juvanni's prettiest sweets. From which rose the moon-dome of the Basilica.

Ghaio would not mind the mass. Although impervious to the holy ritual and the ethereal singing, the gold ceiling was of some interest to him, and the jewels and magenta of the priests.

When his boat reached the bank, the bell began to call.

Ghaio got out, paid the boatman (meanly) and strutted across and in at an enormous door.

Black robes moved at the square's edges. Eyes and Ears noted the pious hurrying in to God.

Ghaio stepped into an alcove, and awarded his gift to the relevant hands, leaving his name as donor for the notice of the Council of the Lamb. He then moved on into the body of the temple. Here the poorest sat on the floor. The better classes had chairs. Several stared up, as now Ghaio commenced to do.

Arch rose through arch, minor dome through dome, until at last the ultimate circle lifted, as if weightless, high above. Gold. It was more like fire. And in the fire, the painted angels flew, pausing to raise their hands in blessing.

There were great treasures hidden here. Relics, standards, icons, thick with bullion and gems. . . . The apartments above, they said, had riches like those of Heaven itself—

How many chests of money would it take . . . ?

Angelic voices rang from the balconies, and Ghaio basked in his insurance. With God. If God did indeed exist, and the afterlife. But Ghaio turned his mind from his own demise. He would live long.

O God, the voices sang, *If I render to You all my heart, I am free. Yet, when You turn to me, You will demand of me everything. For Your love I must forget the world.*

A tavern song—surely?

Ghaio watched the priests, a cross stuck with rubies and chrysoprase.

Nearby a woman wept. They always did.

Not much longer and the show would be over. Then some dinner at an inn. Then two debtors to watch squirm.

By the time the Venus star stood over this City, Ghaio would be at home, and the Fox would come in her rags, bringing wine.

A twitch of feeling moved in Ghaio. After all the spring had found him, there in church. Sap and sea, milk and salt.

After the first dream of the scarlet mountain, for a time Volpa dreamed every night. Not entirely acquainted with dreams, she did not think to ponder that each one followed from the one before. They were like pages torn from an illuminated book, and falling down into her sleep, one after another, telling a story in bright pictures.

In the second dream, Volpa was aware of the summer heat of the wide plain. The sand was a terracotta shade and softly burned the soles of her feet, which in her sleep were bare.

On the land, between herself and the mountain, that in this second vision was darker, more of a maroon color, though glowing like a lamp, a haze of heat trembled. And out of this came walking a figure, slowly.

It was Volpa's mother.

Volpa felt at once very glad to see her. There was no memory that the mother had died. Only a joy which might have indicated some previous parting.

Then, as the woman moved nearer and nearer through the wavering pink air, Volpa saw she was almost naked, and though recognizably still the woman Volpa had known, younger—and darker of skin.

Volpa did nothing, only waited. When the woman reached her she touched Volpa's mouth with her palm. The mother smelled of hot things, stones and cinders. Volpa thought, vaguely, *Oh, it's that she was burned, on the Isle.* There was no terror in that. Here her mother stood, compact and alive.

When her mother spoke to Volpa, Volpa realized it was in another language. Even so, Volpa understood it, and was able, in turn, to utter it.

After this, they walked away over the land.

Waking, the girl never knew what they had said to each other, beyond a phrase of two. Her mother seemed to be teaching her things. In Volpa's infancy, the mother had done this as a matter of course, and necessity. It was simple to resume the manner of it. In the later years, Volpa had perhaps missed her mother's conversation, her advice, her stories. Now the dreams themselves were the stories, and the advice was inherent in them.

After the second dream, came others.

When Volpa woke in the cold spring dawns, to skim frost from the cistern, to cook as best she could Ghaio's porridges and rice, and bake his bread, the dreams did not fade. They sank back a little, as if replaced neatly into the revealed book from which they had fallen to her mind.

They were also, the dreams, very similar, for the most part.

Always the mountain was at the center of them, curved, striated, and a rich red. Sometimes the land had tufts of grass, boulders, even groups of blond trees with tasseled foliage on the boughs. The time of day was always late, near sunfall probably. Things cheeped from the low thickets. Birds of wild dyes flew over, or settled in the trees like topazes, jacinths.

In every dream, however, Volpa's mother darkened. Her hair grew black and her skin like brown ebony. She seemed comfortable with this, changing her skin. Her teeth were very white, and often she raised her arms, lifting by the gesture her heavy naked breasts. She laughed. Every thing which she taught to Volpa—which consistently, as with the conversations, Volpa did not recall on waking— seemed nevertheless good. That is, benign. It made the girl happy, and made the mother happy to dispense it, like nourishing food or the kiss of love.

One of the few phrases of speech Volpa retained was this: that she said to her mother, "Why do you teach me all this now you've gone away?" And the mother had replied, "How could I teach it to you, when I was with you?" In the dream that had seemed, quite reasonably, to explain everything.

Sometimes, other people crossed their path, literally appearing to move on other specific but—to Volpa—invisible roads. They were invariably a little way off or greatly distant. All were black. Sometimes they raised their hands in greeting.

Volpa and her mother wandered. Now and then, the mother would lean and snatch something from the grass or the sand, or out of a tree. These things were often live animals, but curious in form. Either Volpa or her mother then carried them on. The animals did not struggle. When Volpa grew hungry, she and her mother would sit down, and the mother would make a fire. She did this by rubbing her hand along a piece of stick. Volpa watched, fascinated, seeing first a thin smoke, and then a tongue of flame lick up.

When the fire was ready, the mother would shake it off on to the earth, and here it would burn. Then she would place in the fire the animals they had collected. There was nothing horrible or bizarre in this. The animal would vanish at once, and reappear *almost* at once, on the ground a few strides away. There it would run or preen a few moments, before darting off. After that, Volpa would have the sense of having eaten something delicious. She was no longer hungry, but satisfied, as she had rarely been when fed on the scraps of Ghaio's house.

In rather a similar, equally peculiar way, as they wandered, once or twice Volpa saw one of the animals prey on another. There would be a chase or a struggle, but when it was done, the prey animal would only get up and go off, or, on one occasion, it lay down companionably by the creature which had stalked it, and together they sunned themselves under the metallic sky.

The dreams came, if Volpa could have counted, for twenty-one nights. They were very alike in all but slight details. She and her mother, though circling the red mountain and sometimes even seeming to approach it, never reached the place.

Yet the last dream had one great alteration. In this dream, night had come. As Volpa stepped forward into it, the sand was gray under her feet, and ahead of her stood the mountain, as ever, but now it was the blackest of all things, the fount of the night itself.

"Come, make up the fire," said Volpa's mother. So they sat down, and Volpa took the stick, which always came at once, from nowhere, and she rubbed her hand along it as she had seen her mother do. Her hand felt warm, then cold.

Through the dark, the flame birthed clear and yellow. She set it on the sand. The mother said, "Now always you can make fire."

Then they looked up to the sky, which was quite light, far lighter than the earth or the mountain. And it was scaled with brilliant stars. Over the sky too went a shimmering ribboning path, which seemed to rise out of the smoke of their fire.

Winds blew across the plain, that sang almost in human voices. Somewhere things chorused like bubbles opening on the surface of water.

Did mother and daughter speak? What did the mother say to her child? Volpa thought her mother told her a story. That years ago Volpa had come to her as the woman walked, but this was before Volpa had been born. "Let me in," said Volpa. "Who are you?" said the mother. But Volpa had only flown into the body of the woman like a tiny white moth.

"What are the stars?" Volpa asked in the last dream.

"Yesterday," said the woman, now black as the night mountain. "Tomorrow."

When Volpa woke, she began to cry. Worse than at her mother's death, she felt bereft. The mortal City dawn was coming up through the yard. The dreaming was over.

It was sunset when Ghaio returned to his house. The bells of the Venusium, the service of the evening star, were ringing across the City. The bell of Santa La'Lacrima sounded hoarse from over the lagoon, as it sometimes did in the spring.

Ghaio was disgruntled. The two debtors had both paid up all their debt, triumphant rather than squirming. Coins appealed to him less than power, although he was not aware of this, and blamed his mood on other things—the bells, the tedious mass he had attended, the bad cooking of the stupid slave girl who now kept his home.

Red dimmed above the canal. Ghaio's walls darkened, and the alley further along seemed black and ominous, as if robbers might lurk there.

Ghaio scrambled from the hired boat, and in at his door. He locked it thoroughly and let down the great bar. Safe now.

"What's this muck?" he demanded as the bowl was set before him.

"Fish stew."

"That old fool. He can buy nothing any more. Can't see. Can't hear. Useless. Call this fish? You'll have to do it. Market for the food. And improve your kitchen skills."

The candles beamed as Ghaio thrust a lump of bread into the stew and brought it to his snout. The bread was burned, as often now, and Ghaio, having champed and swallowed, turned and cuffed the girl.

The touch of her resilient flesh, springing at the blow, reminded him. He grunted, and drank some wine.

"Tonight," said Ghaio. "Upstairs." Then, a strange caution overcame him. He added, "I want you to help me count my money."

And the naive girl said, "I can't add up, signore."

"I'll learn you, then." This made him chuckle. "Yes, I'll learn you, Foxy. Climb up the ladder as soon as you hear the Moon Bell from Santa La'La."

When her chores were done, Volpa drew water and warmed it, and washed her hair. She had no idea why she did this, for hygiene was irregular among the slaves. The nights were cold still, yet the hearth had some fire left there, and here she dried the mass of tresses, seeing the flames shine through as she rag-rubbed and combed them with her mother's broken comb.

Already the old man slave slept in his corner, but Volpa did not dare lie down. She was afraid she would sleep through the Luna Vigile—the Moon Bell, which called the priesthood again to pray, about two hours before midnight.

Her mother had frequently had to be up late to serve Ghaio. Her mother had never specified what these late duties entailed, beyond the carrying of food and drink.

Had she too helped Ghaio count his cash?

Volpa, despite her care, dozed. She wakened with a start to hear the bell, eerie and far away in the vastness of night.

Her hair was dry, the fire was out. In the yard, as she hurried across it, she smelled the aroma of the stacked wood. And, for the first time, she saw the fig tree showed no buds. She realized with a pang of sadness, almost fear, that the tree had died that winter, even as her mother had died. Ghaio would cut it down to increase his stock. And then only the dead would be there, in bundles in the barren yard.

3

Climbing the ladder, the girl was glad Master was not sitting below, watching her legs—for that had made her uncomfortable. This way, he saw her head first, the hair all crushed in again under its cloth. And she saw him as she never had in her life, sitting on his mattress, which was ancient and stuffed with straw, and contributed greatly to the room's foul odor. He wore a loose robe, rather short, so under it his bony, veined and hairy legs stuck out. If she had been a child, she might have wanted to laugh at this, but now it only faintly repulsed her.

Far, far away, the bell ebbed to silence.

She was afraid for a moment that he would reprimand her for being late.

No such thing. He seemed quite jolly. And his color was high.

"Here you are," he said.

She could hardly fail to be struck—not by his hand this time—but by his changed demeanor.

Volpa did not know Ghaio had decided he might take her even into his bed. She was a virgin after all, and could prove awkward at this first exercise. They were better on their backs for that.

Besides, she was young, and smooth. He did not in the end dislike the notion of her by him, in the night, perhaps convenient for a second game. And this too tickled him, the thought that he might utterly surprise her.

"Now, Volpa. If you're to help with the cash, you must take off your clothes."

She stared at him. Which amused him.

"You see, you might thieve a coin otherwise. I daren't risk it. If you're bare, you can't stow anything away."

Even at the word *bare,* (pleasing him) his tool rose under the robe. Oh, he was man enough.

"Come now, come on," he said, pretending impatience, "are you daft? Do as you're told."

She was a slave. Molded in obedience. With a shrinking that—for Volpa—had no real reason, she pulled off her slave's tunic, and then, in a kind of frenzy of shame, her shift.

Ghaio lay back, and dropping his hand in his lap, fondled himself.

Now this was not so bad. Despite her ineptitude with the food, he had an article of value here. It would not last, of course. A year or so, and she would be dross. Feed well then, while he might.

"And that scarf. Take it off. Not a stitch. Or I can't trust you."

In one wild movement she ripped the rag from her hair.

Five or six candles were burning in the chamber. Ghaio had wanted a proper look.

Now, for a second, he was startled.

His possession was, as he knew, very young, and very slender—but not after all skin and skeleton. Over the fragile bones, the creamy flesh had covered her, well made and perfectly fitted, like a lord's glove. Yet she was so pale, even the round little beads on her breasts barely the shade of watered wine—a match to her mouth. And her eyes, which never before had he noticed, were also pale, a sort of amber color; now he thought of it—just like the eyes of the fox he had seen once, in a picture. In her groin, however, these pallors deepened and flushed alive. She was *red*-amber, there. But that had not prepared him for her hair, nor its evocation.

Had he not once thought her hair like fire? Yes, for so it was. It blew out from her head, framing the whiteness of her body. In length, it fell below her knees. It could be worth cutting, this hair, and selling. But he might let her keep it . . . It gave him quite a thrill, the sight of it, that red mantle round her white.

Indeed, she was *like* a flame. The blanched center, the carmine rim.

"Come over here," he thickly said.

He could scent her, this vixen, this flame. Her rufus tang, the youth of her body. Sweet—

When Ghaio caught hold of her and spun her down on the stinking bed, Volpa thought she had again enraged him, and prepared at once for cuffs and slaps or worse.

Instead, perhaps only slightly less brutal, his hands clenched, one on her right breast and the other on her sex.

Ghaio laughed in her face.

"Now we come to it, eh, Volpa?"

Before, when he had grabbed hold of her, (on the evening of her mother's death) she had not questioned it, though it had filled her with panic. That sexual affront had seemed only one more lashing out. (Another more ferocious extension of the assaults in the market.) Now, a recollection surfaced. She saw again the cart in the rain, and her own mother under the awning and under Ghaio, her body wracked and shaken by his use of it.

This use Volpa had never understood. Nor did she now. Simply, she was afraid. Yet it was a dread beyond anything she had ever known.

"Give me a kiss, girl," said Ghaio. "That rosy mouth. And those white teeth—oh yes. Let me taste you."

And Ghaio kissed her.

At this she managed, her horror acting as a bow, to fire herself away from him.

Ghaio fell on his face and breathed, in place of fragrant youth and charming fear, the smelly bed.

"Come back, you slut. Where are you off to?"

She had stumbled away, but before she could get up from her knees, he caught her leg. Ah, so smooth, like marble, yet not so hard, nor so unfeeling.

"Stay still. I'm your master." He dragged her back and now, turning, not even thinking what she did, she hit him in the mouth.

Ghaio yowled.

No other had smitten him, not in twenty years, and certainly not a female, nor a slave.

His face darkened. A new stench, the effluvia of rage, streamed from his pores.

"You'll lie down here with me, or you'll be made sorry."

She was across the room. She stood by her discarded clothes, not bending yet to snatch them. A weird pose—her arms not clamped protectively to her body, coyly shielding breasts or loins, as even Venus, in certain lewd pictures, sometimes did.

No, the arms of Volpa were outflung. Her head poked forward a little, like a snake's. And the scarlet wind of hair blew all about her, seeming sentient.

Its color—it had increased, become extraordinary—orange, like the golden citruses brought on trees from the East—some effect of the candles, no doubt—he scarcely noticed.

"Lie *down,* you trull. Lie down and take what I give. Or I'll flay your back and peaches for you. Do you want that, eh? Have your master or have the flail—want *that* eh? Or *me?*"

Through Volpa's brain things flashed. Not thoughts, let alone words. Lightnings, gusts of intolerable brilliancy.

She let out a barking scream.

It checked Ghaio.

What was she, this bitch, truly some beast?

A motion, of her body or of some other thing which was in the room with them, put out the candles, every one.

But they were not needed. For now Volpa herself gave light.

She was incandescent. The white of her flesh was blazing, blinding him. He could no longer make out her features, eyes or lips— not even the fleece at her loins.

Yet the outer hair—surely it did burn? Oranges and gold, lava that poured from some erupting mountain Ghaio Wood-Seller had never seen.

"Stop this, you scunny harlot." He got up off his couch. He rubbed his hands together, as he thought, to ready them for violence. But they were slick with sweat. That posture of hers. It was like that of some bird of prey, the wings out, the head thrust forward.

Ghaio stood on the mattress. He could not credit what he saw.

The hair of his slave—was *bursting.*

Who made that noise? It was Ghaio now, screaming. "Holy Virgin spare me—God save me—"

The hair of the slave had exploded outwards, and for a moment the girl was the core of an incendiary storm. It swirled upward, to either side, behind her. Her hair had filled the room.

Ghaio's eyes scorched. The shrill hair dazzled him.

Abruptly he was freezing cold. He clutched his arms about himself and shrieked as flames rushed up them. He was naked too, his robe burnt off, but clad in fire.

Ghaio danced. In the middle of the light, he was turning black. And the shell of the room broke like an egg.

When the roof flew off, he might have seen the night held in a net of glory. But, screeching, he only danced, and swallowed fire, and was made dumb.

Volpa had lost interest in him. She felt herself droop, and as she did so, her mind grew cool and dim. Two wings seemed to fold about her, and her eyes shut fast. She rolled into a silent emptiness, exactly like a sleep that had no dreams.

"What's that glow? Is it morning?"

"No, Lucha. A house is on fire on the Seven Keys Canal."

"Fire—!"

"Lie still. It's not so close. We doused the inn roof with water, to be sure."

Luchita looked out wearily, between the pains, at her husband. "Only one house?"

"Three, to be exact. But they're dipping up water from the canal. It's almost out."

Another pain came, and Luchita cried aloud.

Her husband hurried from the room.

She would lose this child. It was too early.

"Oh God—why do you make me suffer like this? I never even *enjoyed* it—"

She hated God. Pointless to dissemble. He would know.

In the window the red glare faltered, then waxed again.

The girl came in, with the old midwife from the marshes, old Maria with her ten black teeth.

"Best be quick," said this crone, "Venus is afire."

The girl looked scared and sprang from the room. Luchita said, "Three houses only, so he told me."

"Three so far. And the alleys full of wasps—" Luchita stared. The witch pointed straight at the window. Some insects were buzzing there drearily, dropping in and crawling on the floor. "A nest in his wood-stacks. It was the wood-seller's Red House. The heat of the fire hatched them too early. Only one body's brought out. The slave man from the yard, curled up and black. But they say there was a girl, and the miser himself, Ghaio."

Pain came. Luchita cried loudly.

Dying wasps hardly born drizzled in twos and threes into the room. Poor things, like the child, forced on too soon.

The witch trod on the wasps. She would be as blunt with the woman and the baby.

But the fire was dulling now.

The crone peered from the window. "There's a beggar at your door," she said. Everything was of interest to her save her trade, she had seen too much of that.

Below in the street, the beggar looked up at the window as Luchita howled.

Two men, shouldering from the inn to visit the fun on Seven Keys, strode by the beggar, knocking her aside.

Volpa sat down on the ground by the inn door. She had forgotten who she was, and where she was, if she had ever known either. Lusterless wan brown, her long hair flimsily veiled her. Her skin was like unleavened dough. She had been reclothed in something, perhaps her shift—but did not know it. She was cold, so cold. She rested her head on her knees and forgot the world.

Above her, meaningless as bells, the cries came and went for another two hours, until Luchita had brought forth her stillborn boy.

PART TWO

Then saw I a vixen seeming starved.

DANTE ALIGHIERI
The Divine Comedy

1

The night turned slowly as a wheel, spiked with stars. But he had forgotten that. The heat of new summer had brought scents and miasmas. These were shut out. The thick walls fortressed a lagoon of coolness, and the flavors, solely, of olibanum and myrrh.

Heaven was like this. Pure, chilled, perfumed, and silent, save with faint fair musics. A sky of burnished ghostly gold.

The window rose behind the altar. In darkness without tints, until a flutter of summer lightning briefly and inaccurately colored it, the white face of the Virgin, framed in a damson mantle. She maintained her vigil, as did he, the knight of God kneeling at her feet.

It was required of them. But some kept the Vigil (from the midnight bell until the dawn Auroria) only for the six watches obligatory during the course of one year. Cristiano was of that number who kept the Vigil once in every month, save during times of war. In winter, evidently, it was the most taxing. Kneeling straightbacked before the altar from midnight until sunrise—some seven or eight hours. (Some slept, slumping. Others regularly got up and marched about the chapel. Some fainted.)

After his very first watch—he had been seventeen years of age, and it was winter—Cristiano, who had not moved all night, had gone out into the courtyard, his legs had failed him, and he had vomited. Within a year though, he had grown accustomed, physically, to the ordeal.

There was no overt competition among the Bellatae Christi, the Soldiers of God. The proofs of faith, both in arms and in prayer, were a private matter. So Cristiano perfected his skills as a worshipping priest in the same spirit that he honed his fighting ability. By the age of twenty, few could outmatch him in the practice yard of the Militarium. None, in the church.

Of course, the Vigils had long ago ceased to be for him a test of endurance. While he himself had never seen the act in that way. He had understood and believed that the Vigil would bring him nearer, not only to God, but to the *Will* of God. So, even pain had not delayed him. Perhaps, in fact, had driven him the faster to his goal.

For there was always pain, in the first hour or two. Under the lashes of it, Cristiano would rise up into his mind, which soon became then a clear sparkling crystal, not unlike the substance of a star. Here he would wait, timelessly indifferent to the qualms of a body which only youth—and considerable reserves of trained strength—kept in the desired position.

As his soul stood above the body, pain was next burned away by a sheer white radiance.

When the radiance began, which was usually in the first or second hour, but sometimes in the third, Cristiano would tremble. For this coming of white light was the announcement, the *herald,* of the approach of God.

Although he would give way to nothing human, to this Cristiano surrendered.

And then, he would enter into a sphere of ecstasy so otherwise unimaginable, and afterwards so unretainable, that all things, world, time, reason, life itself, seemed stopped or left behind. It was the foretaste of the immortal state, this transcendence. It was beyond any physical pleasure, impossible in its wonder and effulgence, yet nearly always now achievable, by him.

Only the sounding of the dawn bell could bring him down from the height. Then he would sink back, drained yet renewed, into the leaden casque of flesh. Thin sun beams on the stony floor would scatter as his shadow finally crossed them.

That he relished such delight was unavoidable. Was it thus greed, to keep the Vigil so often? No. He had faith that nothing would be given him, should he be found unfit. And once or twice, when the supernal had failed him, that is, he had failed *it,* he had felt a horrible downfall. But despair was a sin. He threw depression from him swiftly, and working the harder at his office of priest, fasting, scourging his body, so pushing this body further off from him, he would find always that the next Vigil brought him again into the realm of the Divine. Into the exquisite duality of awareness and oblivion, which he knew to be God.

Cristiano was a virgin. Among the Bellatae chastity was the code, as with every priest. If any broke the rule and were discovered to have done so, the order thrust them out.

To Cristiano such a thing would have been insanity to contemplate, too stupid to consider. Besides, what joy of the flesh could compare to the crucial and excruciating ravishment gained by communion with God?

In war, there was another joy, it was true, which came also, since such wars were holy, from God. Then the crystal of the mind was not diamond white, but a deep red, like the bloody spinel. The vigor that coursed through the knight was like fire and wine, carnal enough, permissible only since God had willed it. (Such had ignited the Crusades in prior centuries.) When Cristiano rode in a sea of gore, swinging blades of steel in hands of brass, he was, even then, God's instrument, less a man than a battle chariot, and Christ astride him, the Charioteer.

To take life in the service of the Creator was neither sinful nor cruel. It was just.

Returning to the world was always strange. The City, the beings which peopled it, were alien and curious.

Cristiano had attended the Dawn Mass. Now he visited the knight's castra, broke his fast, with bread dipped in wine, and washed in the cold water from the Primo's clean wells. He was no longer tired, and would not look for sleep until this evening.

Less than an hour later, the boat took him through the Silvian Marsh. Today, before the full heat of morning arrived, the smell of salt was strong. Green reeds and brown grasses grew along the water channels, taller in places than a woman. Gulls and other birds soared and sailed, and here and there in the reeds nests were visible, stocked with young chicks. Elsewhere, some men waded with nets and slings.

Houses still stood in the marshland. Many were ruinous. Gardens had become lakes, from which rose dying cypresses. The old amphitheater was only a ghostly hump on the horizon towards the sea, but they passed close to the Roman temple. Ragged boys, who were fishing there, shouting, went stone-still, seeing the warrior-priest rowed by. Between the greened-over columns, they squinted out at him.

Even the boatman was wary. They always were. When the boat bumped home against the bank of the channel, the Silvian Quarter rising in its yellowing summer tones behind, he took his payment and dropped to one knee.

"Bless me, brother."

Cristiano gave him the blessing—it was a fault, but with indifference. The man did not seem yet quite real. Nor any of it.

Only Christ Himself, a deity who had once been human, could take in the fall of sparrows after the height of the sun.

Cristiano walked up the alleys to the inn. The morning was loud with living bustle, like the activity of the birds in the marsh. Washing hung out, and there came the clang of pots, a fug of cooking and dirt.

By the inn door two or three beggars sat on the ground, their backs to a wall. Cristiano paid them no heed. Men had their stations from God, or a calling to some task, as had happened with himself.

His bother-in-law, the drunk, slunk out. "Soldier of God—Cristiano—welcome, welcome. She's much better today. Will you have a cup?"

"You know I won't."

"Yes, Cristiano. She's in her garden."

In the room, the early drinkers glanced uneasily. But the Soldier of God barely noticed them.

He went on through the corridor and out by the little door where he had to stoop.

The garden was not large, but high-walled. Peaches and vines stretched on frames. In the beds were herbs, and salads and vegetables, with his sister moving slowly among them.

A servant girl, one of the inn slovens, carried the basket and a knife for weeding.

Luchita looked no better, he thought. Her body had lost its shape with the last birth. Until this one, that had not happened. Besides, she had borne healthily three sons and a daughter. The dead baby was a shock to her. She had caught Cristiano's hand on his first visit. "You'll say it's my punishment." Cristiano said, "If you feel it to be so, then perhaps it is." At which she had railed against him so violently, he was afraid for her, took her in his arms and said, "No, Luchita. Your sin wasn't such a powerful one. And you repented, you told me so. Be glad for the child, He spared it the agony of this world." But Cristiano did not believe anything he said. She had committed adultery, which only Christ could forgive. And the world was the Militarium of the soul, where it learned to fight and fine itself for Heaven. To be spared was to be cheated, and God cheated no one, only gave what was earned.

Now Cristiano's sister walked to him along the path, and even her walk had changed, less graceful. She kneeled down suddenly, as the boatman had.

"Give me your blessing."

So he stretched out his hand and blessed her, and she became real for him. And the garden, warming, and a bird singing in a small twisted fruit tree.

"How are you doing, Luchita?"

"Oh, well enough."

They sat on a bench by the house wall, and the servant moved alone about the plants, now cutting something, now tying something up.

"This is a thriving garden."

"Yes. I'm the Good Housewife. I do my best. It's never easy. But I like these things. The way they answer care. I sometimes think," she paused, then said, "kindness and love might improve humankind. Better than struggle and suffering."

"God tells us this very thing, Luchita."

He expected her to say sullenly, in her unlessoned woman's manner, "Then why does He never show it us?" But she only sighed.

The servant cut off a large head of salad stuff with a crisp snap. It was forward, he thought, but then the garden caught the sun at this time of the year. He was going to congratulate his sister again, and realized that she bored him, and this was another fault.

"Tell me what you've been doing, Lucha."

"What do I ever do?"

(He had taught her to read when they were children. But she had, here, no chance for or use for books.)

"My poor girl. Remember, care also for yourself. You've received a blow, a wound. It must have space to heal."

"That child? Oh. It means nothing now. If it had lived a few hours, if I'd held it—but there wasn't anything to hold. I blamed old Maria, it's true, the mid-wife. Said it was her fault. Foolish. I always lose my children." Perhaps she saw him frown. She said, "Then Maria said it was a girl under the window who was to blame, a witch, who set a spell on me so Maria's wonderful cleverness was to no avail—"

Cristiano's thought wandered. It was the image of a window

. . . The Virgin in her mantle, the delicacy of her face, beyond beauty. And the light which filled him—He brought his mind back sharply.

Luchita was looking up at him. "You're so handsome, Cristiano. So splendid in your armor. And your golden hair, so thick it breaks a comb—oh, I remember. What a waste. What a *waste* to be a priest—"

Anger moved in him, the dark beast he must resist. "You know, Lucha, I don't like you to say these things. I belong to God."

"You belong to the *world*. Look at you! Any woman could love you. Or a man—"

"Luchita."

"Hold my tongue. Yes. But you might have had sons, Cristiano. Think of that. God knows I mourn the loss of them more than that dead thing Maria pulled out of me."

Cristiano got up. Alerted by his closed fury, which seethed invisibly yet white-hot about him, even the servant cowered, and the bird left off its song.

And at that moment a raucous shouting broke out over the wall.

Luchita jumped up too, wincing and flushed.

"It's mad Berbo, I know his voice. The girl must be there, and he's seen her. The numskull. There are Eyes and Ears all through the quarter today—"

And leaving Cristiano, as if abruptly he had lost his value, she ran heavily back into the inn. The servant girl ran after her, clutching the salad.

Cristiano followed them, irritated, and keeping himself in check.

The inn had erupted into the alley beyond. From upper windows and from doors too, people pressed to see and jeer.

A man in decent garments stood shouting, frothing somewhat at the lips. Pointing.

And from somewhere, probably off the canal, two other men came, in black robes, and took hold of him.

Cristiano disliked the Eyes and Ears of God. But, impartially, he accepted their necessity—in certain areas. Not here, surely? This fellow was crazed, as Luchita said.

But the madman was turning now, clinging to the two black priests.

"Praise God that sent you! Brothers—see—that witch—that Making of Satanus—"

Cristiano turned his head a little. Who was it that this shouting imbecile had singled out for his obsession? It must be the waif there, barely more than a child, skinny and filthy, with matted brownish hair tied up in a cloth. She looked harmless, and unimportant. And yet, thin as a pin, white as sullied snow, she drew his eyes back, and back again.

Her own were downcast. She seemed not to know the outcry concerned her. Containment—guilt—also madness?

"Quiet," said one of the Eyes and Ears to the madman. "What are you saying?"

"I say she's a minion of Hell."

"Be aware of your accusation. *Who* is?"

"That one, there."

"What has she done?"

To his disgust, Cristiano detected a spice of interest in the priest's nasal voice.

The Soldier of God moved forward, and became the center of the scene.

At once the deranged man attempted to kneel to him (the third one this morning) and hung from the priests' grip, They glared, not liking to be, conceivably, usurped.

And Luchita spoke up hurriedly.

"Holy brothers—she's only a beggar. She wanders about. I feed her crusts and the scrapings of the rice kettle, from charity. I gave her a cloth to cover her hair. She does no one hurt. She's addled. And Berbo, too."

Berbo was kneeling, despite the priests, who unwillingly let him go, only looming over him, like black shadows cast up from his turmoil.

"Bellatoro—warrior of God—*you'll* listen. Let me speak."

"Very well."

Cristiano pulled his eyes away from the girl. He was almost glad to, and did not know why.

The kneeling Berbo, no longer shouting, now apparently in control, offered his words with the skill of an actor.

The crowd which had gathered, attended breathlessly. But Cristiano, resistant to such fantasies, set himself on guard.

"It was the night—over a month back—when there was a fire on the Canal of the Keys. Oh, protect me, blessed brothers. A fiend comes and torments me when I speak of it. I shout and stammer and no one believes—"

None uttered a sentence.

Mad Berbo, if he was, glanced round, then, averting his gaze from the beggar girl, continued without a break.

He lived over by the next canal, but came through the alleys to watch the fire. Men were drawing up buckets of water, but he saw no need to assist; as he put it, he did not wish to impede their work. Instead he went through another alley to the back of the houses, only one of which was then alight. It was the Red House of Ghaio Wood-Seller, who was said to have a hoard of money.

The purpose of Berbo was plain to most of those who heard. He had hoped to be able to locate some outer stash of coins and make off with them.

Reaching the back yard, where the smoke was less, he found all neighbors had seemingly fled in fear of the fire's spreading. Some refuse by the yard wall enabled him to climb it, and look over.

In the yard, the timber, in stacks and bundles, shone with the red light of the fire, and sparks spun everywhere, but had not yet caught anything but a tree by the cistern.

Berbo thought time was short for investigation, and besides it would be chancy. As he hesitated, he beheld a very frightening thing. In the upper story of the house was one narrow window, and this was filled by the fire. Until all at once the fire came out of the window, not in flames or sparks or smoke, but in an upright leaping shape.

This, flying into the air, dropped straight down again to the yard, and landed there.

Berbo, who had let out a yelp, discerned next instant that this apparition was only the figure of some hapless person, caught alight in the burning room, and jumping frenziedly forth. He expected it to roll shrieking on the ground. It did not.

Rather, it stood up.

At this very moment, a gust of flame shot through the house top, and rained spangles in the yard. (Sounds of alarm rose from the front of the house.)

Just then too, Berbo was aware of a golden liquid ribbon which ran out from the window. Was this Ghaio's gold, melting?

Something made him forget the gold.

The figure which had sprung down in the yard, and which he had expected by now to be dead, was still standing. Indeed, it had *righted* itself.

There was no doubt that it was on fire. It *blazed.* A woman, as he could just make out. Her hair was a vivid red, and redder from the fire in it. He saw her *through* and *in* the fire.

"She was young, and wearing only a white shift. And it all was burning—the shift, her hair, her body—she was furled in flames that never went out—that never ate her up."

One of the black priests said, "He's mad."

Cristiano, to his own surprise, answered, "Hear him out before you judge."

Berbo exclaimed, "She burned—but she didn't burn, Signore Bellatoro. She burned but never was *burned.*"

"So you have said. What then?"

Irked at the brusqueness of this blond untonsured priest, standing there in maculum and sword, Berbo rasped, "Doesn't the Bible speak of wonders, eh? And terrible uncanny things that attend the Evil One, Lucefero?"

"I'm more concerned with what *you* are speaking of."

Berbo pulled a face. He said he had been transfixed by fear, and as he clung on the wall, the woman walked—*walked,* neither ran nor stumbled—about the yard, and everything—she touched it. And where she touched, that thing took fire.

"Hadn't sparks already set the wood alight?"

"*No,* signore. It smoldered here and there. But where she put her hands—I could see them in the fire—flames burst up. She was a walking *fire-brand.*"

There had been a darkened kitchen in the yard, and until then it had seemed unoccupied, but now it's roof was smoking, and the uprights of the door. All at once the door opened and an old man came out.

"I thought he'd been asleep perhaps, and I was sorry for the poor soul—but then I saw he wasn't in a fix, only standing there looking about at it all on fire, and he was grinning, and praising God."

One of the black priests said, "Too many madmen in this tale."

"I can't help it, brother. It's the truth."

The burning girl was by this time at the tree, which had been all but consumed by then. Still she was circling round and round it, like a sort of dance. "That's when I knew for sure she was a witch. The country witches do it. They dance about the trees. So then I knew the fire was her spell, and that was why she didn't burn up in it."

But, said Berbo, the old man, a slave, probably, now hurried across, and he stretched out his hands to the fire witch.

"Excuse me, signore, but I wet my drawers when I saw that. I went cold in my belly. Do you know what he said to her? No, I'll tell you. I heard him say, *'You are the torch of God.'* "

The crowd which had laughed at Berbo's admission of incontinence, now produced a silence as dense as iron.

Some of them crossed themselves.

Cristiano spoke very clearly. "And could you have misheard?"

"No. *Never*. But then, don't witches call *him* 'God' sometimes—him, the *other* one."

"You're well versed in the manners of witches."

"Who isn't? You have to be cautious."

Berbo said that the fire-witch left the tree and went to the old man and touched him. And of course, he too went up like a piece of fat thrown on the hearth.

"He never cried out once. He seemed dancing, too. Round and round, till he fell down and curled up like an insect. And then the wasps came out."

"Wasps."

"From the burning wood. Must have been three or four nests there in the timber. Hatched 'em. I've seen a man die of wasp stings. I got my legs under me and I ran."

Berbo stood up from his kneeling. He dusted the knees of his leggings, the action of a prudent, fussy man, not a mad one.

"And what has this to do with the girl there?" asked one of the Eyes and Ears.

Berbo said, mumbling now, as if embarrassed suddenly, "It was her, her in the wood-seller's yard."

"The witch you saw was covered by fire, you said."

"I saw her *through* the fire. It's her."

Cristiano did not want to look at the girl again. She was a shred of human life, pathetic, of no consequence. And for Berbo's story, how many cups of ale had he taken, despite the new taxes, before he climbed the wall?

The warrior-priest turned his head once more.

At that second, the beggar girl raised her own.

At the movement, the rag slipped back from her hair a little. Not brown hair, but a dull and dirty red. The face a white triangle with pale yellow eyes. A *fox's* face. The fox which, in legend, was the devil's familiar dog, even his disguise.

"And you, girl. What do you say?" It was a black priest again who addressed her.

And Luchita, again, interposed. "Gentle brothers, she doesn't speak. I never heard her. No one has. Look at her—does she look burned? Does she look cunning or supernatural?"

Yes. The thought jumped starkly forward in Cristiano's brain. Cunning, supernatural, both. And—*holy,* holy in some incoherent, awful and total way, as a fallen angel might, perhaps, that once had been bright winged in Heaven before its fall.

Berbo shook himself. He said, "All right. None would listen before. I've told it now. I'm done with it."

Both of the Eyes and Ears watched Berbo as he marched abruptly away. They would learn his house. He might well receive a call from them, or from others. To accuse, as to be accused, was not always simple.

The girl had lowered her head and her eyes.

One of the priests said, to Luchita, "Will you sponsor her, then? Swear that she's innocent?"

Luchita opened her mouth. Cristiano was quicker.

"The inn-wife is my sister. I vouch for her as an honest woman. But she can't pass judgment on such a thing. She's fed the wretch to save her from starving, no more."

"What then to do, Bellator?" The priests stared resentfully and arrogantly at him. "Should we take her to the Primo and question her?"

The crowd muttered. Ve Nera knew that some taken to the Primo on such business did not come out, or came out damaged. The Council of the Lamb was determined in its service to God: it was better to kill a man than risk his soul.

A woman cried, "She's only a kit! What does Berbo know?

But a surly man remarked, "If she's a witch, she needs seeing to."

Cristiano too was well aware of the interrogations which sometimes were carried on in the under-rooms of the Basilica. They had been a cause of discussion in his own mind. It was a fact also, if he had not stood in the path, they might have been off with her already.

He took a chance, rashly, like a boy. Half offending himself.

"I vouch for my sister, and she vouches for the girl. That's enough. I myself will see to it."

"But," began the fatter of the Eyes and Ears.

"You will leave it with me and save yourselves the trouble. You've enough work in the City as it is."

2

That winter, a high tide had flooded the square before the Primo
Suvio. Now artisans were commemorating, in black and gold mosaic, the large octopus found washed up by the Lion Door.

Fra Danielus, who had not partaken of the—reportedly tasty—
corpse, looked down at the work from a gallery above.

On this sunny day, with its promise of heat, the Magister Major
was conscious of much pleasure in the world. In the beauty of the
Primo. Its enormous dome which, from the Fulvia lagoon, looked
like nothing so much as a gigantic pearl. The courtyards with their
busy yet sedate procedures, the cappella and castra (barracks) of the
knights, their roofs of silver and gold, the pure fountain which
plunged into a basin of white marble, supported by four lions done
in gilded bronze. From the gallery of the Angel Tower, where
Danielus stood, all this, besides the artisans, was visible.

Moving on, around the Tower's huge side, it would be easy to
see, too on such a cloudless day, the phantom forms of distant
mountains. While the Laguna stretched like silvered glass to the sea
wall and the lit curve of ocean, the faint drifts of insubstantial islands like aberrations of some fine mind, profligate only with loveliness.

Yet, to every rose, a thorn.

Fra Danielus considered also this. Like the thorn, it was perceptible, (in the paper he had left lying in his book-chamber.) Like the
thorn, it would not be felt until one put one's hand thereon.

Danielus turned his eyes down to the City. Which thrived and
moved. Not having felt, yet, the thorn.

Last summer, from this very tower, the priesthood had hung out
seven "bird-cages," low enough that the citizens might observe how
the six men and one woman swung in them and starved to death.

They were persons of wickedness, thieves and murderers, the
woman also a whore. But worse than breaking the commandments
of God, they had been caught out in sins against God Himself.

The Council of the Lamb was forthright in its punishments.
Without example, half-blind, Man would stray.

Yet the prolonged death of the malefactors, their cries and con-
tortions, finally their corruption, had been aesthetic blasphemy. The
Angel Tower was for angels to alight upon, not to hang out dying
men like washing.

Though he had thought it, he would never have said it. He said very little, generally.

Fra Danielus was not much more than forty years, and looked youthful for that age. His hair was more black than gray, and his eyes were black still. The thin long nose, the thin but well-formed lips, the long, thin fingers—even without his belted magenta habit, and jeweled crucifix, his body itself revealed him as a man of thought and learning, a calm selective man, self-pared to the service of Almighty God. He had no vices, even those which the Church permitted. He drank no wine, ate sparingly, avoiding all meat, wore beneath his finery the most ordinary undershirt.

All excess, it seemed, recoiled from him. Perhaps miraculously. Fair women became, they said, in his presence more plain. A dog which had once run snarling and foaming at him, dropped at his feet, dying without delay.

At the age of thirty, Danielus had attained his present position, third of the Magisters Major, one of the Primo's highest religious authorities, beside the Council of the Lamb. More, he was the Master of the Upper Echelon of the Bellatae Christi. Perhaps an equal, in all but inherited luxury, to the Ducem in his island palace.

The Soldiers of God were in themselves a power, an essential asset to the City and provinces of Ve Nera. Their Upper Echelon was as famous through the world as some emperor's crack guard. Of course. They were the mortal guard of heaven.

Danielus was not thinking of this. He walked down the stairs of the Tower, then down the ramp, beyond which the cages had hung out. He reached the ground, and crossed through the inner gate to the courtyards of the Primo.

A young man, one of the Bellatae, was in the first court. He had paused by the lion fountain, but now came straight towards the Magister.

Danielus extended his hand. The cool lips of Cristiano pressed the emerald in the Magister's ring.

"Magister, can you grant me a few minutes speech?"

"Yes, Knight. And in turn, I shall speak to you."

"Have I offended?"

The pride, almost insolence, with which Cristiano had responded, amused Danielus slightly. He masked his amusement. He always did. Amusement, rancor, any vivid emotion. Even natural beauty he could regard unsmiling.

"No, my son. This is something our order must soon hear of. You and your brothers first of all."

They walked through a second court, from which led the castra of the Bellatae, and their chapel, in which Cristiano had kept his Vigil. A wide marble stair took them up into the Primo's flank. From here, an indoor stair of stone ascended to the Golden Rooms.

The majesty of these apartments was lost, in a way, on Cristiano. As he expected everything of God, (seemingly this was mutual) so the magnificence of the Primo Suvio was inevitable. Not a marvel, merely a law obeyed.

"Sit, if you will."

Cristiano took a chair in the book-chamber.

Indirect sunlight from a window, paned in glass, burned his hand.

Danielus sat down at his desk, and rested, as he often did, one hand on a polished human skull of abnormal size.

To either side of him, on the wall at his back, were two panels, painted a century before by an artist unnamed, for the glory of God. In one panel the Biblical Danielo faced the lions in the pit. In the second, a single lion, now become the Primo's symbol, was subdued once more by the Christ Child riding on its back.

"I will speak first, if you permit," said the courteous Danielus.

"Naturally, Magister."

"It will be a war."

Cristiano thought, and nodded. "You've had a letter from the Ducem?"

"That's so. Ve Nera's ambassadors have failed in the Eastern city of Jurneia. Failed so profoundly as to have had their heads put up on spikes in that place."

"The Jurneians are savages," said Cristiano.

"So we hear. And infidels, such as we fought in the Crusades. They haven't forgiven us that, the spoiling of their city and capture of their wealth, nor the saving of so many of their kind from damnation by conversion to the one true Faith. Three hundred years and more have passed; they don't forget."

Cristiano said, flatly, "I thought, Magister, it was a war about the price of silk."

Although he seldom smiled, Danielus had a way of conveying a sort of smile, by something in his eyes and brows. This happened now. "So it is. Mankind tends to that, don't you find, Cristiano—the use of new excuses for an ancient grudge?"

"Then it's both a war of trade and holy war."

"As you say. The armies of the Ducem will be called for the first. The Soldiers of God for the second. In tandem, obviously."

"And the fighting ground, Magister?"

"There's some debate. Jurneia is readying her fleet it seems, and building more ships besides. So Ve Nera is to equip hers. But it may take a year for the enemy to be ready."

"Then we go to meet them?"

"As yet, the Ducem makes no decision."

"But that will come?"

"The decision, of course. What it will be is with God."

Both men left off speaking a moment. It was well known the Ducem of Ve Nera, unlike his predecessor, was a weak and idle man, and his advisors supposedly corrupt. Where the Church could over-master the sins and failures of lesser men, the highest-born could, for the most part, only be regarded.

Danielus said, after a while, "There is the letter. Read it, if you so wish."

Cristiano took the letter. It was written clearly in Latin and black ink, on fine parchment.

It was very polite, exact and vague at once. But, without any doubt, it smelled of war.

"You see, Cristiano."

"Yes, Magister."

"There will be a lot to do. I think the Primo herself will need to buy in commodities to safeguard the people of this City, and ensure our interests in the markets of the outer world, to the same end."

Cristiano's eyes, fearsomely clear and steady. "Trade again, Magister?"

"You don't see it, I think. What the delay may mean, if Jurneia is as powerful as she may be, and the Ducem slow, or his decision on the matter—ill-advised." Cristiano blinked. "And now you do."

"Unthinkable—"

"If their ships reach us, those who refuse or are unable to fly, will be besieged here."

"By the Christ—"

"Of course, you don't swear. It's a prayer you uttered."

"Pardon me, Magister—yes, a prayer for Ve Nera under siege—"

"The Jurneian ships are narrow, and oared, reportedly by slaves, although all sources do not agree on this. The rigging is

heavy for the vessels' shape. They have the new weapon, un-
perfected here, cannon. The men wrap their heads in cloth and
worship their mistaken notion of God, facing towards the dawn. A
strangely spiritual image . . . Other than siege, they may wipe this
City from the face of the earth."

Cristiano rose. His hair burned white in the glow of the costly
window. A halo.

Danielus said, mildly, "Please sit, Knight. And tell me your own
news."

Cristiano stared at him.

"It's nothing to this. Some witch by the Silvian Marshes. But she
isn't. The products of ignorance and malice hitched to one cart."

Danielus stroked the smooth pate of the giant skull on his table.
A pious man kept always before him a *Memento Mori*. There was no
life save through God.

He had come across Cristiano when, at fifteen, the boy entered
the novitiate of the Bellatae Christi. Even so young, Cristiano was
striking, and despite his start among the slums, intelligent and
strong. It would be easier to doubt one's faith perhaps, than Cristiano's sincerity, his absolute steely *belief*.

A Magister Major had no favorites. Of course.

"Do I assume, Cristiano, that you intervened."

"Yes, Magister."

"It had caught your eye. I don't mean the witch, evidently. The
situation."

"This happened by my sister's inn. The story's a fantastic one. If
they put such imagination to the service of God, they'd do better."

"Let me hear the story, then."

Sometimes, she thought that she was in Ghaio's house. But the big
room was larger and had many tables. The kitchen was attached to
the house, though entered by a separate door. There was a garden,
she had seen it. It reminded her somewhat of the farm, or estate,
from which she had come. She did not see many people. The blonde
woman who was now, presumably, her owner, kept Volpa mainly in
the kitchen. Here she did much as she had done in the house of
Ghaio, cleaning pots, sweeping the floor, carrying nastier substances
outside to tip into an open drain leading to a canal.

Sometimes people stared at Volpa.

No one spoke to her aside from her new owner.

But who had ever spoken to her, much? Even her mother fell

silent. Only in the dreams following her mother's death had there been conversations. And all those words, now, she had forgotten.

She had forgotten a great deal.

Volpa did not know why or when Ghaio had sold her, and did not recall the process at all. She had one half formed memory, of fierce light, and of being very cold. And someone had helped her pick up her shift, and put it on, and then led her outside into the yard. Who had that been? She had seemed just woken from sleep at the time, and still not fully aware. Was this helper the blonde woman? The helper had been gentle, yet firm. The blonde woman was neither. She pushed Volpa aside or into place as though not liking to touch her. And she vacillated in her orders: Go and do that—no, do this instead. Leave this and go there—no, come back, stay put.

Once she slapped Volpa. "Didn't I say don't let them see you?" And then the woman snatched at her own hand. "Oh—I never meant to strike you, poor thing!" While Volpa, used to blows, waited, puzzled.

The woman was called Luchita. She was the wife of the inn-keeper. This was an inn. The patrons did not like to see Volpa, so she must be kept from their sight. The persons in the kitchen did not like her either. There was a lean piebald cat kept for the mice and rats. Nor did he like Volpa, and sometimes, without reason, approached and bit her. Seeing this, some girl had cried out—"Now the cat's poisoned!"

Volpa remembered a red mountain in a dream—or had she and her mother really wandered there? (Had the mountains been scarlet above the Veneran Plain?) Once they had been on a hill, and looked up, and in the green sky angels passed. Volpa remembered that well. And a snake in a tree.

Luchita rose from her knees. She had been praying to the Virgin, but only in the upper room, while her husband, laved in wine, snored an accompaniment. She had heard the Prima Vigile sound from Santa La'La—two hours after midnight. Useless to pray here. God heard only those who went into a church.

There was never time to make the journey. She was so tired. Too tired to sleep beside the jolting snores.

She struck the tinder and lit the candle-stub. She went down the narrow stair and into the corridor.

It was summer, yet still not warm at such an hour. She suspected

none of the three inn servants slept now in the kitchen. It was a
cause of resentment, her letting the girl come in, letting her sleep
there. But what else was there to do? Cristiano had insisted the girl
have some care. He would speak with his superiors, he said, find a
convent where she might be taken in. That was always his answer.
Everything was only to be found in God. Long ago, he had told
Luchita herself she might be happier out of the world—she, a *nun*!
Damn him, his loins were made of ice and his heart of stone.

No, no. Not so, not so. She loved him, he was good. He gave her
money after the sot drank it away. He was beautiful—oh, to be
chaste when equipped with such an armament. For certain, he was a
godly man.

Luchita cried tears. Wiped them off. Went out of the door and
three steps over the yard and into the kitchen which was built
against the house.

Yes, as she thought. No one was there, only the mad girl lying by
the hearth. Which was out, black and cold as a grave.

Luchita felt angry. Her moods were easily upset after the still
birth.

She shouted.

"Wake up, you slut! Don't you know to keep the fire going?"

As the form stirred—slender and fluid as a serpent—Luchita
glared about to find the tinder. The kitchen was untidy, greasy, and
smelled stale. The tinder was nowhere to be seen. She must use the
candle then, make the fire, put on some herbs and water in a pan for
comfort and perhaps sleep.

At, least the fool was setting sticks on the hearth now.

"That will do. Where did they stow the flint for the fire? You
don't know. Curse you, you wretch. Your brain's turned like milk.
No, I know you're dumb. You can't speak."

(Volpa gazed up, thinking, trying to remember if she could.)

But Luchita was crouching by the hearth, thrusting in the candle. As it met too hurriedly, the sticks, the wick was quenched. The
flame went out.

Luchita laughed with fury. She sat back.

"There. That's how this world is."

The tears returned. She let them drop. Who was to see but this
idiot.

Through the high window a faint light stole. The moon sailed
above Venus, changing every canal, every channel of the marsh,
both of the great lagoons to opal.

A soft, crackling was in the air. It had a sound of burning. Luchita looked, and saw the mad girl running her hand through and through her dirty, sticky hair.

Yet how brilliant the hair was, after all. Its redness shone out, merely from the moon.

She had pulled some of the hair loose. It fluttered in her fingers. She let it pour, liquidly, on to the twigs—

"*Jesus our Lord—*"

Volpa seemed diffident and barely awake. Her voice, unused for almost two months, was hoarse. "My mother showed me how."

Flames sprang briskly along the sticks, from the fire Volpa had made in her hair. The hearth burned with a cheerful domestic light.

3

Down all the winding corridors, the nun glided precisely three paces ahead of him. Either she, or he, maintained the distance, despite his Soldier's stride.

It was a bare place, blank stone, cut here and there with the harsh shape of a crucifix, or a window looking on an empty court.

Then a gallery, steps, a wooden door.

Cristiano entered the narrow room. The door shut.

His sister sat at the table, her hands on a small cross the nuns must have given her. Her face was scrubbed and her hair plaited and put in under a long white cap. She looked older, and younger, both at once. Her eyes were dark and flat.

"You see. Here I am. Where you told me to go."

"Luchita, I never said you must."

"No. Someone has."

"Who—has he thrown you out? I'll speak to him."

"My husband?" She looked momentarily incredulous. "*Him,* that sop? I left his house. I'm to serve here, and then I'm to be taken in among the lay sisters. After a year I can begin my novitiate."

"It's unusual. You're not a widow."

"I told them who my brother was."

"I see."

"You're not happy. I thought you'd rejoice."

"Luchita, you yourself admit you're not a woman for such a life—"

"Now, I am. The rest—was burned out of me."

Cristiano went to the window. He looked down at the empty court. There was nothing in it, no well, no shrub. Only the high walls at its sides.

"You lost a child, Luchita. This—may have been a fancy."

"No."

"She has yet to be questioned. Suppose you were mistaken."

"I never was. She created fire. I saw it."

"Then suppose, Luchita, Berbo was correct and her gift comes from the Devil?" He spoke almost mockingly. He had never, she thought, credited contemporary miracles, only the stupendous wonders of an earlier world.

"If it was from God or the Devil, what do I care? It proved to me, Cristiano, it *proved* to me—what I have *never* believed."

"Which is?"

"Life other than this one. Omnipotent power other than the power of men. God exists." In her face he saw, and did not recognize it, his own adamantine certainty. "You won't shift me. Recollect, you never could. God Himself has done so."

This, she knew, was *not* the house of Ghaio Wood-Seller.

She had been brought here in a black boat, over a vast sheet of water she thought to be the sea. It had been night, when she entered some equally vast building.

The room was small and dark, windowless and lit by candles even now, at noon. Yet there was a sweet smell.

Volpa sat on the stool they had given her, which was uncomfortable, but she never noticed this, being used to discomfort.

Three priests sat at the table, on chairs. Two looked at her, and one wrote down apparently their questions, what she answered. She recalled such priests from the byways and market-place. Everyone feared them, but Volpa did not. It was not courage on her part—she had never been brave. Was there a word for what she had been? It was that she knew that she, a slave, and perhaps insane—as others said of her, she had heard it—was of no importance.

Secure in abasement, she felt no specific awe, and showed none.

The priests for their part had noted as much. Yet neither was the girl rude in her manners. Her eyes were kept down, save now and then. She sat modestly. A humble and demure creature, who answered with a seeming honesty.

Any wrong-doer, blasphemer, murderer, witch—would deny the practice, until the full questioning began. Then all was brought out.

But they had not been permitted to speak of torture, not even to show her the instruments. Was she then only mad? She did not seem to be. She knew her name, her position. When asked if she knew of God, she had said that she did, and crossed herself. Only in the matter of her former master was she somewhat vague. Witnesses had been found to identify her as the slave of the wood-seller on the Canal of Seven Keys. She acknowledged this. But when the priests demanded to be told what had become of him, and his house, (and three other houses besides) she affected not to know.

"The house burned, did it not?"

"Did it burn?"

"I said that it did. And you, girl, burnt it."

Her eyes were raised then, strange eyes the color of the wine of pale grapes. "When I lived there, it didn't burn."

She had told them, in response to their interrogation—apparently not frightened by their voices and louring, used to such things, glad only not to be hit—that since about five years old, she had lived in Ghaio's house as a slave. But one morning, she woke up in an alley and did not know where she had got to. Then, wandering about, she had, she acquiesced, seen some houses that were burned. She did not recognize them. Also, sometimes women gave her a crust or some clean water to drink and she came across an inn, where they gave her food, usually in the evening.

Why had she woken in the street?

She thought Ghaio had sold her. In fact, she had thought he sold her to the inn-woman with blonde hair, because subsequently Volpa had been in the kitchen there, and performed duties. But later she remembered that before this, she had been homeless in the alleys.

Did she remember too making the fire come to the hearth at the kitchen of the inn?

Volpa here seemed to hesitate.

The priests' large white faces swelled. Even the clerk glared up at her.

Volpa said, "Mistress wanted the fire. So I made it."

"How was it made?"

"How mumma showed me."

"The mother was also a witch," snapped one of the priests. Volpa heard him say this, but, it made no sense. Her mother had been a slave. "*How* did she show you? *What* did she show you?"

"In a dream. After she died."

The priests recoiled. As snakes do sometimes, before they strike.

"A ghost? A *demon*? Where did she appear to you?"

"In a beautiful place. With a fiery mountain."

"*Hell*!" exclaimed one of the men.

"*Beautiful*—" said the other—"in what way?"

The girl raised her head and her eyes again. Her eyes were very clear, as if washed in light.

"It was easy and happy there," said the girl.

The priests sank back.

Hell could not be described as easy, nor happy, even by a malefactor. Nor beautiful. But the Devil was cunning.

One of the priests rose. He moved around the table and came to stand by Volpa. He put his hand on her shoulder.

"Now, my girl you're not helping yourself. This business at the inn. Don't you know what you've done?"

She was a slave, with whom obedience was paramount. She said, without guile or omission, frankly, "I lit the fire."

Perhaps she was in that room five days and nights. She was allowed, as most were not, intervals of rest, and to eat, and to void herself.

On the sixth evening, two women came, nuns, with only one man as guard. They took Volpa away up many flights of steps.

In a chamber which had several windows, but these high up, showing only a summer sky fading, Volpa was stripped and washed by a servant, in a bath that had a fountain running into it. Then her hair was also washed. As this went on, both nuns stood by (the guard was outside) and chanted, holding their crosses.

Volpa was dressed in a shift and a plain long gown, and her hair and neck covered by a scarf and cap. This dress, that of a woman neither well-to-do nor poor, most relevantly a *free* woman, surprised Volpa. She said nothing. The non-slavish questioning nature of youth had mostly ended with her mother's silence.

The two nuns then conducted Volpa up further flights of stairs, the guard walking behind.

Until now, the inner landscape of the building had not attracted Volpa's notice, or not very much. Presently however there was a passage, whose deep red walls were patterned by golden flowers. Then came a sort of circular space, in the middle of which rose a marble pillar, painted around in plummy colors, with pictures of robed men. Beyond was a door of iron. Here stood another guard.

Unlike the guard who had come with them, and was clad only as a lay brother of the Church, this one wore leggings, and a tunic embroidered by the sigil of the Primo, the Lion ridden by the Child.

The nuns did not accompany Volpa beyond the gate, nor did the lay brother. Instead, a lean, stooping man in black, and hooded, stepped through the door.

"Is this the woman?"

"It is." The nuns seemed taken aback, anxious.

"Is she named Vixen?"

"Yes, brother."

And turning on her his thin eyes—thin both in width and tint—he beckoned Volpa.

The iron door was shut behind her.

The second corridor was patterned by golden beasts—all of them rare, and mostly uncanny. It opened into a hall less large than high.

Those brought here had been sometimes overcome. Like the vast Basilica that ran below and alongside these apartments, the Golden Rooms suggested the glories of Heaven.

The walls were blood red, so thickly painted and inlaid by gold and gems that they gave the impression of a metallic tapestry. The ceiling was sheathed in silver and gold. There were seven great arched windows, set with diamond glazes of saffron, red and water-green. All this shone into a floor of polished obsidian, and so gave a sense of ultimate light floating on a lagoon—or in a sea of glass.

They crossed the floor, Volpa hesitating, her balance interrupted.

A door, painted and gilded like the walls, let them through into a rose-walled annex. A second door gave on a golden room.

On a backdrop this time of rich yellow, golden angels ranged. Candles burned like stars against a roof that was a sunburst.

Two huge painted images at once confronted the eye, a glowing golden man among a pride of amber lions; the Primo Lion of gold and brass, with a haloed infant god astride it.

Between these paranormal scenes, two men were seated upright at the table. One was another clerk, she discounted him. The other wore the habit of a Magister Major, and on his hand an emerald watched, like another eye.

Volpa, the Vixen, saw him only as part of the whole. (She was not alone in doing that.) He had the face of a disciple from the

pillars of the Basilica, and although she had never entered it until
now, she knew. His face had moved beyond the human. As a priest
should, he poised between Man and God.

4

"Have you been taught the story of Danielo?"

Volpa shook her head. "No, signore."

"He was a Hebrew, made slave to the great and cruel King
Nabucco, in the wicked city of Babylon. There Danielo, through his
wisdom, his visionary skills, and his faith in God, gained such power
that men were jealous of him. They entrapped him and had him
thrown into a pit of lions. The mouth of the pit was then closed with
a stone, and sealed by Nabucco's own royal seal. There is the picture
of this event."

Volpa regarded the picture of the golden man among the lions.

Danielus said, "In the morning, when they opened up the pit, do
you suppose they found Danielo still alive?"

Volpa said, "Yes, alive."

"Why do you think that? There were many lions, all kept hungry. I see you have no answer. But certainly Danielo lived. Because
God had closed up the mouths of the lions as decidedly as Danielo's
enemies had closed the mouth of the pit. God is capable of any
miracle."

The girl sat quietly in the chair. Mostly her eyes were lowered.
She raised them in response to tones of the voice, a slave trying to
divine an owner's wishes. (Had she stipulated that Danielo lived
simply since she believed the questioner wished for this reply?) Yes,
a slave. But even Danielo had been a slave.

"I've been hearing, Volpa," the Magister Major halted, review-
ing her ugly name, then went on, "that you also can perform a
miracle."

She glanced up, away.

He said, "Why don't you do it now? Show me your cleverness."

She sat there, eyes down.

"The woman who saw you do this until now, hers has been an
erring soul. But at once she's come to God because of what you did.
Through your act, this woman has found solace and regained the
hope of eternal life."

Volpa sat silent.

The scraping of the clerk's pen beside Danielus was an irritant. It answered where the girl stayed dumb.

She did not look either deranged or witless. Nor did she look like other women of her type—girls, rather, she was no more than fourteen. In another year, or less, might come the sudden blossoming one saw among the females of this City and this land. For now, she had a boyish quality, despite the curve of her breasts.

"Again," said Danielus calmly, "beside a marvel which seems to have brought only good, we must place men of the Silvian Quarter, who claim to have seen you set fire to the house of your former master, Ghaio. More, to have seen you walking garbed in flames. Can you do such a thing?"

Volpa raised her head.

She was a slave, but when she met one's eyes, it was not a slave you saw. A warrior who stood firm, ready for the blow, and half indifferent to it. Eyes as clear as crystal—where had he seen this look before? It was rare enough among men . . .

"You must, reply, Volpa."

"I don't know. The black priests asked me about my dreams, and I told my dreams."

"I have read your account of the dreams, Volpa. Journeying with your mother, and the curious animals and plants, and the mountain that burned always with red fire."

"She showed me how to make the fire. It's simple." Volpa said, he could have sworn *patiently*, "Don't others do it?"

Danielus' eyes and brows indicated, for a split second, inner laughter. "No. I've never known any make a fire in the way the woman Luchita says that you did. Nor do any walk in fire unburned, save the three friends of Danielo, that Nabucco flung into a fiery furnace. But an angel kept them from harm and led them to safety."

Something fluttered through the girl's own eyes. This was not laughter, more like a passing light.

"An angel then," she said. "Oh, I see. It was that."

"What are you saying? Take care."

She did not. She gazed at him openly, frowning a little, and said, "I was in his bedroom, now I remember it. And he wanted to hurt me. He threw me down on the mattress and pressed his face to mine. I ran away across the room. Then I forget, but I had no clothes on me. And yet someone put my shift on to my body, and led me out, through the window, and then I forget again. But I see now, it was an angel who led me out from the fire. An angel who clothed me in my shift."

Beside Danielus, the clerk gasped and surged up. Danielus spoke quickly, like the edge of a knife. "*Sit down.*"

Volpa said, "I understand it now."

"What, Volpa, do you understand?"

"It was one of the angels I saw with my mother, when we were on the hill."

The clerk had sat, frozen, turning the color of whey.

Danielus said, softly, "You say you've seen angels?"

"When I was a child. Only once."

"Describe them."

The flood of reason, the solving of her puzzle, had loosened her tongue.

"On a green sky against the first stars. They flew over. We thought they were birds—but they were men. Their arms were crossed on their chests. They had great wings. Flames burned on their heads."

Danielus heard the teeth of the clerk chattering. The room seemed very cold. Danielus said, "Volpa, do you know your Lord's Prayer?"

"No, signore."

"I will say it. You must say it after me."

She nodded. Her face was bright, almost happy, as it must have been in the easy, happy, beautiful place she had detailed from her dreams.

"*Father of all, who abides In Heaven*—"

She spoke the words carefully after him. All and every one. With no tremor she pronounced the names of God, then of the Virgin, and the Christ.

When they were finished, he had her speak the prayer over alone. Unlettered, unable to read, and a chattel, she had been used to learning by rote. She was word perfect.

"You perceive," said Danielus to the trembling clerk, "she has no fear of God's name. Write that down."

The clerk wrote. The sound of the pen irritated less.

"Now Volpa," said Danielus without inflexion, "won't you call just a little flame, to start this candle for me."

She looked unsure. But then, her eyes strayed to the frightened clerk.

Danielus saw the peculiar transformation which went over her. He gauged its secret as no other had had space—or mind—to do.

Emotion was her impetus. Ghaio had meant to rape her—lust—and rage? Luchita had been urgent and weeping—sorrow, pain. Now the clerk's religious terror.

Volpa drew off her woman's veil and cap. The hair spilled out—still damp from washing, a dark lion's mane, glorious red as a sunset. And from it, stroking, coaxing, she pulled a tiny little sun, and put it down on the candle, just as Danielus had asked.

PART THREE

MATTHEW: Why doth fire fasten upon the candle-wick?
PRUDENCE: To show that, unless grace doth kindle upon
               the heart, there will be no true light of life in us.

JOHN BUNYAN
The Pilgrim's Progress

1

On the floor, carnations were strewn, as always in late summer. The feet of men crushed them, staining the mosaic with pink and red. At the great ebony table, resting on its ivory lions' paws, these thirteen men who had crushed the carnations underfoot, sat now, all in black but for one.

And above them, hung the banner of white and gold, with its lettering like a spell: *Pax tibi Vene.*

Joffri, Ducem of the City of Ve Nera, (popularly called Venus) to which the banner wished peace, leaned his elegant chin on his slender hand.

His eyes were luminous with distaste.

Once every month, the Council of the Lamb attended on him, as their ostensible lord and patron. Sometimes he was able to make an excuse, as when he had had to have a tooth drawn, or, with more difficulty, when his favorite hound, lovely white Gemma, had died, gored by a boar in the woods of the plain.

But here he was today. And he had listened as they told him, as always, the sins of Ve Nera. How many citizens they had arrested, how many more were being watched over by their Eyes and Ears. Their disgusting black boats, nicknamed for the Styx, Death River, were an eyesore to Joffri. He loved the mass, the drugging incense and beautiful singing, drowsing through the exhortations, with a box of sweets at his side, and wine. He respected God, who had given him wealth and pleasure, and a comely healthy body with which to enjoy them. But Joffri, who as a child had artlessly informed his

confessor that Jesus Christ had said there were but two commandments, to love God and to love oneself, had no liking for shadows.

These twelve shadows about him now were powerful, however.
More powerful than a Ducem? Possibly.

The Magisters Major themselves must dip the metaphorical
knee to this Council. Men in black who had no title save for their
composite Brothers of the Lamb. Hoods or half-concealed, opaque
faces. Repellent faces, like old parchment, cut for lips and smeared
for eyes.

"It occurs to us, Lord Ducem," one of them said now, "that as
war approaches, our authority must be increased."

Who had spoken? He mislaid their names. Besides, sometimes
they changed, one resigning his post (or removed) another mysteriously assuming it. But wait, Fra Danielus, that astute and intelligent
man, had sent a list this very morning. Danielus seemed privy sometimes to the Council's acts, and would, if asked, assist his Prince.

Where was the list in Joffri's brain? Ah, here. Yes, lean, stooping, little-eyed—Sarco, a strange, foreign name.

"Brother Sarco, I thought the Council's authority omnipotent."

"I thank God, Lord Ducem, it is not. We too are bound by
Veneran law, and by the proviso that keeps ambition, even in the
best causes, chained."

"Indeed. Well, whatever you need, naturally."

They rustled in their robes, like things of black paper.

"We hear," said Sarco, "that the fleet of the enemy, when
launched, may number a thousand ships."

The Ducem let out a laugh. Checked himself.

"No, brothers. I pray not. The spies of Venus—pardon my
lapse—Ve Nera—reported less than four hundred vessels, and another fifty perhaps to be made sea-worthy. Our own fleet we have
held at one hundred and thirty ships."

"More ships must be built," said another of them, a bulkier one,
Jesolo, the Ducem thought.

"*Yes*, brother. So they shall be. But we have a small problem
there. To get them, we must add to the taxes. While already the
merchants and tradesmen must pay *yours*. And they're unwilling—"

Sarco interrupted the Ducem fluidly, as if without discourtesy,
"Our taxes, my lord, are necessary to stay men from sin. Since they
lack the will to curb their gluttony, drunkenness and vanity, such
levies as the council sets restrict them perforce, for the benefit of
their souls."

"Of course," said Joffri. "I didn't imply, brother, any feeling against the esteemed council. Only against myself, the poor Ducem, should I require to *add* to the burden."

Far down the table, another man spoke. He was a new one, Joffri thought, swarthy and hoarse-voiced. The name refused to surface.

"Already the City's stirred up with fear of war. When they're afraid, men become more pious, or else they give way and run amok. They indulge appalling vices. Things are done at such times that invite the brimstone of Sodomus and Gomorrah. Do we recall the years of the Death Plague?"

Joffri grimaced. He had been born too late for that horror, and was extremely glad of it. He nodded any way, to keep the unnamed misery in temper.

Sarco finished, "Such scenes must be prevented."

"Oh, quite."

"We have here a letter in which we, the Council, set out that extra scope we consider proper to us, for the season."

One or two of them rose, and came to Joffri, with the thick scroll, bound by a spotless tassel, and stuck with vermilion wax. The wax was imprinted by the seal of the Lamb.

It was a nice little lamb, as it kneeled there. A gentle lamb.

God knew what they wanted now. All a-bed at the Venusium bell . . . a new tax on any traffic along any canal—worth a fortune, that one . . . or on the carnal act, perhaps, within marriage

They could order a rich merchant or even a lesser prince to ride publicly in sackcloth, in a Styx boat, to the Primo, beating himself the while, for some heinous (exaggerated?) crime of blasphemy or sloth. Now and then, in the last two years, they had done so.

"I am grateful, brothers, for your care for my City."

Joffri did not think himself a coward. Only wise.

When Sarco said, mildly, "Your City, Lord Ducem, but also God's," Joffri bowed.

He was so delighted to bid them farewell. But despite the carnations he had had scattered, their odor stayed with him all up the stairs. A sour stale smell of bodies and minds bound always tight in darkness. For a moment, he knew he feared the Council more than Jurneia and her thousand ships.

* * *

After reading a copy of the Council's letter to the Ducem, which Brother Sarco had given him, Fra Danielus went down to the castra, to the practice court, to watch Cristiano exercise.

In the summer heat, all the Bellatae were stripped to the waist. Wrestling, they flung each other over, laughed or complained, and ran back together. They were like battling stags. And seeing the Magister, they vaunted themselves, excelled—or made mistakes.

Cristiano did not do this. He seemed to take no notice. He had tanned from the sun, and standing at rest, was like a statue of the Greeks or Romans, made in planed golden wood. But the hair was silver.

Then he lightly raised up the heavy sword, swinging it in flashing, veering thrusts. He had disarmed his third opponent in the time that might elapse between two strokes of a bell.

Before he walked to the Magister, Cristiano slung on the practice tunic. His was gray and full of holes. No pride? One could not pledge that. But he was young, and God Himself had made him strong.

"Tell me," said Danielus, as they moved through into the castra cloister, which was empty, "have you any curiosity concerning the little slave?"

Cristiano looked at him. He said, "You mean the girl who can call fire."

"Yes, just that little slave."

"Should I be curious?"

"You found her."

"She was there to be found."

"Do you still doubt she can do what she does?"

"No, Magister. Not since you told me that she could."

"I see. Should I then commend you for your faith in me, or chide you for accepting such a story secondhand."

"Either," said Cristiano. He leaned on a pillar of the walk, as Danielus sat down in the shade. In the middle of the sunlit square of grass, a fountain played into a bronze cistern. Insects buzzed. There was the honeyed scent of flowers, but summer had passed its peak.

"And your sister," said Danielus, "how does she manage among the nuns?"

"I haven't seen her for some while. She seemed content."

"Not joyous, then."

"Not joyous. The life's hard for her."

"She will have guessed that."

"Yes. She anticipates nothing now, from this world."

"I'm sorry to hear it, Knight. The world is to be valued, if only as the preface to a greater world."

"On her knees until they bleed, scrubbing floors, awake all night praying, fasting or fed on bread and water?"

"You're angry. Why? You also have done all that. You would do it now, and count it nothing."

"She's a woman," said Cristiano.

Danielus said, "Women are so weak, evidently. She has borne several children. That was probably far worse than scrubbing a floor. Don't you think perhaps God chose the female race for childbirth, because He thought them more valiant? The more able to endure?"

Cristiano said, "It was a punishment, I believed, for talk with a snake in a Tree."

"That too, of course," said Danielus. "But both were punished, both Adamus and Eva. If punishment is a corrective, and her punishment being the worse, did God suppose the woman capable of learning more from it?"

Cristiano laughed out loud.

"I can't debate with you, Magister."

Danielus gazed across the brown grass at the fountain. "I must go and visit my own devout sister on Eel Island. I've neglected her. I leave this evening and will be gone some days."

"Is Veronichi well?"

"Well, but melancholy, and demanding, as ever. I do my best to cheer her. While I'm gone, read this thing the Council of the Lamb has gifted the Ducem. Others know and are reading it. Also, I should like you to visit in turn the slave we spoke of."

"*Volpa*? Why that?"

"Anger again. Why anger now, Cristiano?"

Cristiano bowed his head, a false humility striving to be real.

"Pardon me, Magister. Whatever you wish."

"She's kept secretly, as you know. You know to keep silence. But you'll find her changed—changing. Her name has changed, too. It was a graceless epithet she had. And foxes are enlisted by the Devil, it seems. Now she's known as Beatifica. A name to exorcise all doubt."

"And what would you have me do there?"

"See that they treat her as I instructed. Talk to her, perhaps."

"Of what?" Cristiano shook his head. "Again, your pardon."

"Of God," said Danielus. "Talk to her of God, what else?"

* * *

Like the palace of the Ducemae, the house of Veronichi stood
alone, on an island. Admittedly one that would have fitted fifty times
over in Joffri's gardens.

The Isle of Eels was sufficiently small that, among Ve Nera's
muster of seven islands, it did not count.

Nevertheless, the place was pretty in a drooping, mossy way.
The old water-steps had sunk below the surface only last year. One
wall, which ran down into the Laguna Aquila, was also going, and in
need of repair.

Fra Danielus had given the house to his half-sister a decade
before, after he had brought her from obscurity in the slums beside
the wall of the Jewish ghetto. Though she undoubtedly possessed
their blood, she was a Christian.

Those that saw her, and this not often, (she was reclusive) had
sometimes remarked that she might have caught a husband, if she
had mended herself and looked for one. But Veronichi served solely
one God. Her rumored charitable works and drab clothing were her
only fame.

As the boat was rowed across the lagoon, the sun westered
behind the buildings on the shore, seeming to set them all adrift.

A City built on water, if not sand. Parable enough in that, for
Venus was mighty and rich, and had lasted. Even the threat of war
proved her superior station. Why else fight with her for spice or
silk?

In the apricot light the small island drew near. Over the walls of
Veronichi's neglected orchard, savage pomegranate trees dropped
tangled baskets of branches and budding red pods into the water.
Eels still sometimes swam there in autumn, to gorge. When netted,
they carried the taste of the seeds. Death's taste, surely, since the
pomegranate was the fruit of the classical Underworld?

The sunfall was—voluptuous. Overdone. The words of the
Greeks came to Danielus, who had read very much and widely.
Nothing to excess. Yet God employed brushstrokes of glory. In the
hands of greatness, was excess quite different?

He must read in the library he kept here. This was part of his
reason for the visit, but he might not tell Veronichi so. It would
depend on her mood.

She met him, coming down to the landing-place in a dull gown,
her hair scraped back under a linen cap. Her paintless face was the
shape of a pip, narrowing at the forehead and at the chin. Her eyes

were black as his own. She hid them under lowered lids, as she kissed his ring.

A game?

"I didn't think you would come," she said.

"But I told you I would."

As they climbed the steps, the boat was rowing away, melting into the extravagant sumptuousness of the light. The Council would like to tax such sunsets, no doubt.

2

Because the day was hot, she had come to sit in the yard.

There was shade here from one tall tree. The walls were so high she could not see the canal which ran beyond them, an oily dark green. But hearing it lap on the wall sides, and catching wafts of its summer smell, she remembered it. She had been brought along the canal, and then in at this yard.

The canal was named for the Virgin, Blessed Maria. The building where now she lived she had heard called only the cappella.

Life was not as it had been.

Volpa was not certain if this were a chastisement or a reward. Besides, she expected almost hourly that it would alter.

She rose, as she always had, at first light. A woman, a nun, would come into the cell where Volpa slept, bringing her a cup of water. At first there had been trouble, since Volpa did not sleep on the hard little plank meant for a bed. She preferred the stone floor, wrapped in the blanket. As a slave, she had never known a bed, although the blanket was a luxury prized, if mistrusted. Seeing the nun was displeased by Volpa's preference, Volpa had initially tried to wake earlier and locate herself upon the plank. Often she failed. Then, the nun ceased to be disturbed. Volpa did not ponder on this. She was simply thankful to be left alone. In fact, as with everything to do with Volpa, a report of it had gone to the Magister Major, Fra Danielus. He then advised the nuns of the Little Cappella, saying they should allow the girl to sleep on the floor. ("While we attempt to smite out of ourselves the body's whim for softness and pampering, she must only be envied, in this inclination for hardship.")

After Volpa had dressed in the plain, good clothes now supplied her, she was taken to the Auroria, the Dawn Mass. Here, as the group of nuns intoned and chanted, the prayers were whispered to

Volpa, who, accordingly, learned them all. These prayers were in Latin. However, she got them, and the whole service, by heart, and could soon speak everything perfectly on the cues, and with a pure pronunciation worthy of the Primo. (The diction of the Little Cappella was highly rated.) She did not, of course, grasp one word. Or perhaps, just one, here and there.

She knew the word for God, for example. Although not in all its Latin forms.

After the mass, Volpa broke her fast. In the beginning she was offered many things to eat, at which she stared, and from some of which she turned, revolted.

The nuns' first annoyance was once again translated into reluctant approval.

Volpa's breakfast came to be a piece of dark bread, dipped in watered wine. She took no midday meal, but in the evening might eat a dish of unsalted rice or porridge, or a vegetable gruel.

As a slave, she had lived through necessity as a devout priest of the Church was admonished to. Lack had trained her to accept only lack. To be comfortable only with a hard floor, a meager diet, a blanket and a cup of wine—luxuries valued, if barely tolerable.

To the splendors of the cappella Volpa was also nearly impervious, as she had been indeed to the marvel of the Golden Rooms. *They* had disorientated her, the cascade of gold and crimson, the reflecting floors. Until she put them aside, one more element that she did not understand and so must not waste time on.

Here, shown the carvings, the glass, she looked, and looked away. She was able to recognize the silver cross. Seeing it, she crossed *herself,* as her mother had taught her.

They did not conduct her to any further daily service until that of the sunset Venusium. Again, she quickly learned everything and faultlessly joined in.

Her mind did not wander at these moments. The exquisite inflexions that now came from her own mouth, fascinated the girl as much as they did the ears of those who heard her. Sometimes even she spoke the lessons over, when alone, walking the corridors of the cappella for exercise.

The nuns, finding that, promptly taught her other prayers and holy songs.

Speaking on and on, in company or alone, Volpa's voice fined itself and gained a silvery quality. Only in normal speech did she still sound, sometimes, rough and guttural.

She went to her bed early, after supper.

The nuns had noted she was not quite a child. She had breasts, and every month she lost blood. (Unremarked, she had reached fifteen.)

She was bored, too. The stitching the nuns gave her she did poorly. Also, finding she was not chided, often she left it undone. She could not read. She sat singing to herself the chants of the cappella, or walked slowly about the tree in the yard. At night, sometimes, she stole out, thinking to circle the tree, but the nuns were always about, performing penitential chores, going to and from their devotions, or watching by the altar, from where the yard was visible. Volpa knew instinctively that her dance must not be seen. Less than the interrogatory priests, she recalled the old man slave, and how he had seemed afraid of it, and yet afraid without *fear*. What had become of him?

Had she burned Master's house?

It seemed to her it had only burned. Then the angel led her to safety.

She would like to see the angel again. She could not recollect how it had looked. But presumably it had been like the flying beings she had seen with her mother, on the hill, the great wings spread behind it, and the feather of brilliance on its head.

Seeing the image of the Apostles in the cappella window, receiving the power of God each in a flame that stood up on the brow, she noted a similarity.

She was called now by another name. She liked its sound. She did not really think of it as her own.

Crickets were cheeping in the warm stones of the wall.

A stink of fish rose up from the canal.

The Solus was over—she often watched from the doorway, learning the words of this mass as well. (As, at night, unable to dance to the tree, she learned the Luna and Prima Vigile.) She repeated the orisons clearly now, not knowing what any of them said.

"Gaze upon us, O God, and shed the light, more wonderful than any sun, so that we may see our way."

Cristiano stopped still.

The slave stood in the long shadow of the tree, through which a blade of sunlight pierced to touch her shoulders and the white cap that covered her hair. She was singing sweetly, and in perfect Latin, the words of the Midday Mass.

She had the voice—of nothing human. Not even the genderless beauty of the unbroken soprano of a boy. Cristiano, until now, had never even heard her speak.

Something moved against his skin. It was like a brushing hand made from the air.

He marked himself with the cross.

Then his mind cleared, and the sun shifted. She was a thin young girl with nothing exceptional about her, who turned and blinked at him, then lowered her eyes. And when he said her name—the inappropriate new name the Magister had given her— she mumbled, "Yes, signore," ignorantly and without any grace.

Cristiano wrote to the Magister, who was detained on Eel Island. (It seemed his sister was sick.)

The letter, also in Latin, was formal. Nevertheless honest:

> "The Little Church, as you would hope, as it is your property, and being its chief confessor, is healthy. No summer sickness has manifested. The sisters are hale.
>
> "For the slave, this girl, Beatifica, they care for her as you commanded them. They say she is modest, and shows signs of devotion to the Christ. They do not fault her in anything, especially since you told them to let her go on in her original manner, sleeping on the ground, and so on.
>
> "They say she steals to the door of the Sanctuary to listen to the mass, even sometimes to the Prima Vigile, two hours after midnight. They have noticed that, where the glamours of the carving and windows leave her untouched, she responds to a sight of the cross, and the window which shows the Apostles. She says prayers over to herself constantly, distinctly, and with apparent delight.
>
> "I too have heard and seen this.
>
> "Some of them think she will wish, after some time, to become one of their number. You have not told them of her single talent. And they have had, demonstrably, no sight of it."

Standing with her, under the tree, he felt an awkwardness. He had expected nothing else.

His lowly beginnings he had left far behind. He could read and write, he could do battle, he was a Soldier of God. She was a slave, illiterate and, at her depth, unmotivated, and amoral as any beast. She was a woman.

Long ago (it seemed to him) he had lashed and starved any fleshly craving for women from him.

And a woman, stripped of her potential to satisfy male hunger, or produce therefrom children, was nothing. God's afterthought, made from a rib. Perhaps stronger, as Danielus had mooted, merely in order to bear her lesser life. For what man could bear to live as a woman must? And what woman could tolerate her life, if she had possessed the capacity of a male brain?

Even so, what he had seen—felt—in those brief instants before the sun vanished in a cloud, before she left off her prayer—disconcerted Cristiano.

There had been holy women, transformed by the mysteries of God, and, above them all, the Virgin. Woman was, by the miracle of the Divine, sometimes able to ascend from her body and her lot, and from all things.

"Do they call you Beatifica?"

"Yes, signore."

"Don't call me that. I am one of the Bellatae Christi. God's Soldier."

She hung there in front of him, eyes down. Said nothing.

He said, "They tell me you're a good girl, here."

Nothing.

He said, impatient, "What do you say for yourself?"

She mumbled again.

"*What*? Try to speak out as you say your prayers."

"I mean not to offend," she said, "signore."

"Didn't I say, don't call me that. Say, Soldier of God."

She looked up and straight into his face.

Her eyes grew larger, when she stared at you, or so it seemed. *Yellow* eyes. He had never seen that color save in an animal, a dog or cat. (Woman, the beast.)

"Soldier of God," she said, and then, in clear Latin, "Bellator Christi."

She had been a slave, and the Magister's nuns here had told him, too, her back was scored with previous whippings, one of five and a half ragged scars, perhaps many years old. The stripes would never go.

Inside her white skin he seemed to glimpse now, clusters of bruises, preserved like fossils in marble.

"Sit down, Beatifica." She sat on the bench by the tree.

Sufficient men had been unkind to her. At a loss, thinking dimly of Danielus' words, Cristiano said to her, "Say one of the prayers for me."

"Which one shall I say?"

Naively, although he did not guess himself naive, he said, "One which you like the best."

He had forgotten nobody might have bothered to explain the meaning of the prayers and that she must have learnt them (like the title Bellator) from phonetics alone.

And she any way obeyed, always obedient. She chose a prayer whose *sounds* she liked. And because it had one word she knew.

"I will raise my eyes to the mountains, where God is . . ."

Cristiano was to write: 'She selected the prayer of a king, Magister. She spoke it eloquently. And then there was a change in her, I must admit it to you. Her face became transparent with a kind of brightness. Perhaps only a trick of the sun.'

As he wrote these words in the letter, Cristiano felt suddenly oppressed by the heat of the summer evening.

Moving to the window of his cell in the castra, he saw sailed fisher-boats like dragonflies on the surface of the lagoon. But imposed upon them, the image of the Virgin in the Primo window, her damson mantle wrapped about her.

A slave was not to be compared with Maria. Tonight he kept the Vigil. Before then, he must empty his mind and spirit of this clutter. It came to him again to wonder, as he sealed the letter, why Danielus had sent him to the girl.

During the night, as Volpa-Beatifica slept on the floor, two nuns entered the cell.

"Get up, Beatifica. Put on your clothes."

When they took her through the Little Church and out into the yard, whose gate stood wide, Volpa-Beatifica was uneasy.

Torches burned, and on the canal, black with night, a covered boat rocked up and down.

Another woman would have protested, pleading to know where she was to be taken.

But Volpa was a slave. The small chances of free will she had

had in the cappella were swiftly mislaid. And she had expected change.

She got into the boat without speaking, trembling, and sat where they showed her.

There were also some casks in the boat, smelling of wine.

She was rowed away into the night of Ve Nera, between the high black walls. In some, gratings and narrow slots evicted loud light. Stars littered the sky, forgotten candles.

Some of the nuns stood crying at the water's edge. They had been told Beatifica was to go to a religious house on the plain. They feared their care was not deemed adequate.

3

All the remaining year, past Christ-Birth Mass, Beatifica was at a farm on the Veneran Plain. How many properties, aside from the Island of Eels, and these one or two farms, belonged to Fra Danielus, was unknown. But a Magister, particularly a Magister Major of the Primo Suvio, must have revenues, and also places he might loan or give away or sell, as the Church's needs dictated. Even recently, there had been a sale of another house, in order to supply the coffers of the Church, which in turn leant gold to the City's ship-building.

Beatifica knew nothing of this, of course.

She was aware mostly that from the farm buildings she could see, far off, the mountains. Either she recalled them from memory, or from her mother's told memories. They did not, certainly, seem familiar any more. They were gaunt and gray, and soon helmed with snow. Neither in the brazen sunrise of fall, nor the red setting sun of winter, did they turn to scarlet.

At the farm, she saw slaves. This was a stumbling block, but having stumbled on it, she righted herself and beheld the difference. They demonstrated by their activities, their segregation—unlike her own—that she, now, was a slave no longer.

Like the prayers she still regularly said and sang, this too she had needed to, and did, learn, by rote. Yet, she remained a slave.

She slept in a bare, clean room. When she ignored the bed, which had frame, mattress, and curtains, they removed it. But they gave her for the winter chill three blankets, and a cushion for her head. These she took to. Also there was a brazier for wood. It was kept alight for her, as if she could not have lit it herself. She could not—not, as it were, *cold*. She must have impetus. She would need to be freezing to draw from herself the power—and, still slavish, might only have endured the freeze, as she had always done.

She had candles, too. And a cross the nuns had sent with her, which she liked to hold. It was made of tarnished silver, which with her caresses, grew brighter.

After only a day or so, the woman who came in the morning, (like the nun) a servant not a slave, brought Beatifica new garments.

The girl looked at them, and the woman said, "The Magister Major says you're to wear these, now. They'll be warmer, and handier for your work." A sentence prepared by others; the woman said it with an expressionless face.

Presently she took Beatifica, as usual, down to the farm chapel. It was a vacant stable, perhaps a theosophic pun of sorts. The altar had been sanctified, but stood among wisps of straw. Here were some men of the farm, couth and combed always for the Dawn Mass, and two women, both elderly.

None of them looked at Beatifica any more than they had ever done. Her clothes may have escaped them. Or not.

She ate alone by day. At night, she ate with a man and woman of the house. They corrected her actions at the table as diligent parents might have done. The manners taught her, however, were higher than their own. She did not question this. Could anything surprise her? Little. In her limited world, most had been a surprise, and mostly a surprise that hurt or harmed. Amazements without pain she did not resist. But then, she had not resisted pain either, until it seemed to threaten life itself. (Eventually she might have ceased to resist even that.)

She liked the honey and milk she was given, and the raisins and olives. These became an indulgence.

Beatifica learned the use of spoon and knife and linen napkin, the trencher of bread that was not to be eaten but might be thrown to a dog, should she wish.

Probably she did have a memory of farm dogs, for some reason friendly ones. Where the man and the woman had thought they would need to coax her not to be timid of the huge shaggy animals, they found her careless. Now and then she petted one. Never for long. She was not affectionate, or not in a physical way. And what was lost to her she did not search or lament for. (She had learned so many tenets of the priesthood in her slavery.) Unless, nothing had ever been worth lament or search.

After the dogs, maybe her tutors wondered if she would be frightened, even so, of the horses.

Ve Nera's means of travel, as a rule, was by her canals and other waters. It was true, the Ducem maintained some horses on his island, for riding in the gardens. And more on his estates on the plain, Forchenza principally, for purposes of hunting. Even the Primo kept horses on the plain, for its knights. And sometimes too it was possible in Ve Nera to behold horses, transported on some barge, or gathered, fabulously decked, for a ceremony in the Primo's great square beneath the Angel Tower. But Beatifica had never seen anything like that. To her, a horse was surprising. Therefore, not unusual at all.

Not until two men set her on a horse's back, did Beatifica become alarmed.

For a month before, she had been exercised, given things to do with her body in the new clothes—which were those of a boy, leggings, tunic, cloak. Her body, already firm and supple and spare, had loosened and knit further.

So she kept a grip on the horse. But her mind plunged off. Another would have screamed for help.

The horse was a steady creature of the farm, used to plough and plod. They led him round, and Beatifica sat on his top, her long hair tied off her face and falling down her back in a tail much like his own. Seeing her going like this about the fields, those who did not know—most—took her for a boy.

She kept in her seat; when they took her off her legs gave way, both from the unused posture and from terror.

The woman said to the man, "Is he insane, this Fra Danielus? What does he want from her? To ride like a man—"

"Shut your lips, woman, till you have some sense. How do I know? He's our landlord. We do what he says. Besides, for God's sake, have you forgotten what he did for *us*? Would we be living still, if not for him? So, she's in our charge. If he gave you a priestly robe to sew, you'd use a fine stitch."

"It's a woman we're stitching."

"Shut your lips if you want to stay wife of mine."

Nothing made much sense to Beatifica. No warnings such as were habitual to her tutors' kind of servitude, a *servant's* slavishness, for gain; from thankfulness. Beatifica obeyed, as always she obeyed. What sustained life she did.

So, next day she was put up on the horse again, without cries or struggle. She did her best. By example, doing what she was shown, feeling out the country of the horse's back, Beatifica once more learned.

(She was fifteen. Her mind, unfilled by knowledge, gaping like a hungry mouth of sharp white teeth.)

The lessons she devoured. Unconsciously mostly. From fright she moved to acceptance to an almost—interest, and so to aptitude. She rode. *Bold* as a man now. And when they brought the other horse, sword-slim and brown as malt, *immodest* as a man, she mounted him. She trotted with the horse and her escort through the bare fields, through the woods lashed by the tusks of winter boars. The air was spiked with coming snow. She had never known such freedom. Freedom which had come through obedient enslavement. The goal of the priest.

Nine days before Christ' Mass, the Magister Major Fra Danielus went to inspect one of his farms. Three of the Bellatae rode with him, Aretzo, Jian and Cristiano.

Snow was down in the foothills, and dusted on the plain. The high woods wove nets of snow-blossom. Wolves were seen, a black wind that passed across the distance. A boar appeared near the village of Mariamba, ten miles from the City, and menaced the cavalcade. The young knights killed this boar. It would make enjoyable eating, save for the Magister. But it was not a time for traveling.

Fra Danielus rode in the customary litter jolted between two geldings. The Bellatae rode their horses. Villagers pointed out the white-haired knight, on his silk-white horse.

Snow fell as they approached the estate.

The faces of the young men were flushed with triumphant exertion and cold. (Cristiano had needed this color.) Danielus regarded them from the swaying litter. He himself seemed fatigued. He had been called to his sister's island once more. It was patent she wore him out, this Veronichi, chronically unhealthy, an obscure woman with no proper existence.

The boar gurned on its pole, gutted and dropping thick clods of black blood.

When they reached the farm, everyone came out. The women

were kissing the Fra's hand, his ring, the men bowing low. Slaves ran to and fro. Chickens scattered, and on a post the cock crowed, not knowing six of his wives were due for the pot.

"Is there news of the Infidel War, Magister?"

Jian said, interposing himself between Danielus and his retainer, "No, not yet."

Danielus spoke gently, "I'll send you word, as always. But you will need to butcher and salt down this winter."

"Yes, Magister."

"Don't look so vexed. The number of their ships is exaggerated."

"Over one thousand, so we heard—"

"Less than five hundred. And Ve Nera's fleet will match them, by the spring."

"Thank God, bless the Virgin."

Aretzo said, on the outer stair, "You didn't forewarn us, Magister, to lie."

"Yes, but do lie. A little. For now."

"It's no sin," said Jian, "not a lie of this sort. To save them distress."

Aretzo frowned.

Jian amended, "Truth has varied somewhat in the matter besides. Depending on which spy has sent which report from Candisi. And whether he lived beyond its dispatch."

"Hell waits for Jurneia," said Aretzo. His cheeks burned, as when he put a javelin into the boar.

Cristiano, silent. He had been so most of the journey.

The stair led to the Magister's apartment, when visiting. The farm folk had seen to the bed and hung thick curtains. A fire burned, and there was a dish of winter apples, wizened but sweet. The Magister's three knights would sleep in the lesser room, the four outriders and two Primo guard in the barn beside the kitchen.

As servants sorted the baggage, there came the shriek of chickens chased with knives across the slippy courtyard.

"What's the matter, Cristiano? Sorry for the fowl?"

Jian and Aretzo, worldly enough to like the jaunt, with its hunting and novelty. Cristiano smiled mirthlessly.

"The chapel here's a *stable*," said Aretzo.

Jian said, "So was the birthplace of our Lord. What bag is that? Hey, fellow, where are you lugging it?"

The servant replied, "It's to go up for mistress."

"Oh, take it then."

The woman came in with compressed lips. She did not look at Beatifica-Volpa, but the girl, as so often she did, kept her own eyes
down.

"The Magister Major has sent this. You're to wear it." An order.
A slave obeyed orders, always. "He'll conduct the service of the
Venusium at sunfall. I'll come for you then. Here's the slave to help
you dress."

This (second) slave came into the room. A true slave, Beatifica's
reminder by example that *she* was no longer of that kind.

Over the chair which stood by the window, the clothing had
been laid. It caught the glimmer of the brazier.

Beatifica-Volpa stared one long moment at it.

Then, with the other slave's assistance, she took off her garments of a wealthy farmer's son, and put on the new ones Fra
Danielus had sent.

As sometimes happened, in the minutes before it set, the sun
appeared out of the clotted gray-white sky, a maroon ball, lightless
enough to be gazed at. The sky was torn all around it, bleeding.
Then the sun became a semicircle, and then a slice, and was gone.
Color left the sky, and in the courtyard a boy was banging on a
copper vessel, to summon the household to prayer.

Advancing to the left of the stable-chapel, the women had entered
in a group. There were five or six of them, the farmer's wife, his
elderly widowed mother and widowed aunt, to the front. At the
other side, the right, the farmer and his sons were closest to the
altar.

For the Magister Major, Eastern incense-gum had been brought
from its chest, and lit. The air was fragrant.

Fra Danielus stood by the altar, and by the altar to the right, the
three Soldiers of God. These four, facing the doorway, therefore
saw her come in, as always, alone.

Of the Bellatae, only Cristiano, who had seen her before, did
not take her at first for some unexpected young man of noble birth.

He noted the eyes of Jian slant inquiringly. Aretzo looked
haughty, flaunting his own priestly rank.

In Cristiano a shock-wave broke. He did not know what he
felt—horror? Disbelief?

But then Fra Danielus began to speak the words of the Sunset Mass.

Were the peasant family, the Magister's retainers, aware of what lived among them? This—*changeling*.

Cristiano forced his mind away from the girl, standing now at the back, neither on the womens' side nor the mens', but in the middle, before the door. Her eyes seemed fixed on Danielus, or on the altar, perhaps. When the responses were uttered, and in the chant, he detected her voice easily, silver-pure, the Latin exact.

And when they kneeled before the uplifted chalice, so did she. But on one knee only, as did the knights. Dressed as she now was, it gave her no difficulty.

Cristiano sought for God blindly, and through his great self-discipline, shut out reaction to the girl. But even so, could not quite grasp the majestic otherness of the Venusium, its true meaning and heart.

Religion was his food and drink, desire, rest, his life's love. He rose, cheated. Just as, six times now, from the Vigil he had had to rise. For six times the essence of God had failed him—that is, been failed by *him*. Each month, through the summer and the autumn, the arrival of winter, kneeling before the Virgin window, lifted high above his pain and able to withstand it—but achieving nothing. The sheer white radiance, the overwhelmment of flawless bliss—they had not been his. And though in the past, occasionally, he had not achieved this state, always then it had been his the next time. Now no fast or punishment brought him back to it. Before the last Vigil, Cristiano had stretched out three hours on the floor, beseeching God, requesting to be told what fault of his had barred him from the pinnacle. Frustrated, unanswered.

Was his fault so grave that God refused to reveal it?

Frustrated . . . that now always. Reining himself like the horse he had ridden today, fighting over and over a restless bitter rage, like the boar they had slain.

He must not become a petulant child, fractious because his toy had been taken from him for his own good, seeing that he valued it too highly.

Was this the message God had sent him, then?

Even holy delight might become the sin of greed?

He had believed, while he stayed worthy—Ah, then, he must no longer be worthy.

In what way? What had he done? Reveal, Oh Lord, my *fault*—

Cristiano held himself finally in bands of steel. Self-governance was all that had been left to him.

It was by now dark outside, and a torch burned on a pole in the yard, which was perfumed, after the incense, with chickens and sheep.

But indoors the candles were lit, and they went into the farmer's parlor to eat.

The table was finely dressed tonight with a white cloth, and water for the hands. The woman of the house and her servants brought the dinner. Only the elderly women sat down with the farmer and his five sons. Danielus was placed at the table's head, and his three Bellatae on either side. One place still stood empty.

Then, in came the girl, the abomination of Woman dressed as a man.

Cristiano stared at her. Her lids were not lowered, but she looked only at Danielus.

The perverse garments were white. Whiter than the common white of ordinary things, the old tablecloth, the womens' aprons. Church white. Pristine as the new snow. And the cloak, where it was looped back, was thinly edged by gold. While on her hips the low male belt was hatched with gold. She wore a golden crucifix, not large, but set with one smoldering red gem, to represent the Blood of Christ.

In the candlelight, as she came nearer and nearer, her unbound flood of hair was like the torch from the yard, a water of fire. Cristiano saw her eyes were not after all yellow, but, like her cross, made of gold.

"Beatifica," said Fra Danielus. He spoke casually. No one at the table, or among the women, stirred. As if nothing much went on.

Yet Cristiano felt Jian beside him abruptly alter. And Aretzo across from them, (by whom, it seemed, the changeling would sit down) craned his neck. His eyes started like those of a fish.

"Speak the Grace for us, Beatifica," Danielus gently said.

She brought her hands together, folded one on the other. Her eyes now lifted above them all. Motionless, she moved beyond them. Cristiano saw it, as he had seen it that other time, in the court of the nunnery.

She spoke the Grace.

The table bowed its collective head, even the Bellatae. Cristiano *felt* his fellow Soldiers *listening*.

Her voice—was not like a woman's, not like a boy's—certainly nothing like a man's. It was like an *instrument*. The sounding-board of the sacred words.

(Beside Cristiano, Jian shuddered.)

At the proper juncture, they marked themselves with the cross.

The Grace was finished, and Beatifica took the stool left vacant for her.

It was Danielus who glanced about at them. Who said, "The Maiden Beatifica has learned her orisons, as you see. And here, she learns other accomplishments."

Aretzo said, "To sew, Magister? To make broth?"

Danielus said, lightly, "As you learned to plough, Aretzo, and to break hods."

Aretzo flushed. "I was called to serve God."

"And thus," said Danielus.

The women were placing the central dishes and a rich savory aroma went up. The kitchen had labored to present its best, a pottage of chicken in a great pan, flavored with pears and onions, ginger and pepper; slabs of the boar, roasted, stuck with cloves and powdered by cinnamon and grain-of-paradise. The Soldiers of God, today allowed their fill, reached out hungrily, angrily. Only Cristiano was abstemious, selecting solely from the chicken. The Magister, as usual, touched neither meat, contenting himself with pancakes made with eggs and white wine.

The girl—the *Maiden Beatifica*—was served a separate bowl, some vegetable thing, while from a little wooden dish she took a sliver of boiled white meat.

Cristiano's belly had turned in any case.

The family ate heartily. They seemed to have no troubles. The sons were even becoming sometimes rather loud over their ale, despite the Magister.

The woman though, the Housewife, stood with her servants, her lips drawn in tight. Only when Danielus complimented and thanked her did she wrench them to a smile.

The slave—the girl—the *Maiden*—she ate nicely, like a princeling. But very little. By her trencher the wine cup filled just once, waited mostly unused. She was frugal even with the cup of water.

Danielus spoke to the farmer about the land, crops, weather, the horses.

Later some cheese was brought and winter fruits, and a frumenty with rose-sugar.

They rinsed their hands and wiped them on napkins.

"The Maiden shall say the prayer to close our meal." Danielus looked at Aretzo, at Jian. Not at Cristiano. "The Warriors of God shall make choice of which."

Aretzo spoke at once. "Let her say one of the King's Psalms."

And Jian said, "The forty-second Psalm."

"That has a few verses," said Danielus. He turned to the girl. "Speak this, then, Beatifica—" and he said the first words of the Psalm in Latin.

Immediately she took it up from him, and spoke it all, in the beautiful argent voice.

"Deep thunders to deep, the waves go over me and I drown. Yet the Lord will send to me His kindness by day, and by night His love shall be my song . . ."

There was no noise at the table now, as that silvery instrument played.

Cristiano recalled the silence in the street when Berbo accused her. He thought of her in the convent, speaking alone in the sunlight.

A pressure had risen in him. A child might have identified it as the upsurge of tears. But the man sat transfixed, locked in steel, at war with himself.

The Psalm ended.

Jian sighed. Aretzo, always the redder, was pale.

And the woman among her servants held her hand to her lips as if to hide their relaxation.

Danielus rose to his feet.

The roomful of people gazed up at him, the faces lit from low candlelight.

He called the farmer by name. "Marco, you have been a faithful servant to me. And your wife, a paragon. Now you shall see something to wonder at. Jian, I ask that you will get up and shut the door. And you, Marco, put out all these lights except for that one there, on the chest."

Oddly, from beyond, in the kitchen, at that moment came a noise of the Primo guard, and their servants, some joke told, and laughter.

It was unseemly, and the two old widows clucked their teeth. Marco half turned, scowling.

"No matter," said Danielus. "Always remember, my friends, God gave us the earth also to be happy in. Doesn't the Psalm say this, *benevolentia et carmena.*"

As Marco and his eldest son dowsed the candles on the table, a luminous shadow gathered them all in. There in the heart of it, only the white clothes and the hair of the girl went blazing on—and Cristiano's blondness, too, had he known it.

He spoke quickly, quietly, to Danielus.

"Magister—if you want her to make her conjuring here—"

"It isn't conjuring, Knight. But I value your caution. And—your agitation."

Cristiano's guts churned. There was a swirling in his head like drunkenness, but he had drunk only water. The pressure was rising through the core of him, pushing, scorching, agonized as an arrow working in a wound—insistent and dreadful as nausea.

But he was accustomed to conceal and to restrain his flesh. He had ridden partly unconscious through battles and cut men down like a machine. He had kept the Vigil, eight hours on his knees, even when God avoided him.

Yes, the sea had drowned him. Yes, he cried for the kindness and the song by night—

It was very dark.

Miles off through the stillness now, not the laughter of men, but a wolf's howling arced over the plain. Danielus nodded to his made creature, the Maiden.

"Look, Beatifica."

Cristiano in his locked—fast turmoil, sensed more than saw the crystals of her eyes. Chrysoprase from the breastplate of a High Priest—

It was as if she found him in the dark as he had found her in the obscure alley, alerted by some sound. Did she hear then, in stillness, the wolf howl of his emotion?

Away and away, the other wolf cried slenderly again over the snow. And then no more.

She saw his heart. She, this absurdity, this abomination—this joke cruder than any told in Marco's kitchen.

He felt her eyes upon his heart, cool, like pearls, sliding through his flesh.

And then—Oh God who is in Heaven—then—the light of the fire—

Aretzo cried out. Marco too and one of the sons.

The woman by the door, the paragon, let go a wild scream.

(Did the wolf, searching the plain, in turn hear these animal noises?)

One saw the Christ shown in this way, the halo, the sun, behind his head. And she too, Virgin Maria.

Beatifica—

Her hair had become a score of torches, and behind them shone the summer sun.

And with her thin white hands, she reached upward, and clasped this sun, and it came away in her hands, a nest of flame, sparkling and crackling, *alive*.

She held the fire high up in the dark, and gave them light to see. Then softly let it down, and all the candles caught at once, gushed up with a hiss, and spume of smoke. And on the table cloth, some little rivulets of fire ran off—and faded, harming nothing.

Marco's wife sank to her knees. Men and women knelt.

But Cristiano came to his feet, and as he did so the pressure reached and burst in his brain and all the whiteness of eternity, which for six bitter times he had not been able to attain, entered in. For one second such joy, such ecstasy was there, it shattered him. He died. But only in a second. Only *for* a second. And then he simply stood in the earthly room, and there was low candlelight and the smell of food. And a brown-haired girl in the clothing of a man, her eyes downcast.

4

His two fellow knights had gone out to the chapel. Even though it was a sanctified stable.

The rest of them—God knew. The girl to her chamber, certainly. Slight and dowdy. Her damnable eyes cast down.

Danielus was in his room.

Regardless of the chaos, someone had come in and seen to the fire.

Cristiano looked at the fire, and then at the Magister, sitting in a chair, turning an apple in his hand. At each turn, the emerald in the ring flashed green. But the face of the Magister gave nothing at all.

"You're still angry, Cristiano."

"Yes, Magister."

"Anger is—shall I say a fault, rather than a sin?"

"I'll beat myself later."

"Oh. Sophistry. That's not you, surely, Cristiano?"

Cristiano stood, white with rage.

"Tell me, Magister. Was it a *trick*?"

"I see now, despite your words, you never believed me when I told you what she did."

"*What did she do?*"

"You saw quite well."

"I saw—something. Am I to trust my eyes?"

"Have your eyes lied to you before?"

"No."

"Then, perhaps, trust them."

"*How* can she—for the love of God—"

Danielus got up. He walked across the room and back, and in passing put the apple into Cristiano's unwary hand.

"Look. Here is a wholesome fruit we eat. Meat may be forbidden at certain times, and wine. But apples—never, And yet, Cristiano, on the Tree in the Garden of Genesis, the apples were forbidden. And eaten but once, brought about the fall of Man, as later only the rebellion of Lucefero felled the angels of Hell. By God's will, things may change."

Cristiano gripped the apple. His eyes flamed cold. *So he looks in a battle,* Danielus thought, having never seen it. He pitied those adversaries who had.

"The Bible itself informs us of miracles," continued the Magister Major. "Nowhere, I think, does the Bible say that miracles have ended. Rather that they may attend World's End, or perhaps the dawn of another age."

Cristiano stared at him.

But the eyes of Fra Danielus, as others had found, gave no purchase.

At last Cristiano turned away.

"Magister, does the Bible say a woman should be dressed as a man, and have a man's freedom?"

"Some would tell you it does not," said Danielus.

"Then she—"

"She dresses for her work."

"She's *female.*"

"Do you go into a skirmish, Knight, without your shield or sword?"

"*Yes,* Magister, you amaze me—you dressed her as a noble *boy*—where then is *her* sword?"

Danielus laughed. He tipped back his head and laughed—and this Cristiano had, before, never seen or heard.

Danielus said, "You ask why she wears no sword."

"Yes, then. *Yes.*"

"She," said Danielus, no longer laughing, "*she* is the sword."

"What are you saying?"

Danielus now looked deep into the fire on his hearth.

He said, apparently at random, "Do you reckon they'll keep silent about this? I mean Marco and his brood."

"*No.* Whatever oath you made them swear. How can they?"

"How can they, indeed." Danielus now smiled. "They'll blab. And then go to their priest in the village, to confess the sin of blabbing. And he will send a message to the Church. And soon, between the gossip in the markets of the City, and the questioning of the priests, everyone will have heard of her, a red-haired virgin who can call down fire."

"It was deliberate then, to let them see."

"Of course."

"And I—and Jian, Aretzo—"

"She requires emotion, generally it seems that of others, since nothing stirs her very much. Oh, attempted rape did. That began it. But afterwards, the tears, fright, fury of those about her. Perhaps, their *need.* Her fire isn't always awarded as a punishment. It may be a gift."

"So you employed us, Magister. The Soldiers of God. Our doubt and—anger—"

"You alone were enough."

Cristiano did not move. In his hand the apple, (crushed) began to bleed wine-scented juice that dropped on to the floor.

"Was I."

"Your brother Soldiers gave themselves over quite soon. You resisted. Anger, or terror? Have you ever experienced fear, my Knight, to know it when it comes at you?"

Cristiano reacted suddenly. He flung the broken fruit into the fire. It hissed, as the candles had done, and a wonderful smell rose where the white flesh began to bake.

"How can I credit any of this?" he said.

"You saw it. How can you credit anything, otherwise."

Cristiano's face was bleak and the eyes wide.

"There you have it then. How can I?"

Danielus walked again across the room. Close to Cristiano, they were of a height. Nevertheless, as a father would, he took the younger man in his arms.

"You suffer, my son. Do you really believe God wants only penance and agony? He loves us, Cristiano. He wants us to be happy, too. Yield to Him, only that."

"I always have yielded, to God," Cristiano whispered.

"Do it only this once more."

"But she—"

"What did you feel then?"

"What I've felt only alone—before the altar."

Danielus held the young man; he stroked the blond hair of the bowed head pressed now to his shoulder.

"God is your father. You must trust Him as the child must trust the parent. His purpose may seem unconscionable. But He will know more."

"I've said I can't debate with you."

"Then God forbid you should try to debate with Heaven."

After a moment more, Fra Danielus moved Cristiano from him. The Magister left him to stand there, by the fire, and crossed the room.

Danielus opened the shutter of the small window, and looked out at the snow and the night. Beasts might faintly be heard trampling in their byres. No other sounds now but the emptiness of winter.

"Beatifica recounted her dreams to the priests who first questioned her. Sarco obtained details of all her speech with them. But I found these dreams especially interesting. They're beautiful, and innocent. And bright with power. But they might well have swayed those men further to the idea she was a witch. How lucky they were not beneath corruption."

Cristiano glanced at him. "You bribed them?"

"How else do you think she came to me, after all the fuss that had been made?"

"The Council of the Lamb—"

"Oh, the business hadn't reached high. They thought her nothing much."

Danielus was silent a moment. Then he said, almost tenderly, "There are wolf tracks in the snow, down there. They've circled the farm, poor starving things, and gone away."

"You pity wolves."

"I pity all the world, Cristiano. Myself not exempted. If it weren't blasphemy, I would pity God. So much pain and such a little spice and sweetness."

"That's how we learn. The harsher the school—"

"The greater the achievement? Later, in Heaven, we can be glad of it. Let me tell you what the girl said she dreamed. A country of sands and stones, with slim tall trees that had a foliage like fringes of gold. And a scarlet mountain, which seemed to burn like a terracotta lamp, from within."

"Where did she see such a thing to dream it?" Cristiano's voice was almost idle. Exhausted, he leaned on the wall, watching the apple in the flames.

"Where indeed. She said she saw the people there, and they were black as if burnt. The animals were curious. She describes one like a hare, but taller than a man. And a bear that sat in a tree and ate the leaves. Except, the leaves weren't consumed."

"Her mind—"

"Curdled? Well. Let me tell you something else. Now while you lean there, dying for sleep."

"Pardon me, Magister—"

"Rest yourself a while, Cristiano, from being always perfect. I'd rather have you tired, to hear this. Perhaps then your own dreams will make space for it."

Danielus closed the shutter. The room drew close about them.

"I keep a library in the island house. While I was there, I searched for and found a certain book. The writings of Gaius Suetonius Tranquillus. You will know, he was a Roman much given to anecdote and to history. Suetonius reports the tale of a Roman sea captain who, while questing for a large and unknown island in the Mare Arabicus, was overtaken by a mighty storm. The vessel outlasted the tempest, but lost her course. For some while she was blown southward. Then when the gale dropped, having not enough crew left alive to man the ship, they were driven east of south. The legendary island had failed them. Instead they reached several small islets, which sustained them with water and peculiar fruits. Months passed. Suetonius heartlessly describes their prayers to their pagan gods, begging salvation, and thinking they must die."

Cristiano watched the Magister Major. *Watched.* On guard against weariness, and any miracle.

But up in the watchtower, O sentry, remember night must come.

"At last the ship reached landfall. No island. It was a country large as any they had come from. And in their talk of it, when years after some of them returned, they named it, this place, God's Other World."

Cristiano said, "Since it was so unlike anything they knew."

"So unlike. A land of mountains and deserts and lush forests, filled by plants and creatures never seen, never imagined, not even in the remote East. They had fallen, they thought, from the edge of the earth. But being imperfect, this was not Heaven. Nor was it fearful enough for Hell. Another world then."

"If they returned and said this, were they reckoned liars?"

"Of course. Simply because they had returned, as Suetonius points out. The captain and his men claimed to have brought proofs, nevertheless. Unluckily, if unsurprisingly, none of the animals or plants had endured the journey back, which had been quite as harsh as the setting out. Only the woman survived, and was taken with them to Rome, to be shown to the Emperor Vespasian."

"A woman. Was she as different as the world they said they'd found?"

"She was black. But then, she might have been from Africanus. The Romans were acquainted with Nubians. However, her features weren't of this type, and the language she spoke had never been heard."

"What became of her?"

"I regret to say, she was a slave. The Roman men had made her that, treating her, the writer comments, quite well. They thought her an inferior, as they thought any foreigner, especially one whose skin was unmatched to their own. The white and freckled skins of Britains, for example, seem to have disgusted them. She was disputed over in Rome, whether she should be shown as an exhibit, or carried by the ship's captain to his farm. In the end, bored no doubt, the emperor generously permitted the captain to keep his spoils."

Cristiano thought the apple in the fire perished very slowly. It had not yet burned away. He said, "Is that all the story?"

"She lived as a slave. And died as one. She reputedly bore several children. They said she was docile and biddable, but for all that, a sorceress."

"Why?"

"She could bring fire."

"Yes, I guessed that would be it."

"According to Suetonius, they called her *Cucua*, the nearest they could get to her name. She told them her knack of lighting the fire and lamps had been given her from a mountain, which she visited in her childhood. A red mountain, which was the home of spirits."

"Did her gift pass on?"

"Well, Cristiano. Perhaps it did."

"But it was long ago. And do they say where she died?"

"Gaius Suetonius names the place. I can't discover it. In Italy, for sure."

"She might by now have many descendants."

"Blood dilutes. As water does."

Danielus slowly drew off his cross and put it down. It seemed heavy to him, as he handled it. "Maybe all of it is only my fancy. Or a Roman fancy. Or an ancient lie. But the fire, Cristiano, that's quite real. Go and sleep now. Yes, go on. Throw yourself off into the abyss of slumber. Perhaps the answer is there for you, waiting."

Cristiano straightened.

Danielus looked at him, thinking of the boy of fifteen long ago—the girl's age now, probably. And, strangely, *her* eyes also, here clouded only by another color, by masculinity, and by intellect.

It was in this one he had seen her gaze. And this one who held also her power of fire, but frozen cold as ice and trapped for ever inside.

Cristiano approached and dropped to his knee.

The Magister extended the emerald for him to kiss.

Presently, in the chamber outside, Cristiano's step was firm, then sluggish. The pallet groaned. Then silence.

But even after the candles had been dowsed, the inner room smelled on and on of burning apples.

Beatifica lay curled on her right side, one palm under her cheek.

She was dreaming, and did not know it.

Most likely she would not recall her dream on waking, only that she had been, as always, a great distance from the earth.

It was not Alter Mundi—God's Other World—which now she traveled. Instead, against soft dimness she neither heard nor saw, she beheld an angel.

He was tall and spare, and behind him the great wings had opened, like the wings of a swan she had seen carved in the altar rail of the Little Cappella. They were darkly white, and touched with a watery glow, shifting, elusive. In one hand he grasped a drawn sword. Again, perhaps, like an image she had been shown, this time among the Primo's Golden Rooms, Micaeli, the warrior angel of the

Bellatae. And, like the Angel Micaeli, this angel too wore a maculum of glistening mail.

The girl was spellbound, not awed. She was entranced.

She observed him until he faded in the depths of her sleep. She had not seen his face. Perhaps he had not had one. But within his diadem of flame, the hair hung long, a pale gold almost white.

BOOK TWO

Mundus Imperfectus

PART ONE

And there went out another horse that was red: and power was given to him that sat thereon to take peace from the earth, and that they should kill one another: and there was given unto him a great sword.

REVELATION OF JOHN THE DIVINE
The Bible

1

Apparently he could not visit. She had guessed he might not, despite an earlier letter. She would keep the Festival for the household, any way. It was the Feast of Sweets, after which came the forty days fasting and penance of the Quadraginta, to mark Christ's sojourn in the wilderness.

Veronichi combed her long black hair with the sandalwood comb. A vanity from the East. Crusades had first brought such trifles into Ve Nera. What irony: going out to enforce God among the infidel, they had returned meshed in and trailing infidel pleasures, unguents and perfumes, curious foods and scented baths. Also things it was not wise to talk of—aphrodisiacs, sodomy, the theology of another God passing as the true one.

But her hair was very black; she thought so, almost amused, hiding it now inside her linen cap. The hair of a Jewess.

Danielus had rescued her from that. That is, from living as the Jews of Venus were supposed to do.

To her last day she would never forget the morning that life ended.

The house had stood against the ghetto wall—of course, on its *inside*. Plaster had crumbled from the house, exposing wounds of raw red. It was the same with all the houses of the ghetto. Besides, mostly the ghetto comprised huts. Filth was everywhere. She had thought nothing of it, then, nor the stench of poverty. (She could not bear dirtiness or bad smells now. When the lagoon brought her the summer stinks of Venus, Veronichi's household on Eel Island choked instead on roomfuls of fresh roses and smoking gums.)

She was the niece of a rabbi. He, living alone, had taken her in during her infancy. Her parents were gone, and she learned, then, nothing of them, and never much. Later she would wonder if her mother had been stoned for adultery. For Veronichi—then called Yaelit—was the child of a Christian, a prince of the outer City. And by the death-bed confession he had made, Yaelit gained her escape. For the prince confessed to one of his legitimate sons, Danielus, by then a priest high in the sacerdocracy of the Primo. The confession was not greatly original. On a drunken sortie through the Jewish quarter, the prince had seen the woman who was to be Yaelit's mother. He felt himself enamored, had her abducted, stored a few months in some place he used for such sport, and made love to her until love ended. Then he sent her back to her Jewish husband, and the ghetto. Yaelit was the result.

Following the demise of her actual father, the prince, Yaelit was in turn taken from the slum within the wall.

That scene, never to be forgotten. Her uncle, the rabbi, pulling her back into the room. Threatening he would cut her throat rather than allow her to be defiled, (the inevitable fate) or worse, made into an apostate—a Christian. Already he had been planning to wed Yaelit to a scholar of the quarter, a man even older than himself. She was by then seventeen, and had been kept single so long only in order to tend her uncle's house—his unpaid servant. With marriage, she would have much the same position, but now maintaining two houses. She would cook and clean from the scraps of existence, revere her husband and bow to him in all things, as she did her uncle. But also she would have to lie down under the ancient scholar and conceive for him a son. Worse than all this, though, was the knowledge she must cut off her hair, and put on instead the traditional dry horsehair wig of a Hebrew wife. This proposed robbery frightened Yaelit. Had not the hero Samson lost his strength and spirit when shorn? Her uncle slapped her: what did that matter; she was no hero, but a woman.

The Christian men sent by Danielus came through the ghetto gates, however, armed with staves and knives, and in the end the rabbi, hideously cursing them and spitting foam, let Yaelit go.

How tall the ghetto walls had seemed, and looking back, she saw men and women in black, wailing and gnashing their teeth at her destiny—as if she had been cast out of paradise. Then, the Christian guards outside the gates, jeering and laughing. But then she was through, and she saw sunlight, which seemed now different, and the glitter of the canals, which were that day filled by rippling chains of jewels rather than water.

Her uncle had been right. She had become a Christian, naturally.

Veronichi, no longer Yaelit, pressed home the linen cap. But all her hair lay under it. Her hair remained for her. Whenever she wished, she might let it down. She smiled. She would presently write to the Magister Major.

'Dearest and most respected brother, pray do not leave your promised visit too long. You know I am always anxious at my management of your house, here. And I have not been well . . .'

On the Island of the Rivoalto, the palace and grounds of the Ducem vividly fluttered with pitch brands, candles, hanging Eastern lamps. Joffri had declared the Feast of Sweets must be a "Sunny Night."

As Joffri strolled through the gardens with two pretty women, and with three ivory hounds trotting behind them, he and his ladies tossing candies covered by goldleaf into fountains, dogs, and the jaws of small children, a messenger waited in the shadows of an adjacent court.

He could hear the laughter and the outbursts of fun, the music of harps, bells and trumpets. Distant small topaz explosions denoted runners with torches. But nobody came for him. He sat there, kicking his heels.

It was not particularly warm.

His mind uneasily announced to him that, from what he had been hearing, it had been warm enough elsewhere. Where did those stories start? He had met them at once, coming into the City. Some farms out on the plain, claiming they had seen a naked virgin, clothed modestly in fiery hair, riding a pale horse through the fields at dawn. And from the bare furrows, a flock of birds flew up, all on fire, but not burned, not *harmed*. And later, someone saw a flock of burning geese, rushing down like the sun falling out of the sky. Their wings were full of flames, which gradually went out as they settled to feed. There had been talk of a Plague Virgin half a century before. This was a Fire Virgin. An omen of war? Did it mean God would help Ve Nera—or destroy it?

The dispatches and letters the messenger carried came from Candisi. Later they would be shown at the Primo.

Although not informed of the contents of his satchel, the messenger had some ideas about it. Probably such news was unsuitable for the Feast of Sweets. For this reason, the advisors of the Ducem were making the dispatches wait.

One thousand and ten ships were now, it seemed, assembling at Jurneia. With the first fullness of spring they would set sail. Ve Nera might expect them by the Crab Month—or before, if God did not deter the winds.

The messenger reached into his tunic and touched the old lucky coin, bronze, with the figure of Neptune, the sea god, cut on it. He had already sent his family packing to the hills. A panicked exodus later might have impeded them.

It was said the City had, standing, or building at the shipyards of Torchara, four hundred ships. But more likely that was less.

An enemy could only come at her properly from the sea, and then her channels were too narrow to let them in. But the sand bars of the lagoons would be nothing to them. They would haul their ships over by means of slaves, on logs if necessary. Besides, the tides could flood quite high even in summer. And the sea walls were not very much. The lagoons would fill with ships as well as water . . . Jurneia had cannon. On every vessel?

Screams of merriment burst up from Joffri's gardens.

After this feast came Quadraginta. The wilderness.

An official was approaching.

The messenger rose.

Not an official, a priest. More, one of the Council of the Lamb—all in black, stooping slightly, with fish-pale, worm-thin eyes.

The messenger knelt.

"Holy brother."

"Yes. That's well enough. Take yourself to the kitchens, and eat. You may leave your bag with me."

Again, uneasy, the messenger held the satchel, still.

"My lord the Ducem—"

"The Ducem shall have it."

The documents, in the hands of skillful scribes, would only take an hour or so to copy.

Reluctant yet distracted, the messenger gave Brother Sarco his dispatches. He went to the kitchens, where he fell asleep over his food.

*   *   *

"When your heart is mine
  "You may do as you will to—"
That song had come back. It was a disgusting and lewd song.
The goddess Venus, married to Vulcanus, engaged in lechery with
the war god, Mars. Give me your heart, she said. You will be the
freer without it. But, she warned, if you cause me to love *you,* I shall
make you give up the world for me.

Careless of her admonition, Mars stretched her on her back,
smoothed her nacre breasts, parted the sea waves of her hair and
thighs, and drowned in her. But his spasms, while drowning, rendered her such delight, she loved him, and he was lost.

It had been a chant to God. The soul, loving God, was made
free. But if God should choose to love that soul above other souls,
by which it was meant, *select* that soul for some duty to Heaven,
then the world must be renounced, and all things, but the service.

They knew this, the four priests, (Eyes and Ears) as they stood
by the door. Behind them on the night canal, the Styx boat waited
like a crocodilius from some fearsome bestiary.

Fists slammed on the door.

Within, the noise rose riotous, subsided abruptly.

They had to knock again.

A little boy came, in an apron—a slave—he was pushed aside.

From the drunken inner room, the master of the house came
out, hot-faced with fear.

"Brothers—what can you want here? It's a Christian household—we celebrate the fore-penitence feast—"

"You're Jacmo Leatherer?"

"Yes, brothers, yes, but—"

"Look at your own sins, flaunted there on your body."

In horror, the leather-maker gaped at his own corpulence, his
tunic of good wool trimmed by embroidery—for the feast. The
leather belt his own shop had made, studded with silver.

"I paid my tax on it, brothers—yes, even though I and my son
worked it."

"You're too gaudy always, Jacmo. And too loud. Come. You
must tell us more. We will listen."

Dragged in the boat, and rowed away, Jacmo weeping now.
Once leaning over to puke from terror in the lagoon.

Other boats were stealing on. In each, beside the priests, a man
or two, or three or four, with sagging faces of dismay. One boat with
five whores in it. Bony from malnutrition, or fat with it, fat on

stodges that gave no life. But, "You eat too much. Gluttony. Gluttony and lust." "I never like my work, brother. I *give*." "You give? For coin? You *sold* the flesh the Almighty leant you."

Rowed over water, these lamenting souls. Styx boats, yes. Towards the pearl-domed Primo, which now, by night, was like the gateway to the Underworld.

And in the under-rooms of it, a light like Hell from the braziers, in which weird tools were heating up.

"No—holy brothers spare my hands—I need my fingers for my work—"

"For delving in the dish? For tickling in concupiscence?"

"My trade—my trade—"

"Then repent, my son."

"For what? For *what*? I've done nothing. It's my money you want—for the ships—very well—yes—take it—"

"No, my son. It's your soul we wish to cleanse."

Cries. Such cries.

Prayers. Confessions which were invented to stay the pincers and the iron burning white.

Rumor said the underlings of the Council threw the corpses off a bridge some way over the Laguna Fulvia. Not too close to the Primo.

"Is he alive?"

"I think not . . . No. He's gone. Prayers must be said."

On the long stone stair, a man was standing, watching, as the latest corpse—the leatherer's—was shifted. In the hood, the watcher's face was swarthy. When he spoke, his voice was rough, as if from coughing.

"Remember too, you scour Ve Nera clean. The enemy sails towards us, the Children of Satanus. If we're found wanting, what destruction may not befall us?" They heeded, looking up, their eyes glinting in the brazier light—black rats. "These foul sins of theirs must be cauterized, and the body of the City healed. Or He will blast us all. Remember those other cities of the plain."

One of the Eyes and Ears replied.

"It's true, Brother of the Lamb. Who hasn't heard the story of the creature, formed like a girl, who burns down the houses of wrong-doers?"

The priest on the stair said nothing. Then he said, "This is only some make-believe."

(On the floor now, the dead man lay as if listening too. Make-believe had not saved *him*.)

"But many saw it. She *walked in fire*—and since then several have seen the thing. A being wrapped in hair which burns—"

"They thought her a witch," said another. "But she vanished. It was even thought we took a witch and questioned her, but that witch was only a simpleton. We lashed her and let her go—"

And another said, "Brother of the Lamb, God may already have sent down an avenging angel. It might take any form, to test us."

"A female—" rasped the man on the stair.

From across the black room, yet one more black rat cheeped up. His hands had blood on them. He said, piously, "The Immaculate Maria was at first only a girl. And the luminous Santa Caterina, who chastely wedded Christ."

The corpse was being quickly borne out now. There were others to see to. How many more would perish tonight, to fund and clean the City?

The swarthy priest glanced at dead Jacmo.

"Did he confess?"

"Yes, Brother of the Lamb. He said, beyond his vainglory and noisiness, he had copulated, twice, with his neighbor's dog. A bitch. It might have been worse. Here's the paper. He signed it. That is, we assisted him to sign . . . his hand—Seven hundred silver duccas, and his house, to come to the Council. The fine is just."

"Was he long in his dying?"

"No, gracious brother. And he died in the end in a state of grace, may Christ be blessed."

The corpse was gone now. The underlings would be in charge of it. Off to the bridge . . . deep water could hold so much.

Jacmo, who copulated with dogs. Renzo, who had eaten meat on a fish day, challenging and cursing the Trinity. A whore known as Happy, who had worshipped the devil and boasted she had that month served as many men as Jurneia sent ships.

Into the water.

And for these falsehoods, whispered, shrieked, to save what might be left of a whole skin, these admissions to crimes which, in fantasy or nightmare only they had committed, that place was coming to be named. The Bridge of Lies.

2

It was Quadraginta. The time of fasting and sorrow. The forty days of payment for past faults. But, spring was forward, and took no notice.

On a chair by the high window, Beatifica sat quietly. She was dressed as normally now, like a young man, a lesser prince. Her clothes were white, or gray, and she had learned how to save them from getting dirty, moving carefully about, eating and drinking in the fine way she had been taught. As she generally did when alone, she had spent some time saying over prayers and passages from the Bible, to enjoy their sounds. Now every day a priest came, who was teaching her both Testaments, chapter by chapter, and in Latin.

This priest, young and gentle, blushed on and off and on with confused indecision when he was with her. Even so, he would tell her always the meaning of each passage he was to help her learn.

In this manner, although still not understanding the majority of the individual words, Beatifica was coming to grasp the narrative behind each section she recited. Also the names of Patriarchs, heroes, villains and celestial beings. As others had found before her, the richness of the Bible as a story book was virtually limitless, while the poetry and symmetry of the wonderful, unknown words, consistently pleased her. However, the appalling threats and unearthly inspirations jointly passed her by.

"She speaks so flawlessly, one would swear she knew every sentence, every letter she utters," this, from her flushed teacher. Then, urgently, "Truly, Magister Major, I think she *does,* by some supernal intervention, know them *all.*"

Fra Danielus had nodded. It had been his hope that most would come to believe this of her. Her ignoramus's power of learning by rote was worth much more than mere understanding.

Beyond her window, which was high up in the Primo's side, Beatifica could see down between high roofs, into a small garden, where lay brothers were gathering herbs, the only form of seasoning, with a little salt, permitted for the Forty Days. Tiny flowers covered the lawn like gems and coins. On a peach tree, blossom massed like the white sea-foam from which the goddess Venus had been fashioned.

Beatifica had re-entered the Primo with Fra Danielus and some of his people, scribes and servants. She had been dressed then as one of the lay brothers, in a loose brown habit. No one noticed her. Outside, (unknown to the girl) her fame of fire had spread. But in most of the tales she stayed an uncanny phenomenon, manifesting without human agency, vanishing in thin air.

Into the garden suddenly walked a Soldier of God. He wore the shining maculum, and was girded by the sword belt. The shoulder badge of the Child astride the Lion, from this distance, was just a smudge of sunlight. His hair was dark.

The priests drew back. The Bellator talked to them, shortly. Beatifica heard the voices, but not what was said.

She knew the Bellator, however. He was the one they had called Jian, at the farm on the plain. He had ridden beside the uncomfortable jouncing litter which brought her back to the City. On the journey, three times every day, he had asked her if she required anything. She consistently said No. What could he give her? As always, she expected nothing, and to ask of her her wishes had remained, in her view, at best an irrelevance.

Now the priests left the garden, their baskets laid with green.

Jian, Bellator Christi, stood, foursquare below her. Far down, and made small.

The sun on his hair altered it to silver.

Something moved through Beatifica. This was like a low tide, passing from her heart to her brain, and away again. She did not recognize it. But she leaned out a little way.

And Jian, turning all at once, tipped back his head and looked directly up at her.

Her hair fell round her face and shoulders, over the window's edge, drifting. She wore it unbound and unconcealed now, as a boy or a man would. Sunlight caught her, too.

Jian crossed himself. Then he went down on one knee on the velvet lawn, crushing the little flowers.

Beatifica watched him, puzzled, unsettled as so often by the actions of others, and yet, as usually too, indifferent.

He was worshipping her.

She did not know it. Nor did he.

With a strange sensation of disappointment, (not knowing either what disappointment was) the girl withdrew inside her room.

She went over to the icon of Maria that stood on the chest. It was a small statue, of alabaster, only the veil colored rose, and painted with gold stars, which also appeared, one each, on the dainty feet.

Beatifica now crossed herself as Jian had done. She said a prayer to the Virgin, one of the prayers whose meaning no one had told her. She said it melodiously. She had been taught how to worship, its forms. And this too, for her, had become a valued pastime.

Outside, Jian was still kneeling. Still committing his own act of devotion.

Then the midday Solus sounded from the Angel Tower. Getting to his feet, Jian strode away.

The nun Purita knelt also in the Midday Mass. Here, this fell some minutes later, since the bell of Santa Lallo Lacrima, (lullaby of tears) invariably rang after that of the Primo.

Like all the women of her order, Sister Purita wore gray, her wimple only being white. Against it, her skin looked sallow. Under it, her blonde hair was cropped short—but she had seen, as it fell, some gray also in the strands. At the inn, she would soon have had to cover her hair completely, anyway, or to bleach it with the not-always-obtainable urine of a donkey or horse.

Luchita—Sister Purita—prayed.

Her back ached, but now she had the balm for that, and the herbal drink which helped her to sleep. There was the dispensation too, which allowed her, if unwell, to miss the Prima Vigile two hours after midnight. As a rule though, Purita had one of the novices wake her in time.

He had been so very kind to her. Possibly, it was for the first that anyone had. Even her father had beaten her, and her mother too, as they had all the children, excepting Cristiano. The local priest had taken an interest in the boy from infancy, instructed him in reading and Latin, and entered him for the priesthood. Their parents had been proud. Cristiano, she had always thought, (and sometimes enviously, belligerently) had *escaped*. Now, so had she.

Last summer, when she had knelt differently, weeping slightly from tiredness and soreness, on the stone floors of the nun-house, a man had come for her, a priest. She was taken through the marshes, to the big church of Santa La'La, whose late bell she had so often heard from the inn, and never heeded. She thought she had failed at the nunnery, all her remorse and punishing work gone for nothing. She would be castigated and thrown out. Then what?

When she was taken into the room, and saw the priest sitting there, she had trembled with shock. It was a Magister of the Basilica—more, a Magister Major. She knew him in another moment, from the description Cristiano had once given her.

He had the ascetic face of a saint, pale, and lean, like body and hands. His eyes were black, large and calm, and from his thick dark hair the tonsure seemed carved, like a disc in the fur of a dark cat. There was gray there, too. Like herself, he was no longer young.

He told her she should sit down.

When she had done so, he said, "You must find this road very hard, my sister."

"It is. But I don't mind." She did. She could see no other way.

"How long have they told you you must wait for the novitiate?"

"Until next spring. Then, if well judged, I can begin."

"Tell me, please," he said, "why you came to this? Was your husband harsh? Your children ungrateful?"

"Oh—my children are all far off. One way and another. The boys went for soldiers. Two died in the last war with Candis."

"That is sad."

"Yes." She corrected herself quickly, "You're very good to say so, Magister."

"What of the others?"

"Trade took them away."

"Even the girl."

She hesitated, then said, "My daughter became a whore, I'm sorry to say it. I never see her. My husband—he wouldn't have her in the house. I don't know what became of her."

"Maria Magdelena was also a harlot, Luchita. Nothing is irredeemable. But I perceive why the life of a nun may eventually have appealed to you. Your last child died, I think."

"You'll know from my brother," she said.

Danielus nodded. He had thought she might not be a fool, nor was she. In her scourged and emptied face, he could detect a trace of Cristiano. When young perhaps, she had been fair.

She said, "Magister, *he* must have told you I didn't seek this because of that. But because of the girl."

"Tell me of that, then."

She told him. Her words were halting, not from uncertainty, only through trying to find the proper ones, those which would summon back the event both for herself and another.

When she finished, Danielus said quietly, "And you have no doubt of what you saw?"

"None."

"Someone will have mooted the chance that Lucefero worked in this, not God."

"Many times. How can I know? But I never thought so."

"Why?"

She lifted her eyes and looked directly into his. "It hurt me when she did it. I felt a sort of splitting pain—it was—forgive me, Magister—like a birth pang. And most of my self fell from me. I was left only with my inner self. Not much, you'll agree, I'm sure. Yet no longer—bowed down, laden—*free*. It was as if I needn't cling anymore to the life I'd had. Nor to anything. I could begin again. Do you see? Surely Satanus doesn't give us anything like that? He'd weight us down the more, even if it was with luxuries and charms. It would be *heavy*—not lighter than the air."

Danielus got up. So did she.

"Do you know the symbol which is in this ring I wear?"

She stared at the emerald. "The emblem of your authority, Father."

"It is the stone blessed by the Christ, and from which his final drinking cup was made. Also, it was the stone of the goddess Venus, patron in ancient times of our City." He extended his hand. Unbelievingly, she realized he was allowing her to press her lips to the mystical jewel. She did so. (The emerald felt coolly warm, and smooth as water.)

Danielus said, "You've served your novitiate, Luchita. Now you need only learn your duties as a nun. Do you still wish it?"

Bemused, she nodded. "But I—"

"Nothing is random," he said, "that comes from God. He chose you, Luchita, never forget this. To be the witness and to throw off your earthly chains. Don't cry. You shall serve here in the sister-house of this church. You've paid your dues already in the world. I shall make it my business to see you're well-treated here. The Domina is old and charitable."

Luchita now, kneeling in Santa La'La, raised her eyes to the soft light of the glazed window. She prayed for the charitable Domina, and for the Magister, Fra Danielus. Let God bless him, as Christ blessed the green stone in his ring.

O God, sang the nuns, *I render you all my heart and am free. You demand of me everything, and I forget the world.*

3

The room was very large, and had required to be. It was crowded. The walls were covered by long tapestries, and painted panels that told stories, both colored like jewels, and gilded. Silver lamps hung down twice the height of a tall man, yet well clear of the throng below. The candles were uncountable, and all starred with light. Instantly slaves removed and replaced those which had burned out. Music played. The servants stalked to and fro, kitted in plum silk, the color of the Ducal house. At the long tables draped in white, and set with silver platters and spice-cellars of gold six mid-finger lengths high, (in the shape of towers) guests of the Ducem were eating and drinking. The Forty Days were over. Christ had died and risen from the dead. And here, the taxes and the dangerous opprobrium which hung over Ve Nera's apparel and food, went unconsidered.

Men in stiffened tunics, or long gowns, edged by bear fur and the tails of weasels, velvet hats stabbed by flowers of ruby and beryl. Women with bared lily shoulders pushed up from tightly buttoned over-gowns, which sprouted patterned waterfalls of sleeves, and headgear that was a heart, or padded hoop wound by gilt cord, netted in transparent veils from Inde, and spattered by pearls.

Even so, no joints or poultry were served on this meatless night. Crab flesh and eels had been brought instead, and wide-fish in honey, the scorpion crab in its coral shell, and stew of oysters in the Roman manner. Now, however, a trumpet blew. The salt-swans were coming in. Birds it was true, but, from their greenish tint and fishy taste, allowable.

Each rested on a bronze charger rimmed by gold. Each was re-clothed in its feathers, beaks covered by silver-leaf and with diamonds, no less, set in the eyes. Down the room they sailed, long necks curved, proud on their lakes of vegetables.

Twelve in all. The room applauded. Knives were sharpened. The slender dogs, in collars of gold, lifted their muzzles.

As the feasters tore the swans apart, neatly hacking a way in past the quaint feathery illusion of life, Cristiano watched, expressionless.

"You grasp now the Council's need for curbing the appetite of men?" said Jian softly.

"Yes. I have always grasped that."

Water green feathers littered the floor, among the strewn camomile and asphodel.

Further up the high table, from his place beside the Ducem, Fra Danielus courteously declined the swan. But inclined his head to the two seated Bellatae.

"He says we may."

"You eat it. It isn't to my liking."

"Cristiano, you needn't mask your virtue with a falsehood."

Cristiano grinned suddenly. It was as startling as the rare times the Magister Major smiled. Jian, englamoured despite himself, laughed.

"No, I hate swan-meat. Turbot with feathers."

As the salver came, the riven swan, leaning now, Jian carved off a modest portion. The servant craned near, offering other vegetables, sauce, pickled oranges.

Cristiano had lapsed back into his impenetrable and somber gaze.

He was thinking of the girl, due to be brought in soon, like the swans. Similarly to be hacked and cut up, as by the jeweled personal knives of these rich princes and their women?

On the other side of the Ducem sat two men from the Council of the Lamb. As a Bellator went abroad in his mail, so the Council Brothers did in their night-black, and hooded. One of them was that evil-looking creature, Sarco. And beside him, the man who was coarsely-spoken. He had some ailment of the throat, it seemed. The Magister had called him only 'brother'.

At first Joffri had seemed rather cramped between these two arms of the Church. But as the wine flowed, this lessened. His young wife, Arianna, arrived late. Now she sat along the board in her white gown, neck crystallized by olivines. It was just possible, from the profile of her body, to surmise she might be with child. Joffri looked at her now and then, absently, affectionately, without any passion. She had a sad little face under the extravagant headdress.

A male Jew, Cristiano had heard, thanked God every day for not making him a woman.

And outside, with her guard, for so they must be considered, of seven Bellatae Christi from the Upper Echelon, *she* waited.

A woman, but not solely a woman.

Beatifica.

Since Christ' Mass tide, he had kept the vigil, as he always did every month. But God did not grant Cristiano his vision of Heaven. The ecstasy. Perhaps never again would that rapture be his.

Only at that time she brought down the fire.

Only then.

What did it mean?

He had eaten sparingly. Had not wanted much. These feasts he found distasteful, pointless and dull. Nothing in the world could compare with God.

Where God was, there waited all purpose and exhilaration. Was God—with *her*?

Cristiano dipped his fingers in the water bowl, where petals floated, and wiped his hands on the napkin. He closed off his Cup— it was silver—to the servant with the pitcher.

Tonight, here at the City's temporal hub, was to be recreated that miniature night at the farm on the plain. Joffri had heard the rumors. Of course he had. Now and then, he cast a puzzled glance at the Magister. A puzzled glance lit with a sort of childish wish for surprises. The opposite of the looks he gave his wife and two mistresses.

What do I feel?

Cristiano did not want it to happen here. For it would. She would come in and there would be the sense of startlement, then scandal, and a score of women would giggle at her affrontery, and some of the jaded men, fancying this hermaphrodite thing, a boy-woman clad as a lord, would eye her lasciviously. Then she would call the fire. She could. She would.

He was armored now. He had put a maculum of steel upon his mind and soul.

But they, this ignorant petty crowd, attractive as all the similar scenes of banquets upon the walls, would respond with hysteria. Screams, prayers, women swooning, men falling to their knees.

The smell of smoke.

It was a show-piece, such as could provisionally be faked on any actor's cart, to please the rabble.

Yet it was real.

Had not Christ healed lepers and the blind before a crowd? Had he not, at a festival, changed water into wine? *Died* before a multitude.

Must even the sublime be cheapened to make good the truth?

But—she was only a girl.

The swans lay in ruins. (Twelve—one for every calendar month.)

The odor of roast and grease and burning wax grew heavy, mixed with the squashed flowers, and the Eastern perfumes. Perfumes even from Jurneia, no doubt.

Jian had drunk too much, Cristiano noted. He would stay couth but then need to confess it and do penance. He was not thinking of that. His eyes were bright, thinking of Beatifica.

One saw it among all the Upper Echelon of the Bellatae, for all were in the know. A raising of heads at the mention of the girl. Like the Ducem's dogs just now.

But the seven Soldiers of God who attended her tonight had never before seen what she could do.

The music had stopped. Joffri turned to Fra Danielus, his eyes brighter than Jian's.

Cristiano heard the Ducem say, "Will she come in?"

"Yes, my lord," said Danielus. "If you're ready."

"I long to see it, Father. Trust me."

On his other side, the hoarse priest from the Council said, gratingly, "If we are to believe she can."

Cristiano thought, *How can he doubt?* And then, *The simplicity of it is what is horrible to me. I believe. I know. I wish I could go out— no, I wish before God this was not to happen.*

But God must have decreed it. Miracles were in the provenance of God. God could not make an error. And yet, the Magister had told him she was descended from a witch—

Joffri stood up, and everyone became hushed. A little god upon earth, a man strutting in his crown. *Think of the skull behind the skin, Joffri!*

Cristiano's heart beat, a drum in his side. He tried to cool himself, half reached out for the wine. Took his hand back and sat motionless.

"Generally," Joffri said to the huge, worldly room, "I call jugglers now, and men who swallow birds and let them back out from their ears. Or a poet to sing his latest ode."

They looked at him. Men drunk, feeding their hounds on bits of swan. Women with the upper moons of their breasts shining.

Joffri said, "Christ's resurrection is scarcely past. And God has not forgotten us. Men say, let's eat and make merry and forget the grave gapes for us. But why fear the grave? Christ makes nothing of it. And He, knowing an enemy steals upon us even now, a dragon that slips across the ocean—" They stared. Faces had whitened. Here and there a woman clutched her male companion's arm, or held her own hand, as if to pray. "God sends signs to us, it seems. We needn't be afraid even of a mortal foe." Joffri flipped one nonchalant hand, and the trumpet sounded again. The wide doors at the room's far end were opened.

The Ducem sat. He shot one gleaming look at the Magister Major. The uncaring hand had said, Oh, let's do it then, let's see. The eyes said, You'll need God's help and to spare if you fail now, will you not?

It was exactly as Cristiano had thought.

Startlement first.

He had seen the red horse brought for her. But not reckoned on quite how she would look on it. Here in the City, it was at once a symbol of the rare, and too of war . . . It was a steady animal, despite its lean and graceful, hound-like lines. Ferried through the waterways on a barge, and here to the Rivoalto, it had needed to be. It placed its hoofs with the sure balance of a dancer. In color it was like burnished copper. The saddlecloth was white, sewn with golden stars and suns, and from the white bridle and halter, hung golden bells, which jinked faint but clear in the silence, as it brought her forward.

She was also in her white and gold. Her hair, unbound, was one pure shade brighter than the horse.

The seven Bellatae walked, three on either side, and one at her back. They had come armed into the presence of the Ducem, the only men who might, save for his own guards. And the swords were all drawn, the tips of them dipped earthward.

Down the room the red horse stepped.

Her face was blanker than unwritten paper. All but the wide eyes. Golden. Fixed, as Cristiano remembered, on the Magister. Until, suddenly, they moved, and fixed on *him.*

The drum in his side jolted. Missed, and began again.

But she looked at Jian now. (He heard Jian catch his breath.) And then straight at the Ducem. Straight, straight, straighter than any sword.

Joffri crossed himself. Then he said, very low, "You never told me, Fra Danielus, she was beautiful."

Cristiano heard Danielus answer instantly in his quiet voice, "Of course, my lord. Her beauty comes from God."

Joffri sounded shaken a little. He said, "Doesn't it always, holy Father?"

"By a conduit, it does. On her, it seems, the Almighty has directly breathed."

Cristiano heard another voice in his mind, which contemptuously said that No, she was not beautiful. She *had* no beauty, was more than beauty. Beauty was a tiny word of fools, used to describe what had no word, here on earth.

And a wave of fear followed the inner voice. The instinct to beware.

The horse had passed through the room, and come up to the highest table, where the Ducem sat with his family, and the priests.

They were aware now, most of the crowd, that the young man on the horse was not masculine. As he had predicted, Cristiano heard the quick rills of laughter, the smothered oaths. Until silence resumed.

But the rough-voiced priest spoke loudly.

"This is against the law of God."

The Ducem said, "Holy brother—"

And the priest said through him, not bothering with him, "A woman clad as a man is blasphemous and immoral. She must be wicked and an imbecile, and those in charge of her too."

Danielus now used his voice, pitched not raised, to find the far reaches of the chamber. "God makes the law and God can unmake it."

"You dare to say, Fra, that God—"

As easily as the priest had broken in on Joffri's sentence, Danielus overrode the priest's. "Who am I to speak for God, brother. And who are you to speak for Him. I say this: A sword travels in its sheath for battle. Not in a female gown."

The hoarse priest surged up and now Sarco, the other Council Brother, put out his hand and stayed him. "Let us only see."

The Magister would have told her what to do, and how and when. At some signal from him, now she dismounted from the horse. She did this without flurry or awkwardness, and with no display. She had the coordination of a knight, used to it.

"This," said Danielus, as he had on the farm on the plain, "is the Maiden Beatifica. Speak for us now, Beatifica, the Grace."

She did so.

As Cristiano had expected and predicted. In her perfect Latin.

Hands rose, a roomful of hands, faltering, belated. To mark the cross.

From a side door two of the Ducem's men were coming in. They carried between them a great black pot, and there was oil washing about in it.

They set this down between the girl and the high table, and went away.

One of the seven Bellatae guided the red horse aside. They all drew back, and left the central space clear for the girl and the cauldron.

She would do it now.

Cristiano braced his body and his mind. The Magister had said she drew her impetus from emotion. The room thrummed with it, like the strings of some instrument before a storm. But she should have none from him. Not one jot.

He felt but did not see her golden eyes go over him. He was one among so many.

The Magister spoke. "Bring the fire, Beatifica."

Cristiano, within a wall of milky adamant that could not be cracked, waited.

It would come.

It came.

He *heard* it, *felt* it—felt nothing.

Heard them screaming, and felt the heat of fire, absolutely present. The rasp of the oil igniting with the sound of tearing cloth. Chairs and benches scraped. Dogs volleying and baying in fright, voiding themselves—the silky bundled sound of a woman falling and caught by servants—sparks singeing his own cloak—*the smell of burning*—

Cristiano blinked to clear his vision, and looked and saw the pot full now of fire—and the Ducem, his eyes open wide and lips parted, and little Arianna, the Duccessa, shrinking away.

A column of smitch and smolder flaring into the roof where the banners hung.

A glass goblet, rare, brought to impress, smashing.

Purple light.

Her hair, deep colored now as blood, fading.

Her white face that seemed also burning from within, paling down to a human paleness that was almost ghostly.

She was bowing her head. Her shoulders drooped.

It cost her something to do this. He had never realized that before. Now she was tired. Shivering perhaps, he was not certain. But she kept firm, standing there.

Oh, not as a warrior must. From obedience, duty. She had been a slave. It had been whipped into her.

He had remained on guard. She had not penetrated the wall. But inside it now, for a second, he too felt stunned and drained. Into himself however, he also had beaten the strength to withstand his own weakness.

She and he, some long paces apart, stayed upright and in command. And Danielus, and the Bellatae, and the obviously fire-accustomed horse. While the feast chamber of Joffri gave way.

Cristiano glanced aside at the unnamed Council Brother. He was ranting, slavering, clutching his crucifix, which was of plain and modest iron. Sarco prayed, his eyes closed fast.

The Duccessa was fainting now, and her Ladies gathering her. What had this sight done to the child in her womb?

Joffri swung abruptly back. He glared, then laughed shortly.

"Magister Major, you are to blame for this havoc. Come on, let's go into another room. Bring her, this Maiden. Bring your Soldiers of God. Yes, yes, Brother Isaacus, you and your fellow Council Brother must come with us, of course."

The Ducem's guards were opening a way for them. Others led the red horse off into the courtyard. As it passed by the dogs now, scented with fire, they shied and barked. A young woman with black, waving hair artfully emerging below her headdress, ran to touch the horse with her fingers. Having done so, she turned, crying for happiness. And on the tables sprawled the remnants of the cloven swans.

"She is proof of God's love."

"Of the wiles of the Devil!"

Sarco once more put his hand on Isaacus' sleeve. "Hush, brother. You'll hurt your sore voice worse." And then, "What the Magister says he most truly believes, of that we may be assured."

Joffri put down his wine cup.

He stared at the Maiden Beatifica, who sat now in one of the carved chairs, her eyes lowered, her hands folded together on her right knee. She did not look wanton, nor unsuitable in her clothes. He did not fancy her, either, which, if he thought of it, surprised him. God must protect her from the lewd inspiration. God, Joffri knew, was clever.

They were in the Scarlet Room, one of the three halls which led from the feast chamber. The ceiling rose to its rafters, which were gilded. The walls were sheeted with hammered bronze, and marble.

There was nothing red in the room, (except for the Maiden's hair, which looked any way far less red than it had done in the feast chamber.) The Scarlet Room took its title from the pageantry which was sometimes enacted there. The recognition of sons, and betrothals, when scarlet and crimson garments were worn.

Fra Danielus stood by the Maiden. His Bellatae were ranked behind him. Nine of them now. They watched with professional faces, war-priests. But their eyes were dazed, or sparkling. All but that one, the one called Cristiano. His eyes were like silver discs found on the ice.

Danielus had lost none of his composure, and he was saying not much. He had told them God had sent them Beatifica. She was motivated by Heaven. In the conflict which the City must face, she would give courage in her turn. He did not say, it went by implication alone, the infidel would be afraid, if they heard stories of her.

Isaacus roared, spitting froth, "She must be questioned."

"So she has been," Sarco said.

Joffri said, urbanely, "Let *me* ask her something."

He thought Isaacus, (it had seemed essential to learn that one's name) would interrupt again. No. He only held up his cross, high in one hand.

Danielus said, "Beatifica, look up. There is the Ducem. Answer him."

Beatifica looked at Joffri.

What eyes she had. Were they gold?

"Tell, me, Beatifica, tell me if you're able, if you think God sent you this . . . gift?"

"What gift?" she asked. She did not say 'My lord'. However, her tone was gentle, inquiring, as if she wished to please—or comfort him.

"Your fire-bringing."

"My mother," said Beatifica, "showed me."

"Yes, the monster claims her mother taught her to do it, after the woman had died. A witch—a witch, what else."

Joffri risked a small indiscretion. "Be quiet, Brother Isaacus, if you can. The Council of the Lamb has my reverence, but you are only one of its membership. I am Ducem, and you are very rude."

Did Danielus smile? Invisibly?

Joffri said, "If your mother taught you, Maiden, how did *she* learn? From a demon?"

"She told me nothing of demons. It was angels that she saw."

"Angels—"

"An account of that was sent you, Ducem," said Sarco.

"Yes but—never until this moment did I—" Joffri stopped. He said, "Other than angels, what have you seen?"

Beatifica did smile. She was pleased to speak of herself. In her previous life no one had been interested.

"I only saw the angels once. But also I saw the serpent in the orchard."

Now a great quiet filled the room.

Many had not learned of Beatifica's dreams.

"She saw the Serpent," grated out Isaacus. "Bear witness, Brother Sarco. You heard as well as I. The *Serpent*."

Beatifica said, "Magister," (him she gave a title) "do I tell them of it?"

Danielus said, "I believe you must."

"Then, I saw it in an apple tree. But the fruits of the tree were gold and silver, like the sun and the moon." From speaking the Latin, from talking so much, her voice had changed now utterly. It was a lovely voice, mild but of great clarity. It had scarcely any gender, not feminine—but not masculine in any way. "The snake came down the tree to me. I thought it was a cat—but it hadn't legs, or ears, so it was a snake. It stared in my face with eyes that were profound." (She had learned this word, found it apt, used it aptly.) "But I never picked the fruit. They would have burned my hands. I knew not to. Before the snake could speak to me, I was woken."

In the void, it was Jian who spoke, unable to prevent himself. "Eva, the first woman, heeded the Serpent, plucked the apple, and damned the world with her sin. This Maiden could not—*would not*. And God Himself woke her from her trance."

Isaacus, in his fury, cast down his iron cross on the floor. It rang.

"She is a *seducer* sent by *Hell*. This fire she brings comes from the Pit. Haven't I heard tales that she burns men alive?" He moved fast and ungainly, snatching a lit candle from its spike. "*This* is the natural fire of this world, and what she brings is filth from the guts of the Fiend, a sulfurous belch." Isaacus raised the candle and croaked, in his voice of pebbles, a blessing over it. "Now it is God's fire. Do we doubt *God's* fire is stronger than the flames of Hell?"

He went rolling towards the girl, like some boat cut loose on a lagoon. She gazed up at him, not moving. Changed as she had, still she was the slave.

Jian moved. With a vast thrust, the black priest shoved him

away. Jian had not thought he would need much strength, but Isaacus was brimmed by his virtue.

Isaacus seized up the girl's right hand by the wrist.

"With *this* she calls her dirty genius. With *this* I *punish* her—"

Cristiano saw her start, flinch. Only a little. But she was used to ill-treatment and wounding.

Isaacus dropped her hand.

He waved the candle, victorious.

"She's flammable despite the Satanic influence. She *burns.*"

Cristiano sprang around the chair. It was Jian, staggering still, who somehow caught him back. Danielus who reined him in.

"*Wait.*"

Leaning to the girl, the Magister lifted her hand and looked at it. Tenderly, perhaps. As a father might.

Then he said, "Get up, Beatifica."

When she did so—her face showing nothing, only her eyes, as if bruised—he raised her right hand in his own, and showed them all.

"You blessed your candle, Brother Isaacus, and called on God."

"You heard me, *Magister.*"

"Then God has answered you. And everyone of us."

On her hand, at her palm's center, a red and awful, weeping mark.

"Where else," said Fra Danielus, "have we seen this sign?"

Joffri did not know whether to shout with laughter or hide his eyes. Not one of them was unfamiliar with the cross, the icon of Sacrifice upon it. Nor the holy pictures of its aftermath. How could they be in doubt? The insane Isaacus, seeking to reveal her as devilish, had scorched her hand. With the divine stigmata granted only to saints, the bleeding scar of the nail which had pierced the palm of Christ.

4

Sunset diminished on the sea. They had come far, and had further to go. As darkness bloomed, it gathered the ships, and formed them into one vast single thing, a cloud of wood and sails.

Those that could had answered the cry to pray.

God is great. There is no god save God. Hasten then to greet Him, hasten that His power make you rich in Him, richer than a thousand golden mantles. There is no god save only God.

Suley-Masroor, Master of the *Quarter-Moon,* came from the trance of prayer. He got up from the deck. The warmth of the day was softly going with the light. The sea was very calm. The oars were at rest.

On every vessel now, the lanterns were lighting high up in the fore-towers, yellow eyes blinking to each other. Sails furled in, described two masts or three. The *Quarter-Moon* had three, and the wind-catcher at his stern. He was male, the ship, like all the ships of Jurneia and Candisi, for it was the sea which was female, unpredictable, and lovely.

The Master walked forward to the tower. He climbed the ladder, and the watch stood aside for him.

"It's good to pray," said the watchman.

"Yes, always good. For those moments we become again as God would have us, and are without sorrow."

But after prayer, he thought, the world came back, and this sailing on to make a war.

As if he read the Master's brain, the watchman said, "They are deserving of wrath, our enemies. They cheat us for our silk and spice. They worship a parody of the Most High. A war of trade, but also holy."

"Have the three lost ships returned?"

"No, Master. There's no sign of them. The storm was bad."

"May those men be found, or ascend to Paradise," said Suley-Masroor.

They had lost five vessels in all since setting out. Four in the sudden spring gales, and one which had simply gone down, mysteriously, perhaps previously holed by spies. (They had caught a lot of spies, in Jurneia, prior to embarkation.) With the lost vessels, the fleet now totaled eight hundred and twenty-seven ships. It seemed the Lagoon City of Venarh had almost half that number again, over one thousand. And, as a last spy had confirmed, also ballistas and cannon.

Suley-Masroor remembered joking with his blind old father-in-law, telling the old man the Venarhans had only four hundred vessels. (He would gossip, when Suley was gone, and make his daughter, Suley's wife, afraid. Her three brothers were already with the fleet. It was sometimes best to dissemble.)

"I'll watch. Go down for your food."

Suley-Masroor stood in the fore-tower of the *Quarter-Moon,* staring out at the shining abyss of sea and night. Behind him, like a zircon, the evening star was rising up, Aspiroz, that the infidels of the west named Hesper, or Venus—another name they gave, so he understood, to their City.

He was reluctantly thinking about the dream he had had. Twice it had come to him. If it came again tonight, only then, would he permit himself to consult his sacred talisman. But it was strange, the dream.

In the dream, Suley-Masroor was hunting in the waste, alone but for his horse. The land was spare and dun, as he had often seen it, but then among some boulders a water-spout spangled. As he approached, he saw a yellowish fox, which sat still as the stones. Normally such a creature, of which there were several in the desert, would sprint away. But no, It did not shift itself. Even in the dream, he thought this odd, and hesitated, although the sight of the water filled him with thirst.

Then the fox got up, and trotting to the outlet, drank. But no sooner did the tongue of the fox touch it, than the waterfall changed. Suley-Masroor cried out in horror as spurts of steam and fire burst from the rocks in place of water.

Here, he woke. On both occasions at this instant.

The Chosen of God had, in the dawn of history, struck mountains to produce streams of water. This mocking mimicry of that act lodged like a burning shadow in the Master's mind. What did it mean? Was it only an inevitable anxiety—or some premonition sent to warn?

Cristiano dreamed of the Vigil.

He kneeled, not in the Soldiers' chapel, however, but in some open place of the Primo, which he did not recognize. It had a floor of glass, black glass. Pillars of gold, dull and ancient, rose to the dome, which was luminous and high, sounding with night winds, and with moonlit clouds that curiously passed through it, in and out.

He saw a window. The Virgin was depicted there.

As he kneeled below, slowly transcending his body's pain, as if dragging himself up a steep stair to the bell-tower of his own skull, he became aware that the hair of the Virgin was like copper. It was this, shaded by night, which had seemed to form her damson mantle.

Dreaming, Cristiano knew shame. But why?

More than the hurt of his body, he ached for God. But God did not arrive.

Instead, gradually, Cristiano grew conscious of other Bellatae, kneeling as he did before the window. Jian was to his left, and just at his back, Aretzo. Behind these he now saw, (leaving his body, drifting above them) the ranks of the Upper Echelon, and behind these, the lower militia of God. There were two Magisters Major present also, but not the third, not Danielus.

This concerned Cristiano, and he had a sense of searching for his own Magister, which kept him disembodied, moving on and on. The Basilica was filled, end to end; that in spite of being larger than it was. The priesthood was there, the lay brothers too, almost all the hierarchy of the Church. And beyond them, others knelt, men in mail like the Bellatae, faces locked in casques, their drawn swords held between hands in gloves of steel. Banners hung among them, leaning a little, or straight as the pillars. Emblems of the Lion and the Child, of the Lion and Star, of the Boar and the Bear and the Lynx—Ve Nera's Crusader banners from two centuries before. They were, these men, the first Knights of God. The warriors of the Suvio, the first cry to Battle, which had been uttered at the water's edge, when the Laguna Fulvia was choked with craft, and the sea, beyond the sand-bars, with high-sailed cogs bound for the Holy Land.

In the farthest reaches of the elongated Basilica, last of all, the people of the City stood humbly. They were very still, as if altered to carvings of wood. None of the children made a noise. The men were serious and the women devout. They wore the fashions of earlier times and of current time. He could not be sure of all their eras. But he noted a Roman matron, wrapped in her draperies, and beside her a broad-chested, bow-legged man in the armor of antiquity.

These were not phantoms. Nor quite immobile. Their eyes were living and bright.

At the Primo's end, in the dream, the doors were shut fast. It was here he turned, and looking back, viewed the colossal gathering, and himself, somehow, at their head, with Jian by him. And the Madonna Window, that too, which was like a slender rosy flame. Before it had been raised the secret icon of the Madonna Standard, kept close in the Sanctum, and shown only in extremity. He had never seen it. Now it was allowed him.

His sense of disquiet had left him.

Nothing was wrong, or inappropriate.

And in the upper air, where the clouds were, he saw the white light of God beginning, and was drawn up into it, and knew nothing else.

* * *

Beatifica dreamed a dream she would not remember.

She dreamed the angel had come back for her. He bore her up and flew with her across the sky.

She heard the vast beats of his wings, which were like the drumming of a heart.

Below, the world stretched out. Night was there, and lamps and other specks of light were being born, as stars were, in the higher sky. The sea and the lagoons seemed like salvers of silver, and the Silvian Marsh, and all the canals and channels, like a running of silver threads. Now and then, she saw their reflection on the waters, two flying beings upheld by the wide, beating wings.

In the East, on the sea, the moon was up.

They flew on, out towards the ocean.

She knew that soon the City would be left far behind and all the land. She did not mind it. She trusted her angel. For the very first, since she had been an infant with her mother, she was able to render the *obedience* of trust, which had nothing to do with fear, self-negation, or need. It was easy for her to let go, for there had never been anything to cling to. But now, in the clasp of the gray-eyed angel, she was free. In slavery, free. The earth forgotten, without any goodbye.

5

Caught in the tangle of pomegranate trees, new buds beamed a juicy red. The eels would dine well, this year. If the world went on.

The boatman optimistically sang about approaching summer. It was not a bawdy song. Besides, he had rowed Danielus before, and knew he would not be upbraided. Only when they reached the Isle of Eels did he say, "Bless me, Fra Magister. I can do with it. They say the Jurneians will be here inside three days."

"Not nearly so soon. You have time to get away."

"I? There's my wife and kits, my old dad, mumma, sisters, too, five of them, the youngest only twelve. Where are we to go?"

"Anywhere to safety, perhaps."

"You think it'll come to it."

"I think it may. Entreat God. Take this."

"Oh—Fra—that's generous. God grant you joy."

No one in the garden. (Veronichi had written she was too ill to venture out. Others saw the letter. None had been astounded he must come here, to reassure this querulous, nagging relative.)

Late afternoon. It was warm. Bees had found the waking fruit trees and the beds of flowers. From the highest point, by the house, he looked out over Aquila to the church of Maria Maka Selena. Today, its individual island stood to the waist in water. A riddle, this church. In some years the tides discarded it. Magically it appeared to rise up from the mud. Now it had sunk down. It was scales, like the balance of life.

The girl let him in at the door, and Danielus walked up a narrow stair to the parlor above.

"So you're here."

"As you see, Veronichi. How could I not come to you, after that piteous letter?"

"I had that in mind."

"I know it. Welcome me, then."

It was a small room, off which there led another larger chamber, the door curtained by Eastern silk.

A table had been draped, and laid with platters of silver-gilt.

"Are you hungry, my darling?" Veronichi asked, approaching him.

"Yes. But for what?"

"Whatever you wish. Several dishes have been prepared."

"I see you've put out the gold salt-cellars."

"And the glass cups, look. What else have you missed?"

"Little."

Her raven pelt of hair was down, silken as the curtain—like this, she looked quite wonderful. She had traced dark paint around her eyes, and a pomegranate salve on her lips. She was naked. Smooth from pumice, and almost hairless from a clever razor. Scented like a church and a garden, cream, with a core of black feathers and pomegranate bud.

She wound her arms about his neck.

"And here we are . . ."

As he kissed the delicious fruit of her mouth, she leaped lightly against him. A snake, she wound his body with her slim white legs.

"I am the first of the dishes?"

"Always. And the last."

"Perhaps not tonight."

There were no rushes on her floor. She had heaped carpets

there, from Candisi. She lay back on them, and thrusting away the hindrance of the magenta robe, he possessed her.

There was hardly any play—a sliding of hands on skin, appetite of mouths. She flew swiftly through the gate, and he followed her. They were in a great rush. It had been too extended a wait.

After a few minutes, she left him, and returned with the precious goblets, filled to the brim.

"You seem tired, my love. Shouldn't I have called you here? I was lonely without you. But I can be patient as a spider—"

"Other things tire me, Venus, not you."

"If you call me that, am I the City or the goddess?"

"Let me decide. The goddess was wise in the sexual arts, I believe . . ."

More slow now. He watched her body unfolding like a lily, opening to infinitude, melting in exquisite death.

"Shall we do this when we're old?"

"Of course. I shall need some machinery then, naturally, to support my aged limbs."

"I doubt that."

They walked into the larger room. A great tub of water had been lined with linen drapes. They got in together. The temperature was warm, the surface afloat with asphodel. Afterwards they put on each a loose white robe of Eastern style.

When they went back, the table had been filled up by food. She sent the server away, and saw to it herself. It was a meatless day, but they ate flesh, both of them (all the house would). Braised hare, and a roasted goose, pigs' livers with a janchia of garlic and ginger, also a dish of carp and one of spear-fish. She fed him sweetmeats, candied roses, quinces in honey.

"Do you want to sleep now? The bed is cool."

"Not yet."

"Soon you must. I have plans for your night."

"Indeed."

He took her hand, looking far away. She attended him, stilly. She had learned early on how to wait, and was adroit.

"Veronichi, sweetheart, I'd like best, tomorrow, if you would pack up your treasures and your household. Then a boat will come to take you away."

"If you insist on it, I will. I don't want to, Danielo."

"The Ducem is assembling the bulk of his fleet at the Island of Torchara. They'll be ready in five days. Meanwhile the ships of

Jurneia are almost here. The likelihood is a meeting at Ciojha. But this may not be any solution. If they are unstopped and come on, we should see the Jurneians before the month is out. Picture it. They'll crowd the sea. Break the sea walls, and employ rollers and slaves to get across the bar into the deeper parts of the lagoons. They have cannon. You know all this. And that they think all Christians, especially Christian merchant cities, minions of the Devil. They will be raging from the fight, desperate from the journey, and merciless."

"Yes. They're like the Jews in that. Why else have Christians shut my people in ghettos, save as a man must imprison a tiger. They pull our teeth in case we rip them apart."

He stared, then roared with laughter, drawing her to him. "In God's name, dearest Venus, mankind's decisions are nearly always wrong. Why should they have *that* right?"

She kissed him. She said, "Danielo, may I speak to you?"

"You know quite well you may."

"Of matters where I'm ignorant—where I only *feel.*"

"Veronichi, to me you can say anything. As to your ignorance, you read every day in books from the greatest minds the world has seen. It's your knowledge that knows to be circumspect, not your lack."

She murmured, "Nothing to excess."

"Nothing to excess, beloved, *but* excess."

"Then listen to me, Daniel. Can you give this up? I mean, what you've made your reason and your goal."

"You never said that to me before."

"Never. But now—"

"Now more than ever in the past, I say no. No, I must stay true to it. Remember what I told you, of my youth."

"You were a boy—"

"And now a man. Nor an old man, yet."

She said, "Would you live to be one?"

He sighed. He put her back, and stroked her hair.

"Veronichi my Venus, when I was young . . . I saw two great truths. The truth of the teaching of the Christ, and the lie to which it had been corrupted, into mistranslation, stupidity, and evil. He told us we should live as the flowers live, glorying in delight, hurting no other, loving God and everything that is God's, which means also humanity, and the earth. Christ told us to have no fear of death and also no fear of life. If God had hated life so much, He would never have made it. Having learned these precepts, I saw the churches and their laws and lessons. That man must detest and obeise himself, crawling in the dirt as a worm, damned by a vast sin committed even before his birth. That he must loathe his natural inclinations, and go in dread and avoidance of every pleasing thing—good food, long sleep, the beauty of a woman, of a man, and the divine gift of lust, without which the human race must have ended long ago."

"Danielo—"

"So then, being forced to enter this bastion of lies, I came to think that, only by dwelling within the iron tower, I might secretly break open some windows in it."

"Yes."

"There's little enough I can do, Veronichi. But where I can, I do, I will, I must. Today," he said, "as I came from the Basilica, I saw the seventeen new bird-cages, as they sportively call them, which have been hung out there from the Angel Tower."

"Oh, God."

"Oh God indeed, my love. In those traps of torture, the Council of the Lamb, ever diligent to remind Ve Nera she must cower, has thrown thirteen men and four women. They are shrieking even now, and will do so until they can shriek no more. And below, the populace, trained like vicious dogs, throws sharp stones at them, and rotten eggs. It came to me long ago, and I think it now, that to tell men they are mired in transgression, and will only escape their filth by much suffering and denial, is to make monsters. There will be some strong enough—hard enough, like steel—who can beat and break out of themselves all natural weakness—and with it perhaps all love of life. But most will fail. They haven't the colossal strength the saints have had. And then, failing, what is there left but to become the beast the priests have shown them in the mirror? It's these subhuman things I saw, both in the torture cages—and jeering below. I see them everywhere. This is what the Church has made of men. And it is all—the misery, and even a lingering death—*to save their souls.* Today—today I heard the one called Isaacus, promise that if Ve Nera doesn't mend her sinful ways, we shall have burnings next. Yes, the burning alive of witches and other heretics, in the old Roman amphitheater in the Silvian Marshes. To demonstrate the virtue of this, he reminded us all in his letter, that it had been done there at the time of the Crusades. Am I being too canny if I say, I think he wants this because of the girl who can bring fire, to be even with me? It was plain enough he liked to scorch her. Though she's beyond him, he saw he would enjoy the sport. And these are the men of God, His lawgivers and examples—Veronichi, can't you see, my love, there must be also one or two like myself? Oh, simply for the sake of balance."

"There are tears in your eyes."

"I hide nothing from you. I must hide it from every other."

"And won't God condemn us, Daniel, for our own condition? That we lie together, brother and sister."

"You speak of the laws of men, made to control other men. God condemns those that do harm, Veronichi, not those that love."

She let her face rest against his face. She breathed his breath slowly.

"I won't argue, my lord. I'll do whatever you decree. Only—if you remain here, don't send me away."

"If not, you must still leave this house. They might well come to it, the Jurneians. These men we must call infidels—and who call us the same—in war, we'll *be* the same, no doubt. God has a million names and ten million guises. Man only a few. It's a shabby name, a dirty guise, Veronichi, when angry or afraid."

"Where must I go?"

"To the sister-house at Santa La'Lacrima, then. It's fortified like a castle, and has a storehouse I've seen is filled. I'm sorry. You won't be able to live as you do here, or might elsewhere."

"I'm content. The woman who witnessed your little saint is there, isn't she."

"Luchita. Yes."

"And you have great hopes of the little saint."

"Yes. The wall built by men between themselves and God—she has rent a tiny hole in it."

"She's your pawn, Danielo."

"The means to make another window. God help me to do it."

"And is Luchita also part of your plan? She will be. You waste very little. And besides, she is the sister of your Cristiano." Veronichi slipped from him, stood up, and held out both her hands. "Come and sleep now."

"Perhaps I will."

In the other room, the bath had been cleared. Behind its curtains, the bed was wide, with a mattress of down. He lay back on the pillows. As he did so, with a sudden glimpse of desolation, Veronichi thought she saw how he might look, near death. He was more than a decade her senior. It was likely she would have to behold him, one day, die. But not yet, sweet God. Not yet.

"Don't look sad, Veronichi. You've got your way."

"I'm not sad, my darling, but plotting. Tell me truly, do you love your white-haired knight more than me?"

"Cristiano? Perhaps almost as much. He'll never know. He would drop dead on the spot where I told him. How could I work that on him? But I gain great pleasure, both sensual and possibly pious, from watching him. Man in the image of the Most High. There it is."

The light was fading from the window.

She sat by the bed until he slept, then stole away, her robe whispering.

In another room, a young man got up at once. He had white-blond hair, and was of great physical beauty. He had a look of Cristiano certainly, and being only nineteen, a younger Cristiano, more flexible, less stern.

"You're ready?"

"Yes, lady. And—eager."

"He would refuse you if you weren't. Wait for an hour. Then admit yourself to the bed. He'll sleep a while. Let him find you when he wakes. Love one another well."

When the young man had gone, she sat down to comb her hair. There was no jealousy in her heart. Whatever would do her lover good, did good to her. And he would not send her away from the City. The Jurneians had been nothing to her terror of their parting.

Sister Purita waited quietly by the Domina, as church servants carried yet three more chests up the sister-house stair.

So many possessions for with this visiting lady. And yet, she was said to be frugal and devout.

Of course, there would be things of her brother's, the Fra's, kept in the island house, and now needing to be made safe. The library had already been brought; it had taken all morning to go up.

Veronichi was to have three of the guest cells. They must already be choked and impassable.

An ugly woman, though quite young. Of course she had never borne a child. Child-bearing aged women. It was a fact, she dressed modestly and unbecomingly.

The Domina sat in her chair, her hand on her walking stick. Now she motioned for the other nun, Permaria, to give her her medicinal tincture. (In the outer world, the fleet was gathering. How far off it seemed, here, how slight.)

"Purita," said the Domina, "it is you, there, Purita?"

"Yes, holy Mother." (This was the second time she had asked.)

"Purita, I should like you to read the lesson, as we dine."

"*I?*" Purita was appalled. The lessons read at meals were transcribed from the Latin, to benefit the less able nuns. Even so—"My reading's poor, Mother, despite the help I've had—"

"Your Latin does indeed need work, but as you know that will not impede you in this. And you know the text, Purita. You've heard it often now. I'll go through the words with you. Remember, you may interpret, where you understand. God sometimes inspires us to do this."

Purita glanced at the other nun, who might have been a statue.

The old woman was saying Purita might *invent* the lesson, where she could not decipher it?

"I like you to read, you've read for me," said the old Domina. "You have a clear yet friendly voice, and the accent of the City."

"I'm common, Mother."

"That's not what I said, Purita. Besides, the rose is common in summer. Do we like it less for that?"

She could be crisp, when she wanted. Luchita-Purita wondered sometimes if the Domina acted out her occasional feebleness, her vaguenesses of mind, to trick them all. But definitely her physical strength was failing. They were both needed now, she and Permaria, to help the Mother to her cell.

But then she sat in her room, in the chair, like a cheerful, fat grasshopper, smiling. She loved her room, with its bare white walls lit by the sun, her wide window that looked on the well-stocked garden. You saw her filmy eyes roam over every object, the plain cross and the jeweled one, the hand-high Virgin with white flowers in a vase, the dark religious books, her velvet cushion for kneeling. She liked her walking stick too, which had carved on its top the head of a bird, much polished by use—and caresses. In repose she cuddled the stick like a toy, and now and then spoke to it, apologizing for her weight and her need, telling it, (oddly) that it reminded her of the boundless strength of Christ, who was the walking stick for every frail soul.

Permaria brought the Domina the huge Bible, placing it open at the lesson, where the transcription lay ready.

"Come here, and read it now, Purita."

Purita read the lesson stumbling, flushed with anxiety.

"There. You have it all."

"I stammer, Mother, when I'm nervous."

"That's pride, Purita. Did you know that?" Purita gaped. "In your case, it is. You know you can do well and expect so much of yourself, that you become afraid. Sister Gratzilia stutters, yet she reads. God won't object."

Unwillingly, Purita bent her head, trying to learn the lesson off by heart in the hour before the Solus and the afternoon dinner.

"Permaria, go if you will and fetch me some water. I'm very dry."

Purita, struggling with the words, heard the other nun go out.

Birds twittered in the garden. A ray of sudden sun found the hub of the jeweled cross. Crimson burst from it like fire.

It was harder now to remember the miracle which had brought her here. Had it happened? Surely it had.

"Sister Purita," said the Domina. Her voice was so soft, and like parchment. Startled, Purita looked up. "Listen, Purita. I shan't live many more days. God warned me in a dream. I'm not fearful. His life is lovelier than even this loveliness, which is only its shadow-image. And for all my lapses, I know I shall find mercy. In my heart I think that all men do, at last."

Purita stood, her hands on the Bible.

The Domina said, "I've told them, I want you by me. You must stay near. When the time comes, I have something to say to you."

"I—"

"You. You think they will be jealous? Perhaps. But only a few. And I've made provision. You have no knowledge, have you, Purita, of what you are."

"A sinner."

"Now, that *is* common, for so are we all. The Apostles that Christ chose were common men. They spoke with the accent of the land, some caught fish, they wandered about like beggars. They were his witnesses. And after Christ, his saints too are witnessed. You are the first pure witness to Beatifica, who brought fire from Heaven. The Magister Major has advised me."

Purita stood with her mouth open. She closed it. She said, "What are you telling me, Mother?"

"You're not a fool. You've seen the duties I have been giving you, and so have others. They see too that you're careful, and effacing of self. Above all, practical."

The door opened, and Permaria entered with a pitcher of water.

Purita's heart bounded inside her, blurring her sight, so the words of the lesson now became jumbled and illegible. *I'm willful, too.* They had forgotten or not known that, this Mother of nuns, this Father of priests, Danielus.

She stopped trying to read. She would *interpret* the passage instead. Let them see how they liked that. In such a mood she had several times committed adultery, once met her outcast daughter and given her money, fed the homeless at the inn door, *resented* her brother. The mood of rebellion. Or was it only liberty? As when, rebelling and at liberty, she became a nun?

6

'You will know, since I gave your order my permission—a matter of form, since the Ducem had already desired it—that I recognize your credentials, and your willingness to fight, for the City, and for God. This of you all, jointly and as individuals. But, Cristiano, as I have said to others of your brotherhood, be very certain you are essential there, and not needed here. The Ducem, as you see, is dispatching three hundred ships at last. His aquean army numbers at least six thousand men. Though Jurneia's fleet is larger—and here, we are aware, accounting varies—she packs less men on board each ship. She has perhaps a third again our numbers. Conversely, if the fight is lost at Ciojha, Ve Nera herself must be defended, from the land's edge.

'My gist, Cristiano, is that, while you wait on Torchara, you might think a second time. Many of the Upper Echelon I have persuaded in this. If you rebut my judgment I will, say no more. Christ be with you. Fight well.'

The returning letter from Torchara was, at core, brief.

'I have said, Magister, I cannot debate with you. I shall not attempt it. God be with us at Ciojha.'

It was a glorious summer noon. Torchara, an island of shipyards, showed her greenery high up on her inner hill. From her quays Ve Nera was visible in detail across Fulvia, with the Laguna Aquila, and the Silvian Marshes held, as some poet had said, in her other arms. Out from Silvia on the Isle of the Dead, no smoke went up. They

had left the fires unlit. Instead a hundred bells might be heard ringing clear as glass across the water.

Birds fluttered about Torchara, and the somber gulls circled and
recircled the forest of masts.

They were white-sailed, Ve Nera's ships, almost every sheet
crossed in Crusader red, and every greatest sail painted, in at least
seventy different forms, with the old symbol of the City, the figure of
a veiled woman crowned by a star. She had been Venus, once. Now
they named her *Maria Stella Maris*—Maria, Star of the Sea. The
vessels wore the Ducem's colors in their flags, and the colors of
other lesser lords: plum and saffron, orange, black and gold.

Beautiful. The heart lifted at the sight.

What could stand against it, this perfect entity of wood, canvas
and iron, flesh and bone and steel.

Two days to Ciojha. Propulsion from the slaves' rowing in the
under-deck, a light wind to be discovered, perhaps, when on the
open sea.

Only one Magister Major, not Danielus, had come to bless
them, but nine members of the Council of the Lamb were there,
black crows beside the magenta of the Primo's higher priests.

Boys were singing praise to God the Deliverer, their voices
flung aloft and silencing even the predatory gulls.

Drawing out from land.

Three hundred shining ropes that slipped away. The water
spreading, three thousand shining ropes that pulled them on.

Cristiano looked upward, his heart singing like the children on
the quay, innocent, savage.

A solitary flotilla of clouds, peach-yellow from the sun, sailed
above them, accompanying them.

"It might be some angelic fleet up there," Aretzo murmured,
"some sign from Heaven. Like the Maiden's angels—"

Others had noticed. Gazed and pointed.

A war song rose sturdily from the decks, as the other voices
faded on the shore.

The fleet of Heaven moved away, melting now into the east.

In the morning, after the easy rocking of night, a frisky wind blew
up. The sails bellied out. The slaves were rested at the oars, and fed
with meat and wine.

Ve Nera was merciful. She did not shackle her rowers in a fight.

If a ship was stoven in, they could take their chance with the crew and soldiers.

Cristiano ate meat, like the slaves. Before a battle you did not fast. He drank the wine. Aretzo fretted. "We go like snails. It will be three days at this pace."

"So eager to sink your teeth in an infidel throat," another mocked him.

Jian was not there. He had heeded Fra Danielus and stayed behind. Among the ships there were some hundreds of the Bellatae Christi, distributed mostly in squadrons between five to twenty. On this ship they numbered ten, but all of the Upper Echelon. No one, apart from Cristiano, had received a letter from the Magister Major. No doubt, he had expected Cristiano to persuade others.

The sea was slightly choppy, dragon green in the shadow of the fleet, crushed glass under the sun.

There were a few cannon, purchased from other places. One straddled the fore-castle, an iron vegetable hooped in by iron rings. They were unpredictable furniture, liable to break loose. When fired, they could knock the cannoneer off his feet and slough his eyebrows. Or otherwise blow up and kill him. Cristiano had seen all this in previous actions, when Ve Nera's troops had fought with or by fellow cities.

Cristiano, glancing, noticed Aretzo had put on the new favor, pinned beside the Bellatae badge of the Lion and Child. This was only a piece of scarlet cloth. Many of them had taken to wearing it. He knew, though none of them spoke of it, the cloth represented the Maiden Beatifica's fire.

Some of the soldiers were now seasick.

Over the slap of waves, noises of vomiting and impatient nervousness, dinned the war-song. Or he heard the cannon rattling about in its ties, bound as the human slaves were not.

This ship was named *Virgo Maria*.

The white light of God had failed him. The red glare of war would not. (Hate always more vital than love?)

The red light did not fail. Nor was the voyage quite two days.

On the following morning, soon after sunrise, they saw Ciojha spread before them, perhaps two miles away, like a great whale sunning itself in the aftermath of dawn.

Before the whale, the fleet of Jurneia spread—and spread. And spread.

Like dishes laid for a feast, or the dusky waterlilies smothering some pool.

Sail upon sail, wooden shell on shell.

The sky was pale, losing the brilliance of sunrise.

Men cried out, and fell dumb.

Ve Nera stood on her decks, looking at the flowers of Jurneia.

The priests came quickly now through the Christian ships, shriving men. Warriors knelt, stuffing the Host even down sea-queasy throats. The Blood of Christ was gulped.

"How many ships, in God's name?" Aretzo, angry, priming himself.

"The Magister gave eight hundred as the last count."

"More. Over a thousand. *Look* at them."

"Perhaps."

"I hate a seafight," said one of the *Virgo Maria*'s other eight Bellatae. "I need to get close. Close as a lover to his leman, and sheath in my hot sword."

His coarseness was not rebuffed. Some of them chuckled.

Cristiano, his eyed fixed on the Jurneians, felt he rushed towards them through the air. His blood tingled. His face was to him like metal, his entire body, impermeable. Yet he was light. He crossed himself stiffly, and the red blaze began to wake behind his eyes.

The ship groaned as her slaves rowed.

He felt the straining strokes, although his feet did not seem in contact with the deck. He himself, by his will, powered the ship onward. He and all these men, with whom, now, he was one.

The atmosphere bristled, glowed. From everywhere came the yells and growls of an army, readying itself, bracing itself.

When the first Jurneian cannon spoke to them, they were less than a quarter mile off.

A combusting scatter, like flashing gems—

The roar and hiss of approach.

It was often called *flying fire*.

It flew.

But the range was too great. The Christians saw the Jurneian infidel shot go down into the sea, with gargantuan splashes, sizzlings. Applauded and jibed.

On the *Virgo Maria*, the alien cannon poked its snout forwards. Men swarmed there. Along the line of Christian ships, one or two of the iron monsters had answered too quickly. The boom came of detonations, black fume, men shouting. And this shot too falling short.

But the fleets glided nearer to each other. Now Cristiano, partly out of his body, judged which vessel they would first come to grips with. They were slender craft, this one he had spotted with sails half looped in for the fray. She had Jurneia's picture writing on the side, curlicues and dabs—her name. No, *his* name. Their ships were male.

He noted fresh scurrying about their artillery. Around him, soldiers swore. Cristiano merely waited.

From the forward ship he watched, and from a hundred others, the cannon blast exploded now in a tempest. At almost the same moment, Ve Nera's armed ships replied.

The world reeled. Cristiano saw the great mast of the opposing vessel he had idly chosen, split cleanly. It cracked and tumbled in a billow of broken sheets, holing the deck as it went down. Splinters sprayed like rain; screaming came in another tongue.

But to either side of *Virgo Maria* the Christian ships had also been struck. Through one erupted a mighty water-spout like a dragon, venting. Others were at once on fire. All that beauty spoiled. Figures springing in the boiling sea.

The shots had missed *Virgo Maria*. Through a wall of upsurge and flames, in sudden spark-lit darkness, she closed with a Jurneian vessel—not after all the one Cristiano had selected. That one was listing, going down.

Near enough now to see these enemies—

Through darkness, dark faces they had wrapped about with cloth, as women might. Bearded nuns—Eyes that glittered, white beast teeth—nothing familiar, nothing human.

The sword in his hand was like lightning. Cristiano raised it. It became alive. Eye to eye with them, their animal faces to his mechanical face of metal—nothing human *anywhere*.

The Soldier of God flexed. Marvelous, glorious, the wine red—

The red wine became himself. He stretched now to fill the world, and heard himself bellow far away. Head touching sky. Heart and lungs of sounding brass. The ecstasy sharp as any other sharpest joy, the battle-wrath.

The sides of the two ships bumped, then ground together.

Cannon barked. Another missile tore by above and this time clipped *Virgo Maria*'s topmost mast. A section of wood crashed behind Cristiano as he leaped, oblivious, over the bows.

God—I am Your slave—Nothing save You.

Sword was arm, arm sword. Body unbreachable shield.

He hacked and lunged. No one could come at him. A grinning man of metal, teeth bared—the machine of Heaven.

His voice thundering, *Ve Nera of God!*

God's holy war. They would win. They were unstoppable.

He smashed a man's jaw, treading over him, and cut two others free of life.

On all sides, the holy army, the slick of steel, blood bursting like a poppy.

Ve Nera of God—

(The third ship he had leapt to? The tenth?)

Miles below the stink of gall and offal, blood and excrement, the tinder smell of the ballistas and their iron cooking.

Jumping now across another rail. Ocean irrelevantly glimpsed and gone. Sword and arm, hack and lunge. Roil of brass and red.

A face—quite young—a handsome boy with honey skin and fawn's eyes black as jet, yet with a silver rim—sometimes these momentary images caught in the red net—then vanished—dead of Cristiano's war sword, and that other man-beast, knifed under the chin, both trampled underfoot.

This ship too was going down. (The fifth he had leapt from? The seventh?)

Aretzo punching at Cristiano, dragging him—"Come this way. Jump. She'll pull us under as she goes—"

"He, Aretzo." Lucid a moment, inappropriately lucid for Aretzo, who did not understand.

A scramble, up over the side—help forthcoming—which ship this one? Oh, a Christian vessel—blood-red darkness, heavy, and settling.

Cristiano shuddered.

"Drink this."

He drank the water mixed with wine. It tasted of soot.

This ship lacked any cannon. One mast was gone, chopped like a tree. The sails like wrung-washing on the deck. Men lying weeping, holding in their guts . . . He was coming up from the redness. Movement. Rowers working at the oars.

"What?" he said.

The ship's master, a third of his face a mask of blood: "We're standing off, Bellatoro."

"Yes," he said. Then, "We have won."

The master of the ship that was not the *Virgo Maria,* spat. "No, Bellatoro. Look, can't you see?"

"He's battle-crazed yet," said Aretzo. He sounded sulky. Cristiano saw abruptly that Aretzo had somehow mislaid his left arm. Which was bizarre—it could not have occurred.

Aretzo, losing consciousness, sank back against the washing-sails, coloring them.

Cristiano looked out from the ship.

A bank of cannon was belching once more, from somewhere. The missiles arced and dropped, flaming and smoking, into a wreckage of smoke and flame.

Like a ruined pile of brushwood, trodden on, the mess of ships. Those white sails, the painted crosses and Madonna-Venuses, brave flags, crests, burning, burning, on a water poison green and streaked with oil and fire. Loose spars and oars and planking rammed each other, and floating corpses. And men were swimming everywhere or going under. Heads that bobbed like strange fish, called in mortal voices.

Beyond, towards Ciojha across an interval of sea, the fleet of Jurneia, still clean and whole, grouped in a gracious cluster. Surely one thousand ships still. It was impossible. He—they—had killed Jurneia. But like the Hydra, she had grown these other heads.

The wounded ships of Ve Nera straggled away, picking up survivors, sometimes, where they could.

And now it seemed, Jurneia let them go.

"Ship's master, turn back. I order it."

The master, a head shorter than Cristiano, buckled into leather for the fight, his face divided, squared up to the Knight of God pugnaciously. "I will not. Scan about. Any vessel we have left is making off. If you're so razor-keen for death, signore, there's your way."

Aretzo, surfacing, let out a silly laugh.

"He would, but he doesn't swim."

From the ships of Jurneia a kind of ululation was going up. Mockery—triumph—who knew. They did not follow the retreat.

Not yet.

"Ve Nera requires we return and fight," said Cristiano.

The master spat again, at the feet of this steel-clad fiend. Then turned and left to go about the business of escape.

Cristiano lowered himself beside Aretzo. He bound the gouting stump that had been Aretzo's arm. They must cauterize soon.

Aretzo did not speak again.

The sky beyond the smoke, like the sea, was weirdly green. In it they saw the moon, as clearly as if by night.

7

When he came from the Chapel of Micaeli, by the Primo's South Door, Fra Danielus met Brother Isaacus among the pillars there.

They were like the trees of a wood, the pillars, gray carven trees, with gilded branches. You might expect to meet some creature lurking in a wood, after sunfall.

"Good evening, brother."

"Stay still. I'll speak to you."

"If you wish."

"You keep a woman in the Primo, Danielus. Not a holy sister, a nun. A *woman*. In this sacred place."

Danielus waited.

Isaacus snarled in his half-voice, foul breathed as any bear or wild dog, "You don't speak. Can't. You transgress, Fra."

"Then I must answer, must I not."

"You cannot."

"The woman kept here under my protection, is not a woman."

"Oh, a conundrum, Fra, is it? She is a *woman*. That bitch you paraded before the Ducem, like her whoresman."

Danielus said nothing.

Isaacus swelled like a toad. "If you were not what you are—I'd have our men come to you, our Eyes and Ears of God."

Danielus did speak. "They're welcome, brother. Meanwhile, there is other news than the Maiden Beatifica."

"What news? What?"

"Has no one come to you, Brother Isaacus? This grieves me."

"Ah—the ships. God favored the righteous. There was a victory. The acts of the Council were not in vain, and saved this contaminate City."

"No."

Isaacus drew back. His face in its hood quavered, then slammed itself shut.

"You say no."

"Most of the Veneran ships went to the bottom. A handful are limping home. They sent a messenger, one of the doves they carried for the purpose. Jurneia had the victory. We've only to wait for her."

Isaacus clamped tight his lips. Then rasped some incomprehensible sound.

"Your throat seems worse, brother."

Isaacus turned and went away, leaving only the ghosts of his odors, and the memory of his venom.

She had had her supper, an herbal gruel, and was in her room. Before lying down on the floor, with the blanket and cushion, Beatifica was praying to her pink-veiled Madonna.

Finishing three Latin prayers suitable for the Virgin, Beatifica crossed herself and rose.

Then she felt dissatisfied, kneeled down again, and began another prayer.

Her enjoyment of religion was very great, and had been noticed by very many. "She loves to be at prayer," they said. She attended every one of the services, including Prima Vigile, in a small chapel adjacent to the Golden Rooms. Here her tutor, the young priest, accompanied her for Prima Pegno and sometimes the Solus. Other higher priests came there on their own account, and sometimes Bellatae of the Upper Echelon.

Although clad always as a male, Beatifica's garments at these times were the soft gray of a nun's habit. She had no ornament and carried her little plain cross in her hand.

She should have covered her head, of course, as a woman. She did not.

Some of the priests evidently sought the chapel only to squint and frown at her. These she seemed not to see. (Even now, she expected nothing generous from people. While they did not lay harsh hands on her, she accepted and forgot them)

Jian too was frequently present, for the Venusium, or Luna Vigile. Before the ships had sailed, some hundred or so others of the Upper Echelon crowded by relays into the tiny, elegant chapel, for one office or another.

It was suspected they were her guard of honor, although she scarcely glanced at them, nor did they look at her more than once or twice. They were gazing at her instead clandestinely, with the eyes of the soul.

"It is unwise for these young men, sworn to a celibate life, to hang about so round a female. Especially a female dressed so shamelessly."

Jian had responded, not realizing the Magister Major had somehow laid such concepts in his mind, "To us, holy-brother, she isn't a woman. She is the vessel of God."

"Take care. You're perilously close to the sin of blasphemy."

"Revered brother, I mean, in the same sense as a window may let in the light. She is so clear and open. One sees through her, to the Power beyond."

Besides Danielus, her patron, was himself a power. He had, in all his twenty-eight years with the Church, and by dint of his noble birth, made sure of that. Arguments were suspended.

And the Bellatae remained irreproachable. And the girl—she seemed properly aware, it was true, only of God.

Yes, she enjoyed all the matters of religion. She loved—although she did not fully know it—her hours of talk with the gray-haired priest Fra Danielus sent her as confessor. (She *relished* talking, and to be asked questions with such interest, to know so much—but what?—depended on her answers.) And the kind ancient confessor was swift to say to one and all, "I can tell you, there's no seal of secrecy to break with the Maiden. She is devoid of any crime or failing. I give her penances sometimes because, once informed of their purpose, she asks them of me. She loves to pray. She thinks only of Christ, the Virgin and God." And now and then he had been led to add, "Woman is a weak straw, prone to error. At certain times, God causes to be born a woman who may come to serve as an example, both to women and to men, that even for these faulty ones, grace is possible."

Danielus had always chosen well.

After the ships sailed, for four days, only Jian, with two other Bellatae, had come to every office in the chapel.

But two days before setting out, nearly four hundred of the Upper Echelon had come, in changing groups. And when Beatifica left the chapel, they had stared, for the first, intensely at her.

She felt their eyes, but she had felt eyes searing on her before. She did not look. They did not harm her. Even the few flickering touches of their fingers on her cloak's edge or sleeve, were not the prologue to abuse.

She had got used to them in a way. Perhaps, in a way, she was moved by them, just a little. (Their faces, fierce looks, the young male scent of them, the maculums of mail, their strength, the yearning that sang and trembled when they spoke their orisons.) One more interesting thing. Something else which was pleasant to do.

In the chapel, on the night before the fleet sailed, after the Auroria, one of the Soldiers of God—one only—cried out to her.

"Beatifica—Maiden—before this great battle, give us your blessing."

The disapproving priests froze, scandalized.

The girl turned, and said quietly, "No one has taught me how to bless. But the priests know how."

One or two of the scandalized were caught by this.

They nodded. She spoke the truth, and was modest.

Of course, she had only been speaking a fact.

But the Bellator left his place and went to her, and before she could become unnerved—he was tall and vigorous—he kneeled at her feet.

Beatifica thought. She had an inspiration.

"I'll ask the Virgin to bless you."

And she said one of the prayers to Maria, which began although Beatifica did not completely know it, *O most rare Mother, we entreat you, comfort your earthly sons, and beg from God, who will not refuse you, pardon and deliverance.*

"She dares to intercede—is she a priest then?" one of the still-scandalized exclaimed.

But another one said, "This is a prayer a mother would use. She makes herself their mother, and sister."

And Beatifica's tutor, who had come to the early mass, said quickly, though blushing, "This prayer is allowed to women, brothers. I myself taught it her."

Now, before the Virgin icon, Beatifica at last finished her general praying. She might lie down. Although she slept less well than she had in Ghaio's house, where exhaustion had always felled her.

She went to the window and looked into the night garden below. All blossom had left the peach, its leaves were dark. Thin light fell from another high narrow window, and colored a single red rose.

After all, in an hour she could get up again for the Luna Vigile.

Just then the door was knocked.

This always alarmed her. Not the summons, the recent courtesy.

"Yes, I'm here," said Beatifica.

A servant of the Golden Rooms was outside.

"Maiden, will you come, the Magister Major is waiting."

Beatifica smiled. She was happy: something to do.

She followed the servant at once.

As she entered, Danielus regarded Beatifica closely. A nicer life, coinciding with the ripening of womanhood, had been kind to her. She had not gained any weight, but a soft bloom was added to her skin, and great luminosity to her eyes, and the remarkable hair. She must be almost sixteen.

"Are you well, Maiden?"

She accepted the name. She had always accepted the names given her, and the titles, whether benign or crude.

"I'm well."

No thanks, obviously. Her presumed superiors she would never think to thank, or to inquire after.

"Were you told of the sea-fight?"

"Yes. My tutor told me."

"You know it was lost."

"Yes, Magister."

"This City also lost a great many men. And of the Bellatae Christi, our Soldiers of God, five hundred went out, and less than one hundred and sixty return to us."

No response. No one was real to her. But wait—her eyes stole up, fixed on his, stared straight through him. What did she look for, in that unseen area—which others took for some divine, visionary place, or Hell, perhaps. Which he himself assumed was a kind of vacancy she studied when unsure, to see what might appear to her. Or was she really so uncomplex? Very likely. Light poured through the clearest vessel. Genius and intellect cloudily impaired the way. Most saints were simple. The Apostles had been, mostly, peasants.

She said, contradicting everything, "The Bellator Cristiano?"

Cruelly—was it being cruel ?—he delayed.

Her eyes had focused on him. Nothing to be read from her. Not self-control—more, surely, the inability to demonstrate her emotion.

"Cristiano," Danielus said, "survived the fight."

She looked away again. She said, "Yes. What else."

"What do you mean?"

"God wouldn't let him die."

"Why not?" He spoke slowly. "Beatifica, answer me. Why not?"

And for a second, a breathlessness was in him, not unlike the pressure he had felt, waiting as the first ship back to the outer quays sent in its messages of survivors.

"God," said Beatifica, "loves Cristiano."

"He loves us all, Beatifica. Yet sometimes, through the evil and unwisdom of men, He must let us perish. Cristiano is subject to this law."

She astounded him. She moved, shaking her head. He noticed a wildness in her, as he had thought he had, long ago. "No, no." But her voice was not raised.

Danielus was torn between a strange delight, and a foreboding. That she might love Cristiano tickled him in a hundred ways, both spiritual and profane. Partly, surely, he had wanted it—these two extraordinary beings. Beyond that, she must *never* be caught out in it by another.

"Beatifica, you can have no favorites. Do you understand? That would be dangerous. I warn you now."

She said, flatly, "No, Magister. But he is my angel."

"In the name of God—what makes you say such a thing?"

"You say God shows me things."

"Yes, I have said so."

"The serpent and the angels and the red mountain. And my mother, who taught me to make the fire."

"Yes."

"God showed me my angel. I didn't remember at first. Then I did. It was as I was praying. The image of the Angel Micaeli in his armor, in the chapel here. It reminded me. But my angel was Cristiano."

If she was in love, she was cool. No alteration in her color. Her breathing slow and even. Only insistence had made her wriggle in her seat and shake her hair at him.

Danielus got up. He lifted her to her feet.

"Look at me, Beatifica. Listen to me. Never speak of this to anyone else. Do you grasp what I've said?"

"Yes, Magister."

She learnt quickly. He must trust in that. He was sorry, though, her eyes drooped away, losing for a moment their luster.

"You're our hope, Beatifica." Did that mean anything to her? He thought it did not. "Jealousy is everywhere. Treat all equally in deed and word."

"Yes."

And now, at this crisis point, he must take her to do the other thing, so vital and so risky. But all of it was risk. She had been put into his waiting hand, this slender fiery sword of God.

"Seven ships have returned from the sea-fight, Beatifica. And another five may come. Boats are rowing in the wounded and the dead, over the lagoon. Your white clothes have been brought. They're in the closet there, where you can put them on. Then come out with me. I want you to walk among the survivors and the dead. Beatifica, will you do that?"

She glanced. "Yes, Magister."

"Have you seen a dead person?"

"My mother."

"Forgive me, I forgot. Are you brave? You must be firm. There's no need to do much. Only pass among them. But if they call to you, what will you do?"

Wonderingly she looked. "Answer," she said.

Christ had told them, be as a child. Be simple. Knock upon the door and it shall open. Live as the flower lives and let God have care of you.

Doubt left Danielus.

"Go in then and change your clothes."

The dead, the dying, the crying, were coming in like cargo.

Torches sheered off the night in sulfurous rips.

Much too far away, the square about the Primo Suvio, to see the ruined ships lying crippled out by the bars.

This was enough. A scene from an artist's painting of damnation.

Cristiano stood on the square. He had watched Aretzo taken directly in to the hospice of the knights. (His bleeding had been staunched with heated iron. Now Aretzo was in the rambling stage, feverish, a stranger. Cristiano had seen it often; when sometimes wounded, had entered the state himself.) Elsewhere soldiers, and the crews of the ships, were being put on boats for the infirmaria by the wall of Aquilla. Others, luckier, (or not) had paid or promised payment to be ferried to a church, or to relatives.

Most were, for this while, piled up waiting at the Primo's walls, about the great doors, under the Angel Tower. From which, all but three of the torture cages had been taken down.

His eyes went to those, nevertheless. A pair of criminals, too near death now to move or complain, hung out above the dying army of the City. And in the third cage, now he saw, the momento mori, a skeleton gulls had picked almost naked.

Cristiano felt his gorge rise in a thick wave. Against what he wanted to do, he must sit down by the torch pole, lean there, and catch his breath.

His body was cut all over, torso, limbs. The enemy steel had been superior. Blocked by his mail, the slicings were shallow, but had let out quite a lot of blood. He had felt none of it when he fought, of course. Not even the blow to the temple, which now ached and gnawed, a wolf trying to get in at his brain.

The world was dross. He had always known.

But tonight, Ve Nera was the city of Magni-Diabolon in the Pit.

There was a slight stir, over there by the Lion Door. More priests coming out to add the vapor of incense to the reek of butchery? Yes, here they came.

Cristiano clenched his teeth against a second wave, this one of fury, bitterness.

Here in Hell, what could they do, these black robes, those purple robes behind them? Swinging the censors, chanting over the groans and howls like a menagerie—

This horror was God's world, the making of God—

No—man's world. *Man*-made—

God's.

Cristiano bowed his head on his knees. He heard his own strangled whisper. "Let me lose everything, O Lord, even my life—but not my faith—Oh, God, not *You*—"

Never before had this come to him. Why now? He had been in twenty battles, more—

Dimly, through the rushing in his ears, the echoes of the awful whisper, he heard another noise.

He took it for some delusion. He ignored it. But it grew much louder, a single cry quickly taken up, concentrated by a score, a hundred, two hundred throats.

He turned his head on his knee, and looked.

After the priests, a young man was walking out among the crowd of vandalized men.

The Ducem. It must be Joffri. Odd, the story was Joffri had already fled.

"Maiden—" Close to Cristiano, a man on a blood soaked pallet, was holding out his arms.

Maiden. That was the cry.

Not a young man, a girl. Now Cristiano saw her hair as the torches burnished it. He had not seen her for some while, had not ever been among those who were about her in the chapel. Did he recall how she looked?

She wore her white clothes, and the gold cross on her breast that was only just perceptible as feminine; the gem winked scarlet.

The priests had halted, standing aside, lips closed.

The girl too had stopped, gazing about her.

She seemed serene, yet veiled, as if returning from a distance.

Cristiano heard a man whimper, "See, she's been with God, but she sees *us* now."

And the crying became louder still.

"*Maiden! Maiden! Maiden!*"

It rose to a crescendo, breaking on her stillness like the sea. To silence.

And in the vacancy the shout had left, one man again cried out to her. This time the name Danielus had given her.

"Beatifica, pray for me."

She turned towards the voice. Then, she stepped aside, through the crowd. It was a crowd for the most part lying on its back. Nevertheless, Cristiano stood up, holding to the torch pole, to watch her.

When she came to the man, she kneeled directly down beside him.

He had lost both his legs, and was nearly gone with them. It was a wonder anyone had heard him. But the silence had been vast, and even now it was, and the Primo Square was a sounding-stage.

She knelt in the blood and filth. At once her whiteness was sullied.

Then they heard her silver voice, rising up.

She was doing what he asked. She was praying for him.

It was a minor prayer, quite short. Perhaps, by now, she had even come to know what it meant.

The rumors of her had spread. Been helped to, no doubt, as the clever architecture of the square helped spread the utterances in it. They knew her. They listened.

When she stopped praying for him, the man murmured, "I'm afraid to die, Beatifica."

They heard this, too. They heard her reply.

Beatifica said, clear as a silver pin, "Don't cry. Your pain will be done. God's world is better. Why do you think he damns us for suicide? His world is the best of all, and we must earn it. Long to get there. He will fetch you, by whatever awful way. The road's stones, but the gates are pearl. Fetch him, Lord. Amen."

Something broke in Cristiano. Possibly it was his heart, or some other enclosure less fragile. He seemed to stand in space, all the void about him, in which men lay bright as stars from the souls inside them, and across which Beatifica burned like a risen sun.

He could see the face of the dying man, lit now, radiant and careless. He let her go without any more entreaty.

And only the crying and calling began again, all the others, begging her. And she went to them, everyone. She went to everyone that called.

She went because she was a slave, and taught by vicious tyranny always to obey. He knew that. He knew.

He knew also the sentences she had spoken had been learned from someone else—maybe from Danielus, although they seemed unmannered, fluid—accessible. (He could not guess she had heard them from an old slave man by the wood-seller's Red House.)

But the words had come out of her at the moment of perfection. And she was like the words, made for this time, this arena of history and fate.

Not the pawn of the Magister. The pawn of God. As were they all.

Cristiano stood by the torch, watching her. Watching all she did. Kneeling, praying, answering in the simplest way their questions. So gentle. So soft. Even to the corpses that she passed, or was asked to touch or bless.

(The male slave's instructions had stayed. The second of the meaningful things he had offered her. *Don't shake the sleeping or the dead.*)

Had Cristiano been told this, he would have said, "That too. It was put into her hand for use. God also works most simply. You may see it in everything. Complication is a human failing."

She went by quite near him, once. She was trailed by two Bellatae, Cristiano now saw, one of whom was Jian. But he did not greet Jian, nor Jian him.

Beatifica did not see Cristiano, he thought. He would not have anticipated her to, at this moment. He could not know, of course, how Danielus had warned her.

But, seeing her near, Cristiano saw her for the very first. As other men did, who were on their feet, Cristiano knelt. Some hem of her cloak brushed over his head, and he felt it like a thread of running light.

She was mired in the blood and filth of hundreds, by now. And out of it she shone.

Not until every man who had called to her had individually received her presence, did she go in again.

By then the bell was ringing for the Prima Vigile, two hours after midnight.

They let her go without remonstrance. She had earned her reward, and they knew the Maiden loved best to pray.

8

Not baggage now, but bleeding men were being carried up the passages and stairs of Santa Lallo Lacrima's sister-house.

The nuns pressed back against stone walls. They were in awe. Less at the gravity of wounds, the largesse of damage, than at this general peacefulness. Even men writhing in agony, turning to say through pain-black lips, "Bless you, sister, for your charity." As if to reassure.

Word had come with them.

"It's true then. This girl who flaunts about as a man—"

"But look at her effect."

"Don't doubt, little sister," said a soldier carried by, "God sent her." He laughed, eyes shining.

There had been the usual dispensation of a war. Even the nuns might hear the last confessions.

"I thought I was damned, sister. She convinced me I'd paid, and never was."

Behind the officiating sister, another pursing her lips. "Only God can decide that, soldier."

Shaming her, as she needed to be shamed, the dying man said, "He promised, through her. But He prefers a tender voice, doesn't He, to a spiteful one."

As Veronichi hurried about the church, her arms full of salves, basins, bandages, fresh candles, her hair tied up under her cap so her face looked like a pip, and her gown streaked with ordure and blood, she too thought of Beatifica, this being she had never seen.

But in the rooms, in and out of which she went, she heard the difference Beatifica had made.

Waiting in rows, the soldiers drowsed fitfully, drugged with herbs and pellets of Inde. While a surgeon worked, splashed head to foot in the debris of his trade.

But this man under his knife was bearing it all, choking out between gasps and whines, that the pain of the world was but a lesson. Its suffering cleansed and brought one to the Kingdom beyond life, fit to companion God. It was good to bleed.

At which the surgeon's assistant blurted out, "So it isn't a punishment we're sent?"

"No—she says—she says it's only to learn from. Even God suffered."

At length he fainted.

The surgeon grimaced. "Heaven spare me chatterers."

But the teaching of Beatifica was everywhere now to be found. (Actually, her mother's teaching from the early years of Volpa's life.)

Veronichi labored tirelessly. She was strong and toughened by her first existence among the plagues and illnesses of the ghetto. Also, it seemed, passionless.

Sent on new errands, she passed Sister Purita on the stair behind the cloister.

They went by without speaking, yet each glancing once, curiously, furtively. Danielus linked them, but tenuously.

Veronichi thought, however, prudent and wily, *I must come to know her, I think.*

Purita thought nothing of Veronichi, except that she did not have the Fra's handsomeness, looked properly a Jewess, and had sent all her servants to safety on the Veneran Plain.

All in all, Purita felt prosaic. She had been told her brother had survived the battle—at which had come a gush of relief—and, peculiarly, irritation. Must his way be made always straight?

Then she came about the corner, and scratched at the door of the Domina's chamber.

The fat grasshopper was propped up high in her hard bed. Purita was glad to see she had been made more comfortable.

All about the bed, despite the turmoil of the war casualties below, fourteen of the nuns of the higher offices stood in a pale cordon. Were they reluctant to allow Purita by? Then one stepped aside, lowering her eyes.

Candles burned, but dawn was near. In the window a sort of nothingness had replaced the opaque immensity of night.

"I stayed to see, to behold one more sunrise," said the Domina. "I love it so, how could I leave before—and He has allowed me this."

So she was dying too. With what a guard of men she would go up. But she was worldly in her ascetic way. She would not mind.

Purita was sorry. The Domina was a fair woman. And what came next would undoubtedly be difficult.

Purita had given over trying to deny or evade. Luchita had previously let go her chains, her tribulations. Purita did not mean to take them up. Although, if allowed, the other burden she would accept.

Her own arrogance in that had amazed her, at first. But arrogance and amazement too she had let go.

The nuns in the room, some of whom must also know, struck her now as more friendly than expected. They were conceivably only uneasy. After all, what might Purita turn out to be? She must have already surprised them very much.

The Domina said, "I've been shriven, my own concerns are done. And now I have called you here to witness me."

Purita stood among the other nuns, head bowed, seemingly attentive.

As the old woman detailed her thoughts and wishes, sometimes pausing while they gave her sips of watered wine, Purita's mind strayed back and forth. These sisters had been in the order since girlhood. While Gratzilia there, had entered the religious life as a child.

Gratzilia stammered, but she was often impatient and often brutish. She sneered at the infirm, pinched the novices. In the garden she had, as Purita saw, killed helpful bees, and once shut a little frog under a bucket for no reason but malice. When Purita lifted the bucket, allowing the frog's escape, Gratzilia reviled her, stammering, and incomprehensible. Later Gratzilia scalded Purita's foot with water spilled from a pan.

Now Gratzilia was mute, and her habit had blood-stains as did almost all their clothes, from the assistance given below.

The window was changing further.

This was like any summer dawn. Bird song, color re-invented. There was a trace of golden cloud painted high on the thinning sky.

"Therefore," said the Domina, "it is my wish that Sister Purita take on my mantle. And to this end, I have written to the Primo.

Here's my favorable answer, signed and sealed by Fra Danielus, Magister Major of the Upper Echelon of the Bellatae."

The nuns poised like petrified wood.

Purita thought distinctly, *Will they round on me and rend me in pieces?*

Then she heard their murmurings.

"Yes, Mother. God guided you."

"I have prayed for it, Mother."

To her own astonishment Purita felt her eyes let out two rushing streams of tears. They poured down her face. More fell.

She groped for the bed and crouched beside it.

"Domina. I'm not worthy. Oh, Domina, not me. How can I carry this authority?"

And again astonishing her, she felt the quick light touches of the nuns, smoothing her, softly, almost amusedly reprimanding her lack of faith. And the warm hand of the Domina holding hers.

"There, there, child. Remember how you told me you couldn't do justice when you read from the Bible? And then you read as if you had been accustomed since infancy. Rely on Christ. Then you need never be afraid. And here is my dear walking stick, for you to lean on if ever you have need to."

The window flamed suddenly rose-red. The old woman sighed and died, and her warm hand went abnormally cold. It was as if she had been dead some while, yet somehow stayed animate to see the dawn as she wanted.

Purita wept on, soothed among the flock of thirteen nuns. She did not think of the fourteenth now, the stuttering Gratzilia, gibbering in the corner, her mouth so full of maleficence she could not get it out.

9

The terror came after one more day.

Men fear the worst, and pray the worst will never be. They live only by forgetting that the worst must sometimes find them, as they fear. And sometimes, so it does.

The Jurneian fleet, lit foremost now by a sinking madder sun. Dipped in blood, like the wreckage of Veneran men washed in one day before them.

Up to the sand-bars and the walls that held off the sea. Up to the silver mirrors of the great lagoons.

Jurneia pressed her carmine tiger face against the looking-glass of Venus and was reflected there.

The pitiless enemy.

The ravenous infidel.

And sometimes, so it does.

Joffri had run away. He had been sobbing, as he did it, with humiliation. But he had done it. Taking his dogs, horses, friends, mistresses, and—an afterthought?—his wife. Now the City that had not so far emulated him, began to.

Barges loaded with baskets, furnishings, people in tears, or wailing, toiled through the waterways. There were collisions, drownings. Families fought and cursed each other and began feuds that would last for generations.

Some of the rich and noble had fled, like the Ducem. Others had shut themselves inside their palaces. Yet others opened their palaces and took in the less fortunate, out of the poorer houses and the hovels, before closing and barricading their gates.

Blocks of stone and hand-carts of rubbish were thrown into certain of the canals, in the hope of making them impassable to any of the enemy's smaller craft.

Under the direction of various officials who the Ducem had left with the charge of Ve Nera, soldiers manned the sea walls and the inner islands. Falling back from the former when the Jurneian cannon spoke, just after dawn the following day. This was when the Jurneians had finished their prayers, and the bells in the City were ringing the Auroria. Jurneia was ahead in everything, it seemed.

Belatedly boats had been put across the ocean end of the two lagoons Fulvia and Aquila. These too were all successfully splintered by cannon shot not long after noon.

In the Primo, priests had begun to pray on the previous morning, continuously, at the Great Altar under the Dome.

They prayed in batches. As men sank down exhausted or took sick, they were replaced.

The outer islands were almost deserted—Torchara, Isole. (More inward, also the Isle of the Dead, where the dead had been left to the mercy of God.)

Those who kept the outer (useless) defenses of Aquila and

Fulvia, or on the Silvian Marshes—soldiers and hapless volun-
teers—soon saw the strategy of the Jurneians was to be as predicted.

Within half a day they had blasted flat the sea walls. (The infirmaria, marooned on its strip of land, took one blow almost inci-
dentally. Laid indecently open, it displayed its two stories like
shelves, stocked with corpses, and worse, the partly-dead and
screaming.)

As the afternoon tide shifted, also as prophesied, the Jurneians
used their sailors and their slaves to lay down wooden rollers on the
sand-bars thus exposed. Their slaves then dragged over them the
ships, by ropes. Where the sea had its narrow access to Fulvia, by
the isle of Torchara, they pulled the ships through by means of little
boats, taking no chances.

Into the lagoons, Jurneia came. Making soundings as they came,
sensibly. The lagoons were not to be trusted, their floors uneven.
Jurneia knew everything. Even not to move in too near. As yet.

Last isolate cannon fired from Isole, Torchara, and the marsh.
And from five ships that sailed around the flank of the Isle of the
Dead.

Jurneia returned fire, as if in courtesy not to belittle, and the
Veneran artillery grew silent.

Like the smashed barrier boats, the five last ships of the fleet of
Venus cracked and split, floated, turned over and went down, sails
spread out once more like washing, belly full of water. Veneran men
swam frantically away, and Jurneia let them.

Bells rang in Venus. Not for prayer. Everyone that could was
praying, probably.

The bells, like the ballistas, presently fell silent, too.

Some seven hundred and fifty-eight Jurneian ships had survived
the fight at Ciojha. Now four hundred of them were mounted on the
waters of the lagoons. They jostled a while. Then they were in order.

Now, Jurneia did no more. The ships stood there, hiding the
water, tall and burgeoned with their rigging.

Seen from the City shores, they were like one more city.

They stood there.

Needing nothing else.

The Master Suley-Masroor, in the fore-tower of *Quarter-Moon,* was
looking at Venarh, in afternoon light.

He saw no beauty in it. Like all cities, it had some glamours, the
huge gleaming dome of its idolatrous fane, for example. But it

seemed strange to him, *wrong,* the way this host of walls overhung, or went down into, the water. Besides, it was there only to be destroyed. Not by his will, but by the will of those he served. And through destiny, which came from God.

He was sorry for Venarh.

In the sea-fight he had not felt that. He slew the Christian devils and assisted in the wreck of their vessels.

This thing lay passive, and not well defended. It had its own unlovely but cogent life. Yet, men had souls, even if they threw them away in non-belief; there would be a chance for those Jurneia captured as slaves and converted to the true faith.

But a city's spirit died with its body. Crows would wheel above Venarh, and sea-birds make their nests in its ruin. The sea it flirted with would wash in and cover it.

Among the under-rooms of the Primo, the chamber of the Council of the lamb was lit by candles and by torches. It had no window. An iron room, filled full today.

The Council was in session. But along the great table of polished ebony, there also sat Fra Danielus, and his two fellow Magisters Major, with Ve Nera's Marshal of Arms, who had come here, swearing, from the quays. Captains of the Marshal sat by or stood at his back, and alongside them, nine of the Upper Echelon of the Bellatae Christi.

Of the Council too, eleven were seated. The twelfth was on his feet. And there was quiet, save for this one voice. A hoarse and crackled, hurried yelling, spitting out words like showers of darts.

"If we had cleansed this city—Sodomus, would we have come to this? If we'd done what was there to be done. We were lax—some of us. We let sin run like the water through Ve Nera. Now it will be blood."

The Marshal again swore. Softly as a leaf turning.

Brother Isaacus veered to the tiny sound.

"Ah—be careful of your tongue. These are the filthy things because of which God abandons us—"

The Marshal stared at Isaacus. A look of hatred, rage—and fear. He said, "Forgive me, holy brother. What I've seen has made me forgetful."

"*I* don't forget *you,* Marshal. I shall send to you, when this is done."

Danielus spoke. "If any of us live, perhaps you may, Brother

Isaacus. To thank this man for all his labor on the City's behalf. Or should he have sped away with the rest, and left the City like a trencher for Jurneia's meat and knife?"

The Marshal said, reverting to his role, "We must send to them, and make terms."

"*Send*! send to them—" screeched Isaacus like some scraping, rusty nail—"they are the *Devil! Infidels*—"

"They won't make terms," said Danielus. "It was attempted. The Ducem, while he remained, sent letters. And this was before they brought us low. Now they'll only settle for annihilation. Yes indeed, Brother Isaacus. It will be like the fate of Sodomus. Fire and brimstone. Leaving only a pillar of salt."

The Council shuddered as if a whirlwind raked through them. It was fright. They were the makers and causers of fear, yet themselves not immune to it. Or, only one of their number.

But as Isaacus began another tirade, Sarco got up, holding high both hands.

"Let's be calm. Yes, brother, calm. We are here to decide what can be done."

Isaacus said, almost gently now, "Nothing. It's too late. This City is tumbling in the Pit. Too *late*."

"You will tumble with it," said Danielus, dryly.

"I am of no account. And my soul's clear of dirt."

A silence fell here, as outside.

No sound might be heard, but the rustle of the torches.

Then Sarco said, "For myself, I prefer to let God judge me. And for now, I live. Fra Danielus, have you any advice?"

Standing at the Magister's back, Cristiano observed Sarco, Brother of the lamb, who seemed theirs, but who ultimately was in the service, perhaps the pay, of Danielus. Never before had such a thing occurred to Cristiano. It surprised, disgusted him, but remotely. Much had become remote to him.

As Danielus rose, the other Magisters turned to him. Even the Marshal did so.

Danielus addressed them in the mildest tone.

"We are at the brink. Our defenders are pared to a handful, our defenses ill-prepared and overthrown. Our shepherd, Joffri, has—been called away. The Jurneians don't practice clemency. They kill or enslave. They raze, so one stone fails to stand on another. We need therefore a miracle, sent by God."

Isaacus drew back his head and made some horrible noise of derision from his half-throat.

"Yes, brother," said Danielus. "I was about to say that we've been given one."

Sarco crossed himself. "It may be."

Isaacus cawed: "Satanus—"

It was broad Jesolo who rose from the Council, and he roared across the table, slamming down his fist upon it, "Hold your wind, brother! I've heard enough from you. Even in the Cities of the Plain, God searched for one good man. Are there no virtuous men in Ve Nera? Hold your foul breath and let the Magister speak." And turning he said, "Is it this Maiden they talk of?"

"Yes, Brother Jesolo."

"A virgin, a *saint*—"

"A virgin, yes. The nuns of the Little Capella have examined her. A saint . . . that's for others to decide. But you know her gift, I imagine."

The Marshal said, "I know she brought them comfort in the square. She was there three or four hours with the wounded and the dying. Praying with them."

Isaacus screeched and hopped in a frenzy of viciousness.

The bulk of the Brothers shrank away from him.

There came another voice. Above.

Cristiano recognized it, as did the other Bellatae, the Marshal and his captains, now plunging to their feet.

A long splitting rush. Then a concussion, at which the torches rocked and candles fell. The chamber shook.

"They're firing on the City!"

"The Primo's struck!"

"The roof will come down on us—"

Black dusts trickled down, and up, through the air.

Cristiano watched some of the Brothers crawling out from under the ebony table. There was the sharp smell of fresh urine.

"A miracle, then," said Sarco. "Magister, we're in your hands. All Ve Nera is in them."

Outside, when the bombardment had ceased, Venus sent up columns of dark dust, reminding Cristiano of the candle-soot below. How many candles here had been put out?

The Primo, clearly a target, they had aimed at. But the discrepancies in the depth of the lagoons had kept the enemy fleet bunched up and still some distance out. Range differed, and by a fluke—or divine design—no missile had hit the Basilica. One barrage had struck somehow behind it, however, and smashed the houses there, and the palace of a prince.

Towards the Silvian Marshes, the streamers of rising darkness were more pronounced. And from this square, Aquila seemed hidden by a drifting, horizontal pall, that almost certainly was, or had been, the silk market. Apt enough.

Cries filled the clouded air from all around. Bells came and went, starting and stopping.

The sun westered. Shapes grew flat and without color. As if the condemned City became unreal.

Cristiano stared up at the Angel Tower. In the torture cages, did the two lingerers notice any of this? Were they glad, or made worse?

He put his hand on the carved stone of the Lion Door, to feel it. A war was also in his mind. Pain in conflict—with joy. Exhilaration. Tumult.

Beatifica.

Over the water, you could abruptly make out the huge maneuvering of the infidel ships. Testing, regrouping now, to come in closer and do more.

In the Primo courts a running man ran up to Cristiano, the Soldier of God, and told him Aretzo had died, just now. Cristiano signaled himself with the cross. He could feel nothing new. It was as if he had never known Aretzo, never prayed nor fought beside him. Cristiano was regretful. But it was a politeness.

"Heaven receive him."

"And all of us, Bellator."

10

Sunfall.

Watchman, in your high tower—what of the night?

The order had gone out along the waterfronts to make no light. Cannoneers might take sightings on every such beacon.

Ve Nera, meeting darkness, masked in the dark.

The Jurneians had not fired again, had not sent boats towards the quays. But like wolves they had come closer. And among the shore watchers, armed with pikes and clubs and hunting arrows, the word was that a horde more ships had been drawn in through Silvia, and through Torchara's needle's eye of sea. Five hundred now, in the lagoons.

Why did they wait?

Like the Christians, these Godless infidels prayed very often.

Ve Nera had heard their offices, in the afternoon, and at sunset. A weird howling, it had seemed. Suitable, of course, to wolves.

Unlike the blackened City, their ships were bright with lanterns. They glowed, and the water sparkled under them as if to welcome.

They were wolves and tigers, the Jurneians. They liked best to attack by night.

Activity began to be seen on their decks. They were close enough now, it could easily be made out.

And then, after the stillness which the infidel had brimmed with animal noises, singing burst from the Primo.

Although there had been no bells, it was the office of Venusium, the Evening Mass.

And then the doors of the Basilica were thrown wide, and light, blinding sheets of silver and gold, flung heedlessly on the dark.

From her crannies and corners, Ve Nera peered to see.

The Basilica dome had bloomed like a white rose-bud that sheltered a kernel of flame.

On every side of it, the torches were lighting up. Was this madness?

Among the Jurneian fleet, Jurneia too paid attention. Perhaps asking the same.

Now from the Lion Door, a massive procession issued. The priests in their black and white, their magenta and purple. Boys singing. Sound with light flared and flew into the other upper dome of night.

Incense blew so thick they smelled it on the ships. (Incense, which like the spice and silk, had come from the East.) There were a million candles, delicate butterfly points, yellow stars. And tall brands that burned ferociously.

On *Quarter-Moon,* Suley-Masroor looked, and thought, *They mean to sue for peace, but like kings*—affronted.

At Santa La'La over the marsh, seeing the sudden blaze of the Primo, certain nuns clustered crying that the Basilica had been set alight. They were not alone in this error.

But it was a pageant for those nearer, in the palaces and cannon-spoilt tenements about, as among the enemy fleet.

The priests filled the square, and moved aside. They made an avenue. Their singing ceased. Fearfulness crept back into their faces, which the chant had momentarily eased. The candles shook. This looked only charming: a million butterfly stars, flickering.

And through the avenue stalked the Bellatae Christi, the Upper Echelon, now numbering almost thirty knights. With, walking after them, three hundred more of the Militia of God. All that were left.

Their steel maculums, their mail, the white cloaks crossed with blood; helmed, each with the sword drawn in one hand. Some with a piece of red cloth like a rose above the badge of the Lion and Child. Within the cordon of the priests they too formed an avenue. Lastly, down this narrowed corridor, two Bellatae marched, bearing between them the Madonna Standard from the Primo's innermost Sanctum. Ten feet high, the banner swayed, heavy with bullion and pearls. The moon-pure face of Maria looked towards the ships, unmoved. Her pale hand raised to bless all that knew her.

Murmuring went over the walls of men, armored in mail or purple or black. From the roofs and windows all about. From stations of defense all but abandoned.

Would this special icon protect them? Or did it only signify the end?

Then, out of the Lion Door, behind the Standard, alone, as on a previous night, the figure came, but riding.

On the Jurneian vessels they exclaimed. These fools of Venarh. This must be their Ducem, sent to plead for them. But he was only a boy.

Nevertheless, they honored him somewhat, the men of Jurneia; they had heard he ran away, but no, he was here. A brave boy. Let them take him as a slave and break him, to reclaim his soul—How well he controlled the horse.

Cristiano stood among the Bellatae. As they did, he raised his head, and looked up, at the Maiden Beatifica.

In the Primo, in the floor, were mosaic pictures, parables and allegories. In one, a fox was shown, hoisted up on a pole by a dove, Virtue triumphing over Cunning.

She had been a fox, a vixen. And before her they had carried the image of the Virgin.

The brain, spinning with images, words, memory.

She rode the red horse, which in the torch and candlelight looked like carnelian, as did the waterfall of her hair.

In her white and gold he saw she was no longer a girl dressed as a man, or a female boy. No travesty. She was as she must be. Of neither sex. Of some other gender. Like an angel.

There was a humming note, low and tremendous in his ears. It was the murmuring intensity of all who stood here, priests and warrior-priests. A reverberation, part vocal, partly psychic.

And everywhere about, the City, upturned like a casket of beetles, running every way or petrified. *Attending*.

Emotion was her impetus. Danielus had said.

What had he said to *her*?

Her face was raised above Cristiano now, lifted over them all, as the slow horse brought her on. Could any human face be so white? Empty of any features but the eyes of gold.

Inside him, mounting, mounting, the glory and the terror of ultimate surrender, than which God would accept no less.

Her shadow, cast from the torches, swept over him. He felt his body drain of everything, of life, even. And how many others felt as he did.

He could have cried out, to her. He was dumb. Before this presence, he would not speak. But she had given him back his faith. That night when she prayed among the dying, saving them from Hell—she had saved him, too, from the Hell of a world without God.

Beatifica.

Beatifica.

Her shadow, golden as light, passed. He watched her travel on, his soul caught up, on air.

In some upper room, standing with Danielus, as he showed her the ships out on the lagoon, she would have waited passively, the way she did.

Had those ships meant anything until explained—their purpose and possibility?

Had the Magister said to her, gravely, "Only you, Beatifica, are able to save us"?

But she lit candles, she called flame like a garland and dropped it prettily into oil. She was domestic.

They said, when a slave she had burned her master, the woodseller. But it was a vulnerable wood-yard. The madman Berbo, who was not mad, had said he saw her walk clothed in fire. But he was drunk.

"Call the fire, Beatifica."

Cristiano heard Danielus speak it, inside his brain.

Cristiano thought of the dream he had had, all Ve Nera gathered in the Primo, and the Madonna Standard.

Aretzo was dead.

Death did not matter. The road was stones but the gates were made of pearl.

Beatifica.

If they died now, she would raise them up. They would go with her on her wings. He would go with her, fearing nothing, into the unknown light of eternity.

When your heart is mine
You may do as you will to
When my heart is yours
Then wish the world good-bye

The red horse had come to the edge of the square, where the black water lapped below.

She gleamed, snow white and red as fire.

In the square, in the City, not a sound now. Nothing.

And on the ships also great stillness. They were intrigued, perhaps, by this last show.

Speak the Grace, Beatifica.

All across the short divide of water, aided by the square's design, they heard her voice, which was neither female nor male, speaking to God in the Latin tongue. She did not speak, the Grace. It was an ancient Psalm which invoked assistance, from the mountains. Had Danielus guided her too in this?

Undoubtedly the Jurneians did not follow it. But Cristiano, and how many more, felt his body part along its seams, painless, like a chrysalis.

The world itself is opening like some colossal door, to let another world come through.

The girl stands in her stirrups, well-trained to horsemanship on a farm of the plain. And the horse, well trained, stays steady as a rock. Through everything.

She raises her arms.

Oh Beatifica, the Word is God's, and now the Word is made Fire.

They saw, on the ships and on the land, an invisible great hand, which swept up all her burning pelt of hair, and as it rose, enfurled it into living flame.

Flame *towered*. It raced upward, higher than the walls of flesh and architecture, high or higher than the rose-white dome of the

Primo Suvio. And in the flame, the heart of it, stood Beatifica, the Maiden, burning and unconsumed. (And under her the horse, a rock.)

For perhaps a minute this was seen.

For perhaps a little more.

And then the Maiden gestured with her fiery hands, and all the scarlet whorl of the fire curled over to them like some tidal comber of an ocean. She balanced this enormity in her grasp.

She held the monumental fire. All saw her hold the fire.

Then saw her set it free.

It sprang, the fire, redder than any sun, blinding hot, dry as a desert wind, balled and sizzling, with a shriek that tore the night across. It sprang straight for the Jurneian fleet.

Less than a minute they had. Some few seconds.

The time that was needed for one great breaking cry.

Suley-Masroor beheld, where dark had been, the burning wave, its heat scorching him, and casting up his eyes, saw *Quarter-Moon's* topmost sails alter, from dull white canvas clouds to a fire-cloud bright as day.

Thousand on thousand, all the white clouds were burning.

Flames leaped a hundred feet, tossing up and away huge limbs of masts that shattered as they seemed to hit the sky, falling in tails of gold. Flaming flowers, the rigging of five hundred and three vessels billowed and conjoined above the water, turning it to blood.

Through the roar and bellow, as the ships' wooden sides split wide, here and there interceded the screams of men, with a thin, disembodied sound.

Then thunder detonated, rang round the lagoons over and again as the powder of the cannons exploded. Black metal shapes hurled through the air. The water disbanded to receive them. Stripped skeletal, slender vessels tilted, diving like sharks with blazing backs.

The lagoons drank thirstily.

But now it is all the thunder, the lightning, and a rain of burning red, and sparks like shards of cinnabar, and ruby carbuncles and white gold, and streams of liquid gold that fissure the water of smashed mirrors, and the pillars of smoke that is black-red granite, pushing back the night to give—

this arson room—

this clamour space—

this apocalypse its legend.

PART TWO

By me this way is for the City Sorrowful,
By me this way is for eternal pains . . .
Your every hope desert, that enter in.

DANTE ALIGHIERI
The Divine Comedy
(Part of the inscription over the entrance to Hell)

1

From the Ducal estate at Forchenza, the mountains were visible in some detail. Joffri sat long hours looking at them, brooding.

Those whose business it was to cheer him, tried. He wondered how long they would bother.

The dogs, as usual, were the best. Especially his second white Gemma, who sat patiently at his feet, not minding what he had done.

Joffri attempted to ignore what he had done. This was impossible, naturally.

He saw it very distinctly. Everything. Delay and indolence, not wanting to think of it. Allowing others to decide and make mistakes. Finally a dramatic unavoidable awareness. A bravura (as at the feast, when the girl did her trick with the fire). Even his letter to the Primo, in which he declared his sure belief in his own army, in his ships, in the Bellatae, in God. Then the panic. The packing. The running away.

If Venus survived, she would take him back. She would be, like him, too weak and lazy to demand another lord. But though she might forget with time what he had done, she would never *forgive*.

On the other hand, it must be faced, there was a probability he could not return to his enchanting island.

Jurneia might destroy it, and the City too. (He thought of the lovely colored birds in the trees of the Rivoalto, potted by heathen savages, and wept again.)

After a victorious interval, Jurneia would come inland, up the

plain. They would harry the farms and burn down the old houses on
the estates, this one included. And he would have to run again, up
over those horned peaks he could so clearly see. Into coarse Frank-
ish lands. Or else, he could retreat westwards through Italy, his
house on his back, scorned, mocked, and a beggar in the courts of
other princes.

The Ducem looked at the mountains.

When they brought him the messenger, Gemma the bitch
hound stood up. Joffri meant to, but his legs were like leaden water.

He took the letters, and sent everybody out. Let them question
the man themselves if they were so eager to learn of horrors.

Joffri sat with the letters in his hands.

He said to Gemma, quietly, "I'd do better at once to hang myself." At his voice, and inappropriately, his dog wagged her tail.

He smiled at the irony, and broke the first seal.

Joffri read the letters, one of which was signed by the Marshal
of Arms, and undersigned by three captains, the second and third of
which were signed by two Magisters Major of the Primo, (neither
Danielus). The fourth was signed by five members of the Council of
the Lamb, not including Isaacus. Having read the four letters, Joffri
read them again. Then once more.

He had drunk a lot of wine that night she called the fire. Even
so he had, at the time, been partly overthrown by what she did.
Joffri remembered now the bizarre tale of the man who discounted
Jesus, saying the Christ had only risen once from death, who knew if
He would be able to do it again.

Ah. If only he had had faith.

After this, Joffri sat on the chair.

Gemma came and put her head on his knee, because he was
crying again.

> 'No sooner did the fire take hold, which was instantly, than a great
> many of their ships exploded, from the powder kept for the cannon,
> and stores of oil. The sky was red and the water boiled, and a rain
> fell on the shore of wood splinters and iron nails and other things,
> alight or melted.'
>
> 'Later we learned that the conflagration did further work. See-
> ing the distress of their fleet in the Laguna Fulvia, the Infidel sent
> in yet more ships from the sea mouths at Silvia and Torchara. And
> from Aquila, where the fire-blast did not go, also they tried to come

in, by the wider canals. But no sooner did any draw near, than the fire spread contagiously to them, and so too through into Aquila.'

'The quays and waterfronts, even the roofs, and all the Primo Square, were littered with bits and parts of the Jurneian ships, which had been blown off. The citizens have since taken them for momentoes. One large wooden piece, thought to have been wrenched from a fore-castle, was carried into the Primo and laid before the Great Altar. Strangely no fires were begun in the City from the rain of sparks, and the damage done by objects which fell is slight.'

'The sea and lagoons were full of swimming men, but many drowned, and countless others will have burned. Those we have are our prisoners. Their ships cracked and went down. A few ships left afloat, though shambled, were consequently towed away. In all, the belief is they lost more than six hundred of their craft. As it was learned presently from the marshes and next the outer islands, the rest at length turned tail and fled. We had not the vessels to pursue them. But they have lost very much. Besides, they were shown, God was with us. They will not dare come back. And the word they sow in Candis and the East will muzzle all those cities there which will us harm.'

'For the girl they call the Maiden, whom truly God gave to us, she was carried away dead. Her fire, sent from Heaven, was too vast for her fragile vessel. There must always be a sacrifice.'

2

Before Cristiano was Jian, emerging suddenly from the shadows of the knights chapel, like a moving figure of steel. Defiantly, Jian said, "I am here, as you are, for her."

"Is that my reason?"

"What else, Cristiano. We must keep this Vigile together. We were her first witnesses among the Bellatae. Aretzo would be here, if he'd lived."

Cristiano said, "You know, I keep the Vigil alone. I'll come here tomorrow."

Jian's pale angry face, stony now as Cristiano's face. "You're petty, Bellator. You won't *share* with me? What are we, boys tussling for an onion? I'd use this night to pray for her."

"Yes."

Cristiano turned.

But Jian was after him at once. His hand fell hard on Cristiano's arm.

"*Stay.* Won't you do this for her? No? You're jealous then, I think. You want the Maiden to yourself, Cristiano. No one else must have her—and when they do, you avert your eyes."

"I assumed that was your own argument."

Jian stood back. He said, "You must always be the best, must you not? You treat God like some blind old father, who hears of your wonders and never sees the pride of you." Cristiano stood looking at him. Jian said, "You're swoll with pride, about to split from it."

The white glare of his rage and envy filled up the capella, but Cristiano reflected it back upon him like a polished shield. In his mind, Cristiano heard an inner voice telling him to be still. Perhaps Jian did also. Neither could heed it; And Jian's hand fell abruptly on the hilt of his sword.

"No," said Cristiano then. He stepped forward, and flung one arm about Jian, who resisted him a moment as (Cristiano surmised) a woman might. Then gave in.

"Pardon me, Cristiano."

"I do. I ask your pardon in exchange."

They fell back from each other and stared away in opposite directions.

"She lives," Cristiano presently said.

"So the Magister told us."

"You doubt him?"

"No."

Cristiano considered, as if they were events which another had undergone, the time—hours or moments—after the ships of Jurneia had been riven.

In the upheaval of the firestorm, the flickering light, the detonations, water and land, the City of Ve Nera, seemed equally to be quaking, collapsing.

To this he had come back. Perhaps for Jian too, for many of them, it was like that. But not, Cristiano thought, (*And is this only my swollen, overweening pride?*) as it had been for him, what they returned from.

When she brought the fire—

He had not walled himself away, not protected himself. Rather, he gave himself.

The first time, at the Magister's farm, had been *nothing* to this.

Even to himself, he could neither describe it nor properly recollect.

This alone he knew. The white light of God he had found in the Vigil, the crimson light of war-fury, they were less.

There had been an upsweep, this he did recall. A whirling and soaring, as if in flight. And all the shore of Venus had gone up with him, caught on her fire-wings, to some realm that blazed.

The sweetness of it, and the joy—the *power,* which unlike any power of the earth, came from an assimilation, from a total *loss* of everything—

And no more remained of it, to him, when once it cast him back.

Then there were only the ships burning under their rose-red billow of sails and smoke. And Ve Nera, shaking.

The army of men shouted and screamed as in battle. Thunder. Leviathon the Dragon crashing in the deeps.

After this he saw that *she* had slumped down on the horse's back. It was fire-trained, and—unscathed as she was—had kept stock-still.

In a body that seemed made only from the hollow mail and armor of a knight, he hauled himself forward, to support and guard her, in case she should slip down. He found Jian was on the other side of her, doing the same.

Somehow, through the great confusion and exaltation, they two led the horse.

Men had been leaping and running around them. The Bellatae were howling. Bells rang. A macrocosm of faces lit by fire. And through all this, which Cristiano barely saw, they led the horse away into the Primo's yards.

In the courtyard with the lion fountain, some grooms and servants dashed up.

They lifted her off the horse.

She looked asleep. Her mouth smiled a little, as the mouths of children sometimes did in slumber—or the dead.

But she was alive. The pulse thumped steadily in her throat.

Jian took her from them all and carried her inside the high walls.

She seemed a child, too, in his grasp. Or some creature of another race.

Her hair, hanging down along his arm, was faded and brownish, nearly gray, or flaxen, Cristiano thought, in the uncanny light.

Jian said now, "The Magister keeps her locked away. A secret. They're saying in the City she died."

"She never did."

"Aretzo died in the hospital, days after Ciojha. It could have been like that."

"No."

"The Fra spoke to you? Why to you and not to me?"

"He didn't speak to me. She's alive. Sleeping, I suppose."

"Perhaps it burnt out her mind or soul. Perhaps she's only a shell, the kind the crab-fish leaves."

Cristiano said shortly, "She's no fish."

"You know where she is."

"I don't."

"*Tell* me."

"Jian, take your hand from the sword. I won't stop you again. Do you think you can match me?"

"Can't I match you?"

"*Jian.* No more. In God's name."

"I'd die for her."

"I know it."

"But you—"

Ah, said Cristiano, *she has killed me already.* He did not speak aloud.

Jian turned away.

"Pray for her, Jian," Cristiano said. "There's no greater loving token."

"You talk to me as if—I were her *lover.*"

But when Jian turned yet once more, to confront Cristiano, the capella was again empty, save for Jian himself.

In its black, lit room, the Council sat in silence.

Jesolo repeated. "It's very strange."

Sarco said, "Our dungeons are bursting, nevertheless."

"Perhaps they are."

"Remember, brother," said Sarco, "our task is to recruit for God all those men we may. These infidel may be converted, and their souls salvaged."

Jesolo answered bleakly, "Faced with the prospect, several have already taken their own lives."

"We've seen this before. Not all are so violent, or sinful."

Isaacus' crunching voice stirred in the dark.

"*They should be cinders.*"

"The quick immersion saved them."

"Cinders—ash. Did you not see the fire, brothers? It burned."

Sarco spoke peaceably. "The fleet burned and is no longer a threat. Some of the Jurneians, evidently, drowned. Or died in other ways. And some are burned—"

"Scorches. Singes."

Another of the Council spoke ominously. "Brother Isaacus, what is the pith of these reflections?"

"This devil-witch called her fire. It burnt up the ships and made a show. But the men, these idolators, these infidel, these children of Satanus—these she *spared*. In such a conflagration, how could any survive? Yet many did. Beyond a few slight wounds, they have no mark of it."

Jesolo said, "It's so. It's strange."

"And yet," said another, "the City is rife with tales of men this Maiden is said to have burnt alive."

"*Christian* men," declared Isaacus.

"What are you saying?"

"What do you suppose I say? She incinerates true believers. The friends of Lucefero she spares."

Sarco said loudly, quickly, "Why then destroy their ships and save Ve Nera?"

"Are you a fool, brother?" Isaacus asked. "A fool, or in someone's hand?" Sarco said nothing. Isaacus said, "To gain power over us. Why do men ever turn to the Devil? They sell their immortal souls for help and comfort in this world. She has *helped* us. Saved us. Does she now receive our soul for her master in Hell?"

Danielus sat in his book-chamber, and watched the prisoner they had just brought him.

He was a tall man, dark skinned like most of the Jurneians, although the tones varied through amber and wood to a somber shade like bronze. Curiously, he had green eyes.

"Please sit."

"I will stand."

"Tell me at least where you learned the Italian tongue?"

"In trade. Where else. But you speak my tongue, so my countrymen told me. When they could not speak your own."

"I've studied some of the languages of the East."

Suley-Masroor, his turbaned head unbowed, said, "Oh, a pastime."

Outside, not very far away, came a soft rolling roar, then a sharp crack. The ship's Master started. Danielus said, "They're clearing the rubble of a house."

Suley said, fiercely, "Where we struck your city?"

"Just so. Be reassured. You've left us scars." He added winningly, "Please, do sit. It will make me more comfortable in your presence."

The Jurneian blinked. Then slowly he grinned. He sat down in the carved chair with its golden scrolls. "Are you a priest? You dress like a priest."

"Yes, I am a priest."

"That is astounding to me. You're couth, and quick. Unlike your religious brethren."

"I'm very sorry you were ill-treated. I have tried to alleviate the situation where I can. But we have another authority here, you'll have heard it mentioned. The Council. At this time, there's not a great deal I can do."

"How was it managed?" Suley asked. He no longer looked amused or collected. "The fire that filled the ships. It seemed—"

"What did it seem?"

"Like a magician's trick in the bazaar."

"But apparently it was real."

The Jurneian lowered his eyes. Danielus pushed towards him the crystal cup of water.

Reluctantly, Suley took the cup. He drained it angrily. Then, turning it in his fingers, remarked, "From Candisi?"

"Our own making."

"I thought so. Your glass-makers are inferior."

"Of course. But we will learn."

Suley said, "My fellows say you question them about the nature of the fire. How it took hold. Its swiftness. How we escaped burning."

"They tell me the same things, on every occasion."

"I have nothing to add."

"Did the fire touch you, Suley-Masroor?"

"Yes. Here on my chest, and down this arm. I saw my left leg burning as I went over into the sea-lagoon."

"How did the fire feel to you?"

"Very cold."

"So your fellow Jurneians described it to me."

Suley said, "That's usual, or may be so. At Khibris, when we fought your people years ago, my elder brother was burned across the back. He said it felt like ice and snow from the mountains. And afterwards he lay shivering."

"I'm sorry your brother was burned."

"No, don't lie, lord priest. He was an *infidel,* was he not?"

"But *we* are the infidel," said Danielus, "I believe."

"Yes. You follow the teachings of a great and holy man, but believing he is God. There is no God but only God."

Danielus poured more water into the (inferior) crystal cup. Suley-Masroor drank it. He said, grudgingly, "This water is good."

"The wells are pure, here. I see you have few wounds."

"The burns dried and sloughed from me inside a night. This sore here isn't fire, but from my irons in your prison. And this, from a generous Christian lashing."

"I shall see they are looked at. Forgive my harping on the fire— you suffered little, yet your ship was destroyed."

"How was it done?" the Jurneian asked again.

"Through God."

"Yours or mine?" demanded Suley, his eyes abruptly vivid and dangerous.

"As you pointed out, there is only one God. We merely award him different names, just as I might call Khibris, for example, Cyprus."

The green eyes flattened out, becoming almost opaque.

The Jurneian murmured, "I had a premonition of the fire. I dreamed of it three times. I have an amulet, from the City of the Dawn. When I addressed this talisman, it gave no answer."

Danielus said nothing. Then, almost idly, "Since you speak so excellently the language of this City, I shall keep you here, in the Primo. You'll be treated as a guest. Obviously, you'll be useful to me."

"To betray my brothers?"

"How can you betray them? What's left to betray?"

"What *use* then?"

"To salve my conscience. It will save you the prison and the ranting of men wishing to convert you. I've no interest in that. I will make it appear otherwise, of course. Are there any more from Jurneia you can recommend to me?"

"All. All."

"How I regret, Suley-Masroor, I haven't that much power. But ten or so, perhaps twenty. Write the names here. And I'll do what's possible to me."

"I write only in the script of Candisi."

"Of course. That will do. I can read it quite well."

When the Jurneian captain had gone, Danielus rose and walked about the chamber. He looked at it, at its ornaments, at the panels of Danielo and the lions. Some of the books he touched. Then drew out five of them, pondered, replaced one and drew out another. Had the Jurneian's choice of twenty men been as hard, or harder than this?

Carrying the books in his arms, he went from the chamber and walked through the glowing corridors of the Golden Rooms, where the servants of the Primo bowed, and the Primo's guards unlocked all doors.

Outside, the City was, day and night, loud with festival. Even the stern laws of the Council were being openly flouted. If Ve Nera were damned she would not have been saved. This notion gave them courage to outwit the Brothers of the Lamb.

On the Laguna Fulvia, countless little boats sculled about the glittering water, seeking, normally without luck, yet more relics of the miracle.

But it was noticeable, from the lagoon, that the Primo's nacreous dome had been besmirched by smoke. The smoke of a fire that burned selectively.

Festivals end. Trophies run out. Fear becomes remembered.

Entering Beatifica's room, Danielus set the books down on a chest. The books were not for Beatifica.

She had been laid on the floor, as she preferred for sleep, only her head on the cushion.

Among the priesthood, most were certain the Maiden had been removed from the Primo. Even the Bellatae thought this, it seemed. There had, too, been certain decoys, and misleading maneuvers.

In Ve Nera however, the citizens were convinced their kind angel was precisely here. Where else? Ignorance fathomed where cunning over-reached.

The young woman who sat watching Beatifica, dressed as a nun, had been one, once. Later she was in Veronichi's household, on the Isle of Eels. Danielus had lain with this girl, who was merry in the carnal act, and achieved bliss uttering mouse-like squeaks, which had enchanted him. Later, he had supplied her dowry and seen her wed where she desired.

About Ve Nera there were many with cause to be grateful to him.

That might, finally, have been enough, to see done what he wished.

But then, the torch was put into his hand. Who could resist it, that bright and wondrous thing?

This was not God's cruel and unfair test. God did not perpetrate such deeds on men. They made their own pits, and duly fell in them.

Danielus considered briefly, if he had fallen. For had he, like the other cunning ones, over-reached?

"Has she woken, Milla?"

"No, Fra. Not since that last time."

Milla had told him, just after Solus, the Maiden stirred, and turning, opened her eyes. Looking at Milla, but seeming not to see her, Beatifica had laughed, almost a giggle, like a child's. Then lapsed back into her trance.

"I'll watch her until your sister comes."

"Thank you, Fra."

Knowing him, in several ways, Ermilla knew also this man would do the sleeping girl no disservice. Of how many priests could one say that? To her last day Ermilla would recall the monster, her strict and elderly confessor, who had fondled her when he should have given consolation for her sins, and later denounced her as a strumpet when she refused to go near him.

Danielus sat quietly in the chair.

Just outside some bees had risen up from the garden, smelling the sweet herbs in the room. Perhaps scenting the nectar of a saint.

Beatifica slept.

On her side now. The redness had come back to her hair. She looked thriving and at ease. Ordinary.

"Beatifica," he said softly. "How I've needed you to wake up. Now was the hour when I might have worked a miracle—almost as great as your own. But I asked too much of you. Or worse, expected it. Sleep, little girl. Only return unimpaired. When you will."

Beatifica dreamed a dream which—like the dreams of the serpent and the red mountain, and eventually, the angel—she would recall accurately.

In the dream she forgot the fire. (As had happened the first time, she would have little or no recollection of what she had done when awake.)

An old woman was leading her up a steep white stair. As she often had in the City, Beatifica marveled at the stair—through her early life there had been mostly ladders.

The old woman was black. Who was she? Beatifica thought she might be her mother, grown very old—in the dream the memory had persisted of how mumma turned slowly black after her cremation—but then she had also grown young. Perhaps time passed differently here.

The woman was naked, and though old and thin, was firm, despite her embroidery of lines. Even her breasts, which had lost their flesh and hung down, had a gracefulness and symmetry nothing to do with sexual beauty.

At the stair-top was a terrace.

Below stretched a wide lagoon of silvery water.

Beatifica looked instinctively for the red mountain.

It was not to be seen.

Instead, along the terrace, near the water's edge, many of the priesthood of Ve Nera were walking about.

In that moment, Beatifica realized that she too was naked.

Something in the idea of being naked before men filled her with alarm and distress. Master had hurt her because of it, or had meant to, some new and awful hurt.

"They can't see," said the old black woman, in a smiling voice. She motioned with her hand that was like an artifact of carved ebony. "You so white and me so black. They think us a marble pillar and its shadow."

Beatifica believed the old woman at once. She relaxed her body, and watched the priests moving about.

Some were in the white or dark robes of the Primo, and others in the magentas of higher orders. Some wore black—the Council of the Lamb?

She did not recognize them, however. She could see no one she knew.

"Is Fra Danielus with them?"

"Oh no," said the old woman. "*Oh* no." She gave a laugh, like a stick rattling on a rock.

Something parted the water now. Beatifica thought it might be a drowned ship coming up, for somehow she knew ships had sunk in the lagoons of the City. But instead it was an enormous lizard, plated in a gray-green maculum. Its head was all snapping teeth. It pulled itself aboard the terrace, shiny, puddling. And only then did Beatifica see it too was clad in a purple robe.

When *they* saw it, all the priests began to make a great noise. This noise was not human.

There were squawks and trills, roars and grunts, and long foolish braying sounds.

Beatifica understood the lizard, now upright on its tail, was a crocodilius, for she had been shown one in a book. As for the others, two or three bent over, and then several more, and as they bent, she saw ears stand up on their heads. Cowls and tonsures vanished away. The priests jerked about, hopping heavy-bodied round the crocodilius—they were the huge hopping hares she had seen in previous dreams. And there went others on four little feet, and spines stuck up through their purple. Several had become birds, more gaudy than their garments, with crests, and pink wattles. They fought for perches where there were none. Another, like a pig with fur, rolled grumbling on the terrace, to get free of his priestly gown. A colossal toad sat burping.

Beatifica began to laugh. It pleased her, the silliness of it all. She was yet so young. An adolescent and a mage. She had never been a woman, even in her dreams.

But the black crone, again, was laughing too.

Then she said, "Go back now, girl. They call you."

Beatifica looked over her shoulder. There was a dim doorway behind the terrace, where the stair had been. She stopped laughing.

"Is Cristiano safe?"

"Yes, yes."

"I knew he would be. He can't come to harm. But then the Magister said he might—since, like Christ, he took on mortal shape . . ."

"Even the Magister lies."

Beatifica, troubled.

The beasts on the terrace had all begun to fight. They tore at each other and scratched and bit, snorting, defecating. No longer funny.

The old woman took Beatifica to the doorway.

"Where's mumma?"

"There," said the old woman. Her teeth were long and clean. She put her hand on Beatifica's forehead. Her skin was so richly black, would the fingers leave a mark? Like a flower, maybe, or a star.

"*There's* mumma. You, girl. Me and mumma, and all. *You.* Listen now, listen now."

But then she only shook her head.

The dim door enclosed Beatifica.

The last she saw before she woke, completely and at once, was the purple-robed crocodilius being tumbled back into the lagoon.

And after that, a woman's face, but quite young, and pale.

"God's mercy—you're wakened. Lie still, take care. I'll call to Milla. And the Fra only minutes gone—"

The girl lay down again. She felt dizzy and weak. She had none of the sense of strength and elation that had been with her in the dream.

There was a faint rumbling sound beyond the Primo. Thunder, perhaps.

Had she done what was asked?

What had it been?

Oh, as always. To call fire.

Because she must safeguard her angel.

The room was dark and closed by shadows. In her fluster, the running woman had put out the candle with the breeze of her skirt.

Beatifica took the candle up. She waited to feel the essence, so familiar now, rise in her. When she did not feel it, still she stroked her hair. Stroked as mumma had shown her. For the fire.

It did not come.

Her hand was empty, and warm with cold.

So the women found her, Ermilla and her sister, Ve Nera's saint, sitting forlorn on her blanket, the unlighted candle beside her, in darkness.

3

In a raucous voice, the boatman sang, rowing through into the Silvian Marshes. Sometimes he broke off and glanced at Danielus uneasily. "Be sure you don't mind it, holy Father?" Danielus said he did not. He did not add he wished the man could sing better. "It's relief, and proper thankfulness. Praise God."

"Yes," said Danielus. "Sing if you want."

Ve Nera had sung, and was singing. In the dusk, she was lit up extravagantly by an excess of candles and brands, and faces beaming in windows, at turnings between the walls. Here and there, where Jurneian missiles had struck, they were clearing rubble. The worst hits were about Fulvia. From those places rose businesslike noises, as if in a stone-yard.

On the narrow canals that led through from the marsh, they were out too, trying to gather the rubbish up they had dumped, to choke them off from small craft of the enemy fleet. In some areas the waterways were impassable. Probably they would not flow freely now till the winter tides, and the smell was viler than usual.

A woman pointed in the water, lamenting. "He flung in our bed—our bed we had from my uncle's house. We won't need a bed if the Jurneians come. That's what he said. Now he says, let's couple on the floor, but I say No, no, husband. Buy me another bed first." Seeing a priest rowed by, she made a motion of fake shame. "Forgive me, holy signore." He raised his hand gently.

He was glad for them, glad they were enjoying this respite from fear and worry. Indulging in petty events. It would not last. What could, in such a world?

They went by long outer ways, to avoid the closed canals.

Set in twilight, where the marsh broadened and liquefied to great lakes, Danielus glimpsed a ruin on its hill, the amphitheater of the ancient Romans. It was a smaller replica, a bastard babe perhaps, of their Colosso in Rome. Here, as there, they had watched men fight to the death, and criminals fed to beasts of prey. Through cunning drains and traps in the arena floor, they had sometimes flooded the theater from the sea, and staged mock battles in tiny ships, mock battles where gladiators and slaves died by scores.

Over it the gulls wheeled, crying mournfully. Nothing had improved for the gulls. Worsened, doubtless: ancient Rome and modern Jurneia would both have provided them with corpses to pick.

Santa La'La, also on its hill above the marsh, let him in.

He climbed up the stairs, preceded by two chattering nuns, a servant now carrying the books he had brought, seventeen in all.

Her rooms were not too unpleasant, but she had not been able to soften them much, which, where she could, she had skill in doing. Here, Veronichi stayed circumspect. However, when the servants and nuns were out and the door locked, she lit more candles, and pulled off the ugly cap to let her hair fall, newly washed, blue-black.

"Have you seen your Domina yet?"

"Not yet. After the Luna Vigile I will."

"She was anxious, I think. She's afraid she won't have satisfied you."

"She's only had the post a short while, and in time of war."

"I've seen nothing bad in her. She has a temper, but curbs it. She wept when the old woman was buried."

"Purita has a curious heart. Are you jealous?"

Veronichi smiled. "How well you know me. A little."

"Though never of my lovers."

"No. Never of those."

They ate the meal, which was sparse but well cooked.

"On the island," said Veronichi, "we would have chickens stuffed with pigeons and apples, and sit crowned by chaplets of lilies and peonies."

"And other, better things."

"Do you want—the door's fast—"

"No, dearest. Not here."

The wine, which he himself sent to the cellars of his churches, was very good. They ate and drank in silence. One by one, the candles burned down.

Danielus and his sister rinsed their hands, and sat side by side on a bench before the window of the second room. They leaned close, became disturbed by it, and in mutual consent, drew apart. Their bodies were used to love making, but must be denied. (Beyond, night hung low, its stars obscured.)

"Why have you brought so many books?"

"You also know me well."

"What else, my Daniel, when I've studied you all these years?"

"Your island's safe. Soon I hope you may go back to it. In which case, I'd like it best if you would store these books in the secret place."

"But—Pliny—"

"Perhaps all the Roman books, and the Greeks, must go in there. For a while."

"Carpocrates is there already."

"Wise Venus. Thank you."

You think that the Council will dare—"

"To question me. It's conceivable."

"And to *search* your rooms—"

"Also."

"Oh, Daniel—"

"Hush. Listen to me. Your race of all the earth knows the injustice and the pain of life."

She had put her hands to her face. She took them down. She said simply, "Tell me. I'm ready."

"I have many plans, and many who may assist. However, I'm vulnerable now. I have shown my hand clearly, and at the last moment, lost the valuable weapon—which obviously I considered mine by right. So the arrogant bring themselves to grief. The girl is still in her trance, this I wrote to you. I think she may wake quite soon. But—too late. In the days and nights directly after the firestorm, *then* she was needed. I've been a fool. How could such a power pass through her and not suck her dry? I only pray she'll come back of sound mind. Able to see and speak and walk."

"Pray God she will."

"Meanwhile the Brothers of the Lamb, and others discontented, are working like yeast in dough. The man Isaacus—I have learned his history. He was a felon, a thief and cut-throat, at eleven years sentenced to hanging. They duly hanged him. And he lived. Yes, after a day, when cut down, and as they carried him to the Isle of the Dead, he revived. Now we know the reason for his hoarseness. The rope impaired his voice, but could do nothing else. It seems he thought God had worked a miracle for him. He entered the priesthood. Such was his self-denial, his devotion—his fanaticism—that he rose high. To the spot where now we find him. No one is more zealous than a convert. One has only to consider San Paolo, after Damascus. This Isaacus is stronger than I thought—and still, it seems, immune to violent death. Since I've also learnt certain lords of the City recently tried to have him slain. But he survived the attack unscathed, and the assassins have disappeared."

Veronichi rose. She brought the wine and gave it to him. Danielus drank. He said, "Isaacus sees the world as the mirror of himself. It must be as corrupt and evil as he, in his beginning, and, like him, must go through the school of agony to redemption. Only through suffering can mankind be made whole. But this is the lesson our Church teaches men. The Church has made Isaacus." He sighed. "I was so careful all these years. I spoke publicly only what was permitted, merely seasoning it a little, tempering the whirlwind. And here and there, now and then, trying to let fall a little light. So the intelligent might see through the windows I tried to make. Some have. But the *slowness* of it, Veronichi—Then the girl with her fire. I thought I too had been given my miracle."

"I know, my love. You deserved a miracle."

"If she'd slept only an hour or so. A day. If I could have taken her out to them—I see it in my head a thousand times. The acclaim of her, the shouting and vivacity. They would have swarmed to her—a war won, without bloodshed, *gladly*. Yes, even the priesthood. How could they deny her gift or God's promise? It occurred before their eyes. And I could, by the light of Beatifica, have thrust the Council away, down to Hell where it belongs. Sarco would have helped me—he was primed and ready—not even for gain. From an anger like my own. That man, with his face that men see as ugly and evil—and his good, sensible heart. And Isaacus, who has no look of anything, who at ten years raped grandmothers and drowned cats for entertainment."

"Could you not—"

"No, sweet love. I have said, too late. She slept. She sleeps. The City already forgets. The old order is coming back. I saw a woman tonight who thought more of the loss of her bed than the incredible saving of her life. This is how we are. The many-colored Wonderful is no coat we can put on for everyday. And there's a new story besides. The Maiden, it seems, misled us all. She burned the ships— but failed to kill the heathen enemy, because she is the Devil's dupe. Ve Nera was spared destruction, in order to damn all the souls that are in her. As one spoils a child, giving it only sweets. We are the plaything of Satanus, now."

"I see."

"If the worst comes . . . It won't. It may. You too must deny me." Veronichi turned her head. "*Deny* me. If they examine you, speak of my harshness. That I beat you and kept you ignorant. If they examine you physically, then I forced you."

"Daniel—no—"

"Yes. I raped you, and have often raped you. You were kept in fear, and could never even confess it, for fear—of me."

"Very well."

"Deny you can read any script save Latin. They know you read Latin. I made you learn it to assist me. Of course in practices and strategies you never understood. I beat you worse if you asked."

"Very well."

"You are rejoiced that now you need no longer endanger your soul, but can speak to them freely. They are your rescuers."

"Very well."

He took her face in his own hands, now. He kissed her lips,

abstemiously. "Remember, if I die—I shan't, but I may—I have
faith in God. I believe this imbecilic world is not one half of what
exists. Once dead, I shall know. And I am free."

"I shall die too. The Romans are fine teachers of method."

"Ask to become a nun. That will save you."

She leered now like a wolf. Her face was cruel. "What? And cut
off my hair? Never. I'll die."

He nodded. "Only if it's your wish. I can wait."

Now, with no excitement, they held each other.

He said, "But this may never happen."

Outside, a hand struck on the door, and next moment tried the
latch.

Veronichi got up at once, thrusting her tresses, with a practiced
hand, inside the bald cap.

Into the room came a man from the Primo. He handed the
Magister a paper.

Danielus read. He looked unhurried, almost indifferent.

"Yes, I'll come, then." He sent the man off with the conducting
nun, for refreshment. "Veronichi, seek Domina Purita, will you, and
beg her pardon for me. Beatifica's awake. Tell Purita, too. It hardly
matters now."

"Is the girl—"

"In her right mind? They're unsure. She's weeping and won't
stop. They can make no sense of what she says."

"Send me word when you can."

As she watched him go, Veronichi knew that she might never
see him again. But she had always experienced this knowledge, every time he left her.

I was too proud. I must come down.

Cristiano contemplated the slope, a mental slope, a mortal one.
So steep it was, he could not see the bottom. He had earned that
trek by climbing up too high.

Around him, in the torch-lit dark, other men conferred, or
rested briefly like himself. A woman sat sobbing, cradling a dead
creature you took for a baby, until you saw it was a dog, its neck
broken at once, (days before) by the plummeting roof.

Despise no thing. No hurt or sorrow.

She had loved the dog. Love was love.

Through these days, lending his strength to the soldiers in their
Ducal livery, the desperate Venerans in rags, clearing the rubble of

the buildings smashed by Jurneia's bolts and stones. Carrying out men and women, some living, although given up for lost. While most of Ve Nera celebrated, still this must go on.

He had dispensed with maculum and sword, and all the emblems of his calling. Warrior-priest, he had never been tonsured. No one knew him in his dark plain clothes now thick with blood and dust, (as hers had been that night when she prayed among the dying.) They thought him, so he had gathered, some well-off merchant, magnanimous enough to come out and assist. But his strength and endurance, which the Church had made, were valuable.

When it was finished, and they no longer needed him, he would go back to the Primo, and to Danielus.

"Magister," he would say, "I'm no longer fit for the Soldiery of God. Let me go over to the fellowship of the lay priesthood. I can serve better there. Man and Christ, both."

But would Danielus argue—debate—with him? Maybe. It would be more difficult then. Perhaps that had to be, so that he must fight for this, his fall, his *penalty,* as for the other things he had wanted.

So if he must, he would say, "I love her more than God. That's the greatest sin. I love her."

But Danielus would say, he thought now, "Through such a love, God teaches us the greater Love, which is only possible in Christ. *Love* her. Cease struggling. Let her show you the way back to sanctity."

And Cristiano would say, "I don't seek to cast out my love. I'll strive for her good. In every work of mine. In every prayer. But I must never look at her again, save from a great distance."

If he had to, he would beg. "Let me go. For my soul's sake. Let me go."

And then the circle shaved from his hair, the belt empty of a sword, the dull and mundane robe. He would wait upon men. Not in pride, as he had, but in humility. Their servant.

Let me descend the hill of my pride.

Cristiano rose, and moved to lift up another huge stone.

Ermilla stood to one side. Beatifica moved constantly about the chamber. Her body and limbs, now quite unconsciously accustomed to the liberty of male clothing, strode like those of a young man.

Her crying was of another order.

It went on and on.

At first Ermilla and her sister had tried to sooth and reassure. They had brought the clean water and the dish of ripe, nicely-colored fruits set ready. Beatifica had not spared anything a glance.

"What does she say?"

It was a gabble—the girl had gone back to her former slavish accents and mumbling.

"She said at first she'd failed. That the fire had never come. I told her it had—but she never listened. Then I saw the unlit candle. I think she's lost her holy, supernatural knack—is that why she's crying so?"

Ermilla wrote swiftly to Fra Danielus, and her sister, also clad as a nun, took the letter down.

But the messenger would have to cross all those part-choked canals, to the marsh. It might take some time.

It had. The Luna Vigile had sounded, and still he was not here. And the girl went on and on crying. Poor little thing, her face was swollen, and her gray boy's tunic all stained with wet. Somehow it was worse, the garb and the striding, with this womanly weeping.

Then suddenly Danielus walked in through the door, and Ermilla felt the awful tension shift away from her, like a veering sail.

"Thank you, Milla. Yes, I see how it is."

At the sound of his voice, Beatifica did not check. Ermilla had believed she would. Then after all she made a sort of slight motion with her hands, as if trying to catch hold of something.

Fra Danielus crossed to her. He stationed himself in her path, and as she turned about blindly and came towards him, he said, "Beatifica."

And at this, the girl stopped still.

Ermilla crossed herself.

Beatifica raised her face, bloated by tears, the face of an infant that has lost its mother but perhaps found someone who may help. Ermilla knew this from her own children. Beatifica said, in a small dead little voice, "Magister."

"Thank God," Ermilla breathed, "she knows you."

But Danielus said softly, "Forgive me, Milla. But go out now."

Ermilla obeyed. She was happy to be spared the rest.

Danielus placed his hands on the shoulders of Beatifica, lightly. He had a calming touch. Somehow all the legends of him were true. A lovely woman had made herself plain in order to stay with him. And once, a mad dog, running snarling up to him, had fallen dead

coincidentally at his feet. But that had been because one of the
Bellatae had killed it to preserve him.

"Now, Beatifica. Tell me why you're crying. Have you been to a
terrible place in sleep?"

"No," she said. She hung her head. Between his hands he felt
her fragile as a husk. Something was gone from her. It did not
surprise, though it filled him with a kind of horror, when she said, in
her former slavish voice, "The fire won't come. I do as mumma said,
but it won't come. I couldn't light my candle."

"You mustn't be afraid," he said. He lied. She had reason. So
did he. "What you've done has exhausted you."

"I couldn't—so I didn't do as you asked—the ships—oh he's
dead—he's dead—"

The sword of her, worse than lust or anger, turned in him. *Mea
culpa. Oh God the fault is mine. Perhaps this is what I have always
denounced—a punishment, and well deserved. Tears—water not fire.*

"No, Beatifica. You did all I asked and all the City asked. You
saved Ve Nera, Beatifica."

"How could I? I never can do it now. He died. He died."

Danielus thought how he had stood with her before, explaining
so simply, (just as he had about the farm, and the feast) that she
must bring down fire to terrify the Jurneian fleet. He had not anticipated the magnitude of her response. He might have done. For
when he had told her everything, he also told her the peril of Ve
Nera without her intercession. He had said the Jurneians would
slaughter them all. But, he had told her, that the Bellatae Christi
would be tortured, for the Jurneians hated the knights of God. He
had known, although she did not say this, that she asked him then,
And Cristiano, too? Danielus had replied to her, "And Cristiano. He
too they will kill, slowly and most wickedly."

The Bellatae had become the source of her inspiration, her *impulse,* through which she worked her magic. He did not leave this
crucial act to that alone. No. He let her understand that Cristiano,
whom she loved, her angel—being in mortal flesh—might be sub-
jected to an agonizing death if she should not call down the fire of
Heaven.

Her answer—she had burnt seven hundred ships.

Lovers are selfish. Though she had convinced others that
Heaven lay beyond death, she could not bear to lose her love, even
to God. Who could?

And now, remembering none of it, finding she could not light this bloody candle, she broke her heart, which was that of the purest and most naive of children, thinking Cristiano had died as Danielus had forewarned.

Yes, justly punished, I.

"Beatifica, Cristiano is unharmed. I swear to you upon the Wounds of the Christ. You know, do you not, I'd never offer such an oath for a falsehood. Look about you, where is the enemy? The City stands."

Out of the web of swollen lids and laval tears, her eyes were at once returning. Like lamps through heavy mist.

"Cristiano—"

"Is alive. And whole. You brought the fire, Beatifica. That's why it fails you now. Burnt out, my dear girl, my gentle girl. But he lives, through you."

Never in his life, he thought, had he seen such eyes on him.

And this also was his punishment. To be her savior, when he himself had first thrust her down to Hell.

Sickened, he let her go.

And Beatifica said to him, in the trained silver voice she had recently come to have, "Where is he?"

There was no other recourse. The game had turned into a snare. Meshed as he was, he owed her all the time he did not have. All the risks he must not take.

"I'll send for him at once. And while you wait, you must eat and drink."

"When I see him." Obdurate. As only women ever could be in such a pass. (Veronichi: *I will die.*)

"When you see him. But sit here. And sip the water."

"Send for him."

Danielus, her slave, hastened to the door. He called out into the corridor.

For an hour then, they waited. For another hour.

The secret of her concealment was out. Servants, then Bellatae, came to the door. None had found Cristiano. Jian came, and kneeled to her, and Danielus beheld how she had learned to be truly gracious, for she touched his forehead, and thanked him, only her eyes again going far off. Danielus persuaded Jian to leave.

In the third hour, when Cristiano had not been found, her eyes went right away into the mist.

She began to weep again, in deep, convulsive, low cries.

Water, not fire.

Tears not joy.
The lesson of pain not the teaching of Heaven.
Mea culpa. Mea maxima culpa.

And in the fourth or fifth hour, when the Prima Vigile had long sounded and faded, other steps, other voices.

Danielus, going out, beheld the Eyes and Ears of the Council of the Lamb.

They had not come for him.

For her. This lost and weeping child. For her.

PART THREE

O, Burn her, burn her! Hanging is too good.

WILLIAM SHAKESPEARE
Henry VI Part One

1

One hour after the dawn Auroria, the trial began of the Maiden Beatifica.

The day was, even so early, very hot. It was the Lion month. Soon, the prisoner would be sixteen years of age. And since she had never been sure of her dates, it was conceivable she might be sentenced to die on her birthday.

God's Chamber of Justice was a room kept distinct from the secular justice of the City. The latter was conducted elsewhere by Ve Nera's magistrates, or, in infrequent higher cases, the Ducem. All trials that had to do with the Church took place, as did the priestly inquiries and torturing, in one of the several under-rooms, reached by long corridors that ran below the Primo and the square. Many who had been questioned, (by voice or instruments) had come to learn the long winding walk (or drag) to the Chamber, and back to the cells and the black boxes of pain and terror, most without one window.

By religious law, as by common law, all were supposedly tried. But the trial was often brief, and the accused sent in minutes to be investigated more thoroughly. In some instances too, an investigation was conducted somewhat prior to the trial. For more general offenses—vanity, lewdness, the failure to declare eligibility for, or render payment of the Council's taxes—only the most cursory bow was given to the ethic of a trial. The wrong-doer never saw God's Chamber, having given up the ghost.

For the Maiden, a trial was decreed essential. And, though it had been thought unwise to conduct it publicly, (the rabble would

crowd in and interrupt, mistaking it for a show) even so, representatives of the people must attend.

The Ducem himself might well have been called to do so; this
was a rare case. But he was miles away, lying sick at Forchenza. He
had sent instead two of his advisors, Prince Tizanio and Prince
Ulisse.

God's Chamber of Justice, though underground, was powerfully
lit, night or day, by flaring torches. It was a large room, and the
torches needed for it numbered over a hundred. The rising heat of
the City above would soon be nothing to the heat of this buried
space.

On a raised platform, under the theological banners of the Lion
with Child, and the winged Lion, and the white and gold banner
which proclaimed in Latin *Peace to you, Ve Nera,* sat three judges.

Each was clad, not in black, but a heartening, cloudless white.
They had been appointed by the Council of the Lamb (which sat
now, all twelve members, ranked to the right of the dais). Collec-
tively, these judges bore the name of Shepherds of God. Their duty
was to drive off menacing sin from the soul of the accused. They
would do this as sternly and brutally as any good shepherd faced by
a ravening wolf.

Before the ranked Council sat the Interlocutor, in gray. Next,
sat the Pro-Sequitor. *His* duty was to follow after any hint or scent of
wrong, driving it towards the Shepherds. This man wore red. He was
not Brother Isaacus, and yet, in the strangest way he almost seemed
to be. For Isaacus sat directly at his back, and was speaking to him
often, very low, the hoarse words indecipherable.

To the left of the dais, on a bench, sat one Magister Major of the
Primo. Normally no Magister would be summoned, but in such an
unusual case, his presence was asked. And today his purpose was
dual. He, and they, knew it. But Danielus sat composed, without any
papers or books about him, such as the Council and the Pro-Sequitor had laid out. His hands were clasped lightly. And the emerald
gleamed on his finger, steady, disturbed only by fluctuations of the
lights.

Behind Fra Danielus stood a line of the Bellatae Christi, of the
Upper Echelon. This was not, given the importance of the case,
anomalous. However, the Council had looked askance at it. The
Soldiers of God were counted. In all there were twenty-five of them.
It was known besides that almost all the lower Bellatae Militia sal-
vaged from Ciojha, were above, packed in around the square. There

were also the bemused crowds, some of whom had come to the Primo, it was understood, because they thought the Council meant to honor the Maiden there. And how would it go when they learned otherwise?

Now the Pro-Sequitor rose. He bowed to the white judges, and then to the Magister Major.

The Pro-Sequitor spoke. "I ask you, Fra Danielus, to let off some of these Bellatae. They're needed more urgently to keep order upstairs."

Danielus raised his brows. "Surely not. The Primo guard will see to that. These, remember, brother, are the Soldiers of God."

The Pro-Sequitor, schooled, replied, "Then why are so many Bellatae on the square and walks above?"

Danielus said, without rancor—or concealment, "To wait, brother, on what you will do in here."

The Pro-Sequitor turned to the Council. It was Jesolo who now rose. "Magister, *I* request you then, and the Council requests you, send out the Bellatae."

At his back, Danielus heard no movement among them. They too had been well schooled.

"Church law recommends a presence," said Danielus.

One of the Shepherds responded. "Seven only, Magister."

Danielus nodded. "Seven then. The rest may go."

As all this had been considered beforehand, eighteen of the Soldiers of God detached themselves at once, and left the Chamber, without fuss or formality.

Behind him now, as Danielus knew, waited the five he had selected with, at his right shoulder, the two he must not leave out: Jian, and Cristiano.

By the wall, the table of scribes was writing busily, with many hands, recording all this. Beyond these, down the room's length, the bank of priests and lay brothers sat agog.

The remainder of God's Justice Chamber was a wide space, which had yet to be filled.

Danielus watched, as, to the impatience of God's Court, the two princes now dawdled in, masking their unease with gestures and a great play with cushioned chairs. Once settled, their servants would go out.

The representatives of the people were let in next, men from the guilds and from positions of minor authority. Not more than ten persons.

(But how hot and stifled the vast room would shortly seem.)

Out by the wide doors, which presently would be closed, runners stood, to fetch and carry, to bring in and take away. At intervals also they must, by law, go up to instruct any crowd above how things progressed.

That would be a cause of concern to the court. Or not, if they had seen to things, as Danielus believed they had seen to rumor. Truth was adjustable.

Danielus knew, how well, their motive—also better than they did themselves. To make men carefree was not their aim. Men unafraid and charged with hope—were not governable. When once they grasped that joy was not a sin, as Christ told them, they would no longer be slaves.

And what chance then for the slave-masters?

None of this showed upon him. Nor the fact that he had ascertained by now, Sarco was not among the twelve members of the Council, had been replaced. But Danielus had warned Sarco. Had he eluded them? There was no means of knowing until Danielus might leave the court.

Behind him, the Bellatae were quiet and fixed as seven spears.

A runner now came trotting down the room, as tradition demanded, and standing before the dais, exclaimed, "Are you prepared to receive the prisoner?"

"We are prepared. Let her be brought. God watch over us all to bring this, her examination, to a perfect end."

They had not permitted the Magister Major to see her or speak with her through the days they had kept her here. Danielus had not, beyond the first, attempted it. To his avowal that the Maiden valued above all things her religion, and would need at least her confessor, they assured him they would provide one. They, the still-omnipotent Council of the Lamb. She could not read. He could not write to her. Besides, any letter would be scanned.

Cristiano had entered the primo on the morning after the Eyes and Ears, ministers of that supreme Council, had taken her. Cristiano knew nothing of it, as, then, the City did not.

Light was still gray. Cristiano was like a white flame burning through it. He had all the coolth and self assemblage of the very mad.

"Magister—I must leave off my pride—descend from it—"

"*Where have you been?*"

Never had Cristiano heard this voice from Danielus' lips.

"Helping them," he said. "The buildings that came down."

"More has come down than buildings, knight. Much more."

Danielus told him first how the girl had woken from her trance, and thought Cristiano to be dead.

"Why?—She brought the fire—"

"Now she can't. She believed therefore she failed, the enemy triumphed, and killed you." Danielus did not say that he was to blame for her belief. This was not subterfuge. He knew there was no time for the indulgence of his confession, now. He must shoulder it, if anything was to be done.

And Cristiano's face was like a boy's, all doubts, having missed the absolute way he meant to take—(*downwards* had it been? To Hell or to what? Oh, he had learned nothing. Or everything. Perhaps that was it.)

Cristiano said, "But—I'm alive. And the City—the proof's everywhere."

"She trusted nothing. None of us would do. It's you, Cristiano, who are her angel."

Exasperated at last, as Danielus had hoped himself never to be again—naturally, such a fallacy must fail him, as connivance had—Danielus sampled a moment's acute delight in Cristiano, confused, undone and falling from the sky. But it was not a cruel delight. A loving one. A thankful one. And he became, Danielus, instantly Magister of himself enough to say, not: *She loves you,* but, "She has seen the good in you. Your example shines. It gives her comfort, after the human swine she has had to encounter."

Then he gave Cristiano a glass of wine. Cristiano did not quibble that the glass was ill-made, knowing nothing better. Danielus described for him how the girl had wept like a child, and saw Cristiano go whiter still and then, very red. Red to the ears like a boy, indeed. And next master himself, as Danielus had mastered *himself.* And get out, "Before Christ—why didn't I know—why wasn't I here—"

"Never mind it. Now you are."

Then he told Cristiano, carefully, a little of the poison crumbs at a time, how the Council had sent for her, and he had had to let her go.

Danielus expected anything, despite his care. Cristiano might go raving mad, against the cool madness he had come in with. Faint even. One saw men who were capable of battling bare-handed with a lion, told that their mother was dead, or their son, and dropping headlong.

But Cristiano only stared.

And he whispered, "Is this my fault?"

"No. Dispense with that. How can it be."

"I love her."

"I know it. And she you."

"No, no—"

"And she you. No other must know but you and I and her. And we three *must*."

"Oh God. Oh God forgive me."

"Silence." Cristiano was silent. "Why do you think, Cristiano, God brought love into this world? For us to shut it up in a lead coffin and drop it in the sea?"

"It's sin—"

"Yes. To insult God, the worst sin. Accept His gift. Thank Him."

Cristiano said, after a moment, "The Council—what filth have they invented?"

Danielus informed him:

"She let Ve Nera off her necessary penance of rapine and slow death. She failed to kill all the men of Jurneia, who are infidel fiends. She be-glamored and damned us and is in league with Hell."

"*They* are in league with it."

"Bravo. Now listen. They must have a trial. She's famous here. And they will let me in to the trial, because one at least would like to catch me, too—"

"Isaacus."

"He. And I may summon to the court seven Soldiers of God. Or more, if they're lax, though this I doubt. One should be you."

Cristiano had sworn to himself to end his knighthood. He said so.

"Not yet," Danielus said. "Think of her. She needs to see you as she knows you. Besides, only as a Bellatae can you be present. I wish I could prepare her, I have no means. Whatever else, when she stands before them in that Underworld of theirs, she'll behold you, living and whole. It's all that I can be sure of for her now."

Cristiano looked at him. "The Bellatae would rally to you, Magister. And to her."

"Again, bravo. You reassure me of your humanness at last, speaking as you do. But the Bellatae are no longer enough. Ciojha saw to that."

"The Council's hated."

"And dreaded. Don't forget the power the Church has given them, direct from the highest, in Rome. Others remember."

"What will it come to?"

"At the worst, her death."

It had not been reasonable to prevaricate in this, as it had in the matters of love, and arrest.

And Cristiano said, making the heart of Danielus turn suddenly inside him, "If she dies—have I damned her?"

Danielus thought, *Your cold and frigid sense of only God. Ah, Cristiano. If God had wanted us tied by a rope to Him, would He have cast us from the Garden? The only means He could find to enlighten us was by infantile rebellion, by a forbidden fruit, and an angel with a flaming sword.*

Forget God, Cristiano. He made us in His image. Live in life for one small moment. Or you will never know His Face.

But aloud the Magister said, "If she dies she will go up to Paradise. But there's also the world."

2

"Beatifica, called the Maiden. This is your name?"

As custom ordained, the Interlocutor had risen, and addressed her as she entered. He had ringing tones, big even for the Chamber.

The girl looked at him. She shook her head.

There was some disarray.

Jesolo spoke for the Council. "She must not pretend to idiocy. We shall decide if she is sane or not. This, now, won't save her."

It was the Pro-Sequitor who got up, almost placatory. He said, "A misunderstanding, I think. Woman, what is your name?"

Beatifica said, in her Primo-minted voice, "I forget my given name. Here I have another I'm known by."

"And that is Beatifica."

"Yes."

Jesolo said bluntly, "Were you never asperged for Christ?" Nothing. He said, "Sprinkled with holy water in his name?"

Beatifica said, "My mother told me I was."

"But in another name."

"I forget the other name."

"You were a slave," said Jesolo, "so we hear. How did your master call you?"

"Volpa," she said.

There was quiet then. She had been titled for the familiar animal of the devil. She could have said nothing worse. But she did not lie. Until now, her truthful answers had always been fortuitous.

Jian moved a little. Danielus did not check him, but Jian had quickly restrained himself.

Cristiano stood motionless.

As she came forward now, up the torchlit hall, he waited for her eyes to find him out. If she screamed then, aloud, he must not go to her. He knew this.

She seemed small and far away, as if behind a magus's distorting lens. They had not let her wear her white and gold, but allowed her male clothing, probably to better demonstrate her fault. She wore a padded black tunic, stitched breeches and leather shoes, and seemed inappropriately dapper, a young gentleman.

The princes Tizanio and Ulisse gawped at her. Cristiano thought they had not been at the Ducal feast when she brought the fire, had never clapped eyes on her before.

Behind her walked two of the Primo guards, and two of the Eyes and Ears, who had questioned her, although without instruments.

Her hair was beautiful, shining. It looked too strong for her, there was too much of it, as if it had leached away her vitality. Until she was nothing but the hair, and the gentlemanly clothes.

Now she reached the area where they wanted her to be, in front of the Shepherds on their dais. A stool was put for her and she was shown she might sit down. She sat down.

Cristiano, rigid, saw her head turn now, for the first. She looked at them, one by one, the judges, the Pro-Sequitor, the Interlocutor, the Council. Then, to the left, Danielus, and the seven Soldiers of God. Though no longer only a slave of lowered eyes, there was no curiosity and no interest in her face, and no alarm. There was hardly any face to display a mood. Yet, one by one, looking. And now

And now

And now at him. At him.

His heart twisted. Dropped down.

Her eyes were only a pale hazel.

He might run forward and take her up, and cut a way through several men with the sword. But they would not get more than a hundred steps, if so much. And if still she lived, then they might do anything to her. He must stay, as Danielus had told him, stationary.

Besides, he meant nothing to her. She had looked at him fully, and not seen. She had turned away.

Suddenly her whole body slipped bonelessly forward.

Despite himself, he moved. Wrenched himself back, rigid.

One of the Eyes and Ears had bent over her. Her sliding downward toward the floor was only like the action of someone exhausted, and for a second falling asleep. Was it only that? She had been lifted on to the stool again, seated.

One of the Shepherds said, "Does she swoon?" To Cristiano, the voice was juicy with enjoyment. Perhaps Cristiano mistook.

And she was sitting upright now, she looked straight before her. She looked up at her three judges.

She was changed.

Oh God, how changed. She was ablaze within. Her eyes like two bright flames. She looked at them, these men who might—who must—condemn her to death. She looked at them with radiant happiness and love.

She saw me. What now she is has come from me.

Better than any warrior, she did not say one word, but she was filled by light. The clothes, even her hair, returned to the place of mere apparel. She was alive.

And—she had disconcerted them.

"What is it?" one demanded. "Why do you laugh at us?"

"I don't laugh, signore."

"Call me Shepherd of God. I see you laughing."

"I'm glad," she said. "But I don't laugh."

"Why? You are here to answer dreadful charges."

Beatifica did not reply.

The Pro-Sequitor spoke to her, roughly at last.

"Don't add to your crimes by insolent sullenness. Whatever is asked of you, in this sanctified Chamber, you must give reply."

She glanced at him.

She said, "Then, I will tell you. I glimpsed my good angel."

A commotion. And under it, Cristiano heard Danielus take one abrupt involuntary breath, not exactly a gasp.

"An angel? In your inner eye do you say?"

"No, Shepherd of God. He is here."

"*Where* then?"

Beatifica considered a moment. Then she did smile at the Shepherd, individually for him. She had been warned, and also she had learned a little here and there. She said, without cunning, but only in order to obey them all—these men who demanded, Danielus who had said she must show herself to have no favorites, "He is at my right shoulder. Where I have heard the nuns say, one's own good angel always stands."

The Interlocutor exclaimed, "Take care. You blaspheme."

It was one of the Shepherds of God who rapped out, "She does not. It's some childish thing. She may be addled, or simple, we know that. The nuns do tell the children so. It's harmless. She isn't here to stand on trial for such a toy."

The Pro-Sequitor: "She says she sees him."

"Do you then, girl, see him?"

Looking directly at her judges, Beatifica, burning with her joy, (*Love casts out fear*) softly answered, "Not now."

"We must come back to this. She has always claimed to have seen messengers in Heaven, in childhood. Like her madness, it is a questionable assertion. But for this while, let's get on."

Turning, the Pro-Sequitor and the Interlocutor opened up their books on the bench; were brought, by lower priests, a sheet or two.

Cristiano, shaking and shaken, stood immaculate. And the girl sat facing away from him, like a young bride on her wedding day. She needed only a crown of roses.

The Valley of the Shadow is entered by a million different gates. It has ten million million different names.

For Beatifica it had been this, the world, without Cristiano.

She had so little in her of autonomy. Though she had promised the glorious afterlife to so many, she did not wish to be alone and left behind. Yet, no concept of suicide even, could relieve her. She was, still, the fox. Animal, complex mostly in non-complexity.

To her also, that world of Heaven and this world of earth, were now so little divided that, ironically, she knew of no way to align them or get through. They were like a scene through a window—the angels, the serpent, the scarlet mountain, Paradise—but a window glazed by unbreakable glass. Immediate. Unreachable.

And also, in the midst of love, she did not know what love was. It had never been hers, or if it had, only for a moment. Unnamed, unrecognized, this stranger, powerful or more powerful than death.

What could he be, but her angel? And if through her he perished, what was left?

She had believed the Magister's reassurance instantly. But then, seen him to be wrong. If the lie were some game he played, or unkindness or punishment of her, it did not matter. All that she cared for was Cristiano and his life.

In this state, when the black-robed priests took her, she did not care. She barely noticed.

The Styx boat smelled of recent blood. That meant nothing.

They did not hurt her, physically. (Even the exploration of her virginity, carried out by holy sisters, was not ungentle. She had experienced such things—or her mother had, in early life.)

In every other way, her hurt was all-present. The walls of her cell groaned, the air writhed, the dull light ached.

She ceased to cry. She had gone beyond (lower) than tears. Despair was darkness. In darkness she moved absently about, and answered what was asked. They gave her crusts to eat, which would not have dismayed or offended her, but with which she did not bother. She drank the water, which was sometimes unpalatable. Her constitution was strong, and she survived those days.

Taken to God's Chamber of Justice, she felt no apprehension. Everything—meaningless.

Until, sitting on the stool, she felt somewhere in the walls or the air, or in the light—the groaning, writhing, aching—*end*.

Then, she looked, hesitant, not really knowing what she did—as perhaps she might have done in the cell, if a beautiful odor or color had begun inexplicably to drift about there.

When she saw him, she felt this: an absence of all things. There was no shock—or none apparent to her mind. It was, rather, as if all her horror and despair had been her *silliness*. Of course Cristiano lived. And here, of course, he was. Who has never lost that which is loved, and not felt this—the *certainty* that death is a mistake, a falsehood. Only turn the corner, fling wide the curtain and there the beloved will be. And for Beatifica, he was.

So, she looked away. And then the true shock met her, like a tidal wave. She plunged into a golden void, which swallowed her and then replaced her on the shore. Aspergation? Yes. Rebirth.

Had she ever been happy? Did she know the name of love? Now.

The Interlocutor had finished with most of his interrogation. The Maiden, (and so she was, examiners had made sure of it) had answered without delay, modestly and usually promptly.

The basis of *his* task was to elicit from her the story of her life. He did so.

She had been a slave from the foothills. Then she had served a wood-seller. Then she had been taken from his house—either by another owner, or a guiding, supernatural agency. The house had burned and so had her master, but she had slight memory of it. Presently she was at an inn, then removed to the Primo, and thereafter taught prayer and worship, which obviously she took to. After which she put on male attire, not by her own choice, but because it was given her. She could bring fire from air, having been shown how by her dead mother, in visions. She had prayed with the dying and wounded troops, who escaped the sea-fight at Ciojha. At last she had burnt the ships of Jurneia, although this too she did not exactly recall. She agreed she must have done it. When asked why, if she did not recall the event, she thought so, she said that the evidence was about her, here. With this none could argue. Jurneia victorious would not have left one stone on another.

Asked to say why she thought she had been brought to this Chamber to be judged, she said she did not know. But she seemed indifferent, casual. And, consistently, fearless and elated.

This had made her judges and many of the priesthood present, nervous. Not because it might denote innocence. But since it might mean she could summon up worse defensive powers.

The Interlocutor asked her to say if she understood the nature of the Devil.

She said she did not.

Did she serve him?

Beatifica stared, and answered no.

Who then, would she say, that she did serve?

"My new masters," she said.

"Name them."

She said, without pause, "Those in the Church."

"Who, for example?" relentlessly the Interlocutor insisted.

He had all the booming hectoring tone of any master.

Beatifica said, "Yourself."

"*How* do you serve me?" He was affronted (despite the atmosphere, some of the younger clerks had laughed).

"I am here before you, and obey you as best I can."

"*How*? In *what*?"

"In answering you."

The Shepherds frowned. One, the one who spoke the most, said, "If her wit is natural I doubt."

When the Interlocutor went back, Danielus rose for the first time. He seemed calm as deep water.

"We know, holy brothers, I think, that she has no terror of the name and words of God."

"Do we know this?"

Danielus said to Beatifica, "Speak for us, Beatifica, Christ's Prayer, and then the Psalm of God as the world's light."

And she, knowing them, uttered them. The beauty of the phrases, spoken by her clear as diamonds, stilled the court.

God covered with a robe of light,
Stretching the heavens like a curtain,
Whose beams are laid in the home of the waters,
Whose chariot is the clouds,
Who treads, winged by the winds,
Who for His ministers takes such spirits,
And chooses for his servants flames of fire.

(Let them dwell on those words, these resolute priests. They would have cried out sacrilege, too, if Danielus had told them this very Psalm began in Egypt, the hymn of a Pharaoh to the sun. God, by all his multitudinous names.)

When the girl had finished, Danielus said, "For now, I say no more."

Then the Pro-Sequitor stepped forward, in his fermented red. And an aid of the court, who had just brought it, set up a stand for his books and papers.

"Those that carefully questioned you, and without recourse to persuasion," (he meant torture), "say that, asked if your mother had taught you anything else, you revealed that your mother, while living, made you dance about trees. Is this so?"

"Yes."

"Is this Christian? *How* is it?"

"I don't know."

"Of course not. It's a pagan rite, which treats the tree as a divinity. Yes?"

"She never told me that."

"But she said to dance?"

"No."

"Then who did?"

"No one."

The Pro-Sequitor scowled. He said, "You saw her do it, and followed by example?"

"Yes."

"And this pagan woman then taught you, after death, you say, to make fire."

"My mother taught me."

"How?"

"She rubbed her hand along a piece of stick."

"And fire came?"

"Yes."

"You thought this divinely inspired?"

Silence.

A Shepherd said, "Speak, girl. You have always to reply."

"I thought," said Beatifica, "many people did it. It would be useful."

"But you," said the Pro-Sequitor, "bring the fire from your hair."

"It seems so."

"What are you saying—*seems* so?"

"So it seems."

"Explain how it is done."

"I can't explain."

"Why not?"

"I only do it."

"What makes you do it?"

"Others ask me. And their need for it."

The Pro-Sequitor opened his arms to the court. "She has decided our wants. She rules us."

There was a rumble.

Fra Danielus, the Magister Major, rose.

"Holy brothers, that is like accusing the baker of ruling the man he sells a loaf."

The clerks laughing, and hushed.

From the Council benches, Isaacus spoke like scraping pots.

"Who bids the baker bake?"

The Pro-Sequitor turned and bowed to the Council, to Isaacus.

"Human need bids it," Danielus said. "Even Jesus fed a crowd with bread when they were hungry." He sat down. The clerks were almost applauding him. They were mostly young. The young tended to favor him. And the older ones, not.

The Pro-Sequitor—turned a page.

He said, "There are the burnings we must come to. Do you say you brought fire and burnt the Jurneian ships?"

Danielus rose. "Holy brothers. Many of us saw this very thing. It was a miracle, but it was well witnessed."

"I myself," said the Pro-Sequitor, "saw something of it. I saw the rigging and masts in flames, and the fleet sunk. But thousands of the Jurneian heathen escaped and are now in our prisons. How can this be? Meanwhile we have the tale she burned at least two Christian men in the City. To ashes."

Danielus said, "Her fire seems to find out those who will burn."

"What does this mean?"

"Some men are set for burning. They carry it in them like a spark."

"For their punishment?"

"It may be so."

"Then—why not these infidel? They were *spared*."

Danielus said, "In that instance, I think it may be called mercy."

"We can have no mercy on enemies—the enemies of this City—and of the Church." This, Jesolo.

The Pro-Sequitor raised his voice, unvibrant and thin but carrying. "Beatifica, why did you burn *Christian* men?"

She shook her head slowly.

"You must speak an answer."

"I don't remember it."

"Beatifica, if now an assassin, an infidel, ran into this room, raising his knife against the revered Shepherds, there, and we called on you to slay this man by your fire—*would you do it*?"

"No."

A great muddle of noise.

Again Danielus rose, but it was Jian, standing at his back, who cried, "Her fire's left her. She means only she *can't*."

Danielus turned. He put his hand on Jian's shoulder. Then turned back. Danielus said, across the racket, stilling it, "Answer, Beatifica. Does the knight tell us truly?"

"I can't bring the fire. Not since the night of the ships."

"In the service of this City," said Danielus, "she used up her gift, perhaps. Can it be God gave it to her only for that hour?"

"*Chastisement was the portion of Ve Nera! God willed it*. The City must be cut, and bled to heal. And we—the healers—are bereft."

Isaacus, standing now.

Danielus glanced at him, and looked towards the judges.

"Brothers, God is not put off, if He wishes to chastise us, by a single battle won. Even assuming a battle might be won, against His wish."

"*She is the devil.*"

"Brother Isaacus forgets. Women are the weaker vessels. Why choose a woman above a man, for such weighty work?"

"The easier corrupted."

"The easier found out."

"*So she is.*"

"No, brother. Nothing has been found. Nor is this court to be influenced—resist that error."

The Pro-Sequitor began, "I seek to find if any of these guides she vaunts so, these angels and so on, are demons, who have misled the wench. If that's so, and she will admit it, we may at least save her soul."

This was offered to them all, including Isaacus. But Isaacus gave an appalling crunching roar. He did not sound human, more like masonry knocked down in the aftermath of the cannon-stones.

"She—she—this *wench*—this *woman*—Satanus may take any shape. Who says she's innocent? What has she said of her visions— she rants of snakes and flying things. The Serpent *is* the Devil. Her angels may be *of* the Devil—did some not fall in the Pit with him? And her mountain is red, the very color of Hell fire."

"So," said Danielus sharply, "is the robe of the Pro-Sequitor." A true gasp went up like steam. He added, delicately, "But who among us would think to associate him with the Fiend?"

Isaacus moved about the bench. He came out into the open space. Like some incomprehensible beast from the shadow.

The foaming rabid lethal dog had died at Danielus' feet, killed by Cristiano, long ago.

Isaacus would not crumple. He had survived a day of rope. God was his. He *knew* God. The world must suffer as he had. All pleasure, since foul pleasures had nourished *him,* was foul.

"She speaks," said Isaacus, "of all her sights sent to her by God. But the Church is God's. His beloved and chaste wife. Where does she see the Church in this? Has she never been shown the Church in her visions, and told to heed us?"

"Perhaps," said Danielus.

But the Interlocutor had sprung up. He boomed out, like a bell, "Maiden, tell us then, has God never shown you, in your visions, his holy priesthood?"

She, a bride. Upon her wedding day. Her love. Her happiness. Aspergation in the golden void.

If she had had the sophistry to evade, even if she had, could she have side stepped at this instant? And they had insisted, she must always answer.

"Yes," said Beatifica.

More than silence, a sort of *deafness* which *heard*, this spread from her like ripples in the air.

The Shepherds leant forward. Eager or unnerved?

(Forgotten on their chairs, the sparkling princes goggled like sad fish.)

Danielus stayed on his feet.

She had not told him anything of this. What had she seen or dreamed? And yet, taken aback and unprepared, somehow it was quite expected to him. He knew it, as the spot of blood may be known. It foretold death.

But to gag her would damn her. The same, to let her have her say? She was naive. She spoke her mind. But might this not be only one more charming, spiritually disarming thing . . . Why did he *know* that it was not?

The Interlocutor again opened his mouth. Danielus interposed very quietly.

"One moment, holy brothers."

"What? What is it?" The Interlocutor, scoring on his target better than the Pro-Sequitor was loath to give over. "She must answer."

"That I understand. First, let me ascertain only this. If she has had a vision of the priesthood, when was it?" They waited ominously. He turned to the girl. "When, Beatifica?"

"When I slept, after the night of the ships."

Danielus said, generally, "Her visions have been various. This may have come, waking or sleeping. But be aware of this, she lay unconscious five days and the nights between, after she burnt the ships. We thought her dead. You will be familiar, I think, with the notions of delirium, of a fever dream, and a nightmare. Her vision may not be of that order. Can we be sure? Or she?"

Isaacus let out another awful vocal noise. He was shouting, and none of them made sense of it. Jesolo and another of the Council rose and went to him, and Isaacus thrust them off. They allowed it. He had become, incomprehensibly, disgustingly, a power. Isaacus breathed, then spoke. "Look at him there, this Magister, with his army at his back. His *Soldiers of God—are* they God's? Or do they serve Danielus? His *mercenaries—*"

Danielus heard the shift and rustle of mail behind him, as the Bellatae, despite their discipline, moved. He raised his hand, and they were granite.

But Isaacus said, in his voice of broken bricks, "*See* it there. They hear no man but one. Send them out. Send them out, I say."

Danielus said, "Brothers, the law itself, quoted by you, allows for seven Bellatae in such a court. In fact recommends it."

The Shepherd who spoke the most, answered, stern and cold, "In such a court indeed. But who judges here? Who presides? Sit down, Magister. You're not here to debate. Sit down." Without protest, seeming unruffled and amenable, Danielus sat. "The accused here, before *such a court,* needs her chance to utter, without your interruptions. *In such a court,* she has God Himself to defend her, if she deserves it. You're redundant. Now, be still."

The Shepherd beside him added, "Nevertheless, the words of Brother Isaacus are very grave."

"So they are," said Isaacus.

The third of the Shepherds said, "Let us come back to this. Let us get on. Maiden, if God has shown you his priesthood, tell us now what he revealed."

Beatifica told them her last remembered dream.

They listened.

Of course, she had never considered tact. Others were almighty, impervious. That which is impervious to everything will be impervious to ridicule. Only when Prince Ulisse let out a snort of laughter, then turned his head, (yellow with fear at his lapse) did she half falter.

She spoke of the crocodilius in purple, wallowing up from the lagoon. the priests who changed to beasts. Their noises. How they fought and floundered. Toppled each other down.

Cristiano, hearing her, his heart changing to a piece of ice, thought, *If ever God gave her a true vision, here it is. Just so they are. The Church herself made into a monster, and toppled by their antics.*

She looked about. The lower priests were stunned by horror.

The representatives of the people—picked carefully for their loyalty, their self-serving which the Council aided—were outraged. The judges had faces of white murder. The Pro-Sequitor—a grimace on him almost like terror—The Council blank as stone tablets unwritten on. Even Isaacus.

Beatifica did not speak for very long. The dream had made her, while dreaming, laugh, but now seemed nothing to her. She had been careless with misery. She was only careless, now.

She was not a fool. Nor mad. But what had she ever met or learned to teach her another course? At first beaten almost for breathing, then protected in a shell of glass, and encouraged always to speak.

If Danielus had known, he would have curbed her, and obedient, she would have kept this hidden.

In her despair—she had not thought to tell him. Caught too in her despair, he had not thought to ask.

After her voice, hubbub.

The judges, the Council, waited it out, until it ended in a bloated, rocking nothingness.

Then, the speaking Shepherd rotated himself in his chair. He fixed his eyes on Danielus.

Danielus spoke, not getting up. "Will you give me leave to tender some explanation?"

"No. *No,* Magister. What can you say?"

"She is unlessoned. To her—"

Jesolo said loudly, "Be quiet, as you were warned. The Devil pulls her under. Do you want to *go* with her?"

"The Fra is her patron," said Isaacus. "He is with her, never doubt."

Beatifica's light was gently dying in her face. She had been lost. Did she know?

All the Council of the Lamb was on its feet.

Jesolo spoke to them, and then one or two others spoke. A medley of low mutterings.

"End this session of the court, revered Shepherds," Jesolo said then. "Our scribes need time to put down all these terrible words. And you, Magister, take your Bellatae and go up."

"Yes," said the speaking Shepherd. "Leave this court, Magister. Fra Matteo shall come in, instead. We have no need of you."

Danielus rose. "There are things I should say to you."

"Not yet," said the Shepherd. He said, almost bitterly, "But your hour will come. Be ready, Magister, for that hour."

3

Everywhere, as far as the eye could see, the crowds were roiling, moving together and apart and together, like waves. From the upper windows, they did not seem to matter so much, despite their spasmodic motions, and the whirring, rolling noise they made, now and then split by some higher, vaster cry. And they did not, in a way, matter much, truly. Just as they seemed to be, they had been swayed, and were altering. It was facile, to move them. Avowals and gossip, drinks bought or angers kindled. Not one single man at its back, this campaign, no not even Isaacus. Some almost unhuman force, streaming from the entity of the Church itself, driving the chariot. Powers behind powers behind powers. None quite aware, perhaps, what in turn moved *them*. Sensing only familiar mortal things, a wise rage, an essential piety, the need to survive, the wish not to crack the surface of a colossal code.

It would have been like this, Cristiano thought, in Gerusalemme, when the crosses jutted on the hill. In Rome, when San Pietro had been nailed up like a dead crow. And when a hundred saints were disposed of. Trouble comes in the guise of goodness—or great and perfect good in the guise of an enemy. Kill it then. Be rid of it.

No one had told Ve Nera that the City would have done better to suffer and bleed in order to be healed. Only that it had been spelled and misled by a witch, who performed one rescuing deed, in order to beguile and thrust Ve Nera down to Hell—

Legends surfaced like sea serpents from the ocean of the crowd. Had the woman not burned more than twenty fine Christian men? If they let her go on, what might she not do, with that talent of hers for burning things?

Yet, if she were possessed of fire—how could she be stayed?

There was now no need to fear her. The Church, alerted, had hold of her at last. It was possible to damage her, it had been done, it seemed. Before the Name of the Most High, she was brittle as a straw. God would drive the evil from her. God might, through his priests, do anything; all would be well.

"No, Jian," Danielus said.

"Magister—three hundred men, and more, will rush—"

"*No.* The Bellatae Militia won't turn their swords against their own City. No, not even against the Council. I have never taken a life, and will never do so, even to keep my own. Nor shall you, by my consent, do anything so injurious to yourselves."

"*Magister—*"

"Jian. I've things to do and little time."

"We must get you away. It can be done."

"There are other things to do. I've said."

"How can the Council bring you down?" Jian stammered. He was hushed with fury and disbelief.

"Simply, now."

"God's will?"

"Did I say that? No. The will of men."

Cristiano stayed silent. Danielus offered him nothing, let alone anything for the girl. They had already spoken, before the trial began. What need for more?

When the two Bellatae were out, Danielus went by another way across the Golden Rooms. He noticed, as he passed, their man-made beauty—frescoes, draperies, metal-work and jewels. Beatifica had been indifferent to these things. In a manner unlike her own, so was Danielus, now.

They had passed their days in the small rooms about the little court-yard. Sun came into the court, and by the sun they were able to judge the times of prayer. No one hindered them in this. Nor were they offered any forbidden or obnoxious foods.

Aside from the young male servants, Suley-Masroor and his twenty companions saw no one. But the high priest Daniel had pre-viously described this solitude, assuring Suley he would not leave them to it for longer than he must.

Among Suley's twenty chosen men, were his three cousins, and the three brothers of his wife, four of his crew that Daniel's spies had been able to locate in the prisons of Venarh, and others Suley had named, knowing them to be virtuous and courageous.

These things too, perhaps, Daniel—though an infidel—might be. To Suley he was an enigma.

"Trust none of those benighted dogs," insisted the eldest brother of Suley's wife. And one of the oldest men from the wrecked ship *Quarter-Moon,* announced, "They are not even properly human."

"God has never told us that," Suley had answered. "This man took us from captivity. And their flies of conversion haven't bothered us since."

"Magicians, then. We saw it. They're in league with the Evil One."

Now, sitting under the shade tree in the sunny court, Suley looked up and saw the high priest coming in through the gate in the wall.

All about him, Suley's men muttered. Only the three brothers and cousins, and Reem from the ship, came up and stood with Suley, to receive the priest who had been their saviour.

Daniel seemed older. The skin of his face, untouched by sun, looked thin. But the eyes were as Suley recalled. And he had told all these men to look at the eyes of Daniel, and then say again he was a dog, or a sorcerer.

Danielus greeted them all by name, politely, and with sound pronunciation, as if welcoming guests. Then begging their pardon, in the Jurneian tongue, he took Suley-Masroor to one side, and the men also moved off, glancing at them.

"We have been treated well, lord priest. You have kept all your promises. But one."

"To send you to your home? I will keep it, if I can. But for now you must go elsewhere."

Suley frowned. "Where?"

"To a farm I have, on the plain."

"That's some way to journey."

"You will be given permits, which I regret, as foreigners to Ve Nera, is necessary. My servants will then guide you. I request that you treat them well. From the farm, a method can be found to take you on, by some roundabout means. Others will assist you to the coast, or overland otherwise. As you say, a long journey. But it will eventually bring you where you wish to be. My plans, you see, weren't complete. Hence this unfortunate randomness."

"Then we will wait on you."

"I regret not. I think you must be gone."

Suley said, "There is some dissent over us, and what you've done."

"Not yet. Very few know. Those that do, agree with it, or else have been paid to find it very appealing."

"Then the bowman aims only at you."

"A nice expression. Yes, Suley-Masroor. You are acute."

Suley leaned back on the air, folding his arms.

"You should have left us to be fettered and scourged and made converts to your blasphemous religion, and so destroyed."

"Would you have converted?"

"To a strong cord, or a knife's edge. Am I to lose Paradise to make such dirty priestlings glad?"

"Suley, God is great. This you know. He gave you life to live. Did He ever say to you that to lie is worse than to deny?"

"A riddle."

"No. But there's no time for us to talk. Wait for my servant, and be ready, all of you. If any accost you, I fear you must after all pretend to our blasphemous religion."

"Some won't, lord priest."

"Then let them pretend to having been struck dumb." Over the face of Danielus there passed a swift dark cloud. Suley saw, oddly, how he had been when very young, hotter and more rash than now. But Danielus only said, "Arrogance is a sin, Suley. God knows everything. He knows a man's heart."

"So He does."

"How He must suffer then, Suley, at our idiocy and stubbornness. You will be given an unguent to lighten your skins and so perhaps save you from notice in the City. Think of your lies about conversion in the same vein. Both may be washed off."

"I will tell any who ask I worship your prophet, Yesu. And the others must keep quiet."

"Think of God, made happy by your freedom."

"He will also know to thank you, Daniel. And yes, my God too is capable of graciousness."

The priest smiled, solely with his eyebrows, but the Jurneian noted it. Danielus only said, "There'll also be money, and City clothing. I know you must cover your heads, but use the hoods to cover that covering. Your guide will be an educated man, who also speaks your tongue. He will appear to be nothing of the kind. His name is Sarco."

"Yes. Will we meet again?"

"I think—" Danielus halted. "No, Suley."

"What is this arrow that points at you?"

Danielus said, "That arrow which points at all men."

"Death."

"Death, Suley."

"From your priesthood here?"

"Enough now, Suley. Forgive me, but I have so much to do."

"Before the arrow strikes."

Danielus clasped Suley's hand, and the other men looked on. "Farewell. Go with God, Suley-Masroor."

"Can nothing save you?"

"A miracle."

Suley stood watching as the priest walked from the courtyard. Then, turning about, Suley crossed to these men that, in war, he had given orders. And his face too was the face he had for war, just the same.

The husband of Ermilla, the stone-mason, came from the Magister's book-chamber. Well and plainly dressed, head bowed respectfully, he received no challenge. He had been this way besides, often before. There were, now and then, things to do for the Magister.

But this would be fast work, even with the foundations laid.

How many men would he need for it?

A score, to be certain.

The stone-mason crossed the great courtyard with the lion fountain. From here, the noise of the crowds outside was hideously loud, though it would be worse on the Primo's other side, where the square stood over the Chamber of God's Justice.

A house the mason had built had fallen to Jurneian shot just beyond. He had obtained a right to take back some of the blocks. They might be useful as counter-weights.

Of course, it was chancy, all this. But all life was chancy. And long ago, Fra Danielus had saved this man from penury. From near death. As he had also saved Ermilla.

The crowd boiled under the Angel Tower, from which one last dead rotting thing—that was once a woman—hung in its cage. Ignored.

They were howling now, a gust of howling under the cage and its unspeakable stink of decay. Demanding, jolly with viciousness, to burn a witch.

Changeable as the sea, and not as constant as the sea. She had been a saint not long ago. Though all kinds of provocation, untruth, slander and inducement had been used, to swing Ve Nera about, what scum they were, the race of Man.

Would I have shouted too? Saying that girl loved Lucefero, mocked God and lured us to the brink? Am I such a fool?

But the stone-mason recalled how he had been in youth, acts he had committed, thoughts he still had.

If you never see the light of day, how can you know there is a sun? And some were born blind.

4

She had liked to talk, and to answer questions. The sudden interest of others in herself, enjoyed. But now, so many questions. So much talk—hers, and theirs. And this fume of their emotion, like the slightly unwashed smell of scorching.

Additionally, many questions were repeated.

Sometimes prefaced by, Now can this be a fact? Or, Will you assure us that your meaning is such and such?

They had taken her out. She had been allowed water to drink, and was glad of it for the dark torchlit room was very hot.

When she was taken back, the room was hotter, or seemed so. The priests, even the Shepherds and Council, and the princes in their silks, were sweating. At last, one of the princes, Ulisse, begged the leniency—groveling—of the Council, and went staggering out on the arms of two servants of the court. He did not return.

Nor did the Magister return. Another man sat now where Danielus had. He was old and dry, with sad, accommodating eyes. Behind him, seven Primo guard. Not the Bellatae. Not Cristiano.

Her angel was alive. She knew this. But—where had he gone?

The powers of the court, though overtly threatening to Beatifica, were not fully understood by her. And she had missed many parts of her own trial. Waking dreams had obscured it. The image of Cristiano, thoughts of a cool place, of her accustomed habitual prayers which, now and then even here, she murmured.

(To this, once, the man with the loud crushed voice, had taken exception. He cried out that she recited a spell. But when the judges asked her what she had been saying, Beatifica repeated it at once. Her flawless Latin was received unfavorably. One of them said she masked her actual words. Or, she thought to impress them with her piety. *Deo volente*—God's will be done.)

She was exhausted, took no notice of that—for a slave, it could mean nothing.

But having been brought back to life, she was by now afraid.

She knew herself among extremely harsh masters, and no one to stand between herself and them. As in the beginning.

Beatifica was afraid. And yet, she had learned, inadvertently, to sit there as if collected and proud, to speak clearly when her own heart and breath choked her. But, if ever she had begun to *cease* to be a slave, that was gone. She *was* a slave. Without rights, without redress. No one to help her. But for God, perhaps, for whom she had no real name or true realization. (God, Invisible. Why else send down His heralds, saints and angels.)

"Why then did you dress as a man?"

"I was given the clothes to wear."

"By whom?"

"A servant."

"This woman plays with words—"

"Do you mean the servant of the Magister Major, Fra Danielus?"

Beatifica, unsure.

"Write down: it may be supposed so."

"Beatifica, was a reason given you for this immoral dress?"

"No."

The Interlocutor: "It seems, from other things she says, and that I have learned, that the Magister thought she would be discounted if she appeared as a woman, since women are naturally counted less. For a similar reason, he chose that she should be seen often, mounted and riding on a horse, as horses are not common in the City. The Soldiers, it has been said, took note of her in this way, for they themselves go mounted in war, outside Ve Nera."

The Pro-Sequitor: "That excuses nothing, makes it worse! He must know better than us all. An arch-manipulator."

"Beatifica, when you danced about the trees, did anything appear to you? Any imp or creature?"

"Once I thought so."

"Describe it."

"I thought it was my mother. But then I thought it was a beast that lives in a fig tree and eats men. But it was only a scrap of rubbish."

"What thing is this you speak of? That lives in a tree—?"

She did not know. It seemed she had been told of it.

"Instructed in demons."

"Beatifica, what purpose do you have when you bring the fire?"

"No purpose."

"Come, come. *Why* do you do it?"

"Because I am asked."

"Why then have you killed some—and spared some?"

"I remember neither."

"You have said, you were shown God's priesthood changed to animals and birds?"

She *knew* this they were angry at. (Unreasonably. Why should it concern them?) But she tried now to evade. "I was only dreaming."

"And in the dream, were shown it?"

"Yes."

She had never learnt tact, or to lie. If she had learned either, at the very first might she not tactfully have lied to Ghaio Wood-Seller, words, flesh, allowing him to rape her?

She knew not to ask for Cristiano, or the Magister.

Finally, they demanded, the white judges, if she would confess her fire came not from God, but from the Devil.

Stupidly, truthfully, she told them, "It comes from my hair. So others have said."

Then the one called Isaacus drew close, crouching, creeping, just—as she abruptly saw—like the sort of beast she had seen in her vision. He leaned over her and she smelled his physical uncleanness, the stench of his ruined throat, and of his ruined heart.

"You bring fire, but you too can burn. Do you remember how I burnt you with my candle blessed of God?"

And she perceived then, bending too close, a sort of second Ghaio, almost seeming to be about to glue his rancid mouth on hers. If she had been able, if the fire still waited in her, she would have brought it down. The whole chamber would have gone up, and every man in it. But her fire had left her. She was hot with cold. And with her fire, all else—all love, all possibility.

Instead, some part of her which had borne too much from the day she first began to live, broke in fragments.

She gave her fox's barking scream.

And they crossed themselves, jumping up. As if to scream was a sin. Perhaps it was. Isaacus screamed: "She fears it! She fears the flame of God! Burn the harlot—a rope's too good for her. Oh you strumpet of Hell! Burn to wax, burn to ashes, burn to glass—*burn— burn—burn—*"

Like a tattered flag that voice went with her. It put out all other voices. She had had nothing. She was Volpa, and all that there was—was this.

She was again taken through long corridors.

In a room—where?—cooler, a window—it was night—they bound her hands.

No priest came to her now.

She was an apostate. Could hope for nothing.

(Nothing but this, all there was.)

Beatifica—Volpa—grasped they were about to kill her. She had no concept for death. (Only for pain.) Cristiano's death she had seen in that way—his agony, and hers in loss. What else did death mean? Conversely, her mother had existed after death. The Afterlife, then, opened from the world like one room from another.

This she *knew*. But it made no difference.

When she was brought up on to the square, before the Primo, Beatifica found—but without finding—she was a single particle of a great procession.

Surrounded on all sides by soldiers—not Bellatae, but the Primo guard. Distantly, the priesthood, in black, and there a huge, gold, glinting cross held high. And beyond, everywhere, a wall of people, shouting and shrieking in a kind of merriment which, to Beatifica—to Volpa—was only like a hundred glimpses she had had before of human things.

Darkness, brightness. More torches flaring in this great black room of night. And above, the liquid black of terrifying sky, where no lights showed. And now black water, not liquid as the sky, but chopped and ragged with motion.

They led her, firmly, not gratuitously so, into a barge.

All about, the Styx boats jostling on the lagoon, torch-prowed, and the black priests, staring all one way, the dough-pale faces, and black holes of eyes.

This boat, sidling under her.

Guards either side. *Their* faces like wooden platters, not turned to her at all.

Alone in the world.

Volpa, the Vixen, alone, among these multitudes gathered only to see her.

The fleet of black boats set off, to cross Fulvia, and go in among the channels of the Silvian Marsh.

Bells tolling.

Everywhere the sound of praying and strange outcry.

Water lap-lapping. Oars.

It would be a long route, the choked canals—but had time stopped?

The torches red in ink water, reminded her of something she had seen. But, whatever it had been, she did not know, now.

She knew not one thing, now.

And as before, if any had spoken to her, she could not have used her voice.

She was all eyes. She felt that also. Two erroneous lenses in a flimsy frame. She looked, and saw the buildings of Ve Nera, called Venus, pass. The wooden posts, the overhanging chests of upper stories. From windows railed in iron, people craned and leaned. Pointed her out. *"The witch—the witch—" "May she roast."*

A boy threw a stone at her. It hit instead one of the guards, who cursed, then renounced his curse.

Shades fell, and candlelight, over the prolonged traffic of the boats.

Mumma, she thought. Or a voice said it, in her spirit. What had the world ever been that she could make any sense of it? Harmed and abused, told always what to do, and the pretty prayers she could not translate. And joy and love, only the prelude to this.

Cristiano.

Cristiano—

I will lift up my eyes to the mountains.

Over Venus, Beatifica began to see the scarlet rock of her dreamworld, floating. Flaming red. A hearth or a sunset. On that black, starless sky. ("Mumma, what are the stars?" "Yesterday. Tomorrow." Neither, here.) And the fluted shadows chiseled in the mountain sides. Veins like living fire. All raised on a rosy blazing cloud.

Through the black of night, Beatifica-Volpa saw the tides of day rush in. Sand, not water, filled Venus to her heights. Sand shimmered in her canals. The lagoons a desert.

We suffer on earth, so that we can be happy in another place.

Why? Why? Why?

Let us only be happy. There, and here.

The procession of boats had at last entered Silvia.

The girl did not know, (who would have told her?) they had been building the pyre for her two days already, the platform and the shape of logs and dry tinder. For, without doubt, *they* had known she would be needing it.

In the marshes, the fitful torch light. The boats like a black serpent, some antique story of a monster which lived under the lagoons, surfaced now, glimmering, flashing gold and red.

There were other banks of boats, drawn off. People stood on them to watch.

The bell of Santa Lallo Lacrima, Lullaby of Tears, tolled like the rest. Did she isolate its individual note?

And there, another church going by, with a high and gesturing spire. On an islet in the marsh, desolate, and bell unrung. Gargoyles peered over, and behind, a hill rose free of the encroaching marsh, but a hill bare of anything much, some hovels clinging on there. (From which, people stared.)

Next, Roman pillars marching on either side of the boats, or standing like whitish nails hammered in, and on their tops, the nail-heads, weird beings of wings and draperies, wreathes, chariots—that once had been gods. But they were so high up, like the gargoyles, hardly to be seen.

A square, not unlike the Primo's, but empty, and this waterway carving through it, and on a pedestal a god with beard and weaponry fork—Neptune, the patron, long ago, of Venus, trident lifted, catching fiery crimson from the lights. (And would this god have saved her? He had been partial to maidens, Ovid said, liked them when they looked like young men.)

After that, a hump of darkness, just defined somewhat by other torches, that sprang out like flaming weeds. Ve Nera's little Colosso. The amphitheater where, in the time of the Crusades, the City had burned alive all those who were the foes of God.

Beyond that place, the marshes opened. Though half clotted, spilled with veils of grass and sand, they finally ran outwards to the silvered black of void. It was the sea. Perhaps. Or some other elemental thing that always rings the cities, bodies, *being* of mankind.

To the girl, nothing. Everything—was nothing.

A smell of pitch and salt and stagnancy. Of water. Of fire.

The priests far ahead and far behind, were dolorously chanting now.

Her mountain floated in the air.

Was it only an afterimage of flaming torches, left on the curve of her eyes?

In the day of the Romans, the sea had been farther off. Tunnels had led it in towards the stadium, for their shows of ship-battles and drownings.

Tonight the crowd itself brought a sea into that place.

They were scrambling in among the old crumbled tiers of seats, inconveniencing those already seated there.

In the mouths of entryways, up which victims had been herded or gladiators stalked, the crowd now jumbled. There was no longer an old smell of lions and bears to distress them. The moans of terror had died away.

The platform was at the center of the great arena. It had been built very large, as if for a giant. In former centuries, the pyres had stood in rows, twenty or forty at a time. But she was only one—so things must be exaggerated to display her importance.

There was a causeway. Out of the boat, and along this road of stones, they took Volpa, who had been Beatifica.

As she came into the amphitheater, an awful, incredible sound went up. Itself, the amphitheater knew it well enough. The walls had taken the impression of such noises, kept them better than the odors and whimperings.

One entity, a mob. Wordless. Yet there were words—*Feed me.*

The black and glittering procession, headed by its dayspring of a golden cross, (dragon-like) rippled over the arena floor.

It formed another pattern, with the center left open—for the girl, and the pyre.

Volpa looked up at the pyre. A huge, leaning, stacked pile of wood. It reminded her, the ultimate irony, of the yard of Ghaio Wood-Seller.

A man in black was before her.

He called, in a wild chant of voice, so all the crowd could hear:

"One last time, woman. Will you renounce your wickedness, and disown Satanus? Your body we can no longer, through your stubbornness, save. But we long to cure your soul. It is so easy. You need only throw off your crimes and beg God's mercy, even here at the foot of the stake. And though we, and He, must punish you for your sins, yet you will not altogether die. Oh turn from your vainglorious corruption. Turn from it, Beatifica. I entreat you!"

Volpa stared at him, as the crowd did. A spectator. He might have cried out in another language.

And now indeed, relinquishing her salvation, the priest belled in Latin, long gross sentences of excommunication she did not understand. But the crowd did, even the most untutored of them. They knew, and hung above and about, congealed in a wondrous revulsion at this fear which had missed them.

After that there was some delay. There had been a difficulty
with the structure of the platform, or the pyre. The arena was old
and ill-maintained. Engineers had had to come and make it sure. Or
try to do so.

The eyes of Volpa wandered.

But everything was the same. The reeling tiers of seats, the
circular-seeming space. Human figures, in similar attitudes. Cran-
ing, pointing, mouthing—or, like her guards, the dragoncoils of
priests, motionless.

Her eyes any way were dazzled, and very tired.

She did not see two men, clad in black like countless others,
standing to one side.

If any of the Bellatae Christi—Warriors of God, perhaps,
Knights of the Maiden—had entered this place, which had been
forbidden them, they did so unknown, and disguised. How many,
Echelon and Militia, were there? Careless of the Council of the
Lamb, or God, but not quite of summary imprisonment or death.
Many.

They were known, too, found out, among the crowd. But the
staring mob did not denounce them or go after them. They had prey
already.

Cristiano and Jian had come up by one of the ghastly entrance
ways of reeking, broken stone. Strong, young and male, no one
quibbled that they pushed to the front.

The pyre was perhaps eighty feet from them. But it was much
further. Beyond the moon. Under the sea.

Cristiano stood expressionless. He might have lashed and denied and forced himself on, for this one express moment. And he
was sure, was he not, that no Hell awaited her. He was sure. And
inside the case of steel, he burned already, molten and screaming.

Beside him, Jian, almost as armored. Not quite. Jian's mouth
worked. It was as if he tried to remember speech.

Everything was lost. The world was lost.

Cristiano, burning in Hell fire, accepting.

Jian, writhing in the fire of earth, unable to accept.

Volpa saw neither.

And now, courteously, (at last) the priests and guard were pro-
pelling her to the steps, a wooden ladder, of the type she had often
seen in the first hill farm, and in the house of Ghaio.

The executioner met them there. He bowed to the priests. A
brown man with thick muscles and a brutal face. But the eyes were

not brutal. They glared out in nervous agony at what the body and face consigned them to.

The priests drew off. Somehow, decorously.

The executioner spoke to Volpa.

"Too high, Maid. My boys can't get up again to you. We do, when we can. Break the neck. Make it quick. But not here, not with an audience like this. I'll say what to do. There'll be a deal of smoke. Breathe it up. It'll numb you, take you off a bit. You may die from that. But if the flame gets you, I promise, girl, I've seen it hundreds of times, it never takes so long. Trust me. It'll be over soon. Then you can rest."

Volpa turned and looked at the executioner. He was to say, after, he had never seen a woman or a man so serene. (This being how he interpreted her state.) And she said, "Am I really to die then?"

"Yes, girl. Yes. Don't fret. It's soon over. I swear it is."

And she said, "Cry for yourself not me. My pain is done. I am in God's world now."

The words of the male slave, by Ghaio's house, had again come to her. The executioner was not crying. His eyes always watered at strong light. His eyes wept, but he did not. He caught his breath, though. He did not know she had said these words because, in the shambles of her thoughts, the talk of burning had recalled her mother's cremation, as his watery eyes put her in mind of tears. Because all she had been told was that death was the end of pain. Not the beginning, as a zealot might have assured her.

Or did she say it because some vast intelligence, beyond her and all things, let fall the words on her tongue?

"God will be compassionate," mumbled the man. Then, "Do you need my help, climbing up?" (Sometimes their legs would not carry the condemned to the scaffold.)

"No," she said, listless, almost—he thought—bored. "I'm used to ladders."

5

After tying her securely to the post, the executioner's assistants leaped down.

They had paid her no attention, treating her like a side of meat, or bit of furniture, which needed only to be secured. In the same way, if so instructed, they would, under cover of the smoke, have gone back and snapped her neck, or punched her unconscious. Normally it would be several more decades, if they lived, before they realized what their job entailed.

The executioner came forward with a torch, and then his assistants with three more.

The priests were to bless these brands. How else could the fire work upon this witch who called fire?

Matteo, a Magister Major of the Primo, stood out before the Council. He too wore a black cowl and mantle.

He blessed the torches, calling on God.

The Council of the Lamb raised their hands.

A tableau.

It was spoiled.

Isaacus rushed out of the knot of priests. He jumped forward, and seizing one of the flaring brands, he held it high.

His face was livid, lurid. He waved the flaming staff at the tiers of seats, and at the sky where God must sit, watching.

And the crowd bayed.

How often, long, long ago, some Roman butcher of the ring, in such a stance. And such a crowd.

It was unseemly. The Council folded itself. Jesolo spoke stonily. "Stand back, brother."

"I never shall."

"This isn't your work."

"Yes. My work. God has touched this flame. It will swallow her up into Hell."

And turning, he strode straight forward, and the executioner and his men moved aside.

So it was Brother Isaacus who stuck the first torch in at the platform's base, to light the pyre. (Years after, the executioner himself would remember this. He would say, *The Church lit the fire. Not I, or mine.*)

But the flames at once took a grip on the dry wood, and on the straw packed in behind. Presently, where some of the logs had gone in dampened, there would be, as prophesied, smoke. But not yet.

The crowd, silent again, saw the fire catch. And made its noise once more.

Then the executioner and his men circled round the platform, thrusting in their torches.

And more noise rose. Then slackened off. To a complete silence, in which the rising crackle of fire and wood was plainly heard.

Cristiano looked up at her.

He did not know who she was. Inside his body his psyche seemed riven and pulling apart. He began to pray for her. But the words were meaningless, and even when he knew he was speaking softly but aloud, it did not seem to matter, being irrelevant.

He had been practical. He had willed it to be quick. Then she would be free. Now he saw it would not be quick. Hours would go by. She would see the flames fluttering, like golden birds, towards her. Feel the fangs of them. She would begin to scream.

Instead of Beatifica, better if he had died. He could have borne it. How could she?

Why had he not saved her? Why did he stand here now?

(And over all this, his voice quietly speaking for her. *I shall not be afraid for the sun by day, neither the moon in night . . .*)

Shall I climb up? Die with her?

Half moving. No. They had taken the ladder. He might manage to vault over any way—but the sides of the pyre were not able to support him, now. Or—would they? Why had he not gone up before?

She was not looking at the fire. She was staring away. She did not appear frightened—only—bleak. Like a child abandoned. Acclimatized to it. Indifferent.

Again, he half-moved forward.

As this happened, Jian went by him.

Jian was standing now, in the wide space between the crowds, the priests, and the pyre.

Jian, now, gazing up at her. His mouth working.

The priests over there were conferring. And a guard, summoned, turned towards Jian in his nondescript black.

And Isaacus, prowling like a mangy tiger at the pyre's foot, slavering, all his corded neck showing, as he stretched it to watch the girl. And on the neck a muddy scar, an old injury, that, to Cristiano now, looked like the lusterless loop of some ancient serpent—but which was the bruise of a hangman's rope—

Two guards reached Jian. One spoke. Jian reacted with an offhand blow, and sent the guard sprawling. The other seized Jian.

Jian arched his whole body towards the top of the pyre, as if to shoot himself upwards and join her in the flames.

And his voice came breaking out of him. It was loud and very precise. His mouth had worked and worked to form this and have it right. Not one who did not hear. Like the Primo Square, this arena of death had been fashioned to relay, with trumpets and swords, a footfall or a whisper.

"Beatifica—you are God's own light! And this is the fire of wickedness—of the devil's putrefaction. Oh God, send her your divine spark—let her blast their bloody filth of fire with God's own flame—*Beatifica*—make the *fire* burn!"

The second guard had got up. He clubbed Jian across the head. Jian toppled.

Cristiano moved. Stopped.

A sound had burst out from the pyre. It was like something roaring there, then splitting open.

There was a flash like lightning. And a gush of flames and smoke poured suddenly upward.

The girl had been visible. Now she vanished. She was gone.

Plumes of thunder—smoke billowed, dwarfing the pyre. Flames scratched at the sky.

Was she screaming? Could he hear her screaming? He strained to hear.

No—women in the crowd—in a combination of horror and exaltation—they screamed, not she.

In fire, the throat was swiftly cauterized.

They were pulling at Jian. One of the guards kicked him, and then one of the men from the crowd did so. And a priest of the Council went to them pompously, and spoke, and they left off.

Only the crash of the fire now, was audible. Limbs of trees, laid there, cracked with the note of whips. Through all that pierced a soaring, whistling shriek, which was air escaping, freshening the fire.

Cristiano heard his voice then, saying over and over, "Quickly, let it be quickly. Quickly, oh God, be quick—"

You fool, he thought. *It may be only moments, and seem to her like a hundred years. And for me, it is forever now.*

He strove to see her in the flames. But there were only the flames, and smoke.

Be quick. Quickly. Is it over now? Let it be over for her.

Never for me.

He thought of Judeo at the foot of the cross, and then self-hanged on a tree.

As Cristiano thought this, stupidly his eyes roved back to Isaacus by the edge of the pyre. And Cristiano thought, *That man was hanged.* But some other might have been thinking it.

And then Cristiano saw Isaacus dancing. Presumably a dance of delight, of madness.

No. Isaacus clutched at his neck. His eyes bulged in the sockets. His face was turning to the color of a Magister's purple robe. He was strangling.

A couple of the priests hastened to him, trying to draw Isaacus back from the pyre. Many now were coughing from the smoke, and burnt and daubed with falling cinders. (As yet there was no smell of roasting flesh.)

But Isaacus was down on the ground. He was rolling and bumping there, clawing at his throat. Priests bent over him and jigged abruptly back.

His legs kicked out, again and again. He was like a man dangling from a noose.

All at once a gout of blood and matter erupted from his mouth, and after it a stiff length of swollen and blotched tongue.

Isaacus flopped sluggishly on to his side. He relaxed. His starting eyes had now an uninterested look.

Cristiano watched all this. He did not know what it was, and soon forgot it.

But he did not look up again until a second explosion shook the pyre.

Huge bits of wood and charcoal showered down. A sawn tree trunk, the width of a full-grown man, was catapulted out, and landed with a smack on the arena floor.

The top of the pyre caved in. The smoke, scarlet now, creamed into the sky.

Nothing stood in the pyre. The stake they had bound her to had been devoured. She was devoured.

High in the air, the red smoke formed the shape of a mountain, long and low, fissured with veins of reflected fire.

Cristiano walked across to the guards and Jian, who was sitting half-unconscious on the ground. Cristiano's legs had no feeling in them. None of him had any feeling. His mouth had no muscle, but still said, slurred a little, "Let him go, boys. He's just bladdered on bad ale."

"What was he shouting? Saying the sacred fire was wicked—"

"*Her* fire he meant. Don't you know the stories? Come on, get up," he added to Jian, whom he could barely see, as he could barely see anything. "Get up and come home."

The guard, more interested in the fallen Isaacus, were not uninclined. Cristiano found he had pressed some coins on them, too. (To bribe. Where had he learned that?) They clapped his shoulder. There was a sense of disappointment in the shortness of the show. Other Bellatae, mostly Militia, clad as monks or laborers, were idling over. One got Jian on his feet.

With a sighing hiss, more of the pyre collapsed. And in the sky the red mountain had darkened.

Then wish the world good-bye.

EPILOGUE

Does the Eagle know what is in the pit?
Or wilt thou go ask the Mole?
Can Wisdom be put in a silver rod?
Or Love in a golden bowl?

WILLIAM BLAKE
The Book of Thel

The sky of Heaven was always blue. So this was not Heaven.

Even so, today it was a Heaven sky, and Ermilla was singing in the fields, as she worked with the other women among the sheaves.

Her husband heard her, while he rode down between the long rows. She had a lovely voice, crystal in the sunny harvest air.

Then, through the sheaves, he saw her. Demetrio reined in his horse. It was a solid patient beast, always too ready to stand still. He sat there, looking at her. She was leading the other women in the song. Quite right. Though she worked among them, she was their mistress. But he was always glad, after her other life, to see her so untrammeled. She wore a light dress, saffron color, like the grain, and her hair was tied in under a white scarf.

Then she in turn saw him. She sang the last line of the song, and left everything, moving towards him between the golden land and the summer blue sky.

Reaching him, she said nothing, but put up her face, kissed by sun.

"We're to have a visitor." She only looked. "Yes, who else but Danielus."

Then her face did change. It became serious and thoughtful. At first he had always taken this gravity for unease. No longer. It was simply the face she kept for the Magister.

They walked back together, Demetrio leading the horse. His wife began to pick flowers from the verges of the hilly fields, and clumps of red poppies.

She was not a profound housekeeper. She preferred the work she did in the open, or her garden, where she was successful if haphazard. Peaches doubly ripened on the walls of the farm and great tussocks of herbs bubbled from their beds. She had known this sort of work, before cruelty and religion claimed her. Her cooking though was terrible, and others saw to the food. Demetrio did not mind any of this. Danielus had saved both of them—a thousand years ago it seemed—and now they lived, Demetrio sometimes thought, like the first couple in the first Garden. Except, this was the earth.

Even so, as they saw below the russet roofs of the farm, she said proudly, "I baked bread this morning."

And Demetrio visualized Danielus, chewing steadfastly through the black husks.

The sun had burned. But now the fire was out.

Gradually the mountains were mixed with the sky.

An apron of shadow spread across the plain.

Danielus thought he was tired, riding the slope up through the foothills. He had been in the saddle most of the day, many hours behind his messenger. Before that, he had been traveling three or four days, visiting all of his farms. This hill farm was the highest up. The summer air was sheer and sweet, and birds still rose and fell like notes of music through the twilight.

But he must be growing old, to feel so tired. Even last year, a ride like this would not have wearied him so much.

Then again, might it not be tiredness—more the enervation of a slight anxiety—or an anticipation—

He had not paid this visit to them before, his tenants here, Demetrio and Ermilla.

At his back, his servant, Lauro, had got off his horse, and was walking her. Kind Lauro.

"Not far now, Lauro, I think. Look, there's the path. You see that stand of poplars? Half an hour."

"That's good, Danielo." (Lauro called him always this, when they were alone; the guard had been left behind at the last farm.) "I was beginning to believe I'd fall asleep. It's this air."

Kind Lauro. He saw me flagging. Veronichi was clever, finding him. But, she always is.

He had gone first to her before setting out. She was back in her house on Eel Isle. There, since last summer, they had had five of those dinners, crowned with peonies, garlanded by the making of love. "You see," she would say, "I never had to cut off my hair." *Or die,* he thought.

On this occasion, he had had the new miracle to report.

Veronichi listened solemnly, and then said, very seriously, "Is it true, do you suppose?"

"True, yes. Not a miracle. How can it be?"

"But Danielo—you have always told me miracles may occur. And we know that, because of Beatifica."

"Not this." He had smiled. "I'm glad of it naturally. And it does good not harm. Or, only harm that once."

"He was an evil man."

"Yes. His tragedy."

"Almost ours. And *hers.*"

"In any case, Isaacus' death may not have been so Heaven-sent as it appeared. The rope ruined his throat in boyhood. And he overtaxed his voice. Then his extreme excitement, and the thick smoke—Of course, I wasn't there, but from what I heard described, he choked himself. Or some vital vessel burst."

"It thrills me to reflect on it."

"Ah. Veronichi."

"I can't pretend to your pureness of spirit. Remember, my God is still the Jews' God of vengeance."

"He is God, as is the God of everyone of us."

She had asked, however, for many details of the latest miracle. Possibly, it was that little jealousy of hers, too. For the miracles took place, most of them, at Santa La' Lacrima, where the Domina was Purita.

She had looked, Danielus thought, when he saw Purita again, a proper Mother of nuns. Though she had kept the accent of her inn, her Latin, when she read, had become more clear. Her general speech, too, was finer. So with all of her. She stood straight and quiet in her gray robes, and her face, which long ago was the pretty coarsened face of Luchita, had passed through a gaunt adolescence of middle-age and unhappiness, to this containment, remote—yet approachable. Her dark eyes had grown beautiful, large and luminous. The lined parchment lids enhanced them. Under her hand stood, (at her side) the walking stick with the carved head of a bird. Purita had told Danielus the previous Domina had given it to her, and therefore she cherished it. Also, of course, it had leant her some of the previous Domina's authority, a staff of office. She seemed not aware of that, and now had great authority of her own.

After pleasantries and a cup of wine Domina Purita asked two of her nuns to bring in the sister on whom the miracle had been worked.

Danielus then beheld a dried up little woman, with a spiteful mouth suddenly all softened, and wild eyes.

"Here is Sister Gratzilia, Father. I shall let her tell you herself."

And Sister Gratzilia began to speak. She spoke at great length, and no one checked her.

"I committed a great sin, Magister. I have asked for a penance for it. I went to the casket where the Heart is—the Heart of the Maiden which would not burn—and I said, You heal all these lame and diseased. You give the blind back their eyes. Then why not me? Why not me? Give me my speech like other women." Danielus nodded. Domina Purita had explained beforehand.

Sister Gratzilia did so as well. "You see, holy Magister, since I could talk, I stuttered. It was very bad. And the more I tried not to, the worse it was. In my family, in my family, I was mocked and laughed at. And they said, since I was ugly, too, I'd have to be a nun."

Sister Gratzilia lowered her eyes. Through her casing one saw the hurt and raving, inarticulate child. Then everything eased once more. "I've been a poor handmaid, Magister. I've been harsh and surly. I've taken out my pain on others. But I was miserable. I like this life—but have been useless. And when they let me read out from the Book of God—how patient they were, and only sometimes, the novices would—but I thought they all jeered at me, and made fun of me. I could hardly get out a word. And sometimes, trying to recite properly. I'd spit, not being able to help it—and make noises—like a chicken—or a pig, my brothers used to say. And I thought the sisters here said that, too."

They waited.

Sister Gratzilia resumed, "So I made my rude demand of the Heart of the Maiden in the golden casket, above the altar. And I turned away in anger, sputtering and cawing for breath. And then—"

Gratzilia stopped. Her face, from being only mild, suffused with a blush like a young girl's.

"Oh Mother," said Gratzilia. "Even now, now I can speak, I haven't any words—"

"You must try to tell the Magister," said Purita, calmly. "You underestimate your powers, sister. You always have. Say it as you did to me."

Gratzilia said then, "I felt myself—drop away *from* myself. Like a cloak thrown down. I'd needed it. I was warm enough." She paused. Her eyes went far off and returned. "That was all. I opened my mouth and words came out, and I heard myself offering praise to God, like any other."

"This is a true miracle, Father," said Purita. "Like the rest. And like the rest, it has been written down. I've testified to it. And if you will add your authority and seal, the documents may be put away. Until the next time."

She was very efficient in everything. Of course, she had run an inn.

When Gratzilia was gone, Danielus asked Purita if she had awarded a penance, as Gratzilia had seemed to want, for her rough address to the Heart.

Purita said, "Doesn't Christ tell us only to knock upon the door, which will then open. I think He says nothing about the knock being urgent or too loud. If God rewarded her for it, who am I to punish? I've always felt, we learn better through joy."

"I am pleased with Purita," he told Veronichi.

"I know you are. Yes, I confess I like her too. Sometimes I call on her, and we talk. Of you, rather more than somewhat. Does that please you, too?"

"Very much."

"She believes in every one of the miracles."

"The events do happen. No one can deny it. The lame do sometimes walk and the blind see. And the sick child carried in there, when the box was put by it, recovered. But Veronichi, Purita does not know what is in the casket. You know what is."

"A heart."

"The heart of a dead animal. A large dog found in the canal."

"That too is strange, Danielo. Why did the heart, even of a *dog*—not burn up on the pyre?"

"I imagine because the pyre abruptly collapsed inwards, as it was intended to."

"Most of the wood was consumed. And everything else but for a few bones."

"I wish I had been there when the executioner raked it out."

"You were . . . delayed."

"Indeed. I missed very much. The death of Isaacus at the pyre's

foot, the fire-flash in the pyre itself, doubtless caused as the trap
beneath gave way, but taken for another wonder. And then the
Heart of the Maiden which refused to burn. It was lucky that the
executioner had just had his conversion to Beatifica, and kept hold
of the heart. He would not let the Council have it. He kept it secret,
and finally brought it to me, as he said, a man now above the Council. If only that were so. And this was after, so he explained, did I tell
you? the Heart had cured his watering eyes."

"Since the Heart isn't Beatifica's, nor even human, how do you
suppose it works?"

"Belief. Faith. How most miracles are achieved. Through the
power of God in each of us. It needs only a focus."

"Then all who pray in faith are answered? No, Daniel."

"The strongest faith may be interrupted."

"But—if even once—then these are true miracles."

"The true miracle, Venus, is you." He did not know she saw the
weariness in his face. He thought, naively, he had placated her.
"Come and bind me with your glory of uncut hair. I have to leave
early tomorrow, for the hills."

Men walked out to welcome him, holding lanterns, and Demetrio
went with them. Ermilla came out, too, like the Good House Wife.
And the heart of Danielus sank. He chided himself, but to no avail.
He had hoped, more than he cared to admit, to see—as they said in
the streets of Ve Nera—her girdle lifted. But her belly was as flat as
ever. She was not with child.

She seemed radiant, however. Not at all as he recollected. Certainly, a new woman.

They did not eat tonight in the great stone kitchen, but took
Danielus into the parlor behind it. She sat down with the men like a
lady, and they were served by the cheerful servants. She herself had
only, luckily, baked three loaves.

And you, Danielus thought, *how are you, my dear Demetrio?*

He had noticed that Demetrio and Lauro had given each other
a couple of almost puzzled looks. No doubt each thought he had
seen the other somewhere before. Witnesses more impartial would
be aware that there was a resemblance between them. More than
that both were blond, handsome, well-made. Yet, where Lauro had
grown more gentlemanly, Demetrio had not become a peasant out
here in the hills. One had learned, he still practiced at his former
trade, keeping as fine an edge in play as in earnest. He spoke the

Grace, too, in the old way. The story was he had been a soldier, a captain at Ciojha, who gave up war for the land, and his wife.

Ermilla also spoke a prayer after the food. Nothing omitted there, either.

"And where is Suley?" Danielus asked, when the fruit and cheeses had come in. "I saw him last when he brought your letters down."

"With the horses," Demetrio said. "Of course he never will eat with us."

"Of course."

"When he's prayed, he'll be in. He loves to discuss God with you, as you know, Magister."

Danielus acquiesced. The comforts of old men, to sit debating late into the night, the chessboard between them, the candles burning red and low. Suley had reminded Danielus, in Ve Nera this spring, "The others went home to Jurneia by your generosity, Daniel. But I mean to stay rather longer. If I can, I will win you for the true God. I should hate it, my priest, to see you fall down among the lost." "But Suley, our Gods are one God." "No, Daniel, this you will never convince me of. I know your soul cries out for my God, who is God. One day you will let me feed you the sweetmeat of enlightenment." And Danielus had ceased to argue. Just as always, he allowed Suley-Masroor to speak to him of that one God who was God. And to quote from the sacred and exquisite Book which had proceeded from the depth of this God.

Who knows, one day I may even become a convert to the God of Suley. He will be the God I have always known. Is this not what Suley says to me? But we mean different things. Even so, we are fond of each other. We have each saved the other from likely death. This can make brothers of the basest men. And he is not base in any way. While I am not base in any way which would preclude or offend our friendship. Outside conversion.

Suley had affection, even, for Ermilla. She was shameless, he admitted, like most Christian women, but that was not her fault, she knew no better. She was a child, and a nice child.

He had never known her. Never thought to set together the two halves of Demetrio's wife, to make the whole woman. After all, he had only seen her once before, from quite some distance, and in an unnatural light.

Danielus did not burden Suley with the facts. Few were privy to them. That was usually best.

Beatifica was dead.

Ermilla sat blithely at the table, eating the red grapes which, in this candleshine, matched her hair. She had put on an azure gown, and on her breast gleamed the little cross her husband gave her on their wedding day, set with one stormy sapphire. He had got the cross in some battle. Why he had kept it he did not seem to know. Perhaps he had meant to present it to the Church, and then forgotten even he had it. He could never have thought of it as a bridal gift.

Demetrio and Danielus and Lauro talked about the harvest. That was reasonable enough. Later, Danielus would have some talk with Demetrio alone, and then they might refer to other things. Danielus thought that doubtless, as years went by, those other things—religion, war, the *past*—would be touched on less. Or with less care.

He was glad they were happy. You saw they were. Happy as most were not. Surely it could not be many more months before she had garnered his seed? Perhaps even now it had happened, not visible yet, and Demetrio, embarrassed even would tell him later.

Master of himself, perhaps always, Danielus did not drowse. He did not want to waste the precious time. How often could he visit here? Twice a year at most.

When Suley came in suddenly, winged by night, and with Reem beside him, Danielus caught that tiny flicker of something all about. A Magister did not *have* favorites. Yet the favorites were jealous. All the ones he loved, in whatever way he loved them, in some slight way of their own, subtly vied with each other. Before, Demetrio had had no rival. He had known it, without comprehending.

If he had been sent to the stake, could I have stayed aloof? Could I have planned as well as I did? I never loved the girl. I used her. I was sorry. And between us, I and God—or Fate—

Danielus went out for a turn around Ermilla's savage garden, with Suley.

"You're tired."

"Saddle-tired. It's nothing."

"There is a better horse here for you. Demetrio wants to give it to you. Don't refuse him, he has been perfecting the beast all summer."

Yes, they vied with each other, but also were protective. Siblings. "Then I will not refuse. You're wise to warn me. And you?"

"Look," said Suley. They looked up at the night. "I miss my wife. I make poems to her, which compare her to these stars of

Venarh. And she is only a little plain round woman, with a skin like honey."

"Suley-Masroor, you must go home."

"Have no fear. None of Venarh's women tempt me. While I can stay chaste, I can remain."

"I should convert at once, and free you."

"I would know at once you lied."

"No. Your God is mine already."

"So you say. Listen, Daniel. One day you will die. On that day, you need only cry out to God, He who *is* God, and beg him to forgive and receive you. He will do it. If you do *not* lie."

"If I swear I will do that, will you go home to your wife?"

"A little longer. I shall stay a little longer. Besides, Reem's wife died in Jurneia. He feels more at liberty to enjoy a Christian girl. He has one. He's taught her how to pray. I think she may go with him, to the East. Never fear, for now, they hide it."

Surprised, Danielus gazed at Suley. Suley-Masroor raised his brows into his head-cloth. "Do you forget, Daniel, we also can deceive."

Danielus had been sitting that night in his book-chamber, when the Primo guard came for him. There were twenty of them and one priest. Perhaps not so amazing. The Council might have thought he would yet rally the Bellatae.

He got up at the summons and went with them. He left everything, even the glossily polished giant's skull that sat on his desk. In the end, one must leave all. Others would take interest in those things. Or they too would perish.

He desired that his enemies would not destroy any of his books, or smash the skull as an abomination. But even if they did, all things were always lost at last—and perhaps, nothing was lost. Men had souls, beasts too, he suspected. Why not a book, or an object. One saw, they would recur in other forms, yet the same. All lay in the limitless hand of God.

Noise had drained from Fulvia, away to the marshes, and the amphitheater. He too had considered going there. But he did not want the conceivably ultimate sight he had of the actual world—to be a girl burning alive. He was selfish in that. And immovable.

There were still things to do, anyway. He had made all the provision he could, until the last moment. His final agent indeed had gone down the corridors only a few minutes before he heard the tread of the guards.

If there were any chance, then Danielus had shored it up as firmly as he could. And now that too must be left. In prison he would never know. Dead—bodily dead—he would. Surely, he would.

It was possible, of course, that he was wrong. Although God surrounded everything, might Danielus himself not be strong enough to swim or leap the gulf beyond life?

He pondered this as they marched him across the courts below. It was the simple, the uncomplex who found it easy to enter Heaven. Thought was a wall, a tower. The needle's eye.

Then, leave also thought behind.

Danielus was conducted down into the the under-rooms of the Primo. Above, the silent-seeming City of Ve Nera. And here a silence that sounded in a roar.

He was promised no trial, though doubtless he must suffer one. Neither torture, nor death. Nor life.

Tonight, at the farm, would they again go over it, he, and Demetrio?

Who again would say, "Why did you never *tell* me?"

"I couldn't trust you. Oh, if it had been your life in a battle, then I would. But not with hers."

"I would have had some hope—"

"And if it failed?" Would Danielus then call Demetrio, not by mistake but through recapture of the past, by his former name? "Cristiano, your love for Beatifica was of an extraordinary sort. That's why you were prepared hopelessly to fight to the death for me—I am mortal. But in her you saw the light of her soul, you knew she could only go to God, and to God you gave her up. With *hope,* God alone knows what you might have done. Think. For all I knew, although my men had sighted and seen to the pyre and the platform, rigged up the trap below that led into the tunnel, still they must wait for the flames to take hold, to hide her. By the time it would be safe to bring her down, she might already be dead—or burned so terribly it would be a kindness to let her die."

Cristiano, last year, when this had been firstly discussed, standing there in his black, stripped of everything. No longer a Soldier of God, no longer anyone known. Cristiano, in honesty, might be said to have been expunged already. And Demetrio had yet to evolve and remake him.

And to this displaced being, Danielus outlined the plot and scenes of Beatifica's escape.

How certain men had made sure of the position of the pyre, and others assisted in its construction, supplying it too with the evidential corpse of a dog. The trap below had not been difficult to locate. Beneath lay a cistern and a tunnel. Through here, the Romans had pumped in the sea to fill the arena for their water-shows.

The trap was oiled, counter-weighted. The core of the platform was moveable and the core of the pyre loose, and fashioned to give way at once on the removal of certain props. Danielus' men must only wait and keep their nerve. Until able to precipitate the structure downwards as the trap gaped wide. Masked by fire and smoke, the girl would be plunged to a bed of mattresses and straw, and the trap heaved back above. *Then* water, to put out the flames.

If she lived—in any reasonable sense—they would take her, Ermilla's husband and his gang, through the tunnel, to the open sea. There was a boat in readiness. Along the coast, others were ready, for when the boat would come back to land.

Cristiano had listened. At first antagonistic, next excitable— then dulling down. Until he said, in a cold voice, "So. She lives?"

"She lives."

"But burned."

"There's no mark on her. Even her garments never took the fire. Or her hair."

"Then—"

"I don't know how, Cristiano. Perhaps judgment was unflawed and the men just swift enough. Alive and unscathed. Believe me. At the quay here is another boat to take you to her."

Danielus received no answer. And soon Cristiano, walking like a somnambulist, went away. Danielus sent a man with him, to be sure he reached the boat.

Some days after, on the coast northward of Ve Nera, Danielus married a woman and a man who were no longer Beatifica and Cristiano.

The chapel was a Roman one, but had been sanctified for God. It was a scanty wedding. In its manner also a Christening, for each had been renamed in Christ. Demetrio—the name of a saint chosen, perhaps, at random by the recipient. Since Beatifica did not seem to know her mother's name, nor properly any others for her sex, Danielus gave her that of the stone-mason's wife. Although this would be kept a secret always, the original Ermilla, he guessed, would take a rich satisfaction in it. Beatifica had been a saint.

Saint, and warrior . . . vanished. They were, for sure, two different people Danielus had joined. A bridegroom not stunned, yet very silent. A bride as silent, lucent, and in a gown. Much more than that. Much more. The service which created them one flesh—*superfluous.*

Without festivity, and at once, the couple went inland and turned back to the Veneran hills. The farm Danielus rendered them was far away, the mountains close. If ever they must, they could cross them, and be done with the City forever.

But that they might never need to do.

He had never dreamed of any of that, in the windowless cell beneath the Primo, which was always night, and which always soundlessly *roared.* There Danielus had stayed, (dreamless.) Waiting.

Eventually, as expected, guards came. Only ten of them. They marched him up to the surface. He had *not* expected that. Or, not yet.

Despite himself, he was rather disorientated. It was daylight, besides. Once he could see, he saw the blue sky. Which seemed unending, reducing all this below, to mere stupidity.

There were crowds on the Primo Square.

They were not spent and half-ashamed, as he had assumed they would be, having burned their victim—nor boisterous and seeking new carnage, which he had encountered too, in such mobs.

Most were still sooty from her fire. They spoke in mouthings. And seeing him, went mute.

Then Danielus saw the Council. Twelve men, as ever, for the number of the Apostles. Sheathed in black, and more like avengers from the classical abyss. The Council of the Lamb, which he had wanted, and intended, to be rid of.

It was Jesolo who stepped forward. And then Danielus saw the Bellatae Christi, perhaps all of them that were left, hardly any of them in a maculum, but with swords, knives, burnished in their belts.

Had they risen, done what he forebade? They too did not have that look.

Jesolo reached Danielus. He looked deeply at the Magister from pouchy eyes. Jesolo said, "Isaacus died. At the foot of her pyre. The people are saying he was struck down by the Most High. For his sin."

One of the Bellatae moved forward too. It was Jian. He seemed unsteady, dizzy, or drunk. He said loudly, "She was the saint of God."

The crowd, murmuring, murmured more vibrantly.

Danielus tried not to search the Bellatae, the crowd, for Cristiano, whom he loved. Danielus, Magister Major, succeeded.

Jesolo said, "Some men are here. The men you had charge of. Once our adversaries."

Danielus looked, and saw the twenty Jurneians, and Suley-Masroor. He had not seen them because none of them wore their turbans. Their hair, wealths of it, and blacker than ravens, tumbled about them. They had shaved their faces. Both these things, for them, were fearful crimes.

In the name of God—what had these Christian clods done to them—Danielus felt a whirling fury. He could not quite control it, it was so long since he had needed to take control of such vast rage.

Then Suley-Masroor walked forward.

He called out, in his strongest voice, which seemed to quake the square, "Here is our savior, the Magister Danielus, who brought us to the light."

The sun beat down. God had made the sun. Or caused the sun to be. Or was the sun . . . And Danielus knew, from his reading of the Greeks, that the Psalm which spoke of this had been in the form of a song composed in Egypt, by a Pharaoh, praising the deity of the sun . . .

The guard was falling back from Danielus.

His eyes, stung by the sun's light, blurred.

He saw the Jurneians kneeling. Abominably, they were kissing a cross a priest was offering them, and the crowd murmured, murmured.

Danielus wanted to snatch the cross away and wipe their lips. For them—such sacrilege. As if they smeared themselves with dung—and worshipped that.

He had wept that day they had remade his sister, the Jewess Yaelit, as the Christian Veronichi. Even though he knew it did not matter. God was God. There was no God—but God.

But the skin of Danielus was ill-made glass, and all the light shone through and changed his blood to dust.

He heard Suley cry out, in a lion's voice: "It is he, this great priest there, who has brought us to the one true God. And only he could do it."

And then Jesolo stepped back, and Cristiano stood in front of him. He was white as new skull. His eyes were black. He put his arm about Danielus, and, helpless, Danielus leaned on him.

"They say you made them Christians, Magister, by your preaching. After the fire—after that thing Isaacus died—the mob was turning. Then these men came up. Sarco brought them. See, he's there, in the Council, the twelfth man, to replace Isaacus. You converted twenty-one intransigent Jurneian infidel to the truth of Christ."

Jesolo, a little further off, said, "It's saved you, Fra Danielus. How can we doubt you? Thank God, and Amen."

Then Danielus was kneeling. He did not know why. His legs giving way, no doubt. Cristiano, who had lost his one great love, kneeled by him, holding him up. Cristiano, who was almost dead.

Everyone in the square was kneeling now, and praying. Including the twenty one Jurneians.

They think they damn themselves. And they do it for me.

Oh God, how can I bear this sacrifice?

Danielus thought, as he had done before, of Christ's rejection of the Cup of Agony, the cross, before he put away his human terror, and godlike, drank from it.

But had it been the agony He dreaded or the colossal power, the *godhead* itself, which suffering and death must bring?

No human thing could bear this. Even God-in-flesh could not. How can I?

Then Suley was there, leaning near.

He clutched the Jurneian's hand—"Suley—Suley—*No*—you must—"

Suley-Masroor's lips were at his ear.

"For a great one, great things must be done. But do you think our God cannot *see*—or forgive? Or that *we* cannot *lie*?"

And then Danielus wept. He wept because they had overthrown him quite. He had been returned to infancy, was a baby. And a baby cries.

All this the crowd saw and reported. Misread, it was considered appropriate.

Later, as Danielus, no longer a prisoner, and in command of himself once more, told Cristiano of the plan for Beatifica, and of the message he had received of its success, the first three benign miracles took place. Although they were not broadcast for some days.

The carcass of the dog, put into the fixed part of the pyre as evidence of the Maiden's death, went mostly to black shards. Only the heart did not burn.

And, as the City learned later, a beggar, entreating for alms, when the Heart passed over him, though muffled in a bag, regained the use of both his legs. The executioner's son meanwhile, employing foul language and blasphemy in a wine-shop, took a fit of sneezing and had to desist. And beside the Canal of Seven Keys, where Beatifica, the story went, had once been a slave, a hen laid three score eggs in an hour, and lived.

Cristiano, it was Beatifica you loved, not me.

If ever I am proud, let me remember those twenty-one men who risked their souls for me, speaking the idolatrous prayers of infidels. And let me remember Cristiano, strong as steel to hold me up, until I could stand, and tell him she was not dead.

When I am a child, then I am invincible.

When I am most strong, weaker than any infant.

"Magister—your bed's ready."

"No, Demetrio, I wasn't asleep. We should talk—"

"Tomorrow, Magister."

Am I old, that he treats me so tenderly, like a father?

And he had been in error. Not Demetrio, but Lauro.

Danielus got up from the chair, and now it was Demetrio-Cristiano who went with him. And then the girl came, slipping from darkness.

"Ermilla—thank you. What lovely bread you baked. Yes, a candle. I must light it, mustn't I? Tomorrow then. Tomorrow."

There was a stair, but narrow, wooden. Beyond the parlor and the kitchen, only shadows.

But now he saw her lean forward. Her fox's smile. What a wicked face she had, he thought, this strange girl, like a Maenad almost, from the Grecian myths. Seen in a smooth glimmering—a lamp somewhere . . .

She put out her hand, and set there on the unlit candle stub Lauro had brought him, a tiny light. Not rosy. A hyacinth petal of flame. From her fingers' ends.

"Yes, Magister. It came back to her. She can still call the fire."

Was *this* a dream?

He looked at her clandestine face. Demure now. She was held fast in Cristiano's arm, as he had been, on the Primo Square.

Back there in the shadows, had Lauro seen the flame come? Danielus thought not. And Suley was gone. It was for him alone.

"Thank you," Danielus said, again.

The stair, as he climbed it, was like a mountain. So life was. Only in the afterlife could one reckon to fly.

Before going up to their bedroom, Demetrio went out to look at the horse. It was a fine one, malt-black. He had exercised and groomed it himself. Tomorrow he would show Danielus, ask his opinion on it—which could be nothing but favorable. Startle him with the gift.

He had seemed exhausted, the Magister, and fallen asleep after the meal. That would never have happened—*then*.

Demetrio did not admit to himself, was mostly unaware, that Danielus meant far less to him, now. Demetrio's feelings were of friendship, gratitude, and solicitous respect. Cristiano had seen in the Magister a figurehead, and a man standing in the sky. God, then the Magister. Not much else. And now—still God, but God reflected from the mirror of his wife. Who, in his inner mind, he still named Beatifica.

Before they ended their evening in the world, he should finish reading the letter that Danielus had brought, from Jian. Jian was with the Bellatae Christi at Rome. He served a higher power now. When he wrote to Cristiano, conscientiously, he never called him that. The letter spoke of mundane things, organized combats, monuments, and pageants of the Virgin. It was as if he tried to reassure Demetrio that the cosmos of earthly spirituality safely continued in the absence of a Cristiano. Or to make him envious.

Jian never spoke at all of Ermilla. Just as he did not know where Cristiano had hidden himself, he did not know the name of the woman Demetrio had married. Jian believed the Maiden to be dead.

Danielus had mentioned that Jian, in his other letter to the Magister, had inquired after the Heart and its miracles. *That* now, *was* the Maiden.

There was talk in Rome of another venture to the Holy Land, less a crusade than a processional. Jian would be part of this. He described his ambition to visit the Tomb in the Rock, the way-stations of Blessed Maria on her mule, heavy with the unborn Christ. The desert of fasts and visions.

Was I like Jian?

The horse was peaceful, its coat silk. Demetrio left it, and went to complete the letter under the lantern in the yard.

Jian's world, now, did not seem real. Nor this one.

Demetrio's pulse drummed. He put the letter away, still unfinished.

On many nights, he and she—farming folk worn out—would embrace, and lie down on their pallet on the floor, side by side, to sleep. Sleeping, they went away together, or alone, and in the morning, recounted their dreams. But they seldom did dream, either she or he. Tonight, they would not sleep.

He looked up at the higher window, soft-lit by a single candle. He looked at the window some while, his body tensed, attentive all through. Then he left the yard of the unreal farm, and climbed towards her light, through the unreal darkness.

When she saw the mountains again, she had remembered them. As the year passed, she watched their calendar of winter white, and later their lower mantles of green.

This farm was planted high, almost beyond the foothills.

The life was pleasant to her. At dusk, sometimes, she would gaze upwards, but no longer to watch for flocks of angels. It was her homage to the sky.

In the small room which was their bed-chamber, she sat combing her hair, hearing it crackle, and seeing the sparks fly out, bright blue.

Waiting for her beloved, she had no thoughts for anyone else, not even for herself. None for the past.

"Am I really to die then?"

The executioner had assured her she must.

She said some sentences to him in return. But she was going already to a great distance. She felt sleepy. She climbed the ladder, just as she had in the house of Ghaio.

She was on the pyre in the amphitheater at Silvia.

There were men around her. She flinched from them, although she had become used to the nearness of men, unthreatening and dependent, at the Primo chapel and after Ciojha. These were not like that. And they stank.

They did not surround her long. Having tied her to the stake, they jumped away.

Some shouting was going on below. Crowd noises.

Then a sound like the wind, rising. It carried up to her the smell of smoke.

She had been told to breathe the smoke. But already she did not like the smell of it. She looked outwards.

So many people. But now a silence.

They were burning her. She had no actual fear. What had fire been, but her familiar. Yet, she might have recaptured the pain of the live candle against her palm, Isaacus' penalty after the Ducal feast. No, she did not. Human beings had always hurt her. If fire itself had hurt her, she did not reason it out. It was men, not fire, who hurt. The world.

Rushes of heat began to come. They slapped upwards, soaring against her body. And then the smoke she had smelled billowed between her and everything. It was not yet thick, but wavering and distorting—like water.

Volpa-Beatifica closed her eyes, because they smarted.

She began to leave herself behind.

It was then, on the boundary between flesh and spirit, that she heard a vast voice of brass that shook the outer places, but also the innerness to which she went.

Beatifica—

Beatifica—

Who—what—was it? She thought of the picture the Magister had shown her, the man thrown among lions. She thought of the story of the burning fiery furnace, and how the angel had led the chosen ones from the fire. As she had been led from the blazing house of Ghaio.

Did the angel call to her now?

Beatifica, cried the angel like a trumpet, *God's light. Blast their bloody filth of fire—Beatifica—*

Beatifica—

Beatifica—

*Make the **FIRE** burn*

Who is that walking there? said the king, Nabucco. Into the furnace I cast three men. But there is a fourth man there with them.

In the smoke she saw, the girl, her angel. He wore the steel maculum and mail, the sword gleamed in his hand, his wings were spread, salt-white. His hair burned like white gold in the furnace. Cristiano. He said, now, softly, *Be quick. Let it be over.*

She flung up her head. She felt the torrent of her own pyrotechnic burst through her, as never had she *felt* it before. *She* the candle, *she* the altar. And to *her* fire, this other fire of the world—*nothing.*

A slave. She had obeyed.

And with her slave's obedience, the goal of the priest, directed by her angel, she took back her power and made the world's fire *burn*.

There was an explosive thud, and flash.

Smoke, an indigo column, rushing, thrusting.

She saw herself one moment, garbed in the flames of her own fire. They were cool. They tingled. And her skull filled like a cup with brilliancy.

This was the light of God. She had been told. She knew.

She gave herself to the light. And was received.

When the center of the pyre crashed in and she dropped to the cistern below, the Maiden was burning like a torch. When they threw water over her, shouting, the fire went out. And she lay unscathed, and fully clothed, on the weave of her hair which, for some moments, looked pale as ashes.

They picked her up, the men below, who had also risked their lives. But she slept.

"Is she gone? Is she dead?"

"No. Not a mark. Look, her heart beats in her throat, you can see."

They carried her away through the tunnel under the arena, where, knee high, water yet rippled like snakes. They put her in a boat.

She slept.

"She's cool. Not hot or fevered."

They rowed her from the land, across a web of blackest sea. They rowed her to the land again.

In a columned chapel, partly ruined, that the Romans had built on the stony shore, (to Neptunus) the Maiden lay asleep.

Night ended. Morning began. Day passed. Night returned.

Then the man arrived they had been told to expect.

He had been one of the Soldiers of God, and that was on him still. But he walked as if lugged by a chain, approaching wide-eyed, not knowing why or for what.

"Signore—Bellatoro—she's in there."

He went by them. At the back of the chapel, where a timbered cell had been attached, a red-haired girl lay asleep.

Cristiano stood looking at her.

He did not know that Jian had been, that once, and unrecognized, her angel also. He did not know that somehow she had heard Cristiano's own whispered prayer.

He did not know who she was, or what the world was in which she might have survived the pyre of sainthood and oblivion.

"He's lost. Doesn't grasp what he's doing."

"Come away. Leave him privacy. This is an age of miracles. We're favored and cursed to live in it."

Cristiano leaned above her, and then he reached out and smoothed the flame of hair back from her forehead. As a brother might. But, till then, he had never been even a brother.

It was the first time they had touched.

Her eyes flew open. She was there. Back from a long journey, she thought. Cristiano had been on the road with her. She gazed up at him. Danielus had believed she might not know this man without the mail of Christ. But she said, "You led me from the fire. You're my angel. Don't go away."

She never noticed Cristiano was no longer winged. Nor did he.

For she had burned. But now the fire was out . . .

Their sleeping room was bare, only the sparse mattress on the floor, a chest, a stool. One end, however, had been divided off, making the small chamber smaller.

Beyond the curtain they kept their private altar, where a cross of carved wood was set, a copper cup, and the flowers Ermilla regularly gathered, in a white jug.

They had not fasted. They did not, now. At all times they ate sparely.

They sipped the water from the cup.

It would not matter that the Magister was in the house. He would sleep soundly. Sunrise always brought them back, as it woke them on other summer days, blooming through the unglazed and unshuttered window. Better than a bell, the Auroria of mountain dawn.

They did not exchange a word, he or she. Alone, they did not ever speak at great length. Having no need.

Kneeling, they faced each other, by the altar.

In the warmth of the summer they were naked. As in the Garden, before nakedness became the mark of disobedient knowledge and the stigma of the Fall.

(Outside, soft noises. An owl across the fields. The stirring of animals. Stars turning in sky. The moon, singing, as it sailed its nacre boat.)

Cristiano reached out his hands, and Beatifica reached out her hands. Their hands joined.

The last image each beheld, as always, at this instant, the eyes of the other, silver, gold. And then the wave of eternal radiance, the light of God, swept down and spun them upward.

It came always the same. At the touch.

Together, one thing, they would enter the sphere of ecstasy so otherwise unimaginable, and otherwise so ungovernable. The fore-taste of Heaven, and the immortal state. Beyond any physical plea-sure, impossible in its wonder and effulgence. Yet always achievable. Always.

To this, mere sexual union—which they had never known, nor ever attempted, nor ever would attempt—like the fires of the world—was *nothing*.

In a glory above all delight, they hung together in the firma-ment. Would hang there like stars all night, until the dawn re-claimed them.

Across the wooden places of the house, Danielus, lying yet awake, might dream his waking dream. The Council had not been overthrown, inhuman lies still ruled the City, and the earth. He had lost the sword of flame. But oh, if they, the warrior-visionary, the priestess-saint, if they might produce, from their innocent lust, a child—what might that child not be? What true miracle might that child not work?

Alas, Magister, you must dream in vain.

They are virgins, these lovers, and will be till their death. And from their rare and soaring love, no child can ever be created—unless it is an angel.

For nine further years the mystical Heart of the Maiden Beatifica continued to work miracles in the City of Ve Nera. As belief in these wonders swelled, it became a common cause that the Maiden should be recognized as one of God's saints. At length the Council of the Lamb, eager to end this—as they perceived it—opposing cult, out-lawed the idea of Beatifica, and threatened death by burning to her adherents. On this signal, the City revolted against them. And from Rome came the ultimate edict that the Brothers of the Lamb had exceeded their authority. The Council was overthrown, and most of its members, so the story went, secretly murdered by Ve Nera's princes.

In that year too, the name of Ve Nera was altered by her

Ducem, Joffri, to *Venus*. This after the goddess of love, who also, like the City, had been born from the sea.

The Maiden Beatifica was never officially canonized.

One hundred years later, the golden casket, which contained her Heart, vanished without trace.

> *In heaven's luminous land, in splendour rising,*
> *You, O living Aten, maker of life!*
> *When once you have dawned in the east,*
> *The country of the light,*
> *You brim all places with your beauty.*
> *You, the beautiful, mighty and aflame,*
> *Upon the pinnacle of every land,*
> *Your rays kiss the world*
> *To the boundaries of creation.*

From the hymn of the PHARAOH AKHENATEN
To his one true God, the Sun.